Paradise
Denied!

H. J. Kaplan

iUniverse, Inc.
New York   Bloomington

Paradise Denied!

Copyright © 2010 H. J. Kaplan

This is a work of fiction. All of the characters, names, incidents,
organizations, and dialogue in this novel are either the products
of the author's imagination or are used fictitiously.

iUniverse books may be ordered through booksellers or by contacting:

iUniverse
1663 Liberty Drive
Bloomington, IN 47403
www.iuniverse.com
1-800-Authors (1-800-288-4677)

ISBN: 978-1-4401-7613-5 (pbk)
ISBN: 978-1-4401-7611-1 (cloth)
ISBN: 978-1-4401-7612-8 (ebk)

Printed in the United States of America

iUniverse rev. date: 7/22/2010

Introduction:

I never intended to write a novel. However, over time, I grew highly anxious and worried. Why? I saw that little real progress was being made to defeat terrorism. Fortunately, two recent terrorist attempts on an airline and at Times Square in New York City both narrowly failed. They should be vivid reminders that here are factions that are planning more destruction in the US and the world! Frankly, I'm scared and devastated because people and governments are kidding themselves with their passive approach to terrorism. I'm worried that these attacks will show up in another airline disaster, or a passenger ship being destroyed, or trains, subways or a sports complex being blown up. A car bomb could happen in front of City Hall in any city in any country! Many of you should be worried, as am I, about the additional toll on human life that terrorists are planning. Because terrorism will continue to affect our democracy and our way of life, I want everyone to understand that the danger is still present.

I listened as the experts insisted they were doing everything they could to stop the atrocities. They claimed it was impossible to prevent anyone who is determined to blow himself up. I found that hard to accept. I felt the experts were taking the easy way out, that something was possible, but they couldn't or wouldn't recognize it. They are the experts so who could dispute them? Yet, my brain said *something* was possible, but what?

For years, I thought about this without a satisfactory solution. For years, I worried about the risks we face. One day, relating my experiences from Tough Love to a friend, I remembered a lesson I had often taught families about how to deal with their misbehaving teens. The lesson is this:

NO ONE CHANGES THEIR BEHAVIOR UNLESS THERE IS A COMPELLING REASON TO DO SO

This means that if the consequence of an action is worse than the act someone commits, he (or she) will, most of the time, consider changing his (or her) behavior. I frequently applied this principle to adults in the workplace, as well as to teens in home or at school. It proved highly effective.

I questioned how that concept could apply to terrorists. To answer that I first examined the obvious problem. When someone is willing to sacrifice their own life, what punishment can be worse than death itself? Why would anyone be willing to be a suicide bomber?

I found a plausible explanation. Terrorists are convinced of two things. First, they are willing to fight and die for Allah against anyone who violates the teachings of the Qu'ran. Second, by their death, they believe they will reach Paradise. If their path to Paradise were denied, terrorists might not have a motive to kill us. I further postulated that this might eliminate their willingness to become terrorists.

The second part was much more worrisome. Why do the people and governments who support terrorism get a free pass? Aren't they too terrorists? Why is the world not pursuing them with the same intensity as the guys with the guns? Those are more daunting questions that demand answers, issues that carry much greater significance and implications than even the frontline terrorists.

Paradise Denied! was born.

The story concept rapidly began to unfold in my head. The more I thought about it, the more I determined the story needed telling. Characters began to take shape. Who they are, what they needed to do, and how they could do it.

This gave birth to a secret organization who called themselves STN (Stop Terrorism Now). STN's reason to exist is to destroy global terrorism in *all its forms.* I accept that the solution offered in Paradise Denied! is hardcore. I make no apologies for that. People need to understand that if we are going to stop terrorists, dramatic actions are required. I thought about how, during World War ll, both sides fought against each other's armies, but they also tried to cut off the supplies and weapons needed by the frontline troops. Both sides took great risks to stop the supplies by bombing their cities and factories. The same applies to fighting terrorism. We need to cut off the means for them to continue their fight against the West and democratic countries around the world.

Once I created STN, I realized I needed to prevent them from becoming the new breed of terrorists. This gave rise to the Peace Envoys, whose covert mission was to destroy STN.

Now that the framework was set, my imagination ran wild. I explored the consequences of actions by STN and the Peace Envoys, and the men who controlled these opposing forces.

The storyline grew from a concept of how to stop global terrorism into a message for people who seek freedom and peace. Paradise Denied! developed into an intricately woven tale that examines the impact that people's actions can have on themselves and on society. From there, I examined the role that governments play in this scenario. I also began to explore the level of morality in real-life government and society. Of course, my primary goal remained to draw attention to the risks we all face from present and future terrorist actions.

Paradise Denied! evolved into a multiplicity of sub plots and ironies, of personal and governmental achievements and tragedies that are realistic, believable, and sometimes frightening. I subtly pose questions about government actions and their problem solving techniques, especially when their actions focus on an illegal vigilante organization that actually is performing a vital function to society. Another question arose about whether the end justifies the means when the means violate your legal and moral beliefs.

Throughout the course of writing my novel, I constantly thought about the future and what steps we need to take to carry us forward in peace and security. I remain adamant that we must pursue all possible paths to defeat both the street fighters and their supporters. I'm not necessarily advocating that a secret organization be formed to destroy terrorists as I propose in Paradise Denied!. However, I am demanding that the free world pursue a real solution before it's too late! By taking an insightful approach, I hope to open the political door to a more focused and meaningful campaign to defeat terrorism.

I believe Paradise Denied! is a stimulating novel that could result in an exciting movie. Regardless of the future disposition of my novel, my solution does raise an intriguing question of "What if?"

The characters in my book are purely a result of my own imagination and bear no resemblance to anyone living or dead or who has been or is currently in my life. In my search for names for my characters, I took the liberty of using the first names of people with whom I am familiar.

Dear family and friends, please do not read anything into the traits and actions of the characters that might bear your first name. I meant neither disrespect nor any implied criticism of you or our friendship. I thought it was cute or easy to select names from those people around me and use them in my book, regardless of the person or the situation. Mostly, I wanted to acknowledge our relationship by using your name.

Foreign names and places, such as Bilal and Farook, are real. I harvested them the internet. I selected the names of my International characters from lists on the internet merely because they appealed to me. If I inadvertently used a name that defames anyone or any religion, it was quite accidental, and I apologize in advance for any oversight.

The task of creating *Paradise Denied!* was greatly hampered by my lack of typing ability. Hunt and peck is tedious, difficult and dumb. Why did I not learn to type? I was too busy writing (and rewriting and rewriting) the book to take precious time away to learn a helping skill. Had I learned to type, I could have saved hours and hours of precious time that I took from family and friends. Without the invaluable resources offered by the internet, I could not have easily presented the authentic descriptions of foreign furniture, food, Muslim burial rites, and places with which I lack personal familiarity. I grew to marvel at the skills and patience that authors or the past had to endure to compose a novel before spell check, or the cut, paste, and copy features of a computer were available. I have a newfound appreciation of difficulties they had to overcome.

My thanks to the many people who volunteered to serve as my guinea pigs to read the initial draft of *Paradise Denied!*. Without your invaluable input and honest criticism, I would never have known how many pages of writing I forced you to endure. I took every criticism, every correction, every question, and every suggestion you offered to heart. I listened and adjusted the story and the text to the best of my ability. I deeply thank you for your time and effort. It meant the world to me. I hope that our collaborative efforts resulted in a book that others can enjoy.

I would like to believe that *Paradise Denied!* will stimulate the readers to ask their own questions along with those that I raise about morality and beliefs, and especially of how individuals and governments react under trying times. I especially hope that governments will soon include *all* terrorists as part of the problem, and that they take appropriate actions to stop terrorism now.

Paradise Denied! has been a true journey for me, one that has been illuminating, thrilling, exasperating, frustrating, and eminently satisfying. Not to mention the many hours of lost sleep. It is also a sincere message of concern for you, the readers. Be active, tell your government you want real protection, that they need to fight terrorists on all fronts, wherever and whoever they exist..

I hope you enjoy *Paradise Denied!* and consider the issues, the people, and the difficulties that confront us all in these difficult times.

Thank you.

H. J. Kaplan

ACKNOWLEDGEMENTS:

No author can exist in a vacuum. I frequently turned to friends for their input and criticism, of which there were many. My sincere thanks to the following for the time and energy you spent on my behalf. It is deeply appreciated:

Carol Cavalier
Professor Florence Fay
Steven Kaplan
Julie Kaufman
Debbie and Sid Klein
Dr. Bonnie May
Karen and Irwin Terach

You each helped to make Paradise Denied! a reality.

A special note of appreciation to my wife, Judi, who tolerated my absences from her life as I tirelessly typed away at the computer for long, and I am sure, annoying hours. Without your willingness to give me the space I needed, Paradise Denied! would never have been written.

Love to all.
HJK

Paradise Denied!

1

SEPTEMBER 2009:

He couldn't put off reviewing *Red Sunset* any longer. The first time he read the report, it frightened him, even though he had not absorbed all the details. What he did remember was enough to make him dread reading more. Today, in spite of his apprehension, he felt compelled to do his job.

"Alice, please bring me the Findings Report," Ed Walker requested of his secretary through his office intercom.

"Sure thing. I'll be right there."

A few moments later Alice Hennings entered his office, walked to his wall safe and expertly manipulated the complex dual security combination lock of the safe. Ed always had Alice open his safe because it frustrated him. As often as he tried, he usually managed to screw up one of the six maneuvers. He hated to appear stupid, especially to himself, but for some inexplicable reason, he couldn't remember the number sequence. Alice, timid, mousy looking in her badly tailored two-piece steel gray business suit, her gray hair tightly tied in a bun and held in place with a black hair clip, easily managed to implement the six steps needed to release the locking mechanism of the safe.

Not that I couldn't do it, he reassured himself. *I merely avoid another little unnecessary frustration at the office.*

She placed the report on his low luster cherry wood desk and asked, "Need anything else?"

"No. I'll buzz you when I'm ready. Please close the door and hold my calls for the next twenty minutes. Thanks."

Ed Walker glanced at his watch. 8:21. He had been in his office at the CIA complex in McLean Virginia, Building 2, since 7:20 that morning. Even leaving his home early he could not avoid the McLean traffic that slows to a crawl when the rain is heavy. This morning was no exception.

The black bound think-tank report was a heavy eighty-seven pages thick. This was the second time he read the report since its publication five days ago, and he wanted to be sure that he understood the full implications before over reacting. With documents this long, Ed preferred to skim it first and highlight items that caught his attention or needed further review. His initial impression of *Red Sunset* was disbelief laced with a touch of uncertainty. That alone was enough to warrant a thorough examination before jumping to any conclusions.

The government published and distributed only seven classified copies of the report. The official title "Findings of the Commission on World Crises over the Next 20 Years," prepared under the authority of President Alan T. Schuster. Report submitted by the Commission, chaired by Russell K. Schreiber, August 28, 2009, had a code name: *Red Sunset*.

Early in his first term in 2009, President Allan T. Schuster commissioned a panel of his brightest advisors from the intelligence community to develop an analysis of what worldwide scenarios might be in ten, fifteen, and twenty years. The President's premise was for the committee to make the worst-case assumptions and to evaluate their impact on the security of the United States. Part 2 was the impact on the rest of the world.

The Commission issued its report eight months into the President's first term.

Ed Walker's initial impression of the report's conclusions was unsettling.

Despite the fact that the committee excluded the possibility of nuclear weapons use by rogue states, they concluded that world chaos would be a likely consequence of Islamic Fundamentalist terrorism. Their analysis clearly pointed to a major global disruption of society and business. The projections suggested that millions of innocent people would die, the global economy would be on the verge of a major financial crisis, and worse, many governments would be seized or paralyzed by militant, terrorist, or fanatical religious groups. Under the Commission's worst-case assumptions, one or all these groups would control a majority of the free world. Multiple small wars or police actions would be the norm as countries tried in vain to counter hostile takeover attempts. Disrupted lives, governments overthrown or dissolved, and the progress and scientific developments of the past century would be overturned because of the emerging dominance of the Islamic Fundamentalists. Once the free world governments dissolved or are overthrown, people's lives would change dramatically, and world progress would stop or even regress.

Walker rubbed the back of his neck as he reread the portions he had marked for review. The more he read, the slower his hand moved. When the rubbing ceased, it was a subconscious indication he was engaged in deep thought. Troubling ideas made his wiry body stiffen to a point where he barely could move. His fingers clenched his neck in a desperate attempt to prevent his head from falling off his body.

During his first reading Ed highlighted in yellow the most unnerving and riveting conclusions of the report. Items four to seven drew the most yellow.

Conclusion Four: "It is our opinion, with a probability of over 78.4%, that terrorism, however defined, and wherever based, would become commonplace." The related footnote further explained that fanatics willing to kill themselves are impossible to stop under present day attitudes, policies, and capabilities of the free world governments. Suicide bombers acting alone, emboldened by their own outrage, or that of their leaders, had the capability to create and sustain world chaos.

Conclusion Five: "No present day global government or military, acting alone or in concert, could prevent or deter terrorists from accomplishing their devastating killings." The footnote referenced the long held axiom of traditional wisdom that emphasized the impossibility of stopping or detecting an individual intent on destroying others by blowing themselves up.

Conclusion Six: "Structured terrorist organizations, such as al Qaeda or the Taliban, who are funded from multiple unknown sources and whose members can blend into the civilian population, operate under the same general safeguards as normal citizens." The footnote claimed identification of the individual members of the group is nearly impossible. "That puts society at the mercy of the terrorist attackers," it stated.

Conclusion Seven, the one that Ed had highlighted and underlined in red and yellow, the one that slammed his mind and body, forecasted:

"The chaos and control of the terrorists will, in all probability, get much worse across the globe. As terrorists gain access to more sophisticated weapons, or even nuclear weapons, they could potentially achieve geographical dominance within 10 years in the Middle East, within 12 years in Asia and the Pacific Rim, Europe within 12-15 years, and the US a year after Europe." The footnote reminded the reader the stated period was within *Red Sunset's* twenty-year exposure window.

Salty sweat dripped from his brow, into his eyes, past his lips into his partially open mouth. The salt stung his eyes and dried his throat, while his rigid body barely reflected the tempest churning within. Waves of nausea accompanied a sudden shortness of breath. He wanted to scream, to run away, to stop the sudden fear that was shattering his nervous system. Pounding. Exploding thoughts. Exhaustion. Immobilization. Despair. And Fear. Everything happened simultaneously.

He wanted, he needed help...relief from being lost... from being confused... from the terror that was sucking him dry. Alice? Janice? God? Anyone?

For Ed Walker, there was nowhere to turn, not at this panic filled moment. He was lost in a world of vivid and scary images.

"Get a grip," he admonished himself. "Breath slowly, relax." He repeated these words over and over. Two, three... five minutes lapsed. Slowly he allowed himself to escape from his self-imposed hell.

"I...I... can't believe what I just read," he whispered to himself. "My life, my family, my country, all at risk? In less than sixteen years? And they say we probably can't stop it from happening? What does this mean? Surely something can be done, but what?"

Ed rapidly reviewed his knowledge and conceptions about terrorists, knowledge he had accumulated over the past eleven years as a CIA analyst of terrorist funding sources. It was his job to trace the financial dealings from selected terrorist groups in the Mid East, including how they obtained their money, where they banked, who supported them and anything else related to their ability to financially sustain them.

His thoughts drifted to the presently held perceived reasons people joined terrorist organizations. Some theories depicted the terrorists as coming from well educated or financially well off families who are attracted to terrorism because they believed their religious freedoms were under attack by Western societies. Others concluded that religious leaders had mesmerized their young followers into joining, with the promise of a better life in Paradise if they die while fighting infidels. Others depicted the West as Satan and against Islam, and declared a jihad, a religious war, to destroy their enemies. Still others theorized terrorists were people who had gotten the taste for killing, and who fed their passion though ever more bizarre acts. The reasons or suppositions didn't matter. Only their results did. For some, as long as they killed in the name of Allah, that in itself was their ultimate achievement. Paradise was their promised reward.

Based on these many profiles, police and special security forces throughout the US and free world were trained to recognize typical terrorist personality traits, and to prevent, interrupt, or to react to their actions. In spite of the huge amount of money spent and the emergence of sophisticated prevention or detection technologies, *Red Sunset* concluded, terrorists could not be stopped. The difficulty of infiltrating terrorist organizations further limited the levels of intelligence about their structure, their members, their intent, or their plans. The committee further concluded that little would change this paradigm.

The body of the report cited the example of the aborted efforts by the

Palestinian Authority in the Middle East, who organized Death Squads to control terrorists within their borders, and accomplished little.

The report ranked, in descending probability, the most likely countries to fall under terrorist control. The top of the list were the Middle Eastern countries. Once the Middle East region fell under Islamic control, they postulated, Islamic Fundamentalism would spread to Asia, The Pacific Rim, Europe, and finally to the Western Hemisphere. They estimated these events could happen in less than 16 years. They offered frightening statistics in which South American countries would succumb to the Fundamentalists ideals, beginning with Venezuela. Canada would be next to fall, and the pressure on the United States would result in the US engaged in a war against the rest of the world. Eventually, as United States depleted its resources, the Fundamentalists would gain sufficient political and military power to control the country. The report did not specify by what means governments would succumb to Islamic rule, whether by force or through elections. They only offered their conclusions. They stated in bold print, under a worst-case scenario, that it could become a reality, if all their assumptions were met.

Red Sunset panicked and deeply rattled him.

"I've got to talk to someone about this. I need to know if anyone else feels the same as I."

He immediately focused on Dr. Leonard Winslow, his immediate superior and the Deputy Director of the Foreign Activities Department. He waited another ten minutes before he buzzed Alice on the intercom.

"Alice, see how fast you can set up a meeting with Winslow. The subject is the Findings Report."

"When do you want to meet?"

"The sooner the better. It's not urgent, but really important."

"How much time will you need? You know he likes to know that in advance."

"About 45 minutes."

"I'll let you know."

Ed wasn't quite sure why he had reacted so adversely. It was only a report, and a worse case one to boot. Yet, he understood he desperately needed to talk to someone about *Red Sunset*. Now. Later was too late. Never before had he felt such a sense of urgency or of impending doom. Intellectually he knew the report was theoretical, but it seemed more real than not.

Perhaps Leonard can help me. I know he is on the approved reading list. IF I DON'T GET THIS OUT OF MY HEAD, I'LL GO NUTS, he shouted internally.

Minutes later Alice buzzed to tell him the meeting was set. 2:15 today. Ed felt a small measure of relief.

Len'll help; I know he will, he convinced himself. The remainder of the morning, lunch, and the next hour dragged. His concentration shot, his nerves jangled, and his stomach ached from this morning's trauma.

He walked the polished and near immaculate tile corridor that lead to Winslow's massive office located three aisles from his, roughly ½ a block away. He arrived five minutes early.

"Hi Gwyn," he greeted Winslow's secretary, busily pounding at her computer and hadn't seen him approach.

"You scared the crap out of me."

"Sorry," Ed said somewhat seriously.

"He's running a little late, probably 15 minutes or so. Want to wait?" she asked.

"Yeah, just in case he breaks earlier."

Experience taught him that any scheduled meeting with his boss usually happened on time, or as close to on time as possible. Even if he was running late, you'd better be there when he was ready for you or he moved onto his next appointment.

"I thought so," she giggled. "How are Janice and the kids?"

"They're doing great, thanks."

"Looks like you've gained some weight. Still refuse to go to the gym?"

Ed looked wistfully at his slight paunch protruding above his waist, broadly smiled, and laughingly replied,

"I guess I have gained a little weight. Must be Janice's good cooking."

Gwyn and he had a long-term work-related relationship. She had worked in his office pool years ago when he first joined the CIA, and they become quick friends. Nothing romantic, just friends. She had a nice figure for a forty-two year old. Beautiful blue-gray eyes set symmetrically from her button nose, and always dressed tastefully yet fashionably. He often thought of how pleasant it would be to kiss her full and sensual lips. In spite of his mild fantasy about her, he never pursued any closer relationship, nor would he. He was happily married to Janice. The respect he felt for her, coupled with the fear of being caught, outweighed notions of a sexual encounter with Gwyn. It however didn't stop him from fantasizing when in her presence.

Occasionally they would lunch together when they had time. Years ago, she came to him when her husband of fourteen years told her he was gay and wanted a divorce. She was devastated and depressed. Ed helped her through her crisis by being a friend and offering sage advice. She never forgot it.

"I'll let you get back to work, Gwyn."

"No problem. I miss our little talks from yesteryear. I guess we all have to move on, don't we?" Gwyn had never remarried, which puzzled Ed.

"Guess so."

Seven minutes later Leonard Winslow emerged from his office.

"Come in, Ed." He closed the door behind him.

"Thanks for seeing me on such short notice."

"Glad I had the slot open. So, what's on your mind?" he asked as he gestured for Ed to sit on the deep brown leather sofa he had personally selected for his office. He never sat behind his desk when talking to another CIA employee. He reserved his desk position for official business with outsiders. He preferred to sit on his plush brown leather wing back chair carefully placed opposite the sofa, at a slight angle to allow him to look directly at anyone sitting on the sofa. At one time, the chair was a favorite of former President Jerome Mathews. After he was promoted to Deputy, he rescued the chair from congressional storage where it sat covered by plastic for eighteen years.

"I just finished reviewing *Red Sunset* in detail, and frankly I'm really upset."

"How so?"

Winslow was an astute manager and person. Tall, athletic, with gray hair cropped close, bright blue eyes that were capable of digging into your soul when he chose, a nose pushed out of place too often from his collegiate basketball days, and glistening white teeth. He dressed as though he had stepped out of a GQ ad. His suits were always pressed, fashionable, understated, and appropriate. At work, he wore only a heavily starched white shirt with a traditional narrow spread collar. He felt that colored or striped shirts conveyed an image of casualness, and he preferred to be thought of as a dedicated professional. He believed it gave him an air of authority. He refused to deviate from his self-imposed office uniform that he accessorized with a plethora of conservative ties perfectly color matched with his suits.

Co-workers called Winslow and Glenn the fashion couple; they were always prepared to step into a meeting, a party, a photo op, or a clothing magazine ad, whichever came first.

Winslow was in sharp contract to Ed. Winslow stood six foot tall, two inches taller than Ed. Ed was a paunchy 42 year old whose suits were clean, slightly out of balance, sometimes slightly wrinkled, and didn't fit his body. Colored shirts with out of date ties, and shoes frequently in need of a good shine, completed his mundane appearance. Unfortunately, his extra fifteen pounds of weight settled mostly in his stomach, which didn't match the rest of his wiry frame. Light brown wavy hair, graying at the sides, framed his long sunless pale face. Ed was fairly good looking and had a winning smile, marred only by his slightly yellowing teeth. Although he had tried several commercial whiteners on the market, he saw little improvement. This troubled him so much that he consulted a local dentist about a solution. A relatively new procedure was available that required home preparation and three or four

7

prolonged bouts in the dentist's chair. As usual, he procrastinated committing to it.

In spite of his fastidious and authoritative appearance, Leonard Winslow's personal demeanor encouraged people to talk openly, to feel safe to discuss any matter, official or personal. His managerial philosophy encouraged freedom of expression without intimidation. His listening skills and patience gave people confidence to talk about their issues in depth and in their own time. He never minimized their feelings, and instinctively understood that good listening skills permitted hidden issues to surface quickly and honestly. He allowed them to happen naturally.

"I'm really disturbed by that frigging report. I know it's a worst-case scenario, and I should be able to accept it as such. But I can't. It makes too much sense to simply ignore it as another think-tank mental diarrhea," Ed started.

"Why?"

"It's hard to put my finger on it, other than my gut tells me that the likelihood of Islamic Fundamentalists controlling the world is more truth than fiction. Just think. What do we really know about terrorists? Do we know their background, their ideals? What drives them? Who funds them? And, what or who will stop them?"

"What specifically bothers you?"

"I've tried to figure that out, and it comes down to this. Although the report takes a worst-case approach, when you dissect it closer, many of the assumptions made by the Commission coincide with what is already happening. A new terrorist organization crops up almost out of thin air, we have no in-depth intelligence data on them, we can't find or stop all their money sources, and they are causing major disruptions throughout the globe. What was only a theoretical study now seems to be a realistic probability. Everyday we learn that they're expanding their target base, just as the Commission assumed. They continue to target military and civilians with impunity.

So what really bothers me? I'm worried that the US will become targets like everywhere else in the world. I don't want our wives and children at risk. How can we, you and I, protect them? Does anyone have a real plan to stop terrorists, anywhere?"

Ed's voice quivered slightly with his increased pace, his face drawn as his emotional outpouring continued.

"Do you think we have time to wait while the next generation of Islamic children is taught that democracy is achievable and desirable, and that Americans and the West are not their sworn enemies? In fact, we know the opposite is true. They are taught hatred and violence in madresses throughout the Arab and Muslim world. Who is going to stop the mullahs from preaching their venom against us? I don't see anything happening now or in the near future that tells me that things will get better. Wherever I look, I see the opposite. Unemployment, poverty, and fanatical religious leaders working overtime to reinforce their terroristic concepts while rebuking democratic ideals. Frankly, I'm frustrated and scared. I'm scared to death that the President and his advisors will reject *Red Sunset* as too far-fetched. They will keep it in their files along with all the other dead Commission reports they ignore.

We could wake one day to discover that it is happening right here, under our noses. By then it might be too damn late to do anything about it!"

"Whoa, Ed, take a deep breath. Calm down, you're getting too emotional about this. Care for something to drink?"

"No... but... I'm... CONVINCED," he emphasized, "that... the... time... to... act... is... NOW. And...we're... not... doing... a... damn... thing... because... we... WON'T RECOGNIZE THE DANGER!"

Throughout his soliloquy, Ed reacted to his own words. The longer he talked the angrier he became. His speech grew rapid and choppy, culminating in him shouting his last words. By the time he finished his face was red with anger, and sweat had formed on his upper lip and his forehead. He was unaware that he had clenched fists. His fingernails had made deep impressions in his palms.

"Whoa, whoa, whoa, ...calm down, Ed", again extolled his concerned boss in a calm voice.

"I understand, your concerns, but you need to calm down first. I think you need a break. Let's have something to drink, OK?"

Ed nodded yes. Winslow pressed the intercom button.

"Gwen, would you please bring us coffee, you take cream and sugar, don't you, Ed?"

"Yes."

"OK, one with cream and sugar for Ed."

Winslow verified the intercom had disconnected before he spoke.

"You know I've read the report too, and I don't see it as threatening as you. Not to say that you are wrong, just a different interpretation, that's all. As I see it, the Commission considered only the worst-case scenario. I suspect they had to discount the good things that are happening. Let's wait until after our coffee before we move on." Ed neither agreed nor disagreed.

A few minutes later Gwen entered carrying a hand oak carved wooden serving tray with two cups of steaming coffee in footed bone china cups sitting peacefully on their matching saucers. Winslow liked to show off his fine bone china coffee to visitors that he had received as a congratulatory gift from his world-traveling parents when he first entered government service.

Somehow, it made him feel more civilized, especially when discussions of the US security were involved.

"Thanks, Gwen. Please reschedule my next appointment. I'm going to be later than I expected. By the way, who's being blown off?"

"Senator Richards."

Winslow grimaced.

"He's not going to be happy with this. Use your feminine guiles to pacify him, will you?"

She nodded affirmatively and left.

"Hope I'm not causing you grief with the Senator, but I do appreciate you spending this time with me," Ed muttered.

"He'll get over it. This is payback for when he cancelled me two months ago with a rather lame excuse. Don't worry about it."

They sipped their coffee and passed the next ten minutes by exchanging pleasantries about their families. Twelve minutes later, Winslow got back to business.

"Here's my take," started Winslow. "From my perspective, I see some things happening now that are beginning to be successful, or at least have the chance to be successful. You are aware of the International agreements to attach the terrorist supporting funds in banks in the US and most of our allies, especially since you and your team identified some of their major funding sources. I believe we are making significant progress to shut down these accounts and their laundering schemes. Everyday we identify more places where they are hiding their money. I agree they're taking more time than what either of us like, but we're doing better.

Some countries are actively fighting terrorism rather than supporting or passively ignoring them. Think England, Pakistan, Saudi Arabia, Philippines, Spain. That's progress. Increased efforts to attach the terrorists' funds will be made by more countries as we move forward. We now have intelligence sharing relationships with over eight countries, which we never did before. Homeland Security has prevented terrorist attacks on US and German soil. Don't forget, the public's awareness has also increased. That's a big help, too.

Look, Ed, we both know things aren't perfect, but I believe in my heart that we are on the right track. If we continue to stay vigilante, if we continue to build foreign alliances, if we sustain our commitment to fight, then we'll continue to tighter the noose on terrorists and render them ineffective or neutralized. Add these things together you will come to the same conclusion. The *Red Sunset* committee fulfilled their duty by making the worst-case analysis. Let's face it, their report complies with typical White House studies. They're obsolete three months before they're published.

I challenge you to name any think-tank study in the past ten years that changed policy or the government's direction. Frankly, I can't think of one. They waste money conducting these investigations, writing, and publishing their reports, and take so much time to complete that they're virtually useless. But, they sure make for good politics, don't they?" Winslow chuckled.

"What you say makes sense, but this time, I don't believe the terrorists are following the script," Ed calmly replied.

"In fact, I believe they're actively creating more actions that don't follow our assumptions. Here's the problem. In the past, terrorists weren't coordinated, and they acted as separate individuals or groups. They didn't cooperate with each other. They had no central authority or guidance. Now, we're seeing greater cooperation among terrorists groups and increased support from Iran with weapons and money. We've seen coordinated attacks against our troops in Iraq and Afghanistan. Though we've cut off some important sources of funding, it hasn't slowed them down. We have no idea how much money they actually have, who's funding them, or the extent of illegal activities they're using to get the money to operate. They're into drugs, counterfeiting, laundering money, identity theft, and God knows what else. I believe it's so pervasive that we may never be able to completely shut the spigot off, and so they go on and on, indifferent to our actions against them," Ed responded as his voice once again took on the sharp edge of anger.

"What you say is true, but I believe that by being aware of their activities, we're in a better position to recognize and stop them. Sure, any person acting alone can still do damage, but we can and are stopping some of their more organized operations. And, I believe, with continued International cooperation, we'll prevail," responded Winslow emphatically.

Ed had placed his hand on the back of his neck, and left it there.

"I don't see it that way," Ed insisted, "though you make some good arguments. The problem is that when I step back, when I try to eliminate traditional government hype and bullshit, and look at reality, I'm not as optimistic as you."

"Look Ed, we obviously don't see eye to eye on this, and I'm not sure what I can say at this point to help you with your concerns, except that historically, thousands of reports are written and most of them are marvelously flawed. I suspect *Red Sunset* is too, but we'll need more time to learn what the flaws are. Perhaps it's best to give it a rest, give it and yourself some time to see how it plays out, and to see what progress we make. It will drive you crazy trying to apply reality logic to a theoretical study, however troubling it might be. Make sense?"

Reluctantly Ed acknowledged Winslow's assessment. His head nodded *Yes*, but his mind screamed *No*. He still felt frightened, agitated, and certain

Winslow had become a typical politician. Put your head into the sand and ignore the truth.

I know he's wrong. Red Sunset is closer to reality than he's willing or able to recognize. I know in my heart it's more than a study, in fact it's a direct window into the future, and that future is getting closer and closer, Ed internally reasoned.

"You're right, to a certain degree. I suppose it would be better to wait and see what happens. I'll try," Ed replied.

"Good. I suspect in six months we'll have another talk about *Red Sunset* and we'll both laugh at the naive assumptions the Commission made. We'll both chalk it up to another false alarm."

"Thanks for listening, Len. You've been a help." Respect for his boss was gone, replaced by Ed's realization that he was now alone. No one understood. No one will listen. And he knew he could not now and would never accept Winslow's conclusions.

He's blinded by the hype, blinded by his own desire to believe in the Pollyanna image of the free world effectively fighting terrorism. I KNOW Red Sunset's conclusions are true, he thought while he walked back to his office. *Blind, naïve, and typical Washington bureaucrat, that's Winslow. I guess I can't blame him, since I became one too. But no longer! We need action, but what can be done?*

The rest of the afternoon, he accomplished nothing of importance. Fear of the future dominated his thoughts, clouding his thinking.

Thankfully, 4:13 PM arrived. Time to leave. Ed felt the intense urge to be cocooned in his own home, to be safely surrounded by his wife, Janice, and his two loving children, Alicia, 13, and Brad, 11. A pervasive brooding took hold, deep, deep within his body, invading his body and his mind.

Walker headed to the parking lot, his heart heavy with the deepening fear that the committee's findings were becoming a reality faster than he imagined. His thoughts alternately skipped from the love of his family to dread for their future. Images of a life of pain and suffering became entrenched in his head. He was unable to relegate them to a secluded memory space, where his troubling thoughts and feelings resided, often forgotten or ignored, but never reconciled. They were always present. He knew they would not go away. They never did.

He unlocked his 2007 red Cutlass four-door sedan, wedged himself behind the padded gray steering wheel, locked the doors, and slowly edged out of the parking lot. He absently flashed his badge to the uniformed Marine guard who saluted as he passed, and began the short drive to his home in McLean. It was still raining. Giant puddles had collected along his route.

2

HOME:

Ed pulled into his driveway and flew into his home. He craved the normalcy of his life, without the fear that now possessed him. Janice was in the kitchen, ready with her special pork loin dinner and sides of Lyonnais potatoes and broccoli. The kids were watching TV, their usual reward for completing their homework before dinner. Home was his respite from the stress at work. Here, he could enjoy his family's daily routine of discussion at the dinner table where each member has a chance to talk about his or her day, the best and the worst. Today, Ed was not ready to remember the worst, let alone talk about it.

His thoughts flashed back to the first time he met Janice. It was at a college party in his senior year at Drexel University in 1989. His first impression of her was her choice of clothes. No fashion there. She wasn't the fashion model type. Although she had pleasant facial features, she was not a beauty queen. Her skin, slightly pocked from a childhood bout with chicken pox, was light and soft. Her round hazelnut eyes set slightly apart, filled with love and contentment, a small button nose and full soft lips were her distinguishing features. She wore a size twelve dress. He smiled thinking of how men and women still remark about her perfect and sensuous lips. Bright and quick-witted, Janice had a remarkable penchant for details that fascinated Ed from the day they met.

He felt many college women lacked sophistication and world awareness. Most had difficulty expressing opinions about history or world events. Not Janice. She displayed a keen mind, was articulate, and unafraid to voice her opinion. Not that he considered himself an expert, but he did have an unusual interest in world events because he felt it gave him a perspective on global issues of the day.

Somehow, this not-his-type-of woman, had captured his imagination as no one before. He thought about their conversations on politics, sports, religion, and relationships. Everything seemed to flow smoothly, seamlessly going from one topic to another. Never had one awkward moment existed before one of them introduced a new thought, or a new feeling about many diverse subjects. No topic was excluded, no area protected.

Four dates later both realized they had found the perfect mate. They contemplated immediate marriage, but squelched the temptation with reason. They agreed to stay together in a monogamous yet committed relationship until they graduated in three years. Ed's long-range plans were to move to the Washington, DC area because that's where government employees lived.

He made that clear to Janice. She loved the idea of moving back to the area, since she originally came from Towson, Maryland.

After graduation, Ed applied and accepted a position with the FBI as a foreign analyst. Shortly thereafter, they were married in a small church in Philadelphia, the Church of Ascension. A low budget honeymoon in Atlantic City was all they could afford. Besides, Janice loved the ocean sounds and smells. They gave her a sense of peace and tranquility, a place for contemplation and clearing of the mind. He hated the sand, but loved the junk food offered by the numerous stands on the boardwalk.

Ed deferred to his bride. The honeymooners went to Atlantic City. They both had student loans to repay, and neither would be earning decent money for a while. Janice had one remarkable trait. When she was happy, sex was incredible. He'd rather have her respond to her animalist sexual urges the ocean brought out in her more than anything in the world would. Life was good when you were twenty-three, recently married, both employed, and facing a bright future.

They settled in McLean, Virginia, and rented a small, cozy, and barely affordable apartment. After four years in the FBI as an analyst monitoring the increased activities of terrorists and terroristic rogue states, Ed transferred to the Foreign Studies department of the CIA in Langley. His assignment: track the cash flow of terrorist groups, identify the paper trails of money transfers, analyze their spending habits, review charitable organizations that fronted for terrorists or terrorist organizations, and collect, analyze, and report the data that posed a national security risk to the government of the United States.

Janice took an entry-level job working with mentally disturbed children in the area. She helped to monitor their lives, raise funds necessary for their health, and generally assisted the staff in whatever activities needed. Her salary was borderline poverty, but she enjoyed the work experience. Her dream as a teenager was to be actively involved with helping children survive the gallows of poverty and despair. She had fulfilled her life's dream. She was in the area she loved. She married a wonderful and sensitive man and was now working with needy children.

He parked the car in the driveway and almost leaped to the front door in his anxiety to reach his cocoon to shut out his oppressive worries of *Red Sunset*.

Ed loved and adored Janice, and deeply admired her for her mental acumen. She possessed incredible insight into most things, and could analyze any situation and offer an intelligent solution. He often found himself using her as his sounding board for new ideas or problems at work. He attributed much of the success he had at work because of her insights. He often wondered where he would be without her, trusting she would see solutions or raise an alarm on issues he hadn't considered. She was his built-in safety net. Her opinions made him safe. Several times she had saved him from promoting bad ideas at the Agency. She worked hard to insure no one labeled him indecisive or incompetent. The Agency considered him a bright star because his proposals and decisions were usually correct and well thought out.

"If they only knew, I'd be in deep shit," he often said to her. She would smile back.

Relief remained elusive. That night, tucked in their California king bed, the report still on his mind, he decided to talk to Janice. Perhaps she could put his mind at ease.

Before speaking, he scanned his thoughts one at a time as though he was using the skip button on his DVD.

It's only a worst-case study. The committee that wrote it could be wrong. It wouldn't be the first Presidential report that was wrong. In fact, most miss the boat and are obsolete before anyone reads it. Yet, the report said no more than sixteen years from now. This is stupid, to get myself so worked up over a what-if report. Len reminded me that dozens of other special committee reports were wrong. And things can and do change rapidly. Let it go stupid. Let it go! he admonished himself.

Still, I can't shake this feeling of doom, of my fear for the future. Logic says to forget about it, I can't. I will never do that!

It was there, firmly embedded in his head, in his belly, in his body, and it was going to stay there unless he, or Janice, figured a way to neutralize it.

"Janice," he cautiously started, "I need to bounce something off you. I'm stuck with some dumb thoughts and need your opinion." Of course, he could never reveal that he had read a highly classified Presidential report, not could or would he acknowledge that such a report existed. The CIA had four unwritten rules regarding classified information.

One: Never bring your work home.

Two: Never disclose information to family or friends. They could be in danger.

Three: Even if they have top security clearance, all information is on a need to know basis.

Four: Don't violate Rules 1, 2, or 3.

The rules protected the country and individuals. To involve families in secret government business placed everyone at risk. Spying was a recognized and established International technique to gather information on friends and enemies alike. Nearly all intelligence agencies honored at least one rule: Families were off limits.

His lingering fear was that terrorists might decide to attack families of government operatives. Terrorists don't follow any spoken, written, or unspoken rules.

"Can't it wait until I finish this chapter? It will only be ten minutes or so."

Experience with Janice made him comply. Once she gave you her attention, she was committed. The extra time gave him an opportunity to rethink how he wanted to phrase his question without alarming her. Twelve minutes later, she closed the book, turned to face him in bed, and coyly said,

"Wouldn't you rather have my body than my mind? The mind can wait, but my passion can't."

In the sixteen years of their marriage, Ed knew they had the best sex when she was aggressive. Wanton, reckless, and electrifying sex. Once they started, she reacted like a possessed sex maniac. He loved it. If only it could happen more frequently. She was usually willing to mess around, but those fits of passion defied boundaries, explanation, and logic.

"I hate turning you down," he muttered, "but right now I really need to talk."

Surprised, and somewhat annoyed since he never turned her down, Janice looked at him with a puzzled look.

"It must be terribly important for you to say NO, so talk," she said sharply.

He wanted to blurt everything out, but he managed to control himself.

"I've had this nagging thought all day about criminals. They are guerrillas who attack the innocent then disappear into the general population. The police are at a disadvantage because they fight an invisible enemy. What would you do? How would you protect people from criminals who use violence to get what they want. They do not care who they hurt. What would you do to stop them?"

"What the hell's wrong with you? You're asking me, now about something that's been going on forever! That's your big problem? For that you're willing to give up sex?"

"You know I can't talk about the real issue, so I used criminals because they're convenient. OK? Don't get all pissed off now. Believe me. This is legitimate. You'll be a big help if you just humor me for a few minutes."

"Idiot." She took a deep breath and disdainfully replied,

"OK, but this better be important and not just some stupid anxiety of yours. It just couldn't wait until after we had sex, could it?"

"No," he meekly responded.

Janice stared at him with fire in her eyes.

"Alright, but I promise it'll be short. Criminals do what they do for money and power over people. We value life. They value death or prison. They're willing to fight and die."

"So what is your question? What can be done to stop these illegal or frightening acts?"

"That's it."

"Is there a real question here?"

Janice seems perplexed and uneasy. Ed realized he had hit a nerve with her and unless he was able to explain his concerns further, the discussion would end in a disaster. Sensing her uneasiness, he offered some calming words.

"I've stated this wrong. Nothing is wrong. I've just been bugged by this ethical question. Let me rephrase it."

He took a deep breath, allowing his words to have the desired calming effect on her.

"Is it morally acceptable to stop criminals before they act? he asked.

"Are you serious?" she asked, disbelieving what she just heard. New lines of tension gathered around her lips and her eyes.

"It that what has you so worked up? You'd give up sex to talk about the morality of dealing with killers and thieves?"

"Yeah, eh… that's the essence of it," he sheepishly replied.

"I don't get it. You're worrying about a hypothetical question that has you so concerned that you can't think straight. Worse, you refuse me sex during my passion time? Are you sick or hiding something from me? And do you mean terrorists, not criminals?"

He tried to reassure her.

"No, it's not terrorists. It's just something I couldn't get out of my head. It's been bugging me all day."

"Let me get this straight. You're asking if it's all right to stop criminals before they act. Since when have you lost your morals or your humanity?" she said forcefully. He heard anger and fear simultaneously.

"Is this what you've become? That's not the man I fell in love with, and certainly not the man I married."

The high pitch of her voice worried him. When Janice's voice changed, he knew she was angry, very angry, and usually at him.

"I'm still the same man, I just need your input," he lied. In his heart he knew something in him had changed. He felt under attack. His life, his family, his country was being threatened by an evil force. He languished in the throes of fear, confusion, and anger. He was angry with the terrorists, with the government, with Winslow, and now Janice. They were all the source of his increasing terror. He always prided himself on his Christian morality to do the proper thing, to respect people's rights, to be open to other's views, and to abide by the adage that people are innocent until proven guilty. All that changed when *Red Sunset* entered his life.

I'd be better off if I wasn't on that fucking reading list. Damn the terrorists, damn bin Laden, damn the government for stirring up terrorists in Iraq, and damn Winslow for being an ostrich. Don't they understand how close we are to losing everything? Where the hell are their heads?

Janice's voice jarred him out of his near catatonic state.

"Ed, Ed, Edddddd…are you OK? What's happening?"

"I'm. OK… just… eh… lost in thoughts, … I guess. Sorry."

"Are you sure?'

"Yes… yes I am."

"You scared the shit out of me. I've never seen you like this before. I thought you had a stroke or something."

"Let's just forget about the whole damn thing. It really wasn't that important. I got off track, what with all the pressure from work. I shouldn't have brought my thoughts home with me. It won't happen again. Promise. Just forget about it."

He ripped his pajamas off in a flash.

"OK, I'm ready."

"I'm not. It's gone. Just forget it," she hissed.

A worried Janice Walker reluctantly kissed him on his cheek.

"Maybe you're right. Let's chalk it up to a bad night. Get some sleep. Good night Ed. Love you."

"Me too."

She turned the lights out. Easy sleep eluded them both.

Ed's troubling thoughts would not stop. He couldn't let go, though he desperately needed to chase it from his mind. Sleep was elusive. He laid there, eyes open, staring at the blackened ceiling. A faint glow from the hallway's night light for the kids cast an eerie soft glow at the far corner of their bedroom.

The light is like my thoughts. I'm in the dark, with just the barest hint of light. Maybe Janice is right. I've allowed my fear…of what?… to screw with my head to the point that it's grown a life of its own. But things have changed. I'm not the same. I'm different, very different. I'm afraid of the future. Is there a future? I don't know, I just don't know. Yet, I believe Red Sunset. We're doomed unless something happens. But what? By whom? When?

Ed heard these same questions repeatedly as he lay awake in the darkened room.

Maybe I'm the one who is naïve. Maybe I'm over reacting to a dark "what if" report by people who might have a hidden agenda, who might want to capture the President's eye. What better way than to scare the shit out of him? It's possible, I guess.

A barely audible "Nooooo," escaped his lips, low enough that Janice couldn't hear.

I'm right damn it. I am! Everything I've learned about terrorists tells me I'm right. I see how little we've done to stop them. They still have money, lots of it. They buy weapons, they make bombs, and they kill people. We've tried to stop them, but we haven't made a dent. I suppose, here and there. But not enough, certainly not nearly enough to put an end to their terror.

He managed a little over three hours of fitful and restless sleep.

Sleep also eluded Janice. Her thoughts were on Ed and his questioning. Though she intellectually understood there HAD to be something really troubling him, his question seemed dumb. Was there a hidden message? *Was he, she, or the children in danger? Did Ed say criminals when he meant terrorists?* A kernel of panic welled in her chest. Her barely perceptible shallow breathing escaped Ed's view. He was in his own world and wasn't prepared to have Janice join him. She wasn't ready to join him, either.

She felt helpless, alone, and frightened. She slept sporadically, an hour on and off. Mostly, she too lie awake with her fears.

They got out of bed about the same time, and prepared to do the morning chores, which were to get the kids dressed, fed, and onto the school bus.

Ed's thoughts continued to plague him. He barley spoke to Janice; she returned the favor.

I never lied to her before. Now, he rationalized, times are different, more dangerous, and more frightening. Instead of traditional warfare, terrorists have changed the rules. They don't want our land or our resources. They want our lives, our minds, and us. They don't give a fuck about following the rules of warfare. How do you stop fanatics? Rogue governments and private citizens are financing, training, sponsoring, and covertly protecting these terrorists. What's worse, there is no accountability by anyone in government. World leaders pussyfoot around, permitting them to do whatever they damn please. They claim they're not involved. Yet, I know they approve of these terrorist. They support them with money, provide safe havens, and give families of the jihad martyrs cash when their son dies in a suicide attack. The simple fact is that terrorists really want to control the world. Red Sunset proves I'm right.

It was too early to go to work. He had an hour to kill. He watched as Janice glided through the morning routine of cleaning the kitchen after the kids for school. Her silk pajamas clung to her figure. The more she moved, the more excited Ed became. He suddenly needed to make love to her, to feel the warmth of her body pressing against his.

"I apologize again for last night. I don't know what got into me. I know it freaked you out. Me too. Couldn't sleep well because of it. Looks like you didn't get much either."

"No, I didn't. But I heard you breathing heavily, and it wasn't because of me, so I knew you still had that crap on your mind," she said dripping with sarcasm.

"Yeah, for some reason the question became an issue for me, and I couldn't see the forest for the trees," he quietly responded. "Now that that's out of the way, let's go back to your body question from last night. The answer is YES!"

"Yes what? Now? Too bad! The moment's gone. Mind if we wait until tonight, or whenever we're both ready?" she pleaded half-heartedly.

Oh fuck, I really blew it, Ed wanted to say, but decided on "Alright," rather than antagonize her further.

She's still pissed. My stupid fault for rejecting her. Ed quickly left to shower.

Janice knew the rest of the day wouldn't get any better. She still felt deeply frightened. She didn't know the source of her fear. That frightened her.

3

SEPTEMBER 2009:

He needed to feed his family or they would not survive. When Bilal first joined the ExecProtect Agency (EPA) in South Africa, he was looking for a way to protect his family. As a construction supervisor in Pakistan, he earned about 3300 PKR (Rupees) per month. That ended when terrorism became Pakistan's main export. New construction fell to nearly zero and he became expendable. No longer able to earn a living, Bilal struggled to support his meager existence through a variety of odd jobs. He drove a taxi, sold fruit in the market, and even resorted to begging when necessary. He heard of ExecProtect from a friend and decided to discuss it with his wife, Nasrin.

"The thought of leaving you and our family is offensive, yet, without money, how will we survive?" he sadly lamented to her.

Short, stocky and powerfully built, Bilal recognized he fit the profile ExecProtect recruited, despite the fact that he was Muslim. He felt that since he was not very religious, they would accept him.

EPA was recruiting fifty-four security people with military or security training. A sergeant in the Pakistani Army for three years, he had commanded an elite rifle squad that saw action against India over Kashmir. That was enough to qualify, he deduced. He spoke Pendjabi, Sindhi, Urdu, and English. That, coupled with his military experience, were valuable assets that ExecProtect would surely find quite interesting. He decided he had the credentials EPA sought.

The pay of $87 US dollars per month, about 5200 Pakistan Rupees (PKR), was more than enough to compensate for the risk he was taking and for being away from his family. He anticipated sending almost 4000 PKR per month home to his wife and their five children.

He and Nasrin discussed ExecProtect during the next week.

"I fear for your safety and how your absence will impact the family. The children and I need you and your strength, your love, and the protection only you can give us in Pakistan," she sobbed.

Tears of anguish and great trepidation swamped their conversations. Bilal, although fearful, tried to allay her fears.

"It wouldn't be long. I promise. Just until we accumulate enough money to pay for our needs. The extra money will help us until new construction begins. I will have to be away only twelve months."

"Twelve months is a lifetime. I don't know how we will manage. The money will pay the bills, but the family needs more. It is you we need more than the money," she pleaded.

"We must be practical. I will miss you and the children too, perhaps even more. You have each other. I will have no one. But, I have no job. I tried to earn enough, but failed. I cannot feed you on the small amount I earn from driving a taxi. People don't have money for taxis or anything else. Everyone is hurting. We need to do something, however painful. I've made my decision. I must join ExecProtect, if they'll have me," he replied. His eyes became misty. Hers were red from crying.

Sadly, they conceded that joining the EPA was a necessity and their only practical option. Because of the one-year's employment requirement, they agreed to seek one concession from EPA before he signed the employment papers. He wanted permission to return home two times a year, without pay. If EPA wouldn't agree, Bilal agreed he would not take the job, in spite of the fact there were many opportunities to earn a living. Although two trips a year would dip into their savings, they conceded he needed to be home. The family needed to be together. The children needed to see their father.

He applied by mail. Three weeks later, he and the EPA representative met at a local restaurant. Within a half hour, both sides agreed to a deal that included six weeks of non-pay leave to allow him three consecutive weeks at home for each trip.

After he had signed the employment papers, Bilal confessed to Nasrin he was thinking of accepting the ExecProtect's offer to extend his employment for a second year of service. Resigning for a second year meant a bonus of two months pay. It was too much to reject, he explained to her. He planned to accept, although they both agreed they would review their situation before Bilal signed the papers.

Bilal left his tearful and distressed wife and five children for Preiska, South Africa two weeks later. The date was September 3, 2009. The temperature had soared to a stifling 109 degrees.

It took a combined thirty-eight hours for him to reach EPA headquarters in Preiska through a combination of commercial and EPA private planes. Preiska, located in the foothills of Doringberge on the bank of the Orange River, was a dry and desolate desert area of South Africa. Its remoteness was the primary reason for EPA to locate their business there, away from government scrutiny. It offered them the freedom of moving their aircrafts and people without concerns about cargo or personnel manifestos.

Preiska, according to the Korana Qua language, means the place of the lost she-goat. The EPA employees referred to it as the place of the lost souls. It is a vast and sparely populated area. Farmers grow vegetables, fruit, and maize. Sheepherders and EPA employees are the remaining people who live in and around the area. Farmers draw irrigation water from the Orange River. Springtime arrives in August or September, depending on the amount of rainfall the previous month. Until 1996, Preiska was an active copper and zinc-mining town until the mines became unprofitable to operate.

His second week there, he and three other recruits went to see the area's only attraction, the Wonderdrall, where the Orange River forges a horseshoe-shaped island that creates an illusion that the water runs uphill.

Time wasn't kind to Bilal. He felt miserable, lonely, and depressed. He resented that he had to leave his wife and children alone for extended times. Nasrin and he had never been apart in their ten years of marriage.

He worried his carpentry skills would disappear through inactivity, and his sons would be the ultimate losers. Pakistani fathers teach their sons their skills. He had become an absent father and teacher.

Bilal's father had dutifully taught him house framing for the construction industry when he left school after the eighth grade. His mother, a beautiful woman with wide deep brown eyes and a warm inviting smile, died giving birth to his younger sister. Bilal's family of two brothers and one sister died through disease or auto accidents. Only he and his father Syed remained alive.

Bilal quickly discovered a propensity for woodcarvings and was elevated to carpenter apprentice. There he applied his carving skills into cabinet making and built-in construction. He feared his hands would lose the delicate maneuverability necessary to retain his skills while in Africa.

His busy training program as a security guard and mercenary did not lessen his need for Nasrin. He deeply longed for her touch and the loving hugs from his children. His training program focused on the numerous skills to become a personal security guard. Not just any security guard, but for special assignment to the CEO of Metalique LLD.

Metalique is a multi-national company with extensive mineral rights throughout Africa. They had a standing order with EPA for a replacement as each man's employment term ended. It was automatic business for EPA.

Bilal's specific security guard training, in addition to mastering weapons, included personnel profiling, protection of the client from a crowd, safety precautions in a variety of terrains and geographical conditions, and building and vehicle protection techniques. Hand to hand combat and close range fighting techniques were also a vital aspect of his training. All EPA recruits spent many hours practicing their sharpshooting skills.

Bilal Maqsood Ahmed, short, stocky and solidly built, sported a full dark beard that hid his round face. His dark brown eyes set close and deeply in his head, made him look fierce and menacing. Deep down he was a loving and dedicated father and husband, and showed respect for both men and women. Quick to smile, and quick to laugh, he was not popular with his fellow mercenaries and officers. He preferred to be alone most of the time. He found idle talking a waste of time, so he did his best to avoid the typical barracks chatter. He never participated in horseplay, cards, or jaunts into town for drinks or women. Though not a practicing Muslim, he adhered to the principle traditions. He didn't drink whiskey and didn't chase after women.

His intensity and dedication to excelling in all aspects of the training program earned him the respect of his fellow trainees. They appreciated his hard work, his natural ability, his leadership, his strength of character, and his fierce loyalty. He soon developed a reputation as someone they could count on in a personal fight or a gun battle, even if they were not friends. He never shirked from his responsibilities.

Individually, they worried about his glaring personality flaw. Bilal had a temper that seemed to be waiting for an excuse to erupt. Most accepted it as part of his Sunni Muslim temperament. Though Bilal was not devout Muslim, he accepted the sect for what it offered him and his family, mainly the security of the majority religious group in Pakistan.

Within the first five weeks of training, Bilal displayed his dormant anger for the first time. Nasrin had recognized this and pleaded with him to control his temper. There were always young men looking for work, and an unsympathetic boss might quickly fire him by labeling him a troublemaker.

He recognized the wisdom of her advice. He trained himself to clench his fists instead of hitting someone when he felt his anger building up. It worked, Bilal kept out of trouble, for a while.

He was feeling sorry for himself. Bilal soon lost interest in controlling his emotions. In fact, he was looking for an excuse to release his pent-up frustration. His reward came quickly. Another trainee foolishly spoke disparagingly about Pakistan in the barracks common area. Bilal instantly leaped from his chair, and brutally thrashed the man. In the process, he broke the man's nose, knocked out three front teeth, and put him out of commission for three days. The assault ended when another trainee whacked Bilal on the back of his head with the butt of a rifle. The EPA fined him 700 PKR to cover the medical costs for the injured man. Bilal received nothing for the massive headache he had for two days.

A second incident happened less than twenty days later. An Irish recruit laughingly poked fun at Bilal because of his short stature. It took two men to pull him away from the fallen perpetrator, but not before he kicked and broke the man's fourth rib on the left side. He paid a fine of 1000 PKR for that one. Bilal's fines were mounting. He knew he needed to control his temper or see his paycheck disappear in fines. He promised himself to behave.

Bilal constantly worried about the safety of his family. New recruits could not carry their cell phones during training. Management ordered all trainees to turn in their phones until they had their work assignments and left EPA. EPA claimed recruits became distracted with news from home that tended to affect their training. Management feared an angry or worried recruit would miss valuable training that could potentially result in the client's or the recruit's death. Letters were the only mode of correspondence. Bilal felt cut off from Nasrin. It exacerbated his worries and his loneliness.

Bilal's home was only forty-six miles southeast of the area where terrorists were active. The war against terrorists, especially against al Qaeda, remained unchanged. Bin Laden was still at large, in spite of over 15,000 Pakistani and US ground forces stationed in the foreboding and treacherous mountains of the tribal area. Bilal feared that extremists would spread their tentacles beyond the hills to threaten his family.

The Ahmed house was a small simple stucco single story building in the village of Sam Khel-Alang, midway between the two towns of Sam Khel and Alang, about 60 miles north of Quetta. Life was simple in the village. People were more concerned about survival than the politics of the day. Only the affluent seem to care. Politics don't affect poor people. To eat, to work, and to provide for one's family is more than enough to occupy one's day.

Two and a half months of difficult training in the 90 degrees plus daily temperatures, coupled with the separation from his family, took its emotional toll on Bilal. He longed to return to Pakistan to be with his family, to talk with his friends and live under his own roof. He wasn't satisfied with the three weeks he had negotiated. He wanted to return home permanently.

He dreaded the thought of extending his one year service with EPA. Rumors that conditions were improving in Pakistan circulated within the barracks. Bilal quickly convinced himself he'd be able to find construction work when he returned. He desperately needed to believe the rumors. It was the single point of hope he embraced to make his remaining service time tolerable.

He sent most of his pay to Nasrin, with instructions for her to use what she needed and save the rest. He kept enough to take care of his immediate needs. His pay was many times what he earned as a construction worker, and he felt confident that she could manage the bills and save enough to carry them through future bad times.

Without his family and in need of a friend, he hooked up with Bruce MacCardle, who bunked two apartments down the hall in the same barracks. Current employees were assigned to the barracks during advanced training or when between assignments. Each employee had his own small private apartment, which actually was a large single room, equipped with modest yet functional furnishings. A single sized cot hugged the rear wall. Two built-in night tables and lights, a medium size steel desk and plastic desk chair on wheels, a larger than expected closet, a small dining table with two cane chairs, a tiny living room that included a two-person sofa, a lounge chair that had seen better days, and a 19" color TV. An apartment-sized refrigerator sat in one corner, beneath an array of brown wall cabinets. The barracks had a central community room for the employees for conversation or recreation. EPA equipped it with a ping-pong table, a large 52" Sony color TV, dartboards and a pay bar where beer was the beverage of choice. Each of the four EPA barracks had a central bathroom furnished with six stall-enclosed toilettes, a large trough-like washbasin and an open shower area with six showerheads to service the inhabitants.

By the time Bilal moved into the barracks, Bruce, a two year EPA veteran between assignments, had moved into the same building. Bruce wanted to upgrade his skills. He came back to EPA to attend three-month training on counter intelligence methodology and management. Bruce and Bilal roomed adjacent to one another. Bruce had returned to South Africa from Brazil where he served as one of six round-the-clock bodyguards to a wealthy oil executive.

Bruce walked into the common area one evening to find Bilal sitting in the corner by himself. He walked over to Bilal, and warmly said,

"Hello, I'm Bruce. You look like I did when I first came here. Alone, quiet, and ready to kick ass. I don't mean to intrude on your space, but trust me; it will be easier to get through this training when you have a friend. Besides, I'm really good at kicking ass myself. Want to give it a try?" he asked with a wide grin on his lanky face.

Bilal looked up and burst into laughter. "What makes you think I want to kick someone's ass?"

"Aren't you the one who already had two fights? My guess is that you'd like to fight again, someone, anyone, but it would cost you too much money or even your job. Right?"

"I don't think I'm looking for a fight. They just come. But you're right. I can't afford to be kicked out of EPA," Bilal replied. "I doubt if I would make a good friend to anyone. I prefer to keep to myself."

"Pakistani?"

"Yes."

"Scottish myself."

"Well Bilal, it's your choice. Do you want someone to cover your back? I'm one hell-of a good fighter. We can watch each other's back. You never know when you need a friend, someone you can trust, and someone with whom to talk."

"Why should I trust you?" Bilal questioned.

It was Bruce's turn to laugh. "Of course you shouldn't trust me. But at least you know where I stand, and that's more than you'll ever learn from someone who pretends to be your friend, but isn't."

Bilal thought about it for a few moments, then answered,

"OK, you can be my friend. But aren't you taking a chance with me? How do you know whether I am a good or bad friend?"

"In this business, anyone who can fight is worth having as a friend," Bruce replied.

They agreed to be friendly. Friendship would have to grow.

Bruce MacCardle was the antithesis of Bilal. His 6'3" lanky frame housed a wiry set of muscles. A sharp angular jaw drew attention to his wide mouth that covered his face when he smiled. Glistening white teeth, straight, even, and beautiful, gave him movie star status among his peers. His friends called him *Million Dollar Man* as a tribute to his pearly whites. Bruce took great pride in his teeth and spent a large portion of his money in their maintenance. After he joined EPA, he decided that he wanted perfect teeth. He committed to a full dental care program that included braces, whitening, caps and regular dentist visits.

Born in 1974 in Melrose, Scottish Borders, Scotland, he managed to live down to his and everyone's expectations. His family moved to Inverness, the Capital of The Highlands when he was 3 years old. Inverness is on the banks of the river Ness, at the head of Great Glen. It is here where the famous Lock Ness monster is reputed to live. Inverness has a population of 65,103 people, and is the site of the ancient Fort George. After linking to the west coast of Scotland by the spectacular Caledonian Canal in 1822, Inverness flourished and became the Capital of The Highlands.

Bruce's father had become a master gardener whose specialty was the care and cultivation of flowers for both commercial and family consumption. He worked for Gregors Nursery, the major supplier of fresh flowers in Scotland. The bulk of their business was International. Sixty-five percent from Germany and Spain, twenty-five percent from England.

Bruce was infamous for his unremarkable school career and life. He failed to complete high school, failed to learn a trade, never earned a sustainable paycheck, married and divorced twice. No children. Yet, those who knew him loved him. He sparkled with personality, was honest, and one of the most loving people proclaimed by those who had the pleasure of his acquaintance. He willingly gave of himself, regardless of the request, the time, the cause, or the person making the demands. Bruce even granted total strangers requests for assistance for everything except for money. People willingly slipped money into his hands to help him with his daily sustenance. Yet, his personal pride prevented him from directly asking for assistance. Strangely, and fortunately, he didn't have to. People gravitated to him with offers to help of their own volition. Simply because he was Bruce. No one prodded him to change his life style, to get a job, or to repay them for their kindness.

That is, of course, except for his two wives. It was the primary cause for their divorces. Each woman knew and understood Bruce, or so they thought, and were convinced they could change him into the perfect husband. All they asked of him was to earn a decent living, have children, and live happily ever after. They believed he was worth the trouble. Who wouldn't want to spend time with a universally loved person? Each woman embraced the same question. Each later decided it was folly to expect him to be willing or able to change.

Bruce saw no need to change. He was happy, had a considerable number of friends from all lifestyles, and was extremely gregarious and fun. He was the pied piper of his town. Surrounded by happy friends and strangers, Bruce had isolated himself from the troubles of the world.

His single scrape with the law was inadvertent and unexpected. With his bottomless kindness and naivety, Bruce was asked by a casual bar acquaintance, Joe Morton, to deliver a bag to the Caledonia Canal, the popular yacht area. Morton explained that the bag belonged to his girlfriend that she left it in his apartment. He was leaving for a long business trip directly from the bar and couldn't return it himself. He gave Bruce the taxi money to and from the Canal. He explained to Bruce that in two hours a woman named Kathy, wearing a blue and while sundress, would be waiting for him in the coffee shop at the end of the retail area of the pier. Bruce willingly agreed. For his efforts he paid Bruce 50 Euros, about 75 dollars US. Morton insisted that Bruce arrive on time since Kathy could not stay long since she had to get back to work. Bruce promised he'd be there on time.

Instead of the woman, the police greeted him, handcuffed him, and carted him off to jail. When word spread what had happened, twenty-three of Bruce's friends swarmed the police station demanding his release. The local Magistrate, a kindly older man, explained the matter was out of his hands because of the estimated 75,000 Euro street value of the heroin Bruce was carrying. The law demanded incarceration until his trial.

His friends quickly pooled their money and secured the services of Gaylord P. O'Donnell, one of the top criminal lawyers in Inverness. There was no bail.

Bruce sat in prison for over two months, devastated by these sudden turn of events. He withdrew from everyone, and barely acknowledged the frequent visitors to his jail cell.

His trial began two months and three days after he was caught. O'Donnell presented his case to the Magistrate. He explained how Bruce MacCardle, universal friend, master dummy, become a mule for the drug dealer, only because the stranger duped him. He called forty-two personal witnesses who spoke eloquently and passionately about Bruce's virtues as a friend and caring person. Each spoke about his naivety, his acceptance of strangers, and his passion to help anyone, anywhere, at anytime.

O'Donnell cited multiple events when other unscrupulous people took advantage of him. He explained Bruce had a fundamental desire to help friends or strangers alike. Bruce had no previous record, and had never done anything to injure another person. Though, he argued, Bruce was unemployable and not educated, he still lived by his own set of high morals. His golden rule was to do nothing that could harm another being. For him to entertain distributing drugs was "absolutely unthinkable." It went against Bruce's moral principles.

McDonnell further argued Bruce was a model citizen. He never threw trash on the street, didn't take a neighbor's paper, and always waited for the light to turn green before crossing the street. His argument was so compelling that Bruce easily won acquittal. He left the Court a free man.

But he was no longer the same person who first entered jail. Bruce was deeply depressed while incarcerated. He hated knowing he had become the unwitting tool of drug dealers whom he despised for the evil they inflicted on society. In the two months of his incarceration, he examined his life, his beliefs, and his status in the community. He didn't like what he saw. The truth was painful, yet he managed to turn it into a catharsis. He was easily duped too often, not educated and couldn't hold a steady job. He now found it disturbing that he chose to live off the kindness of others. He needed a job and a new attitude. He would have to leave Inverness. He needed to change, big time.

He saw an advertisement in the evening newspaper for ExecProtect and applied. Although he wasn't a man of violence, he decided he needed to experience a different life, one that would teach him how to function. With great emotional difficulty, he joined the real world. He applied for the position of security guard. This, he decided, would teach him the perspectives of both ends of life, and once he learned those lessons, he might be able to find his place in society. EPA seemed a good place to start his new life.

Amid genuine cries of anguish and pleas by his friends to reconsider, Bruce remained steadfast with his decision. Three weeks later he was on his first-ever plane ride to Johannesburg South Africa, and then to Preiska. He left with trepidation and anxiety. Concerned that he might have made a wrong choice, as he so often did, he wondered if he could fit into this new and frightening life style. He never lived with restrictions before, and he dreaded the thought of the consequences if he was unable to adjust to the loneliness and the violent nature of the job.

Bruce surprisingly made the adjustments as an EPA recruit.

*

The series of high profile kidnappings in Africa, mainly in the Niger Delta and The Ivory Coast, resulted in a demand for protection by oil company executives. Efetobore Uko, former Captain of the Special Forces for the Democratic Republic of Congo, along with two close associates, created the ExecProtect Agency in 1996 to meet the need for highly trained security personnel. They expanded their capabilities with mercenaries trained to support coups or to combat the rising insurgencies in Africa. Consequently, EPA trained their employees in all phases of armed conflicts, both open and covert. Security guards normally specialized in training for assignments dictated by the customer to meet their specific needs. Metalique demanded their security personnel be equally efficient in security and armed conflict operations. That required an additional two months training. Because this dual capability involved greater personal risk and training, employees received an additional 30% compensation pay. Few rejected this offer. Bilal had accepted it without a second thought.

EPA's policy was to dual train all new employees in all phases of security operations, even if their prospective employers didn't require the complete skills set. Employee flexibility and multi-capabilities resulted in increased EPA earnings, while also extending employment opportunities for their people. In the past, many EPA employees found themselves stationed in high conflict areas such as Iraq, Indonesia, and Kuwait. Sometimes they supported a coup attempt, supported local military, or civilian authorities in their local operations. EPA became the largest armed labor supplier in Africa. The three owners became rich men on the backs, and sometimes the deaths, of their employees.

The nature and danger of their work forced ExecProtect to become self-sufficient. They insisted their employees learn multiple skills of personnel, weapons, and warfare equipment use and deployment under a variety of high-risk conditions. To support their varied and often unusual operations, EPA owned their own fleet of four Bush Hawk planes capable of taking off and landing on the roughest terrains. Their weapons training included a variety of Swiss and Weston M & P 45 caliber 10 round pistols, AK-47 assault rifles equipped with grenade launchers, and FN-Herstel 5.7 armor-piercing guns. Recruits received their work assignments only after they become proficient with each weapon.

EPA used specialized tools or weapons to support their variety of missions and customer's requests. Items that fell under the South African import restrictions had to be smuggled into the country. EPA used their Hawk fleet of planes to bypass the restrictions. The borders of South Africa are long, porous, and impossible to patrol. EPA used private airports to deliver their personnel and their legal and illegal cargo. The airport owners readily accepted cash and asked no questions. Those airports that were not available to EPA for whatever reason, EPA simply used any convenient open field. The Hawks were ideally suited for such use.

Most EPA employees joined the company for the money, although some preferred the adventure of danger. A major problem for the EPA employees was how to get their pay to their relatives at home. Cash in the mail invited thieves, and most people in the rural areas didn't have banks or checking accounts.

Sympathetic to their plight, EPA took responsibility for delivery of their employee's paychecks. They established a network of global couriers to insure the cash reached the designated recipient. EPA willingly shouldered the added expenses. In return, they received a fierce loyalty and commitment from their highly trained employees. Their skills and expertise were useless without the loyalty and the continued employment of their members. Families relied on EPA for their survival and became beholden to EPA for safely delivering the money.

EPA made the necessary International money conversions and transfers according to each employee's wishes. They used the most favorable currency exchange rates as a small bonus and an incentive for the employee to send their earnings home. They enjoyed a widely held reputation as an employee-friendly company, which, in turn, enabled them to recruit more employees. Word of mouth was their biggest recruitment tool. It worked successfully for them for over twelve years. EPA's reputation as a caring employer was as impeccable as it was unusual.

4

DECEMBER 2009:

"What now?"

The double-ring intercom buzzer shattered his concentration. Barrows was in the midst of his Monday Priority One ritual of reviewing the morning intelligence report.

"Mr. Barrows, guess what," Mary Jackson, his three-year secretary said excitedly. President Schuster's executive secretary, Judi Ritagoli, just called. The President wants to see you this Thursday in the Oval Office. You need to be there by 10:20 AM, and she said to keep it quiet. Tell absolutely *no one* she emphasized. How exciting for you. So, what's this all about? Is he making you the Vice President?" she teased him.

"This is the first I've heard of it, and I doubt he's making me anything," he snapped. The unexpected demand from the President stunned him. Normally a calm and calculating Deputy Secretary of Homeland Security executive, he instantly turned into a mass of irregular pulsating nerves. For one of the few times in his life, he felt out of control. Worry became his unfamiliar and disturbing partner.

For the next three days, Barrows was nervous, agitated, and highly apprehensive. Usually upbeat and confident, he re-evaluated his career plans, his life, and his future. It had been eight months since he met the President in person, and that was for a major debriefing in support of the Homeland Security Secretary, Sidney G. Kleinerman. His part was so brief he doubted President Schuster would remember him, although he remembered the event vividly. He mingled among the inner circle, shook hands, and the President personally congratulated him on his achievements as the Employee of the Year.

Now the President wants to speak with me in three days, and I have to keep it quiet. But why? Is he firing me? I've worked my ass off as the DHS (Department of Homeland Security) and it could disappear overnight. Nothing feels good about this. I wonder if this is a private meeting, or will others be there. How could I defend myself if the President asks for my resignation? But why would he be involved? He doesn't fire people at my level. If anyone's going to fire me, it'll be Kleinerman.

These thoughts swirled in his head. He felt confused and uneasy. At home, he snapped at his wife Lynette and their two teenage sons. He barely slept that night.

"What's the matter, dear?" she asked the following morning.

"Nothing that concerns you! Work issues, that's all," he barked.

"I've never seen you like this before."

"I told you to forget it! It's none of your damn business!" He stared at her, left eyebrow slightly raised. "Don't bother me again," he said in a raised voice.

"I… I… I'm sorry, it's just…"

"Just be quiet!"

She lowered her eyes, submissive to his anger.

What the fuck will I do if I have to leave the Service? My position could vanish in an instant, at his whim, he thought.

Now, his dream seemed to be in jeopardy, and he didn't know why.

Years of careful planning, execution, and hard work. For what?

"My career was on target until the President called, but for how long? Everyone, especially my father, the damn control freak, assured me that by accepting the Deputy position, my pathway to the Presidency would save years of effort. So did I," he grumbled quietly to himself.

When the opportunity arose, he had eagerly accepted an entry-level position with the CIA, primarily because he believed, as did his father, that terrorists would become a major force with which to contend in the future. As long as he was involved in a project dealing with terrorists, Barrows knew he would always be in the midst of the action. His father's access to multiple reports that predicted major uprisings in the Middle East by disgruntled Muslims and Arabs provided him insight to select the best long-term position for his son.

Barrows Senior correctly assessed that increased levels of animosity and discontent by militants, possibly fueled by Iran or Iraq, would become a major headache for the free world. He recognized that the tensions in the Middle East could erupt and become the focal point of the US long-term problems, problems that would strain the leadership and influence of the United States. He deduced these upheavals in the early '70's and '80's, when the world was focused on Russia, and little attention was paid to the growing unrest in the Middle East.

When his son came to him for advice on the CIA position in 1982, Senior urged him to accept the position "because this is the best place to learn about the troubles of the future. There," his father had explained, "you'll be ahead of the curve. With the world in chaos from terrorism, your experience in the CIA will prepare you to handle the biggest issue on the President's plate, which, I believe, will be more troublesome than the domestic economy, or some crap country's civil war. Learn how to succeed against terrorists and the country will beg for your leadership."

Barrows took the job without hesitation.

For the moment, Barrows' future seemed less than bright.

If I'm out, I might be able to convince my father that I suffered the same political setback as he did when he sought the Presidency. Hopefully, he'll accept that and not cut me out of the will. Yet, I think I can still earn a great living. I can be involved in politics in some form or another. I could try for a seat in the Senate, or become a lobbyist. I'll get another job, but it won't be in the White House. Goodbye Oval Office. I'm sure some lobby firm will welcome me with open arms and wallets. I have connections they'd all love to have. Between my congressional connections and my father's financial muscle, I'm a catch!

These thoughts weren't convincing enough to help him through this sudden crisis. His worries were so murky he couldn't see a future. His plan, so meticulously structured since he was in his twenty's, now looked like a pile of crushed and rusted metal piled stories high in a junk yard. Rust and dust, dust and rust. That's how he saw the fragments of his soon to be shattered life.

Negativity shrouded him with its twisted and decaying arms. Timothy Barrows felt certain he knew what to expect. It made the wait for his meeting with the President interminable. He wasn't sure if he would be able to attend the meeting before he collapsed from mental exhaustion. Heeding the President's instructions, he didn't discuss his meeting with anyone, especially his father, Barrows Senior.

He knew his father well. He feared Senior would twist some arms or call someone at the White House in an attempt to learn what was happening.

If he does that, it will get back to the President. I'm not ready to piss Schuster off any more than what he might be already. On the other hand, he surmised, *perhaps he wants to discuss a special assignment.*

It's the only conclusion that made sense to him in light of his excellent government record of accomplishment, his father's connections, and the fact that both had donated considerable money towards the election of President Schuster. Thoughts of *All that should count* prevented him from exploding as time inched slowly towards his Thursday meeting. That evening while watching the evening news, a special report on the suffering children in South Africa appeared. He immediately turned to another channel. All his life the one sight he could not handle was to see the despair and hopelessness of children. Especially tonight.

Thursday morning arrived in its own agonizing time. Barrows was in no mood to fight the nearly five inches of snow that fell the previous evening in Washington. Traffic was never good heading into the Capital, but he knew today would be especially frustrating. The morning traffic report didn't help. Cold and shivering in the biting eighteen-degree temperature, KTX TV's meteorologist Julie Levow reported from the steps of the Washington Monument that the snow removal throughout the city was proceeding more slowly than hoped. Snow mixed with sleet prevented the crews from reaching their depot destinations. But, she added, she had been assured the city would be cleared by 2 PM. She urged motorists to take the train or public transportation into the city. "All government agencies will remain open," she cheerfully interjected.

Barrows left his house at 8:15, two hours before his White House appointment. It usually took less than an hour for him to drive from his home in Manassas. He drove his wife's 4-wheel drive Lexus LX SUV instead of his Porsche. He pulled into the While House underground garage and parked in the visitor's space. After having his credentials checked and rechecked at the guard station, he was ushered into the waiting room adjacent to the Oval Office.

"Hello, I'm Timothy Barrows to see the President," he said rather perfunctorily to Judi. She already knew why he was there. She smiled at him and replied,

"Yes, I know. Please be seated. You're a little early. The President will be with you shortly."

Judi and three other assistants were busy handling the mounds of papers that altered the topography of their desks while attending to the constantly ringing phones. Barrows watched the activity as though he was a casual observer at a scripted play depicting people in planned chaos. This small diversion wasn't enough to ease his tension. He fidgeted nervously in his chair, compulsively shaking his left foot. He wasn't sure how or where to put his body. Judi was aware of his anxiety and offered,

"The President is running later than expected. I expect he should be available within the next 20 minutes or so. Would you like some coffee, tea, cold drink, water, doughnuts, or cookies?" she asked. He graciously declined. His stomach was churning enough and he feared anything going in might want to come out. *Not a good prospect to toss your cookies in the President's waiting room,* Barrows mused.

Finally, after what seemed hours, the President buzzed Judi to escort Barrows into his office. The previous occupants had already left through the side door. Barrows followed her through the huge mahogany double doors. A sharp staccato knock, she quietly opened the right side door, lead Barrows into the Oval Office, and quickly exited. She closed the door behind her.

Barrows had always been impressed with the Oval Office, though his only previous glimpse was through a picture that hung in his father's office. Clark Barrow Sr. and then President Walter T. Zanger consented to a photo op session years ago. It was his reward for helping to raise over a million dollars for Zanger's election campaign.

The Oval Office reeked of history, of elegance, and authority. He felt impressed, even awed by the sense of sheer power emanating from the President's office. The President's seal behind him, two flags of the United States of America on either side of the emblem, hovered behind the massive mahogany wooden desk. Barrows' only concern was what was going to happen in the next few minutes that would determine his fate.

President Schuster moved around his desk and extended his hand.

"Thank you for coming, Timothy."

The President had a serious yet faint smile on his face.

"Thank you sir, it's my pleasure to see you again," Barrows softly responded. They shook hands, and the President motioned for him to sit in one of the two brown wing backed leather chairs positioned in a corner opposite his desk, the ones facing each another.

"It's less formal here than at my desk. Easier to talk."

The chair's lack of comfort became immediately evident. It only exacerbated Barrow's uneasiness. It was hard and unyielding, and hit his lower back enough to give him a backache. The designer had shorter people than he was in mind. His legs extended well beyond the firm padded seat. He'd generally preferred sitting in either a hard wooden chair or a soft fluffy chaise lounge. But, he wasn't in the Oval Office for comfort. If things went badly, he'd probably never see this chair again, let alone sit in it.

At least whatever the President is going to do, he intended to do it face to face and not separated by his highly polished desk, Barrows reflected.

As expected, the office had no paperwork in view, no In/Out baskets loaded with papers in transition, and no signs of drinks, cups, or anything to eat. Almost sterile, now that he thought about it.

The President smiled and began speaking.

"How are your wife and children, Timothy? Everything OK at Homeland Security?"

"Both doing well, sir," replied Barrows.

"Excellent. I'm sure you're wondering why I asked you here, so let me get right to the point. If you followed my campaign speeches, you might remember I promised to do something concrete about global terrorism. I've decided to implement a plan that I feel will help us for the future. As you know, the roots of terrorism are complex and sometimes obscured, but I believe there are things we can do to reduce the fascination that al Qaeda offers to young men. My plan will accomplish two things. One, it may help to eliminate the fertile grounds that allow terrorists to flourish, and two, it will definitely help the world economy and productivity, and hopefully, bring global peace.

Recent discussions with world leaders during my trip to Europe, Asia, and Russia have solidified and clarified my commitment to being pro-active in the pursuit of peace. I know this sounds far-fetched, but I think it's possible. With the support of all the world leaders with whom I spoke, I am creating a special sub cabinet committee called Peace Envoys. Its mission will be to identify and to recommend programs to assist third world countries to utilize the knowledge and expertise of the developed countries. We will bring the technologies and advantages currently denied them. These countries are poor and loaded with corruption. The leaders of the free world are hoping to change all that. We have put together an interesting plan to pool our money, resources, and personnel to bring the necessary changes to these countries. We know it will take time and patience, but we feel it's achievable. I have received hard commitments in funding and personnel from twenty-eight nations. Let me show you something."

The President reached into his inner jacket pocket and withdrew a blue bank passbook, opened it. He handed it to Barrows, instructing him to read the printing out loud. There was only one entry.

"Thirty-five million dollars!" exclaimed Barrows.

"Now," instructed President Schuster, "flip to the first page and read the name."

"Timothy R. Barrows, Jr." Astonished, Barrows quizzically looked up at the President.

"I… don't understand."

Schuster laughed. "I didn't think you would. It's simple. We want you as Chairman of the Peace Envoys. The money is to support the programs you will recommend for the poor countries. Nineteen countries have committed their money and people to this project. Each contributing country has selected one or two people with excellent credentials to be part of the Peace Envoys, reporting directly to you. Before I continue, I'd like to hear your thoughts and questions."

"I'm honored, Mr. President. Thank you for thinking of me for this position. I… err… guess I do have some immediate questions. First, why me?"

"Why you? Let me review your file."

President Schuster moved to the front of his desk and pulled out a file from the drawer, opened it, paused, and read out loud,

"Graduated Harvard Law. Joined law firm of Thorsten, Jefferson, and Verdez as an insurance litigator. Studied politics in the evening after work. Appointed US District Attorney for the Northern sector of Maryland. Main claim to fame was the jailing of seven leaders of three corrupt gangs in Maryland-Chips, Bloods and MS-13, for drug dealing and ordering the assassinations of their rivals. Elected Governor of Maryland in 2001. Served a six-year term and created the *Governor's Office of Homeland Security,* a partnership with local and Federal Governments in the fight against terrorism. Moved to Homeland Security, accomplished enough to be appointed Deputy Secretary. I think your credentials speak for themselves, Timothy."

"Thank you, Mr. President," Barrows responded in as humble a tone he could manage.

"I guess I do have several other questions, sir."

"What's involved, for how long is this appointment, where and how will I operate? How will you measure my performance? What are your expectations? How can I fight the corruption that exists in these countries? To whom will I report? How do I account for the money spent? What if we need more money?" quickly responded Barrows.

"You guess? That's some list! I never expected anything less. First, you and your group spend the money as you see fit, on your own authority, based on proposals you submit to me. I'll pass them along to the other leaders. That's why all participating countries are on your committee to be certain you have considered all interests and submit meaningful proposals. I will resolve any conflicts that arise. On the corruption issue, we are resolved to apply adequate pressure to remove or minimize corrupt or ineffective leaders. We will demand the resignation of those who will not cooperate, from the top to the bottom. We will also provide workers, administrators, and materials required to implement your proposals. Your money will go towards researching the problems of each nation, the costs of running your organization, and the start-up funds to kick things off. We understand the difficulty of the job, and don't expect immediate results. It will take time and a massive commitment. We want you to get the ball rolling. It will be up to us to give you the support you request.

By the way, your salary will be $195,000 per year, for at least three years. Are you up to the task, Timothy?"

"I am, Mr. President, and I accept," enthusiastically responded a wired Barrows.

"Do you want to consult with your wife about this?"

"It won't be necessary. She supports me fully," responded Barrows.

"Excellent."

"Anything else Timothy? If not, I've arranged to move your office from Homeland Security to the White House. I didn't think you'd refuse the assignment. I expect you at work Monday morning, ready to work for world peace. I'll let you know when I plan to make the official announcement of your appointment as Chairman of the Peace Envoys. That will certainly feed the media bloodhounds. Thank you Timothy and good luck to us all. Anything else before you leave?"

"Not now, Mr. President."

"Excellent. My security advisor, Tom Peaksman, will contact you to help with your White House ID, security, and garage privileges. You can spend some time together to be acquainted and to make your preliminary plans. Your office furniture, your personal files and effects from your Homeland office will be packed and set up in your White House office. Natalie Spovel is your secretary. She'll show you around when you arrive. She comes highly recommended. She'll be a real asset for your scheduling, meetings, and correspondence. As I understand, she can handle even the toughest people without causing an International crisis. She'll be expecting you in the morning. You can replace her if you're not satisfied.

Use the West entrance to the garage. There's a parking space assigned to you on level one, three slots from the elevator. By tomorrow, your name will be on the "Reserved For" spot.

In addition, Timothy, when you've completed this project, come see me about the next phase of your career. I expect to be around at least that long."

The President chuckled again at his joke. What he meant to say was "If you don't succeed, I'll be out of office and who knows what can be done for your career, or even if the next President will continue this operation."

"Thank you, Mr. President, for this opportunity and the confidence you have in me. I won't let you down. I'll take you up on that offer. You can be sure I'll finish the job as quickly as possible."

"I'm sure you will. I'm sure you will. Good luck Timothy. Keep Peaksman informed." They shook hands as they parted. Barrows took one more look at the President's office before he left. He fully expected it to be his one day.

Barrows' multiplicity of thoughts began to coalesce into concrete plans even as he left the Oval Office. Judi lead him out of the White House office area.

By the time he reached his car, he already had mapped out the initial steps needed to organize the Peace Envoys.

"I guess dear old Dad was right. Be in the right place and opportunities will come your way. If I hadn't been working at Homeland Security, the President never would have known about me. This will surely lead me to the Presidency. Schuster has a little over three years left. If he's re-elected in 2012, then my chance will come in 2016. By then the world will know me as the man who helped to promote world peace. I'll be a shoo-in," he exuberantly said to himself.

Now, home to tell Lynette we're moving to the DC area. She won't be happy, but she'll have to get over it. She always does.

5

JANUARY 2010:

"In two weeks, Thursday, December 17, 2009 at 10:00 AM. Be at the Oval Office by 9:00 AM."

So stated the opening line of the note from President Schuster to Barrows of the President's intention to announce the creation of the Peace Envoys. The President promised to include some lofty and inspiring verbiage to introduce the Peace Envoys' lofty goals. Lasting peace to the world, eradicate poverty, famine, and genocide were the key words he thought would get world attention. He indicated that leaders from England, France, Russia, Israel, Saudi Arabia, Canada, China, Jordan, and Egypt planned to attend the news conference. The President wanted to stress the cooperation and commitment of the industrialized world to the Peace Envoys mission and Barrows as the Chairman. His note ended with, "Any suggestions?"

Barrows immediately shot back his reply.

"Thank you again for your confidence in me. I will do everything in my power to bring a new order to the world, under your direction. You might want to include phrases such as:

...Will develop a comprehensive program to assist third world countries to industrialize and to compete economically with the wealthier countries....Goals are to eliminate the causes of discontent through education, compassion and fair dealings with other countries.. Help feed and care for the children ...Nations are committing significant funds, manpower, and knowledge to attain our goals... Expect a series of recommendations from the Peace Envoys that is comprised of

representatives from countries around the world who are interested in achieving lasting peace… Looking for global cooperation from all nations…No intention to remove or undermine existing leaderships in the third world countries…Expect many recommendations from Tim Barrows and his team of highly qualified experts… We envision a continual stream of recommendations and fine-tuning to insure programs are implemented in the best interests of the receiving country and its people….One day we will look back and recognize that what we have done today will benefit all of mankind.

President Schuster's public spokesperson, Max Trillings, issued a press release indicating, "a special and important announcement will be made by President Schuster on Thursday, December 17, 2009 on behalf of the leaders of the industrialized world from the United Nations building, main auditorium."

Barrows awoke early that morning and quickly jumped into the shower. He paused long enough to admire his nude body before dressing for the morning's festivities. Over the years, he made a habit of checking himself before getting dressed. Five -foot ten and a half, well-built, broad shoulders and highly muscular from his days as a college wrestler and weight lifter, he marveled at how he had been able to maintain his physique with minimal exercise. His slightly olive skin made his white teeth glisten in comparison. Handsome, rugged, with thick eyebrows, and coarse brown straight hair slightly graying at the temples complimented his aggressive personality and pointed determination.

"Excellent. Fifty-two years old and I look better than most thirty year olds do. Perfect 'V' shape, and still well toned," he said loud enough for Lynette to hear.

"You are dear," she replied in suppressed tones. "Which suit are you wearing?"

"The one I always wear to official functions. You know that, so why ask?" he responded with an obvious edge to his voice.

He put on his black Mondo Uomo single-breasted suit, black silk socks, polished black Moreschi black oxfords, a narrow spread white shirt, and accented with a red power tie. He knew the President preferred his pale blue tie, and he did not intend to compete with him. At least for now.

At ten after ten that morning, President Schuster addressed the assembled global dignitaries. On the dais, flanked by International representatives, his cabinet, Barrows, Lynette, their children, an additional 179 global representatives plus seventy-six assorted media staff in the audience, President Schuster announced the formation of the Peace Envoys, with Timothy Randolph Barrows Jr. as its Chairman.

"We recognize that global peace is and has been the goal of mankind since recorded history. Peace is elusive and fleeting. Although we still have many conflicts throughout the world, the absence of peace does not preclude making honest attempts to look towards the future. It is incumbent on us to reach out beyond the traditional restraints and arguments to make a sincere effort to bring the gift of peace and prosperity to our children. To achieve peace demands hard work and a continual and long-term commitment. To preserve and enhance what has already been achieved, my fellow world leaders and I have jointly decided to create an organization dedicated to making the world a safe place for us all, not only for today, not only for tomorrow, but for the future.

Today, I am excited to announce the formation of the Peace Envoys, headed by Timothy Randolph Barrows Jr. Their mission is to establish guidelines by which to achieve global peace by actively pursuing all possible avenues. The Peace Envoys will provide recommendations and propose ways to share the world resources, and to assist the poorer countries of our world with education, agriculture, and proper healthcare.

We recognize that in the past we have not focused enough on eradicating poverty and suffering, elements that lead to discontent and global disagreements. Through our own negligence, we have encouraged the growth of terrorism and dissent. We have turned our backs on the millions of people who live in squalor and filth, and those whose voices we silenced by our indifference and intolerance.

Today we declare a new era by our commitment to right these wrongs to provide the financial and personnel aid for those need our support the most. The Peace Envoys will spearhead programs to resolve these problems and to strive to bring to everyone a life of peace, prosperity, and freedom. We will help those who seek help, and listen to those in need.

Through the Peace Envoys, we promise to make this a better place to live, and to eliminate hunger and despair. We will establish better education systems, better healthcare, and jobs to keep the economies of the world moving in an upward direction. To address the global needs of our neighbors are not only the right thing to do, but also the moral thing to do. Although this may seem to be a formidable task, especially in light of the present threat of terrorism," explained President Schuster, "we are confident our goals are achievable and sustainable. The Peace Envoys will also recommend changes and programs to insure peaceful solutions to International disputes.

This is an historic time and opportunity for us, to learn from the past and to look forward towards the future with hope and great expectations. It represents the first time in history of humanity that there is universal agreement to abide by the new rules or operations we expect will be outlined by the Peace Envoys. This is truly a new beginning for us all.

Every major country has selected representatives to serve on the Peace Envoys to address and to recommend global solutions. We expect to increase representation in the Peace Envoys to include those countries who are not currently involved. The door is open to all who wish to participate. There will be no closed doors, only open hearts and open minds. This we promise."

Amid the gaggle of microphones and video recorders, President Schuster continued his speech for an additional sixteen minutes.

The world cheered as governments and individuals offered their silent prayers for success and fearful of failure. President Schuster ended with a brief introduction of Barrows and his accomplishments.

He yielded the microphones to Barrows.

"Mr. President, noted dignitaries and world leaders, I want to thank you for the honor you have bestowed on me through my selection as head of the Peace Envoys. I can add little to what President Schuster has already said. I feel deeply humbled by the confidence you have shown in me. As Chairman of the Peace Envoys, I promise three things. First, my speech today will be short. Second, my fellow Peace Envoys and I will work diligently, fairly, and honestly. We will work with as much haste as possible to develop programs that will meet your goals and expectations. We will work tirelessly in pursuit of these goals. We will try to establish a framework that will produce future prosperity, peace and good health to all children, to all people of the world, to all countries, and to friends and foes. We promise to listen, we promise to learn, and we promise to bring specific recommendations that provide solutions to specific problems. My third promise: short future speeches. This is my commitment to you, the people of the world. Thank you."

Smiles and applause erupted from the surrounding dignitaries and audience. There was no mention of the troubling obstacles to peace. Terrorism, massive corruption, and rogue nations who had no interest in global tranquility. Each separately had the power to dismantle the best of intentions.

Barrows leaned over, kissed Lynette, and held her hand with apparent affection and triumph as they left the dais. As least the triumph part was sincere.

On the drive home his Blackberry rang. He checked the ID. It was his father, Barrows Senior.

"The bastard wants to talk with me. Probably watched the news on TV," Barrows mumbled angrily.

"Are you going to talk to him?" Lynette asked

"If I have to."

"Hello."

"Hello, son. I wanted to congratulate you on the Peace Envoys thing. It's a huge step upward isn't it? I guess all our planning was on target!"

"To an extent. I've been working my butt off to get here. It hasn't always been a smooth road," Barrows tersely replied.

"No road is smooth, I've told you that. However, those bumps don't matter now do they? Do a good job and I'll guarantee you the door to the Presidency will automatically open," Senior shot back.

"It's a long way from here to there, so don't count on anything happening for a long time. Schuster has at least three and possibly seven more years as President."

"You've got the time. You're young and can afford to wait. Call me when you want advice." Barrows Senior had a bounce in his voice.

"I may lose you soon. I'm entering a dead zone. I may lose the connection. I'm…"

Barrows turned off his phone.

"It's a trick I learned a while ago," he said smugly to Lynette. "Hang up on yourself. Everyone accepts that a cell phone conversation can end unexpectedly. I didn't want to hear any more of his crap. He's always wants the credit for everything. This is my day, and I refuse to allow him to enjoy any part of it!"

"He's getting older and he's sick. Can't you be a little more tolerant?" she quietly asked.

Barrow ignored her the rest of the way home.

Reaction to the President's speech was immediate and positive. People around the globe applauded this new global initiative to bring justice and lasting peace to the world. Never before had such an ambitious and far-reaching program been announced with such fanfare, and received with such excitement. Never before have the people of the world been lifted to such heights of expectations. The dreadful turmoil of the past three decades was lost in the euphoria of the moment, as was the possibility of future chaos. His speech became the most significant and breathtaking announcement made to a world weary of war, terrorism, and poverty.

The President gave them a reason to believe, a reason to live, and a reason to hope. Barrows gave them the expectation of fulfillment. President Schuster himself was impressed, as he eagerly embraced his newfound global leadership. Now, all that remained was for the Peace Envoys to do their job. Even if the Peace Envoys failed, or they made no progress against poverty and corruption, he believed history would acknowledge him for his leadership and vision. President Schuster sat back in his easy chair at home thinking,

My legacy is secure. I wonder if the historians will mention me in the same breath with Washington, Lincoln, Roosevelt, and Reagan.

6

Bilal received an unexpected letter from home the sixth week of his training, shortly before 8 PM. It wasn't from his wife. He ripped the envelop open and read the hand written note from his father Syed.

> *Dear Bilal,*
> *Please forgive me for writing this letter, but it is my duty to tell you that your beloved wife, Nasrin, and your five children died by a terrorist bomb today in Karachi. They were traveling by bus to see my sister, your aunt, when the bus exploded. HuM (Harakat-ul-Mujaludin) took credit for the bombing. Please hurry home. You must arrange for the funeral. I grieve for you, my son.*
> *With great sorrow,*
> *Syed, your father*

His uncontrollable scream shattered the evening quiet. He shook violently, yelling in anguish, in anger and in disbelief.

"My family? Killed? By a terrorist bomb? Why? It must be a mistake. I need to call her. I need to speak with Nasrin. She'll tell me it was a terrible mistake. She'll tell me she lives. She and the children."

He ran to the office, burst in, grabbed the desk phone in front of a startled clerk, and dialed his home number. No answer. He dialed again to be sure he had dialed the right number. Again, no answer. He let it ring over twenty times before he hung up to dial his father.

"Tell me it's not true, it's not true! I know it's not true. They can't be dead!" he demanded.

His tearful father sadly replied, "It is true. I… I'm so sorry. Please, come home. I…."

Bilal never heard another word. He ran out of the office, leaving the phone dangling in mid air. "Noooooooo," was the only sound he could make as he ran towards the barracks.

Overcome with anguish, his fury demanded action against anything or anyone. He staggered into his apartment completely out of control. "Noooooooo" changed to a primal scream without words and without meaning. He attacked his apartment. He smashed lamps and tables; tossed chairs into the walls, and ripped his mattress from his cot, flinging it across the room. He viscously trashed anything not tied down. Alarmed by the noise, Bruce ran to Bilal's apartment.

"Bilal, what's happening? What's wrong?"

Bilal ignored him and the others who had gathered from the barracks. They tried to consul him, to talk with him, to help him, but to no avail. He pushed and lunged at them, beating them with his fists and the 38-caliber sidearm he always carried. They backed off at a loss, not knowing what they could or should do. They feared he would shoot them if they interfered.

Someone found the letter that Bilal had dropped on the floor before he ran out of the office. A recruit who understood Punjabi read it aloud. Now they understood.

Hate, anger, and disbelief drove Bilal's actions. Bruce tackled him, wrested the gun from his hands, and grabbed him in a bear hug to restrain him. Bruce needed the help of four other men to subdue the enraged Bilal.

"I know, I know what happened," shouted Bruce. "Let me help you. I know, I know!"

By then the camp doctor arrived with a needle of 5 milligrams of Haldol to calm him down. He injected Bilal during a pause in his thrashing.

It took another twenty minutes of struggle before Bilal's strength gave out and he succumbed to the medicine. He grew limp in Bruce's arms, continuously sobbing his wife's name. "Nasrin… Nasrin… Nasrin… Nasrin…" before Bilal recognized Bruce was holding him. Sobbing and weeping, Bilal was a broken man.

Bruce said, "I'm so very sorry. I'm here. I'll help you get through this. But you need to arrange to fly home. I'll do it for you and I'll take a leave of absence so I can be with you. Stay here and I'll be right back." Bruce replaced the mattress on the cot and eased Bilal into it.

"No," Bilal mumbled. "I need to do this myself."

"You can't do this yourself, not now. Come with me if you must, but I'll take care of everything for you, for us."

Bilal numbly nodded his acceptance. They walked to the Executive headquarters a block away. Bruce held him by his waist as he guided Bilal to the office. Bruce was prepared to explain the situation to the night manager, but he had already heard about Bilal's misfortune and was ready when they entered the office. The manager, a massive Ukrainian named Dmytro Kovalenko, came to greet them as they entered. A long-standing ExecProtect policy allowed early resignation without penalty when an employee faced a family crisis, especially the death of an immediate family member. The stricken employee received a full two months severance pay, with the opportunity for reinstatement at EPA whenever the employee was ready to resume his duties. No repayment of the advanced funds was required.

"I am very sorry, Bilal. I've taken the liberty to begin processing your paperwork for your separation. Everything will be ready in less than an hour," Kovalenko said.

Looking at Bruce MacCardle he asked,

"Are you going with him? Should I begin papers for you too?"

"Yes."

"No, he is not coming with me!" interjected Bilal. "This is my problem alone, and no one can help. These are things I must do alone."

"No man should face this alone," Bruce argued." I'm going with you."

"No! Although I appreciate your offer, I cannot accept," Bilal strongly responded.

"There is no bloody way in hell that I'll not go to Pakistan with you. That's what friends are for."

"We will talk about this later, as we wait for the arrangements."

Dmytro interrupted.

"I will have one of the company planes flown in tonight. Your journey home will begin after refueling. The plane will take you to Vereeniging airport. A car will be waiting to transport you to Johannesburg. From there you have a direct flight to Karachi, and another flight to Quetta. I believe you live about an hour from the Quetta, is that right?" asked Dmytro.

"Yes, the arrangements are fine. It is very kind of you. I will not forget your kindness, or EPA's, Dmytro."

"If there is anything you can think of, just ask."

"I will," Bilal softly answered.

"I should have all the arrangements finished –your pay, the plane schedules, and any other transportation you need, will be completed shortly. Do you need to make arrangements to go from Quetta to your home?"

"No. My father will meet me," sadly whispered Bilal.

"I'll send someone to find you as soon as I confirm your flight schedule. A car will pick you up at the barracks 20 minutes before flight time. Be sure you are packed and ready to go."

"I'll call my father when I know the schedule, Dmytro. Again, thank you, thank you. We'll be at Lollo's bar. I don't want to go back to the barracks."

Bilal and Bruce left the office towards Lollo's to await word from Kovalenko. Lollo's was the local bar and coffee house where EPA employees spent their free time. It was their single form of outside entertainment. Bilal could only focus on the image of his wife and children and the single question that defied an answer, the one question that burned deeply in his gut.

"Why? Why? Why were they murdered by HuM?"

He wondered if they suffered or died instantly. He wondered if the killer knew him or his family, if he targeted them, or was it an unlucky circumstance that put his family in harm's way. Though he heard Bruce talking, he could not focus on what he was saying. His mind was filled with rage and the loss he felt. Rage and emotion quickly morphed into revenge and determination. He swore to avenge their deaths. That was his solemn oath to his wife and children.

He shared his oath with Bruce. He forced Bruce to acknowledge that he had made this vow, and to serve as his witness to his sworn duty to avenge his family. Revenge was all that mattered now.

"What will you do?" asked Bruce as they sat quietly at a small table in the bar.

"First I must bury my family, and then I will find their killers. I might join the Pakistani Intelligence (IB). I might even join the terrorists themselves, if I can. I don't know yet, I'm can't think clearly. Whichever course I select, it will have but one purpose. My family's death will be avenged."

"I'm going to help you find them. When you're ready to make your plans, I'll be by your side. Together we will do this. We'll find them and kill them."

"But I already know who murdered my family. My father told me that Harakat-ul-Mujaludin, HuM, claimed responsibility," answered Bilal.

"I will track them down and kill them as I have sworn to you and to my family. Please, no more questions. No more talk. Tomorrow is the time for talk and action, but not today, not now."

They sat together in silence throughout the evening and into dawn, Bruce drinking beer and Bilal drinking tea. A Muslim devoid of his beliefs and a Scotsman in the process of finding his, mirroring life's cruelties in a small bar in South Africa, an unlikely place that marked the beginning of a new life experience for both men. Within months both men's lives would take an unexpected turn, one that would dramatically influence them in a manner that neither could have guessed, imagined, or believed.

The messenger found them, told them the car would be at the barracks by 7:10 in the morning, and the plane would leave as soon as Bilal arrived at the airport. He immediately called his father's cell phone.

"I will arrive at Quetta airport, but I don't know exactly when. When my plans are final, I'll call you." Bilal spoke as soon as he heard his father's voice. He didn't know or care what time it was in Pakistan, as long as his father knew his plans.

"No more talk. Forgive me. Goodbye." His father never uttered a word, nor did he expect to have a conversation with his son at that moment. There would be time enough to talk after his family had their proper burial, he presumed, after his son's torturous journey home, and his own oppressive wait for his arrival.

Despite his anguish, Bilal remembered he was to leave for the airport about seven in the morning. To his added chagrin, the time with Bruce didn't do what he hoped. He desperately wanted to dull his senses, not to think, not to feel his pain, not to hold his anger, and not to remember the guilt he was experiencing.

If I were home, Nasrin would not have taken the bus and they would still be alive. It's my fault. She begged me not to go, but I did. Now they're dead. I did it. I allowed them to die. But I will avenge their deaths. This I have sworn, and this is what I will do.

Repeatedly he retrieved the letter from his pocket and reread it, hoping that the message would magically change, or that he would awaken from this horrible nightmare. Nothing, except more pain. He repeated the name of the terrorist organization, sometimes aloud, mostly in his head, perhaps afraid he would forget who they were and what they had done.

Harakat-ul-Mujaludin, Harakat-ul-Mujaludin, Harakat-ul-Mujaludin.

He left the table only three times, two to pee and once to throw up. His anguish and pain remained steadfast. By 6 AM, Bruce reminded Bilal they had to return to his apartment to pack, which they promptly did. Bruce helped to collect his belongings and put them into Bilal's duffle bag.

At precisely 7:10 AM, the camouflaged Hummer pulled up to the front of the barracks to take Bilal to the airstrip. Dmytro was in the passenger seat.

"Here is your travel itinerary and tickets. You will arrive in Quetta about 38 hours from now."

He turned to Bilal and handed him his final pay. Dmytro stepped out, they shook hands and said goodbye.

"Should you ever decide to return to ExecProtect, there is always a place for you here," he said.

"Who knows what the future may bring? For now, many things need my attention. Until they are finished, nothing else matters. But I thank you and EPA for all the kindness you have shown me," replied Bilal.

Bilal turned to Bruce. They sought each other's eyes, and locked their gaze for nearly thirty seconds. Neither wished to speak, yet each spoke volumes. Of such are true friendships formed. Bruce spoke first.

"Goodbye, Bilal. May your peace of mind come quickly. Call me here or on my cell number. Call me whenever you are ready. If you want anything or need me, I'll be there."

Bilal got in the passenger seat, closed the door, and looked sorrowfully at Bruce as the car accelerated from the front steps of the barracks. He neither spoke nor gestured goodbye. It wasn't necessary for either.

Threat of rain darkened the sky. It fit Bilal's mood, and he was glad he didn't have to face a sunny day to travel. He wanted nothing to intrude on his dark feelings. He placed a call to his father and assured him he would keep in touch as he got closer to Karachi so his father could make plans to meet him in Quetta.

A Bush Hawk airplane, painted in camouflaged colors of green, sand, and brown, was waiting, its single engine in idle. The side door opened and Bilal climbed into the black leather front passenger seat and closed the door behind him. He pulled the silver latch down into the locked position. The Chinese pilot, Duyi Sun Yee, after extending his condolences for his misfortune, instructed him to secure his seat belt. The rear seats were unoccupied, except for Bilal's large duffle bag. The plane had the top of the line interior-black leather, black carpets and black side panels. Bilal didn't notice nor care. Pilot Yee gunned the engine, released the brake, and the plane bounced down the short grass runway.

The Bush Hawk needs only 750 feet of runway for takeoff, and its single Lycoming 300 hp I0-540-LICS engine quickly launched the plane into the gray sky. Bilal had never flown in such a small plane, and certainly never this close to the pilot. Those things didn't matter. He was returning home to bury his family and to avenge their deaths. Lee explained that he was taking Bilal to Vereeniging airport, a small airstrip located about an hour from the Preiska headquarters. The Johannesburg denied small propeller aircraft landing rights, so EPA had arranged for a car to transport Bilal from Vereeniging to Johannesburg. There he would catch a Cathy Pacific commercial flight directly to Karachi, and then a local carrier from Karachi to Quetta.

The rugged Hawk was not designed for cockpit noise reduction so both Yee and Bilal donned headsets to muffle the engine and wind noise. What the Hawk lacked in noise suppression was more than made up in reliability, power, payload capacity and its ability to fly in rough weather, characteristic of the South African area. Surprisingly, the passenger seat comfort was better than most commercial aircraft.

Scheduled to arrive at Vereeniging airport in slightly less than an hour, Lee made several insincere attempts to engage Bilal in conversation. Bilal ignored his attempts. Numb from the pain, stoic in determination, Bilal chose to sit in silence. The last thing he wanted to do was to talk. He was thankful the engine noise made conversation difficult.

They arrived at the cow pasture they called Vereeniging airport. The car was waiting. They immediately drove to the Johannesburg airport. Thirty-five minutes later he walked through the dual sliding glass doors that lead to the main terminal, picked up his electronic ticket on Cathay Pacific, and waited at the boarding gate for an intolerable hour and a quarter to board his flight to Karachi.

The quieter cabin that modern jets offer allowed Bilal to catch three or four mini-naps of fifteen to twenty-five minutes at a time. His last nap abruptly ended when he awakened with a start, sweat pouring down his face and through his shirt. The image of Nasrin, calling his name as she lie in a pool of blood next to the shattered and smoking bus, rattled him. The dream seemed so real, so agonizing, and so desperate. The look in her eyes as she called to him scorched his brain. Bilal was convinced that his wife had reached out to him in death. She wanted him to know that he was on her mind and her lips, even as she lay there dying from a terrorist bomb. Awakened, he nodded slowly and said to himself,

Thank you, my love, mother of my children, for coming to me. I swear by Allah I will avenge you and our children. I promise.

Her plea, her look, her pain, would remain with Bilal the rest of his life. It would serve to inspire his resolve to avenge Nasrin, or die trying.

I love you Nasrin.

He nibbled on an apple offered by the flight attendant. His demeanor was that of a warrior preparing for battle against a formidable foe, assessing his strengths and weaknesses, seeking the way to insure victory. For Bilal, victory meant death to his adversaries, slow and painful death. He wanted to see the terror in their eyes before he killed them. He wanted them to know why they were dying. Their death had to be personal, not anonymous.

He was anything but relaxed. He sat upright in his seat, his eyes tense, lips drawn tightly. He asked for nothing. He wanted nothing. He remained silent the entire flight. His former life was over. It died with his family, with the letter from his father.

My life is over, except for the promise I swore to keep. I will live to fulfill my promise.

He tried to concentrate to develop a plan, a place to start, but the ideas remained trapped in his head. He wasn't thinking clearly, but knew it was only a matter of time before he would regain control.

For now, I must make the burial arrangements for my wife and children at the People's Cemetery.

Free burials for all residents of the village at the People's Cemetery are available to those in need. He decided Nasrin would prefer burial there instead of the private cemetery that families of officials and dignitaries chose.

After the burials, I will complete my last mission, was his last thought before he dozed off in a shallow troubled sleep.

7

MARCH 2010:

Confusion and anger were no strangers. For the next three months, they co-habited in his body as uninvited guests. They were always gnawing at him, demanding a solution, and disappointed when none came. Ed Walker buried his fears in the recesses of his mind. If he didn't, he knew his life would be hell. He did the best he knew. However, it was there, lurking, waiting to pounce, and threatening to devour him like a piece of raw meat.

It's not like when I was a kid. I could handle anything then. But not any more. I've changed.

Sometime between being a defiant kid and becoming an adult, Ed's personality dramatically changed. At ten years old, he was defiant and strong-willed. As an adult, he become indecisive and reluctant to take a stand, a trait he fortified when employed by the CIA. Janice became his rock, his crutch, his point of reference, and his guidance counselor. Without her, his career, his existence would have been difficult. Success would have been a fleeting thought were it not for Janice. He thanked God everyday for having her in his life.

The evening news rocked his stability. The talking head said,

"Three suicide bombers blew up the Shiite Khalani mosque in Bagdad during morning prayers. The attack was coordinated to inflict maximum damage to the building and the occupants. A truck bomb filled with cooking oil and explosives detonated, and as rescuers rushed to the scene, two additional powerful car bombs went off. An estimated sixty-one people died in the explosions, and 130 severely wounded. Al Qaeda in Iraq claimed responsibility. Two walls of the 350-year old mosque shattered, causing the roof to collapse on the praying occupants. Officials declared there were no survivors. Hospitals and the morgue were overflowing with the dead and the wounded. Thirty or more of the wounded are in critical condition and not expected to survive. This was the highest civilian toll in four months."

Stunned, Ed gnashed his teeth in anger.

"Sixty-one people killed!"

"They were just praying," he snarled to Janice. "What threat were they to the terrorists? What was the bomber's purpose? Make a statement to the free world? Was he acting on someone's orders? Acting alone? Who knows?"

Dana Ross, KTX TV, interviewed Timothy Barrows Jr., newly appointed Chairman of the Peace Envoys.

"As a former Deputy Director of Homeland Security," she started, "thank you for appearing on such short notice. I know I'm speaking for the American public when I express my outrage at these continual killings by terrorists. It seems like very little is or can be done to prevent these attacks. Can you tell us what steps are being taken by the government to prevent this from happening in the US?"

"Glad to be here Dana. My heart goes out to the families who suffered losses from this latest cowardly act. The Unites States military is cooperating fully with the Iraqi officials to track down the group responsible and to bring them to justice. Of course, that's one of the reasons our military is in the Middle East, to identify and destroy the terrorists' capabilities to wage uncontrolled warfare. Closer to home, and to answer your questions, we are continually upgrading our ability to prevent terrorist infiltration into the US. We have stepped up our air and seaport security. The newly installed Traveler's Identification Security System has undergone extensive trials and I'm happy to report a 99.9 % success rate. I can't go into the details, but rest assured that this system is a major step in preventing undesirables from gaining entrance to the US. We are working with several countries to install these systems. Our goal is to stop them at their point of origin, before they have a chance to land on our soil."

"Isn't the threat of a home grown terrorist as much a concern as outsiders?" she pressed him.

"Yes, as you know, that's a different level of concern. Through Homeland Security, we have been doing a better job of coordinating our efforts with all the law enforcements agencies through the country. That includes the CIA, FBI, NSA, and state and local police. We're not perfect, but I expect a significant improvement in our ability to recognize a homegrown threat, and to be able to respond quickly and efficiently. Of course, we encourage our citizens to be alert to anything unusual or out of the ordinary, and to contact your local authorities if anything strikes you as a problem in national security. I no longer can speak for Homeland Security at this time. As you know, the President has just appointed me to head up the Peace Envoys. You'll have to confer with Homeland Security directly."

Barrows sounded confident and authoritative as he voiced the party line.

"Haven't we heard this before?"

"Probably, but look at the results. Since nine-eleven, we haven't had another terrorist attack in the US, have we? Doesn't that count for something?" he responded with a slight smirk on his lips.

"Yes, but…"

Ed turned the TV off.

Same bullshit. I know better. Those systems are far from perfect. Who's he trying to fool? The intelligence agencies still don't talk to each other. And I doubt if we're talking to anyone else!

Barrows remarks rekindled Ed's deep seeded fear. His thoughts turned towards global terrorism, and how everyone acts paralyzed with inefficiency and inaction.

"Someone needs to figure out how to stop these assholes," he lamented to Janice.

That damn report is consuming me! What can I do? I'm a peon trying to find where they keep their money; it doesn't matter and neither do I. We sit with our thumbs up our asses hoping to find a solution or praying the terrorists quit on their own. Fat chance of either happening, were his real thoughts.

He slammed his fist on his leg in frustration. The rest of the evening, he and Janice sat silently watching a stupid movie. It helped to numb his anger only slightly.

The following evening, reports of another vicious attack on civilians in Iraq dominated the evening news. The program featured a graphic video showing mangled corpses, people screaming in pain, dazed, and bleeding, many with limbs torn from their bodies. The traditional warning, "The following contains graphic material," preceded the video.

He saw their terror, felt their panic, and reacted to their bewilderment. Anguished cries for help. Severely wounded people bleeding profusely. People screaming, running, stunned by the carnage. Wailing ambulance sirens pleading for people to move from their path. Shouts of relatives, themselves in distress, calling out to mangled loved ones caught in the rubble.

"Horrible, just damn horrible!" Janice heard him bellowing from the den.

"What happened?"

"Another bomber. Fifty-three people killed in Iraq, and over a hundred wounded. It's unbelievable!"

Flash images of a similar scene in McLean, or Washington, or New York, or Los Angeles fixated in his head. His heart was racing. Sweat formed on his forehead. The possibility that a suicide bomber could strike within the US was all he could emotionally stand.

I have to get control of myself. I can't react like this every time I hear about a terrorist attack.

He flipped the channel aimlessly, searching for anything that would bring him relief. In disgust, he turned the TV off, announced to Janice that he had a bad headache and needed an hour to sleep before dinner.

Ed retreated quickly to the quiet of his bedroom to think, not to sleep.

I can't sit by and do nothing. Think! Think! I have to do something!

Sweating and badly shaken, Ed Walker collapsed weakly on the brown and gold patterned bedspread neatly resting on their king sized bed. He wasn't worried about ruining the expensive spread. Survival from himself was all that mattered.

Suppose I was killed, and Janice and the kids would have to go on without me. They'd have to live with the memories of how I was murdered by terrorists. How could they survive thinking I failed because I didn't do enough to protect them or me? He shuttered at that daunting prospect.

He was now completely obsessed, dedicated to find a solution to save the future for his family and all of mankind.

I will not allow Red Sunset, I won't! If I could only think of something…. Exhaustion prevailed. He slept.

Janice checked on him several hours later.

An incoherent husband begged for more sleep. She helped him undress and tucked him into bed for the night, without dinner.

Ed dragged through the remainder of the week in zombie-like fashion. He moved slower than usual, barely sleeping more than three hours at a time. He fought desperately to avoid meaningful work at the office. He ate because Janice badgered him, not because he was hungry or because the food had appeal.

Concerned, Janice pleaded with him to see a doctor or take time off from work. Ed refused both. He wanted to be at work where he felt he'd be more likely to find his answer, to find THE solution he desperately craved, yet feared it might elude him. Worse, he wasn't confident there was a solution.

He worked overtime racking his brain for an idea, any idea that might work. He brainstormed with himself, hoping for a solution. His list of ideas covered three handwritten pages. He rejected them all as inadequate, unworkable, or dumb. One question haunted him. Is it possible to make terrorists feel enough pain to force them to stop?

Nothing. Hour after hour, day after day, week after week, no ideas came to mind. The harder he focused, the more confused he became. Agony and frustration settled in. The constant pressure took its toll. He usually returned home from work feeling edgy, nervous, and intolerant of Janice, the kids, the supermarket bagger, the gas attendant, and anyone who had the misfortune to cross his path. He was miserable to be with or to be around.

Worried friends and co-workers, aware of his abrupt personality changes, tried to talk with him, to beg him to take time off, to seek professional help, or to confide in them. Perhaps they could help, they pleaded, if only they knew the problem. Ed assured them "it was temporary and he was sure he'd get through it soon."

Still, depression was hiding in plain view outside the door, for Ed Walker.

Ed swore a solemn oath to protect his family and his country from falling prey to a life under the rule of radical Islamic Fundamentalists. He knew he was failing, badly. Weeks went by without answers. Moreover, the vicious terror attacks continued unabated in Iraq, in Afghanistan, and in Turkey where markets, mosques, and mass gatherings exploded with increasing regularity. Carnage ruled.

He was convinced that terrorists would eventually be on his doorstep sometime in the near future. He became obsessed with finding a solution.

I must find a way. My family, my world, they depend on me!

He continuously racked his brain for ideas. He critically reviewed each idea, only to reject it as inadequate or unworkable. For every idea he generated, Ed found a reason for rejection. Nothing pointed to a solution. Nothing screamed, "Look at me, I'm the one!"

8

FEBRUARY 2010:

Week three of his torment, Ed collapsed in bed at 1:37 AM, no closer to the elusive answer he so desperately sought. He awoke with a start, breathing heavily with excitement an hour and a half later. Was it a dream? A vision? He wasn't sure and didn't care. He saw the solution. It flashed in his mind as he slept. One huge word at a time. Each word appeared on a giant white sheet the size of a newspaper. Page after page, flipped by an unseen hand, exposed the words for him, to read and to remember. There it was, so elegant, so simple, and so right!

"My God," he blurted out. "Oh my God!" He sprung out of bed, raced down the steps to his first floor office, and wrote the solution on a scratch pad in long hand, afraid he'd forget something important. He recalled each word, clear, big, and in bold print. Once committed to paper, Ed reflected on his dream.

"I can't believe... I can't... understand what just happened. How did it happen and why? Why did I see hands turning the pages? Was God speaking to me? Telling me what needs to be done, and... and how? Why me? I'm... I'm not very religious. I believe in Jesus, even if I don't go to church but... why? Is this like the prophets in the bible? Is that how they got their information from God? Is this a godly decree to save the world?"

He remembered reading about people who had dreams about winning lottery ticket numbers.

"Could this be a psychic thing? It never happened to me before. I don't even believe in psychics. Is my mind playing tricks on me?"

Confused, but thankful, Ed decided it didn't matter whom, how, or what gave him the solution to fight terrorism.

I accept it for whatever it is. No questions. It doesn't matter, not now... probably it never will. I wanted to find a way to defeat terrorists, and now, I know the way. It's up to me to do something with it.

He read his scribbling three times before satisfied it was accurate. "Oh my God," he whispered again. "This is so remarkable. It was right in front of me, and I didn't see it until now."

He slowly ran his hands through his hair in disbelief. There, before him, was the answer. Weeks of anguish, of fear, and doom, turned to ecstasy, excitement, giddiness, triumph and satisfaction, all lumped together in a giant rush of monumental relief. With help from who knows where, he had discovered the pathway. The hours spent racking his brain no longer mattered. The lack of sleep no longer mattered. The oppressive feelings no longer mattered. He had the solution!

Ed sat at his desk, hands clasped in his lap, released from the pressures of the past three weeks, to savor the triumph and the success of this moment.

He turned on his laptop and waited impatiently for it to boot.

His fingers stumbled across the keyboard, trying desperately to keep pace with the plethora of thoughts erupting like a volcano in his head, spewing hot words one after the other. He typed until he was satisfied he now had a true plan to save the world from terrorist domination. A plan to defeat *Red Sunset.*

It was 5:48 AM. He felt exhilarated. He could hardly wait to shower and get to work.

He loaded and started Mr. Coffee, made the kids' lunch, and cleaned up the kitchen. Janice ambled into the kitchen by 6:42, startled by Ed's presence.

"Are you OK? Why are you up so early?"

That engaging smile, the one she loved, spread across his face. She hadn't seen him smile for weeks.

"What's going on? You're smiling again. Does that mean you're back? No more dread and gloom? What happened last night?"

"Just thinking of you, my love. That's what, " he said excitedly.

"Really. What...?"

"I have to apologize. I know I've been miserable and I'm sorry. I had some work things on my mind and couldn't let them go. I woke up, and it was...

just there. Everything's going to work out. Everything's back on track. I put you through hell, but I promise I'll make it up to you and the kids."

"Want to share?"

"Love to, but you know…"

"Yes, I do. Ask no questions. I was worried about you. I thought you'd lost it. And I wasn't the only one either. Everyone's been on my back, offering to help. It's been brutal. The kids have been upset too, but I've managed to keep them busy. They're OK, I think."

"I… really…eh… thanks for being there for me. Without you, I might have lost it. Really, just knowing you were around was a big help, especially when I felt alone."

"This is too much Ed. If this is going to happen to you whenever there's a problem at work, maybe you should leave the Agency. We'll figure something out. Maybe a business, go back to school, whatever. I can't go through this again. Neither can you."

"You're right. It's too tough. But I have to tell you, what I just figured out is a solution that might make a huge difference. Now that that's behind me, I promise it will never happen again."

"You can't promise that," she sneered "and you know it."

"You'd be surprised, you'd… be…very … surprised."

"What's next?" she asked.

"I've spent all night putting together a plan, this plan," he said enthusiastically, pointing to the stack of papers. "It'll change everything, you'll see. Have to shower and get to work. We'll talk tonight."

"Thanks for the coffee and the kid's lunch. Appreciate it. I really love you."

"Me too, more than you can imagine."

He bolted up the stairs two at a time. He needed to get to work. Fast.

Only the fear of a ticket or an accident kept him from speeding, but he pushed the limit. He shaved four minutes off his normal trip time.

There's one person who needs to read my proposal, and that's Alan T. Schuster, President of the United States.

He needed a favor. Washington exists because there are people who need favors and people who grant them.

I need someone to help me get my proposal to the President. The most likely candidate was Ralph Madison, Secretary of State. He and Ralph had worked together many years ago on a variety of projects. Ralph Madison was a rarity in Washington. He spoke his mind without fear of pissing someone off or losing his job. Ed considered him bright, a free thinker, and independent enough to confront the President on issues or policies he felt were wrong or politically foolish. President Shuster regarded him as one of his confidants, and relied on his opinion whenever he needed a sanity check. He relied on Ralph not to be a YES man. Ralph never disappointed. Their relationship was a Washington rarity. They trusted each other.

Ralph is perfect, Ed decided. Ed knew Ralph always arrived at his office in the White House by 7:15. He called at 7:16.

"Ralph, this is Ed, Ed Walker. Sorry to call so early but I need your help."

"What going on?"

"Nothing out of the ordinary, but I need a huge favor."

"What kind of favor?"

"I need you to deliver something to the President, for his eyes only, and that includes you. You need to trust me on this one. It's very important. I have a proposal for the President, based on *Red Sunset.* I know you read it. I saw your name on the distribution list."

"What kind of proposal?" he questioned.

"I'm sorry to put you in this position, but I have no choice. Will you give it to him, no questions asked?"

Silence. Ralph Madison was smart enough to be cautious when necessary. He would never jeopardize his standing with the President without first understanding the reason the President had to become involved, and second, that he had enough time to evaluate his own position. He wasn't about to violate either of those two now.

"This is quite unusual for a CIA agent to send a secret message directly to the President and bypass normal channels, even for highly sensitive information," Madison said.

"Understand. But this once?"

"You know me. I'm not going down that route without knowing why."

"Ralph, I need an answer, even if it's NO. I'll find another way if you aren't willing to be involved. I can tell you that it affects our future, and doesn't involve any individual or government agency. Let me assure you that it has nothing to do with the way the government is conducting its business, it's not an expo, and no one will get hurt. It's just some special ideas I have. I'm positive the President would like to be aware of them, especially since they relate to *Red Sunset.*"

After a long pause, Madison firmly replied,

"No, not unless I know what's inside."

Ed knew unless he agreed, his proposal would never reach Schuster. Reluctantly he responded, "I guess you're entitled to that. Can we do it now?"

"No, I have an important meeting that can't be put off. Let me check my schedule, hold a minute. What about Monday, AM, say, 9:30 ish. Will Monday work for you and is an hour enough?"

"Don't you have your weekly debriefings on Monday's?"

"Yes, generally from 8:15 to 9:15, so 9:30 should work. See you then, OK?" replied Madison.

"OK." Ed left his office.

"Shit. Monday will never come," Ed grumbled to himself.

The rest of the week Ed forced himself to concentrate on his work. Waiting for Monday would be difficult, but that was the easy part. Waiting for a response from the President, if there was one, would be hard, very hard. Probably impossible.

Secretary of State Ralph Madison was a frequent visitor to the Oval Office, and could easily hand the President Ed's proposal, once he knew the contents. If he decided to forward it to the President, his political capital might diminish if the President Schuster wasn't happy with Ed's proposal. The President expected Madison to act as a filter so that only important matters reached his desk.

The last thing I need is for the President to question my motives for asking him to read Ed's proposal. It had better be as important as Ed believes, Madison thought.

Madison was a career politician. Throughout his thirty-three years in Washington, people at all levels from both sides of the aisle sought his advice. His reputation as a straight shooter had been carefully cultivated and maintained. His non-partisan opinions were valued and sought. People considered Ralph Madison a true patriot, a man with an unbridled and uncompromised belief that politicians should act for the good of the country, not for the expediency, and certainly not for themselves. The word on Capital Hill was "check with Ralph before you put your foot into your mouth." Most were grateful they did.

Ed hurried to Ralph's office Monday morning. Madison's secretary, Debbie Tuttleman, ushered him into Ralph's office as soon as he entered the area.

"He's ready for you, Mr. Walker."

Not one to waste time, Madison motioned Ed to sit on the side chair next to his desk, extended his hand for the proposal, opened the envelope, and began to read.

Ed remained quiet, anxious, and apprehensive, waiting for his reaction.

Twelve minutes later, Ralph-balding, lean, pressed suit, white shirt and pink tie, crowfeet at the corners of his eyes, reading glasses perched at the end of his narrow nose, politician extraordinaire, confidant of the President, leaned back in his chair, removed his reading glasses, and pensively stared at Ed. He replaced the papers in the envelope without a word.

"This is quite a piece of work," he said softly. "It's pretty radical, don't you think?"

"It is. It took a lot for me to consider this approach, but after reading and rereading *Sunset,* I knew something dramatic was required. We can't go on pretending *Red Sunset* is fiction. We can't let the terrorists win! I believe we're already along the path to self-destruction because we're not doing all we can to protect ourselves and our future," he passionately replied.

"Let me get this straight. You propose to violate our laws, skip trials, jail, and due course. You say when we find a terrorist, or suspect someone is a terrorist, we should kill them on the spot. No questions asked. Is that right?"

"Yes."

"What makes you think this will work?"

"I haven't seen or heard of anything that will make terrorists stop killing innocent people. We've tried to shut down their funds, but you know that hasn't worked. Here and there, for small groups, perhaps it's had some effect. But, what about al Qaeda, the Taliban? Has anything shut them down? No. We're *still* fighting in Iraq, Afghanistan and Pakistan. We haven't made a dent. Be honest Ralph, can you point to any real long-term success we've had? Our intelligence stinks and our soldiers are tired from extended tours of duty. We're alone in this fight, and our economy is taking a beating because of it. We lose ground every day. If we choose to do nothing, we'll find ourselves facing *Red Sunset's* worst-case scenario. You, me, and the world, will be living under Islamic rule."

Ralph listened intently, patiently, waiting for Ed to finish. The only movement was his tongue wetting his lips. His hazelnut eyes never left Ed's face.

"So you're advocating being like them. Kill indiscriminately, whenever it suits us. Doesn't that make us them?"

"No. I'm not advocating indiscriminate killing. I say we should target only those involved in terrorism, those who want to destroy our way of life. I believe that taking this approach, we raise the stakes for terrorists. We must make people take responsibility for their actions. Fear will turn them around. They don't mind dying, so let's accommodate them. It's the least we can do. It does sound brutal. But,.... I'm betting it can work."

"And if you're wrong?"

"Would we be any worse off?"

"Perhaps."

"The real question is whether we can afford, no..., are we willing, to take the chance to see democracy defeated? You know that's their goal. They're willing to wait years for it to happen, waiting to control the world."

Agitation, anger, and determination, replaced Ed's initial fears that Ralph would reject his proposal.

Ralph has to be convinced to fight, or all will be lost. Ralph has to take this to the President, he has to! I must find a way to convince him. I have a real solution and no one, including Ralph, will stop me from getting my proposal to the President, he passionately vowed to himself.

"We have different opinions, Ed, but…," he hesitated before continuing, "I think President Schuster should be aware of your suggestions. I'm not promising to endorse them, but I will suggest he read your proposal. It may stimulate other thoughts that could be useful. That's the best I can offer."

Ed was stunned.

"I never thought you'd agree. Thank you, thank you so much, Ralph. When?"

"Christ you're pushy." Ralph smiled. "I never saw this side of you. I like the change. It's great to see someone who has convictions stand up and fight for them. Don't see much of that around here lately."

"I only hope to contribute to our country's safety. We can't stand by and let her sink through inaction, can we? Thanks for your support and your comment. I appreciate both."

"I'm not saying I support your ideas. I only promise that President Schuster will have your proposal in his hands," Ralph corrected him.

"That's good enough. That's all I can ask." Ed backed off.

"What's the next step?"

Ralph replied, "I'll see the President tomorrow afternoon. I'll give it to him then. After that, it's up to him. He'll decide what he wants to do, if anything. You may or may not hear about it. I won't ask, I never do. If he wants my opinion, he knows where to find me."

"If you hear anything, will you let me know?"

"Not sure if that's in the cards. Again, it depends on whether the President wants to do anything or not."

"That's fair. I can't thank you enough Ralph. I know you're putting your relationship with the President on the line over this. What can I say?"

"Let's start with Goodbye. I need to get back to work."

"Thanks again." Ed nearly skipped out of the office. He never noticed the wintery February cold as he walked back to his car parked in the White House garage. He drove back to McLean, elated and extremely satisfied at how well things had gone.

Once Schuster reads my proposal….

His emotion soared to heights he had never known before, one that made him feel he had reached the zenith of his life. He didn't know the strange and unexpected path his life would soon take. If he did, his attitude would have been different. Quite different.

*

Never one for second-guessing himself, Ralph felt uneasy. He couldn't predict the President's reaction to Ed's proposal, or to him.

Would he be angry or disappointed? Lose confidence in me? So why am I jeopardizing my standing with the President?

He wasn't quite sure, but something told him he needed to get Ed's proposal to the President. Call it his sixth sense. He worried what he'd tell the President if he asked for his opinion. He hadn't decided if he'd be willing to support Ed's ideas. It *was* radical, but it might work.

Yet, it's against everything I've fought for and believed in my life. Have I become a hypocrite by violating my beliefs to save my country? But, what else can I do?

He said quietly to himself,

"I've read *Red Sunset,* and it scared the crap out of me too. We need to do something, much more than we are doing now. Ed's proposal is the only idea I've heard in a long time that makes sense."

Hopefully, he reflected, *my decision to present it to the President will not bite me in the ass.*

Tuesday afternoon Ralph handed the sealed envelôpe to the President.

"You might want to read this, Mr. President." He offered no further explanation.

*

Ed's sudden decisiveness was the most startling revelation that came out of his meeting with Madison. He felt strangely proud, yet incredulous. He knew he had grown indecisive over the years. He lacked trust in his thoughts and his decisions. He didn't believe in himself. Through the years, he had learned to lean on Janice to help him with his decision making for the major issues at home and work. Amazingly, his self-confidence was now elevated. He wasn't sure why, but he liked this new feeling. He thought back to when he was a young boy. He was defiant then, especially with his Mom.

"I guess I was too immature to understand how to sustain that into my adulthood. Too bad. Things might have turned out differently."

He reviewed the President's options. Reject the proposal as dumb; shove it into his file and never look at it again; not act on it; forget to read it because he was too busy; accept it or sit on it long enough until he believed it was his own idea. Two out of six. Not very good odds for success, he concluded.

Ed had made a list of pros and cons the President might consider, leaning heavily towards the pro side. He recognized the President might want to understand all sides of the issues before he would accept the ideas in his proposal. He wasn't happy knowing he'd have to wait until he heard from either the President or Ralph to learn the fate of his proposal.

In his proposal he had stressed that waiting until terrorists committed an act of terrorism was too late, a point he tried to emphasize. He wrote, "We must act, not react. We cannot allow their leaders to influence the youth to commit acts of terrorism by filling their minds with slogans and ideology about Allah and his demands. Typical is that Allah demands the death of any infidel who commits an act against Allah, Islam, or the Koran. Be a Jihadist, fight for Allah. Die for Allah. Your reward is Paradise."

Ed wanted to remind the President that terrorists came in many forms, including the young men and women who commit the heinous acts of terrorism, but also clerics and national leaders who brainwash them.

He used the same logic as the clerics. Anyone who is a terrorist, calls himself a terrorist, or acts as a terrorist, should be put to death immediately. No trial, no bulldozing of homes, no prison camps, no Geneva rules, no exceptions.

I know I'm suggesting a concept that violates traditional US attitudes of morality and law, he mulled in his head. *But why should we legally protect people who want to destroy us? Terrorists break our laws and flaunt our democratic values. We need to turn the tables on them.*

His proposal emphasized that the *only* way to stop terrorists is to give them a reason to stop being terrorists. If we eliminate their opportunity to reach Paradise because they die without fighting in a jihad, they will stop being terrorists. Ed projected a decline of 80-90% of terrorist attacks in the world within nine months to two years, "providing global leaders join our crusade, led, of course, by you, Mr. President."

Entire communities, Ed predicted, would do a 180-degree turnaround, and go from terrorist supporters to benign citizens. Some might even work with us to expose known terrorists. We can expect that some terrorists will go underground. For the majority, terrorists would become isolated with less money and less popular support.

My solution is simple, concise, and elegant. Terrorists will quickly understand the consequences of their actions. When they understand they will be executed without a trial or state protection, they'll fold like a paper napkin. Terrorists will feel the same level of fear they instill on innocent people, he said to himself. *Hope the President gets it. He has too!*

"My concern," he reasoned aloud, "is the automatic reaction of the bleeding hearts that will recoil at the prospect of instant death for terrorists. Bypassing humanitarianism might offend their Judeo-Christian sense of values." He expected to hear the old clichés of:

"That would make us the same as they," and "Too barbaric."

But what if the President himself is a bleeding heart?

"Even if he feels that way, I have an answer that will satisfy even the most docile person. Terrorists changed the rules of engagement by attacking innocent civilians, including men, women and children. Why should we obey rules they don't accept or follow? We're in a different fight, one without rules, one without boundaries, one we cannot afford to lose. The only thing that matters is winning. There is no other option."

At the end of his proposal, he inserted a direct and personal appeal to President Schuster's sense of history and his legacy.

"Would you, Mr. President, like to be known in history as the President who refused to take action to preserve the world from terrorism, or be applauded as a great leader, as the man who led the way towards their defeat? Which one fits you better?"

Late Monday evening, after Ralph delivered his proposal to the President, Ed had second thoughts. He worried he may have been too forceful with the President, *but damn it, he needs to hear the truth.*

The more he thought about his proposal, the more he justified his approach.

His rationalization continued.

We have the right and the responsibility to defend ourselves by any means available. We want to play by the rules, yet our enemy doesn't. Are we to become sitting ducks and claim that nothing is possible, or are we to fight back with whatever means available? If we have to abandon our morality to win, we must do it. How can we justify sticking to stupid rules when we're fighting terrorists?

Terrorists bank on the freedom we provide to live and to operate within our country, to meet and move around without controls, and to plot against us right under our noses. Our laws are inadequately structured to prevent them plotting against us. We do nothing until they act. Then, we react, vow to find them, form an investigative team, capture them, and follow up with a long and involved trials from which they often receive no or limited jail time. Many return to their homelands to continue their fight against us. Some get off on a technicality. I believe…no, I know President Schuster also wants these heinous crimes to end. I have confidence he will accept his duty and act against terrorists, just as I propose.

Ed was immensely satisfied with his long yet elegant rationalization he intended to use to neutralize any Presidential objections to his proposal, assuming he had a chance.

Not that this will be necessary, he concluded. *President Schuster is the Commander in Chief of the United States, the leader of the free world. Certainly he'll understand the value of my proposal. He'll do the right thing. When he does, he will lay the foundation for a new world, a place safe to live in and safe to raise a family. Freedom and democracy will prevail. I'm sure of it!*

He gloated at the prospect of the President's actions.

It was my idea. Thank God I was shown the solution, the only one that will work!

9

Pakistan, 38 hours later:

Thirty-eight hours and twenty minutes from the start of his homebound journey, the PIA plane pulled into gate number twenty-three in Quetta. The movable steps wheeled into place. The ant-like procession of single file passengers began exiting their hive. Bilal quickly passed through the two-person inspection lane. Pakistan inspected everyone entering or leaving any plane, regardless whether it was domestic or International.

His weary father stood at the exit door, waiting to drive Bilal home in his cousin Habib's 15-year old Hyundai truck. Habib was one of the lucky ones. He still had a job with Al Nahzid Engineering, one of the largest electrical manufacturing companies in Karachi. They operated a sub-branch in Quetta where Habib worked. Although he had to travel 60 miles a day to Quetta, it beat unemployment. Pakistani high-end businesses survived only through the blessings of high-level political connections. Al Nahzid had the right connections. Government-sponsored contracts meant big profits, even after the demanding government officials received their bribes and kickbacks.

The moment Bilal exited the customs area and saw his father, he openly wept. It the first time he had allowed himself to display his grief. Though Muslims are not supposed to weep, he did. They stood for several minutes clutching each other tightly, sobbing, distraught, and united. With tears in his eyes, Syed led him to the parked truck.

They drove the sixty minutes drive home in silence. No words were needed and none offered by either the younger or the elder Ahmed. Only an occasional angry outburst or gut-wrenching sighs of pain from Bilal punctuated the silence.

The sky seemed eager to share their grief. Ominous dark clouds splashed onto a slate gray sky, mirroring the cruel tragedy they shared. Green fields with the early harvest of wheat and vegetables huddled together, unwilling to open their bounty to the passing truck. Bilal's world had closed and nothing would be the same. He interpreted the menacing sky and the fields as their personal proclamation of his own fate. He accepted that the rest of his life to be filled with torment, emptiness, and pain. His new way would be an existence but not a life.

The village mosque served the living and the dead. Quasim Nasim-ul-Ghani had been in charge of insuring proper burial preparations for seventeen years. He and Bilal quickly made the burial arrangements for the next day. Syed informed Bilal that Nasrin's sister was already in the village and she would perform *ghusl*, the traditional washing of the body of Nasrin and the children. Ghusl is the Muslim way to prepare the body for burial. She would assist in wrapping each body in the *Kafan*, sheets of white cotton cloth used to cover the body before burial. Reverence and dignity surrounded the wrapping procedure, known as *Takfeen*. After the wrapping, rope tied at the head and feet of the corpse seals the Kafan before burial.

Syed drove Bilal home after the arrangements were made.

"I'll stay with you this evening," suggested his father.

"No, I want to be alone."

"But there is nothing in the house to eat, no meat or fresh vegetables. Only some canned food. I checked before I came to pick you up."

"I'm not hungry. I'll manage."

The old man told Bilal he would arrive at his house by at 9:30 in the morning.

"You can trust Quasim. He will be sure the arrangements are correct and proper. We will meet him at his barn. Quasim will provide the coffins for transport to the burial site. He will notify the male mourners selected to carry the bodies into the cemetery. At your request, your family will be buried according to our tradition," his father told his grieving son. "May Allah be with you."

"Thank you. May Allah be with you too," replied Bilal.

Bilal slowly entered his home with tears in his eyes. He struggled with his grief and anger. Although he hadn't eaten since the morning, he felt no hunger. Darkness settled over the village. He turned on the single wood-based lamp on the small round table in the corner of the room and surveyed the contents of his living room and kitchen. The dim light revealed the starkness of his humble dwelling. It startled him. There was no distracting children playing or vying for his attention. There was no greeting from Nasrin, who would be near the stove or sweeping the floor with her worn straw broom.

The room looked different, as though he saw it for the first time. Nasrin kept the house in proper and clean order. It seemed always ready for inspection. She found it near impossible to leave the house without insuring everything was in its proper place. He found it just as she left it that fateful day, the day she and the children took a trip of joy, but found death instead.

Things looked old and tired, and seemed in mourning for the lost family. The three-cushion pale green sofa especially looked the most dejected. Threadbare in areas, fading in others, with throw cushions beaten down through the force of continual use, wept in its isolation. The single upright chair that Nasrin had purchased from an aging man who moved from the village after his wife died stood forlornly in a corner. She had been so proud of the acquisition. It was a maroon over-stuffed chair with wooden exposed arms fitted with a hand made skirt to hide the legs. She had given it a place of honor, near the window, so that Bilal could see the distant mountains when he was home. She would often sneak prideful glances his way while he sat there, gazing out the window. It represented royalty to her. She was proud to see him relaxed in the chair, reading the paper or listening to his favorite music from the tattered radio.

Nasrin's other most cherished possessions were the Balock ottoman with woolen taimani barjasta upholstery and the hand woven rug from Punjab. Her mother had given them as a wedding gift when they got married. Although they were second hand, she didn't care. To her they represented the spirit of Pakistan and symbols of love.

Seeing their possessions, her possessions, forced him to accept the finality of her death. Nasrin would never again be able to see and revel in the happy emotions these simple treasures brought her.

He spotted the wooden toys he had carved for his five children. Each was a gift to Nasrin to commemorate a new birth. He used his skills as a carpenter to create special and unique carvings. He carved a camel and a ship with a mast for Esmail, his first-born. His first daughter received a camel and a teething ring made from cherry wood that he carefully carved and sanded to insure a smooth finish. His wife wrapped a piece of soft white cotton towel around the ring as a soft cushion for their infant daughter. Resting beside the ship and the teething ring were the three other gifts for his next three children. Their individual camels, the good luck baby necklace with carved hearts tied to each other by thin leather laces, the hollow dark bracelet, and the small car with non-moving wheels.

As each child reached the age of three, he carved them a personal wooden camel to remind them of his love. The camels measured 9 inches high and

4 inches wide. Bilal trimmed each with fancy cloth so they looked as if they belonged to the same family. The camels for his children reminded them they are each part of a family unit. He hoped they would always remember they were family, that they would love, respect and support each other after he and Nasrin passed away.

Seeing them together, lounging on the huge shelf he put up in the kitchen, made him gasp. He choked to hold back the scream exploding within. His wife's favorite apron, the one she had made for herself from the same cloth he used on the camels, was hanging on a nail, beseeching her to slip it over her delicate body when she prepared for the next meal. She had embroidered the seven names of the family members in a circular pattern to show the love she felt for her family as a mother and a wife.

The long slotted kitchen table had seen better days, but remained sturdy and functional, preset for the next meal. The seven chairs, garnished from many sources, didn't match, yet somehow exuded warmth and happiness when the family sat together. Now they stood, empty, cold, uninviting.

Bilal wandered through his small house in a daze, room by room. Old wooden plank floors ran throughout the house. Bilal used his knowledge of wood to sand, polish, and seal the planks. Nasrin was pleased because it dressed up the home.

"Our floors are just like the rich, only better," she liked to remind him. Bilal was thrilled to see her so happy.

He peered into his bedroom. The barren bed, the small table, the winged chair in the corner gathered in mourning. He stumbled to the two moderate sized bedrooms that housed his five children: two double bunks, a cot and a single table with a small camel colored table lamp squeezed tightly together; the second bedroom had two single beds separated by a small desk and chair. A desk forlornly sat in the far corner.

The cramped quarters made exiting either bedroom a challenge for the children. They giggled it was their daily exercise program. They called it "the obstacle course." It was especially hard for his wife because she insisted on sweeping the room everyday. It always saddened him to see her struggle as she moved each piece of furniture to clean. She would get on all fours, tie a rag to the bottom of the broom and sweep under the beds. It saddened him because he couldn't afford to provide better surroundings for his family. No one complained but he knew the difference. He always wanted to do better for his family. In some small part, his guilt helped to drive him into the arms of EPA.

Nasrin took enormous pride in her home. Though they didn't have money to spend on frivolous things, she had a wonderful sense of color and spatial coordination. She seduced your eyes with harmony and pleasure.

"The warmth of Nasrin. Her tender touch. My children's smiles and joy, are gone forever," he sobbed.

He finished touring his empty house. He collapsed into his chair, her chair, desperate, dazed and devastated. It was time to weep in solitude, to grieve, to remember his vow, his rage, and his anger. Slowly the tears and the pain subsided, replaced with his final purpose. Revenge.

He turned off the lamp to sit in the heavy darkness, swallowed by the stillness and the emptiness of his life. He sat alone in the dark, in his chair that once was his refuge of peace. Nothing of his past remained. He had no future except revenge. Revenge *was* his future, one to which he was now totally committed.

"Death to HuM! I swear my vows will not go unfulfilled."

He sat throughout the night, married to the darkness.

"I need a plan, but what? Where do I start? How do I start?"

Radically swirling emotions of pain, agony, grief, anger, hatred, determination, revenge, and confusion tortured him.

"Too much to sort for now. Tomorrow, after I bury my family. Tomorrow I will know how to honor Nasrin. Tomorrow…"

He unwillingly fell into a shallow and troubled sleep in the chair. He hadn't slept for a day and a half, not counting the brief catnaps on the planes. His body demanded. His mind yielded.

*

The screaming startled him. It came from his throat. Shrill, agonizing groans mixed with hesitating sobs. His simmering rage collided with the emptiness of his house. His dominant thoughts, as always, were death to the perpetrators. He focused on tracking the HuM killers. He wanted to make them suffer, to suffer beyond their wildest fears.

Early morning light confirmed the time was approaching for the burials.

"I swear to Allah that I will not stop, I swear it, I swear it, I swear it!" The sounds of his shouting rippled throughout the desolate house.

For nearly 40 minutes, he repeated his vow, inducing a near self-induced hypnotic state. He rose from his chair, disregarding his stiffness from sleeping upright throughout the night. His torment stalked the stillness of his home, looking for an object upon which to focus. Numbly he surveyed his surroundings, scanning the contents in slow motion.

The table, preset for seven for dinner, which Nasrin habitually set in anticipation of his return home, drew his focus. Without regard to Muslim law, Bilal's rage superseded the rule that mourners must not break things in their grief. A single swipe of his arm sent the plates and silverware crashing to the wooden floor with a violent clatter. He went to the window to retrieve his chair and returned to the dining room, the chair poised above his head. It became his battering ram. He swung it wildly from side to side, destroying everything in its path. Lamps, books, chairs, mirrors, pictures, clothing-nothing escaped his fury. Exhausted, Bilal collapsed to the floor, tears flowing from his swollen eyes red from the unending stream of tears. The disorder in his head matched the disorder of his house. Everything lay in tatters, broken, disfigured, and silent. He caught a glimpse of the picture of Nasrin amongst the shambles.

"Nasrin, Nasrin... how I love you. My heart is heavy with your absence. How will I survive without you?" he crawled over the debris, lovingly cradled the picture frame in his left hand. Carefully he removed the picture from the shattered glass frame.

"You will always be in my heart, and never will I forget you, never will I forget your love. Never will I forget what happened to you, I swear to my death," sobbed Bilal.

He tenderly placed the picture of his wife into the pocket of his shirt.

"There you will remain until those who killed you are dead."

Anger turned again to grief. The onslaught of the events of the past several days took its toll. The shock of the letter, the endless travel, seeing and entering his empty house, the ruins, the anguish, and the unrelenting grief sucked his remaining energy. He lay there on the floor, amongst the ruins of his home, amongst the shattered ruins of his life.

A small sliver of sunlight caught his eye. Like a hammer, the truth once again smashed his mind into reality. He surveyed the damage.

"It is fitting that my former life be destroyed with my family. From these ruins will grow a new terror within me, one that my adversaries will learn about as I extract their last breath from their wretched throats. Only then will they understand, they will suffer, and only then will I avenge the deaths of my wife and children."

He lovingly and softly touched the pocket where the picture of his wife nestled, close to his heart.

I must prepare for the funeral. I must bathe, for to appear in tattered clothing for the funerals would desecrate the memory of my family. He stumbled to the battered porcelain tub in the bathroom. Impatient with the speed of filling the tub, he jumped in with the water only half filled. He quickly washed and dressed in his black long robe he reserved for funerals or weddings.

"Now," he soulfully whispered aloud, "I wear this for the last time. There will be no joy, no reason to laugh, no reason to celebrate, and no more funerals." He walked out the front door to sit on a stool in front of his house to wait for his father.

Syed arrived at precisely 8:43 AM. It took 9 minutes for them to reach their destination. Flatbed bullock carts pulled by buffalo had to be used instead of men due to the large number of bodies. Traditionally, men of the village would carry the wrapped body of the deceased on wooden planks to the cemetery. Because of the unusual number of bodies, there were not enough men to fulfill this ritual. Quasim Nasim-ul-Ghani, had to borrow five sets of carts and buffaloes from the townspeople. Quasim used the carts as a last resort.

The carts, the buffalo, Quasim, and the six deceased members of the Ahmed family patiently waited for the arrival of Bilal and his father. The order of the procession follows the tradition of the village. The six bullock carts carrying the six bodies at the head, their order dictated by the age of the deceased, with the eldest of the dead first, followed in descending order of the others. Nasrin's body was on the first cart, followed by their children, from the eldest to the youngest. Immediate family mourners assembled in single file behind the last cart, followed by relatives and friends. Others who wished to join would do so at the rear of the established procession. Bilal, his father, Nasrin's sister, and their relatives queued to begin the torturous ½-mile processional walk behind the last cart.

Mourners, unless physically unable, lined up to walk behind the cart as the carriage moved slowly through the village. Bilal and his father positioned themselves behind the sixth cart, nodded to the drivers, and the slow-paced mournful procession began. The wooden cartwheels made small creaking sounds as they rolled over the tiny stones in the road, almost with a special cadence specifically reserved for these sad occasions. As the procession of carts and mourners passed the homes of the other villagers, each person fell behind Bilal and his father to form a snake like train of wagons and mourners, growing in size as the residents joined in the processional to the cemetery, all in single line, until the entire village was walking behind the men in mourning. Every man, woman and child, was dressed in their mourning clothes as a sign of respect to the deceased and to share in Bilal's sorrow. Never had so many from one family died at the same time. Certainly never from a terrorist attack.

Muslim mourners, by tradition, are to remain calm and silently offer prayers from the Qur'an for the departed. Muslims believe that death is a departure from life, but not the end of a person's existence. Rather, eternal life is coming, and the funeral prayers, called *Salat-l-janazah*, said with the hope that the deceased find peace and happiness in the life to come.

As the carts slowly proceeded through the village, other townspeople who wished to join the procession formed a single line behind the distraught and solemn mourners. Men walked slowly and silently, while the continuous chanting of prayers fell to the women and children. They began their prayers when the carts began to move.

Eighteen minutes later, the long procession arrived at the entrance to the cemetery. A wooden arch announced the cemetery location. It had no fence. The archway notified the mourners it was time to separate the men from the women and children. Muslim law permits only men to participate in a burial. Women and children remain outside the cemetery grounds and continue their prayers until the Imam, the prayer leader, begins the *al-dafin*, the burial rituals.

One by one, the men respectfully removed the six bodies from the carts and carried the bodies to the gravesite, making six separate trips. They placed each body on a wooden platform, set between two long poles, adjacent to the gravesites.

Two large gravesites had been prepared, one for the male members and the other for the female members of the family. Two open anticipating mouths were waiting to swallow their newest members. Muslim graves are dug so that the heads of the deceased, when placed in the ground, point towards Makkah, or as the non-Muslim world refers to it, Mecca. Two men climbed into each grave to accept the corpses and to place them on the ground, their right side facing Makkah. Bilal's wife first, then each female child. Duplicate procedures followed at the male grave.

Six times Bilal witnessed the bodies of his family lowed into the earth. Six times, he weakly uttered a prayer of respect and love, barely audible even to himself. One by one, his voice became fainter. One by one, a portion of him remained, buried with his family. When the body of Habib, his youngest son, reached the bottom of the male grave, ropes were tossed into the grave to extricate the men performing the burial positioning. Bilal was without energy or tears. Lost too was his soul. The magnitude of his personal tragedy filled the hearts and minds of all at the mass funerals, a feeling none would be able to erase from their memory as long as they lived.

Markers of any sort are not used, including stones or flowers, to identify the gravesites of the deceased. Instead, Muslims are required to humbly remember Allah and his mercy, and offer prayers for the deceased. Nasrin and their three daughters, Seeta, Azra, and Shirin, his two sons, Esmail and Habib were settled into their respective graves.

Iman Abdul-Mutaal, proceeded over the burial ceremony. Muslims do not wail or scream at burials. Prayers and praise for Allah are the centerpieces of their eulogies. The Imam opened the ceremony with:

"When the Prophet Muhammad's own son died," he said "The eyes shed tears and the heart is grieved, but we will not say anything except which pleases Allah."

"Today is a day of deep sadness for our beloved friend Bilal Maqsood Ahmed, and his father, Syed, who today witness the passing of the senseless death of a happy and peaceful family whose only crime was to be in the wrong place. Their lives were cut short. Their deaths are wrong, for they were not combatants, and harbored no offending religious beliefs or actions. We pray that the spirits of these six will ascend to heaven, where Allah waits with open arms. We are witness to this family who only wished to live in peace with their husband and father, Bilal, a good man who loved his family, who honored his father, and our village."

The Iman proceeded to offer four prayers, called *Takir*, to conclude his portion of the burial ceremony.

"Allah is great. Praised be Allah. And now I call upon our dear friends and fellow villagers to offer their final prayers to Bilal's family."

Bilal, drained from the emotion of the short, devastating ceremony, barely able to stand, aimlessly gazed around at the gathering of his fellow villagers. He looked at each person, yet saw no one. He barely heard the words spoken by the Imam, though he did see his lips moving through his gray thick beard. He only knew that it was time for him to pray, to say a final goodbye to his family. He wanted to shout with all his strength that he did not want to follow the Muslim ritual of daily prayer for his family or to forgive his enemies. He wanted to scream, a primal scream, with mournful and powerful anger. Instead, he stood silently, not to pray but to reaffirm his commitment to seek revenge.

To conclude the service, Bilal and Syed each grabbed a handful of earth and placed them into Nasrin's grave and recited:

"Out of it We created you."

They scooped a second handful of earth, let it fall between their fingers and recited:

"And into it We deposit you."

Then:

"And from it We shall take you out again."

Male and female children require separate prayers. Bilal recited them as he placed the handfuls of earth into the two gravesites. With his last handful of earth, Syed prayed for forgiveness. Bilal silently prayed to complete his vows of destruction.

The village men, along with Bilal and Syed, hand shoveled the earth into the graves until a mound of eight inches formed above ground level.

Syed turned to his son.

"Preparations have been made to receive the townspeople at sunset to show their respect for you and your family. Two hours before the women will bring the food and drink. I must remind you. It is your duty to receive your fellow mourners in your home in honor of the deceased. I will arrive with the women later this afternoon. Until then, you must look inward for your strength to sustain yourself during these four months and four days of bereavement. To mourn, to pray, to begin the healing process. That is your obligation."

He turned and motioned to Bilal to follow. They painfully made their way back to the truck left at the starting place of the procession. His father drove him to his house and quickly drove off to oversee the food preparations. Bilal was alone, alone to confirm the course of action he decided on during the morning destruction of the inside of his house.

Numb with pain and suffering, he thought only of his plans for the future.

I must tend to this empty house. Then, I'll move to Karachi where they were killed. There I will hunt for their killers.

He entered his house for the last time. He desperately wanted to imprint his last memory of every item in his home, though all lie in tatters, broken, strewn about, or smashed. He fingered the picture of his wife Nasrin to be sure it was secure in his breast pocket. Systematically he threw the combustible items into a pile in the center of each room, every paper, every book, every article of clothing, and any remaining pictures. The single item spared was the picture taken a year ago of his wife surrounded by their five children. He placed that picture in his pocket, next to that of his Nasrin in his breast pocket.

In final tribute, he carefully placed the carved camels he had made for his children at the top of the kitchen consumables. He remembered how proud Nasrin felt because he carved the camels.

To her it was a sign of my love and dedication to our family and to her.

Bilal formed the piles of flammable material in each room until he was satisfied nothing was left behind. He poured the scented bath oil his wife so loved over the pile in his bedroom, and lit the first match. Symbolically, he gazed into its flame, mentally commanding it to do its job, then threw the match onto the pile. He moved from room to room methodically igniting the oil-laden piles. Ritualistically he continued to inspect the flame of each match before setting the pile ablaze. This was his way of finalizing the process of destroying his past, of freeing him for the future.

By the time he reached the last pile in the living room, the house had solemnly accepted its fate. Quickly it joined the macabre by assisting in its self-destruction. Flames frantically licked the drapes, walls and furniture. The house embraced its final memorial to Bilal's family.

Bilal stood in the doorway and watched the flames do their duty. Satisfied, he walked fifty feet from the burning inferno that once was his home, to sit on the ground and watch the funeral pyre as it inexorably consumed the last of his memories. He sat and watched, waiting for the last remnants of the house to die. The afternoon temperature had soared to over 101 degrees, made hotter by the rapidly spreading flames. Bilal sat, hot, sweating, yet numb in the stifling heat.

Some villagers noticed the smoke and ran towards the fire, anticipating a heroic effort to save Bilal from even more tragedy. As they approached, Bilal stood in their path, raised his hands to stop them, a blank look on his face. Reluctantly, confused, yet obedient, they stood by and watched as the entire house was engulfed in billowing black smoke and orange-red flames. They gathered quietly, without conversation, without tears, to watch the flames reduce his house to ashes. Silently they respected Bilal's unannounced wishes to lay waste to this final portion of his life.

He accepted their compassion, their intended support, and shared with each their heavy and breaking hearts.

Within twenty-seven minutes, the flames reluctantly receded. Walls collapsed, and the smell of charred wood and fabric filled the air. Soon, all that remained were pieces of unburned wood, charred clothing remnants, and melted or twisted household items that managed to escape the intensity of the blistering flames. The choking smell of smoke hung in the oppressive summer air. Bilal and the villagers watched in silence as the last remnants of his house vanished into smoke. What was once a symbol of a happy family, living in a small but friendly and warm home, crumbled in ruins.

Sometime during the burning of his house, Bilal experienced the second and last metamorphous of his life. His first change was the normal transition from a shy and down trodden boy to adult manhood. For most people one dramatic life change was all they needed and all they received. Bilal was not the average man. He transitioned from being a kind, caring and loving man into a new and menacing machine, devoid of feelings, compassion and love. Hate replaced love. Anger replaced tolerance. Ferocity replaced decency. Bilal had only one reason to live-kill those who destroyed his family. Life had no meaning without Nasrin. He would kill those responsible even if it meant his own life.

Without a word or gesture, Bilal, satisfied that nothing remained of his once happy past, stood and began to walk towards his father's home. No one questioned him, no one understood him, and no one stood in his way. His father, still in his mourning clothing, rose inquiringly as he saw his son approaching.

"What are you doing? Where are you going?"

"To avenge my wife and children."

"But where, but...?"

"No questions, father. I need to borrow the truck. I'll let you know where it can be picked up, But I must leave, this instant. Goodbye."

Syed reluctantly gave him the keys. Bilal entered the truck, started the engine, and drove away. He couldn't bear to see the pain on his father's face, or the tears that he knew were there. Nor did he want his father to see his tears. They had both seen and tasted enough in the past three days. To revisit that again might weaken his resolve, and he would not let that happen.

They instinctively knew they would never see each other again. His father was old, and would probably die before he finished his mission. Or, he might die first. He was certain one or both would happen. It saddened him to think that his father and he were the last members of the family alive. There was no one to follow him, no son to carry his name, and no one to teach his precious carving skills. Death had also come to Syed's brothers and sisters through disease, accident, or war. His mother had died in childbirth when his younger sister was born. A friend from another village cared for and raised her as a member of the family. His father understood he was not equipped nor expected to raise a girl-child. Had she been a boy, things would have been different.

Bilal had returned to the village as a man in pain, filled with dejection, eyes red and swollen with tears, and a heart burdened with hopelessness. He left a man-machine, focused on killing, committed to his revenge, with his heart hardened and drenched with hatred.

He left the truck at the airport in Quetta, phoned his father about its location, and secured a seat on the next flight to Karachi. Three hours later, he boarded PIA flight 233 to start the next phase of his existence. He didn't think of it as the beginning of his new life, rather, the beginning of his eminent death.

10

BARROWS- WASHINGTON, DC:

Monday morning was hectic, but satisfying.

This is a great way to start the New Year. First work day, first job at the White House, and the first day of establishing my Presidential credentials.

These thoughts made Barrows a happy man, enough to not care about the Washington DC traffic. In fact it didn't bother him at all. He reported to the White House garage to meet Tom Peaksman.

"Good morning Mr. Barrows," Peaksman greeted him as he entered the gate. "Follow me to your parking spot." He climbed into an electric scooter and directed Barrows to follow him.

Barrows had expected a lean and sharply dressed man to greet him. Instead, Tom Peaksman was anything but that. He was short, fat, balding, and pale white skin with eyes overshadowed by thick bushy eyebrows. His brown ill-fitting suit needed pressing, and his tie looked like he purchased it in the 1970's. The combination of the brown suit and his pale complexion gave Peaksman a sallow and washed out look. Tom Peaksman was the antithesis of what Barrows envisioned a trusted Presidential confidant would be. It took him by surprise. He wondered about the President's judgment. He needed someone who was sharp, energetic, and a power broker in the government. Peaksman didn't match up.

They reached their destination at level one of the underground garage. Peaksman motioned him to park in the designated spot. His title, *Chairman, Peace Envoys*, looked like the painter stenciled it on the wall moments before he arrived. Barrows parked the car and got out to greet the man with whom he was to work.

"Tom Peaksman, Mr. Barrows. Nice to meet you." They shook hands.

"Call me Tim."

"OK Tim, I'm Tom. Sounds funny together, don't they?"

When Peaksman smiled, only his upper teeth showed. Large while teeth with a wide gap in front. Barrows thought he resembled a cartoon character he remembered seeing on TV.

"OK, where to now?"

"To your office. You'll have a chance to settle in. Later we'll get your security badge and clearances taken care of so you can enter the building on your own. Electronic monitoring is everywhere. Without your badge and eye detection registered, your life will be miserable. Your Homeland badge doesn't work here. When you're ready, we can talk about how I can support you. Based on how excitedly the President spoke about you, I'm sure you already have some plans and tons of questions that need attention. He's really excited about you."

"That's good to hear."

"I'm sure it's well deserved. I'm looking forward to working together."

"Same here, Tom, same here." Barrows lied. He was less than impressed by this ragged person.

Tom opened the door with his eye detector and badge, signed in at the security desk, where Barrows' name had been pre-registered and together they cleared security. They took the elevator to the fourth floor, walked down the polished marble corridor to a corner office protected by a secretarial station.

"Natalie, this is Timothy Barrows, your new boss. This is Natalie Spoval."

"Welcome on board, Mr. Barrows. Good luck with your new position. Be sure to let me know how I can help. Your desk and personal belongings are here already. If you would like anything moved, I'll see that it gets done."

"Glad to meet you Natalie, and thanks. I'm sure it's fine."

She unlocked the large wooden door to his office, gave him the key, and returned to her desk.

His office faced north, where he had an unobstructed view of Lafayette Square and the historic Hay-Adams Hotel. Once spring came to the large barren trees, he deduced the foliage would obstruct his view. Barrows couldn't care less about what view he had. He came to work, not to daydream. As the President had promised, the entire contents of his former Homeland Security office shipped over the holidays, including the pictures of his family and the Japanese scenic cork picture he bought years ago.

"Tim, I'll leave you for a while to get organized. Would you like to have lunch together? We can eat in the Executive dinning room. It would be smart to meet the chef to let him know what kinds of foods you prefer and how you like them prepared. You'll find that Chef Tang is excellent and most accommodating."

"Great. 11:30?"

"Done."

He buzzed Natalie.

"Do we have any bottled water? I drink a great deal when I'm working."

"Certainly, Mr. Barrows. I have a well-stocked refrigerator in the galley kitchen. Do you prefer still or bubbly? Do you drink coffee or tea?"

"No, I don't drink coffee and I only like unsweetened iced tea. Still water is fine, thanks."

Natalie knocked, brought him the water on a dual handle wooded serving tray, and left. She automatically closed the door behind her.

Someone trained her real well. She does her job and doesn't dawdle. We'll get along just fine.

He made phone calls to Sid Kleinerman, his ex-boss, to the President to thank him again, and the White House travel staff to acquaint them with his travel preferences. As Chairman, he expected to travel extensively. Stupid or inefficient travel arrangements irked him to a point of distraction. He spoke with Staci Cove and her assistant Howard Mark about his needs, including airport and seating preferences, hotel accommodations, and car rental choices.

They assured him they would do their best to accommodate him. He spent the rest of the morning arranging his office.

Natalie buzzed him at 11:15 to remind him about his lunch date with Tom Peaksman.

"Is this something you would like me to do for you, Mr. Barrows? I'm used to maintaining schedules, and if you prefer, I can manage yours and alert you to your commitments. As long as you identify what and who are important to you, I'll do my best to control the people and phone traffic in and out of your office," she stated.

"I like that. I prefer efficiency at work. If you can do that, we'll get along just fine," was his crisp reply.

Peaksman showed up at 11:25, and escorted Barrows to the executive dinning room. It took over twenty minutes before they sat down at a table. Peaksman walked him from table to table introducing the Senators, Congressmen, and the few cabinet members who were present.

"It's a good thing we came early to meet the government," Barrows laughed.

"It gets worse. Wait until they want something from you. You may never come back here again."

Chef Tang made his appearance, and he and Barrows discussed his food preferences. Though he usually didn't eat desserts, Barrows indicated a small piece of dark chocolate candy, if available "would be nice."

Peaksman pointed out whom he felt needed watching.

"There's a lot of political back stabbing here, as you can imagine. I'll do the best I can to cover your back, but it doesn't hurt for you to watch your front." Barrows nodded his thanks.

They exchanged family history information-wife's name, kids, schools, living area, etc to get to know each other. They moved onto the business of the Peace Envoys.

"I know it's early, but have you any questions I can answer? One thing you need to know is that I've been around for a long time at the White House in many capacities. As advisor to the President, you'd be surprised at what I can get accomplished. Just let me know what you need, and I'll see if I can help."

"Thanks, Tom. That's reassuring. I'm sure I'll ruffle some feathers. I usually do. Anything you can do to steer me on the right path would be appreciated." Peaksman laughed.

"Its easy to believe you will crush some toes and fingers. Your reputation from HSD precedes you. We'll get along just fine. We come from the same piece of cloth. Let's just try to not hurt each other, OK?" He laughed again, harder.

"Agreed," replied Barrows, though he found it hard to believe this frumpy man would do what he claimed.

Nevertheless, he has been around, and he's an advisor to the President. Maybe I'm wrong. I'll wait and see what develops.

Barrows was always good at recognizing any opportunity that presented itself.

They separated after finishing their turkey sandwiches. Chef Tang sent over a bar of Dove chocolate for Barrows as dessert.

Back in his office, Barrows' thoughts turned to his wife Lynette and their life together. Periodically, when he thought about it, he tried to show an interest in Lynette and their teenage sons. He chatted about his job and his desire to become President. Sometimes he remembered to hold her hands, especially when she was upset. Fortunately, the boys usually managed some sort of interruption to break up these very awkward and unusual caring moments. Lynette refused to take his actions seriously because she understood he wasn't sincere. She knew he really didn't care how happy or unhappy she was. It wasn't that he didn't love her. He did, the best way he could.

Barrows never experienced open love between his parents. His experience with his father, Barrows Senior, was of a man driven by intense ambition, fueled with arrogance, distrust, manipulation, bitterness, vengefulness, and controlled by the power-money demon that resided in his head. His father was always on the phone, traveling, or attending closed-door meetings in their mansion. To him, love meant you didn't hit your wife or children, you made sure they had sufficient money and safety, provided good social status, and lived in a beautiful home. Intimacy was an alien concept. Barrows learned the art of manipulation from Senior. He never failed to use it.

I'm smart and know how to manipulate people and situations have made me successful. I expect the same success with the Peace Envoys summed up his approach and attitude to life and Lynette.

He knew she was confused about what made him tick. He acknowledged his best times were when he made money or committed some self-serving act. Then he was less moody and sometimes more tolerant of Lynette and the boys. It generally stemmed from the fact that he had screwed another person.

She learned that early in their marriage to stay out of my way, especially when I'm angry or upset. She learned quickly not to challenge me.

He recalled her first lesson. After six months of married life, she accused him of lacking compassion for her and her friends. He flew into a rage. His face reddened, his eyes narrowed, and the veins in his neck throbbed. It was apparent he was battling to control his anger. Though he had never hit her, she wasn't prepared to test his breaking point. When he was happy, she benefited.

"You're a narcissist," she once accused him. She decided it was his personality flaw and she was powerless to change it. She swallowed her pride for the sake of their marriage. There was no other valid option, except divorce. She wasn't prepared to take that step.

I cringe thinking about Lynette making decisions or doing things on her own. I made her that way, and now I'm paying for it. Well, she'll have to make the best of it. This is my opportunity. No one is going to fuck it up. Not her, not Schuster, not Peaksman, not anyone.

He flipped his laptop open and began to plan for his success with the Peace Envoys.

11

PEACE ENVOYS:

Barrows decided to wait until mid February to tell Lynette, his wife of twenty-three years, they would be moving from Manassas closer to Washington. One evening, after a tiring day at the West Wing, and a long traffic filled drive home, he broke the news to her. They were having dinner with their two teenage sons, Lewis and Steven, ages 16 and 14, when Barrows asked for everyone's attention.

"I have an announcement, and I want everyone to listen. We will be moving to a new house closer to Washington so I can be closer to my office. I have selected a place, that I want you to see this weekend. It's in Fairfax, Virginia, about ½ hour drive for me."

A collective groan came from the family. Lynette was the first to react.

"What do you mean we're moving? Why can't we stay here? This house is perfect, the children are doing well at school, they have their friends, and I belong to several social groups that I enjoy. I'm happy living here."

"Here's the way it is. We're moving. Period. You and the kids will make new friends. It's important for me to be close to the White House. This job should propel me into the Presidency. You've known since we married that the Presidency was my goal, and now that I have this opportunity, I'm not about to waste it."

Lewis, the elder of the two boys, complained,

"I don't want to move. I love my school and my fri…"

Barrows interrupted him. He glared at his son with a look that said volumes. He thrust his jaw directly at Lewis. His voiced elevated to a partial shout.

"What part of we're moving didn't you understand? It's done. I don't want to hear any complaints from anyone!"

His two sons looked at their angry father with total disbelief, shrouded in sadness. They knew arguing any further was not only useless, but also threatening. They learned over the years that when Barrows made a decision, either you acquiesced or you suffered later. He had his ways to punish them by withholding favors, or preventing them from being with their friends. One time he pulled Lewis off the soccer team for three weeks because he spoke disrespectfully to him.

Both looked tearfully at the mother, hoping she would intercede on their behalf. She returned their pleading looks with a slight shrug and a lowering of her eyes. She too learned not to cross her husband. He usually turned silent whenever she annoyed him, sometimes for days at a time.

The teens left the table to complete their homework.

Lynette turned to Barrows and tentatively said,

"You're acting just like your father. You always said you hated him, and now you are acting exactly like him. It's just not fair."

Disdainfully he replied,

"I know." He left the table to go to his office on the second floor.

"Have work to do."

They didn't speak for two days. Lynette cried most of the time. Barrows ignored her.

For some inexplicable reason, his thoughts turned to his father. The man he was, how he lived, and the relationship that Senior so completely dominated.

He recalled how his father had planned his career from the time he was twenty-three.

The senior Barrows decided his older son belonged in politics. The goal was the Presidency of the United States. In thirty-two years. That was in 1984. Five years remained.

Barrows respected his father, but bore deep son-father hatred towards him. Nor was he excited about politics during those years. Clark Francis Barrows Senior, seventy-two, cancer ridden, wealthy, powerful, business innovator, owner of 243 US based Collette's Luxury Boutique and Spa centers, arrogant, mean and vengeful, doubly so after his failed attempt at the Presidency in 1980. Barrows resented his father for believing and acting as though he was always right, and expecting everyone to meet his demands, whenever and whatever. He was used to getting his own way. No one in the family ever challenged Senior.

Timothy Randolph Barrows Jr. graduated Harvard University following the Barrows' family tradition. His father, his brother and their cousin graduated Harvard, each with honors. His valedictorian father graduated first in his class, receiving undergraduate degrees in Poly Si and Business Administration. He attended Harvard Law and graduated first in his class after just two and a half years. Barrows Senior joined the prestigious law firm of Watts, Ingraham, and Goldberg in New York City.

After three years, Senior grew tired of law and having to answer to all the people above him at the firm. He looked for another means to become rich, and hit on an idea to create a women's luxury hair boutique and spa. He opened his first store in the City. Within a year, he added three more. It took only fifteen years for his 243rd store to open. He grew independently wealthy. He turned his attention to politics, becoming Mayor, Senator, and finally the Presidential candidate from New York.

During his candidacy campaign, he locked horns with the Republican Party boss, Richard Trunican. Trunican feverishly worked behind the scenes with the party's largest financial backers against Clark Barrows, and effectively killed his bid for the White House. Senior left politics bitter and vengeful.

Timothy Barrows had not lived up to his father's expectations. Though he graduated ninth in his class, his father never let him forget his failing.

"You must have been loafing," was his greeting after his graduation ceremony. "You should have aced everything. You're better than that!"

During his first year at Harvard undergraduate, he made the mistake of expressing an interest in politics to Senior. His father latched onto that like a pit-bull clamps down on its victim. Senior applied maximum pressure on his son to think and act everything political. Barrows, though himself slightly leaning in that direction, reluctantly succumbed to his father's ambition and disappointment. Senior dictated that he, Timothy R. Barrows Jr. *had* to achieve what had denied him.

Clark Barrows channeled his anger, his time, and his vast fortune to clear the path to the Presidency for his elder son.

"I know you're smart, ambitious, and determined. I'm going to do everything in my power to get you into the Presidency. No one is going to deny the Barrows our destiny ever again."

Barrows recalled how he cringed when he heard his father speak.

I knew my fucking father wouldn't stop, not when revenge and embarrassment controlled his life and actions. I knew it, and was young and powerless to stop him. There was no escape from under my father's continued influence. I'm older now, and don't have to put up with his bullshit any longer.

Senior habitually reminded his children early in their childhood that he had the money, and without it, they had nothing. He hung the threat of expulsion from their inheritance if they didn't accept his directions in life. His sister, Kate, had no ambition, so for her to have a dictatorial father was of no consequence. She wanted nothing except his money, and that made her subservient to her father. Barrows was the opposite. He wanted to get as afar away from his father as possible. With the money, of course.

Barrows knew unless he followed his father's direction and moved into politics, he would see little of Senior's wealth. He suspected, even in death, his father would deny him his inheritance, if he felt Barrows was defying his wishes. He would punish him by cutting him off. If nothing else, Barrows was practical. He responded like an obedient son. Openly he accepted his father's control to insure an easier future life. In his heart, he loathed him.

Life is better with money, he conceded. *Even if I don't become President, I'll still be wealthy. Dear old Dad will take care of that, as long as I don't screw up.*

Over time, Barrows surprisingly caught the political fever himself. He was bright, arrogant, ambitious, and ruthless, possessing the same traits he hated in his father.

Anxious to right the wrong done to him, Barrows Senior marshaled his energies and power to influence his son's career. Convinced Timothy had the makings to become President of the United States, he laid out the plan and continually reminded his son,

"Just follow my plan and the Presidency will be yours."

Barrows adjusted his actions to follow his father's career plan. Senior had programmed his son to fulfill his own unfilled dream. Eventually it became his son's dream too.

A key element of the plan was for Barrows to accept only those jobs that added experience, contacts, or a political opportunity that fit the Presidential plan. If the position didn't expand the skills or the opportunity for his personal enhancement, he withdrew his name from consideration. His father's money behind him, Timothy Barrows Jr. enjoyed the luxury of choice, and he took full advantage whenever he could.

Damn you Lynette for reminding me of that bastard! As Peace Envoys Chairman, I'm on my way to establishing my own international credentials. With just a little success, the Presidency is mine.

12

KARACHI, JANUARY 10:

Karachi is a city with a violent past and a marginal future. It is a populous city of religious and non-religious families, terrorists, and a variety of people from assorted backgrounds going about their business. It is a city of intellectuals, poverty, trade, banking, art, cricket and one with a colorful history. The attitudes of the people seem behind the times, while much of the infrastructure remains neglected. Karachi is old and tired, though its population of over 17 million people makes it the largest city in Pakistan. It is home to the biggest shipping port in the county. Jinnah International Airport handles more traffic than any other Pakistani city. Muslims dominate the population demographics by a whopping 96.4%. That fact allowed Bilal to easy blend into the city without calling undue attention to him.

Bilal decided his destination was Saddar City, a Karachi province, with a reputation of being highly infiltrated by al Qaeda. He rented a car and drove to Saddar City, one of eighteen towns of Karachi. He headed toward Old Haji Group, a poor section of Saddar City. The January weather was typical for Karachi, cloudy and cool, reaching 32.8 degrees Celsius (91 degrees Fahrenheit) in the daytime. He felt comfortable driving, even without the air conditioning working. Once he arrived in Old Haji Group, he searched the local paper to locate a furnished apartment. One ad caught his eye. He called the number listed and made an appointment to see the apartment later that afternoon.

The building proprietor was not concerned about Bilal's past. He only wanted to know how long he intended to stay and if he had the money to pay the one month rent in advance. The uncertainty of the political situation in Pakistan forced everyone to be virtually invisible and to ask no penetrating questions. A breach of either could easily result in a visit by the Intelligence Bureau (IB), which, if they were not satisfied with your answers, might result in a beating or one's death. The locals quickly modified their behavior to remain intact. They chose no political sides, kept their personal affairs to themselves, and never talked about or showed off their material possessions. Carelessness could easily label you as a collaborator for the enemy, whoever that was at any given moment.

The political uncertainty suited Bilal's purposes to hide in the open. He wanted no one to probe into his past or his present intentions. He understood every community had it eyes and ears finely tuned to strangers or unusual events. For a modest fee, there were many in Karachi who would eagerly reveal

Bilal's presence and his activities to anyone willing to pay. For an additional fee, they would quickly voice their opinion about who he was and what he was doing in Karachi. With luck, they might receive payments from multiple sources for the same information.

Bilal paid the advance rental fee with cash. The landlord led him to his modestly furnished three-room apartment on the third floor. It had a living room-kitchen combination, a bedroom, and a private bathroom equipped with a tub, toilette, and a pedestal washbasin. The apartment was clean yet well worn. It suited his needs because it was located in the heart of the area where he suspected terrorists and civilians regularly co-mingled. It was accessible to the general market area, and, he hoped, to al Qaeda. Because Karachi was the leading seaport and airline location in Pakistan, the inflow of people with sorted backgrounds and intentions found the city accessible, hospitable, and a perfect place to conduct business.

Karachi presents the best chance to meet the people I want, or for them to find me, Bilal thought during his two-block walk to the market.

After a brief buying spree for food and other basics, he settled into his small living room and surveyed his outside surroundings. The view from his small single double-hung window revealed typical signs of area neglect. He overlooked the winding cobblestone street suitable for bikes and very small cars. The buildings on either side of the street stood, or leaned, in various stages of decay, and quietly flaunted the effect of years of neglect and poverty. Pedestrian traffic was limited, since it was a side street and offered no stores or fruit carts. It was just a street, dirty, narrow, in need of repair, and unremarkable, so typical of many poorer areas of Karachi. It was perfect.

Despite the recent building spree in the early 2000's, many of the older sections of the city remained untouched. The large influx of Muslim migrants, known as *Muhajirs*, during the 1970's, prompted a rush of new housing building to accommodate the ten-fold increase in population. The buildings, hastily assembled, quickly fell into disarray through neglect. Newer affluent sections provided a direct contrast to the older Karachi. New hospitals, schools and government buildings sprung up. Because of the wealth behind their construction, the newer construction was sturdy and attractive.

Bilal was determined to fulfill his vow of revenge, and developed his plan accordingly.

I must become part of the community. I will be no one special. Special people stand out among the faceless and soulless roaming the streets. I must become faceless to be approachable by my enemies. I will portray myself as a dissident, angry at the US and Israel, and unhappy with the Pakistani government. I will be a man without direction.

He hoped that this portrayal would encourage members of the Taliban or al Qaeda to contact him. Through them, he hoped to gain an entree to HuM and to find those responsible for murdering his family. Then they would die.

He decided to maintain a low profile for several months before beginning his plan of attraction, as he called it. He spent hours each day wandering around the neighborhood, buying his daily fruit from two or three street vendors. He lingered nowhere in particular and everywhere that people congregated. He avoided asking even trivial questions. People had to believe he did not wish to be part of society, at least the Karachi society. Once he finished shopping, he walked directly to his apartment and remained there until the next day. A few times each week, during the early evening rush hour, he went to the local teahouses as a regular patron. He did not encourage unnecessary attention to himself. Hide in the open became his mantra.

The third week of his weekly teahouse visits a man whom he had seen in the area approached him.

"Excuse me, but I have seen you here many times, and you are always alone. Would you like some company? My name is Emir Fida Hussain," he said with a smile.

"Bilal Maqsood Ahmed. Yes, that would be nice."

"How long have you been in Karachi?"

"I arrived three weeks ago."

"What brings you here?"

"Looking for a change of scenery, I guess," replied Bilal.

Emir Fida Hussain, dark, tall, and lean, sported a full black beard typical of the Muslim faithful. His threadbare white turban matched his well-worn white shirt and brown baggy pants, yet the intensity of his dark piercing eyes belied his physical appearance.

This is a man of passion and purpose, Bilal observed. *He may be the first step in my quest.*

"Everyone needs a change sometime, is that not true?"

"I suppose."

"Are you working?" asked Emir

"Not yet, I'm looking for construction work, but have not found anything."

"What about you?" Bilal asked.

"I own a car repair shop about three blocks from here. I've been here several times and noticed you always sitting by yourself. Are you alone here in Karachi?"

"Yes, my family died in a car accident four years ago," Bilal lied.

"Sorry."

"That is one of the reasons I decided to come to Karachi, The City of

Lights, to begin a new life. Too many bad memories. I needed a new start and decided to move here to find work. Construction work is not available in Quetta."

"I understand."

Emir abruptly stood up.

"Please excuse me, but I have a previous appointment that I must keep. It was nice to meet you, Bilal. Perhaps we can meet again."

"That would be nice, Emir," he said, as he watched Emir exit the shop and briskly walk up the street, opposite to where he said his car repair shop was located.

Bilal sat there for another fifteen minutes before he paid his bill and slowly ambled back to his apartment.

Good, my first contact. We'll see if Emir makes contact again.

From his training at EPA he learned to pace himself when engaging in a covert encounter with your enemy. Go slow, never arouse suspicion with questions, and do not appear too eager to make new friends. Although he was anxious to meet Emir again, he remained cautious. The first step was to determine who and what Emir represented. Once he knew that, the next step was to gain Emir's confidence. Emir would have to accept him as a lost and lonely person, who was out of work, unhappy, and a disgruntled Pakistani. And, who posed no threat.

Bilal purposely did not return to the teahouse for four days. If Emir was a terrorist on a recruiting mission, Bilal needed to avoid any overt action that might make Emir suspicious. His absence for four days would re-enforce that Bilal was not directly pursuing Emir. If however, Emir was pursuing him, he had to allow the direction of their conversations to be dictated by Emir.

My job is to convince him I am a malcontent with no personal agenda. He will feel safe to approach me if he chooses.

In the afternoon of day five, he went back to the teahouse area. He mingled with the throng of people crowded around the line of street vendors, directly opposite the teashop. He pretended to be a potential buyer. He casually examined their wares and questioned the quality and price of whatever he seemed interested in buying. From this vantage point, Bilal had a clear view of the teahouse while maintaining a degree of indifference. He would be able to spot Emir if he approached the teahouse from any direction. Emir would assume he was a typical shopper.

Twenty minutes later, his reward appeared. Emir headed directly for the teashop. He stepped inside, looked around, and then headed back outside before taking a seat at a favorably positioned table, one that allowed him to see and be seen.

Bilal nodded approvingly to himself.

So he does want to meet me. If he's here for me, then my revenge may soon be satisfied.

Bilal remained alert.

Emir is certainly not in the car repair business. That means he has a reason he wants to meet me. Soon I will learn his purpose.

Bilal approached the shop and pretended to be surprised to see Emir. He walked directly to the small table where he was sitting.

"So, we meet again," he greeted him with a friendly smile. "May I join you for some tea?"

"Hello Bilal," Emir grinned. "It's good to see you again. Yes, please sit."

"How have you been?"

"Well, but very busy cleaning up some family issues for my father. He's been sick and I wanted to be sure that the doctors could provide the proper care. It's hard being separated," Bilal answered.

"You are a good son, Bilal."

"How is the car repair business?"

"In these uncertain times, I never know day to day. Sometimes very busy, sometimes I think I could close the shop and no one would care."

Bilal casually glanced at Emir's hands. He found no dirt or grease under his fingernails or imbedded in his pores. In fact, his were smooth, not what you would expect of someone who performs manual labor on dirty cars.

Emir is not in the car repair business Bilal reminded himself. *But what is his real business? Who is he?*

"You are not Pakistani. Where is your home?"

"Egypt, Al Minya, a small town about 250 kilometers from Cairo."

"What brought you to Karachi?"

"I was in the export business and had a lot of dealings in Pakistan. I met my wife through a mutual friend. We married and I decided to stay in Karachi. That was about six years ago. Unfortunately, my business varies, depending on which government policy is popular. As you know, the cost of staying in business with the local officials is very expensive. I often think of moving back home, but conditions are not much better there. Besides, my wife would be unhappy moving away from her family. I would move if the business demanded it, but... Politics control us all, don't they, no matter where you live, true?"

Surprised that Emir had so quickly turned the conversation to politics, Bilal wasn't sure if he should follow Emir's lead or continue to play the waiting game.

It is better to set the trap and catch the prey, then to allow the prey to escape because of carelessness.

"I understand. Who in our times *is* satisfied?"

"I agree."

"Have you found work?"

"No, not yet," Bilal replied in a soft tone.

They spent the next twenty-two minutes discussing their likes, dislikes, and other benign non-committal issues. Neither chose to discuss politics, the Iraq war, or even US foreign policies. By the end of their conversation, each felt they had established a rapport with the other sufficient to warrant further contact. Bilal could not have been happier. As was Emir.

They parted and agreed to meet at the local cricket match the following Saturday. The locals were up against their archrivals from Lahore. Cricket is the principal sport in Karachi and usually draws over 30,000 people per match. The National Stadium has the second largest seating capacity after Goddafi Stadium in Lahore. Critics claim the single stadium is inadequate for the population of Karachi. The local government artfully ignores the frequent criticism.

Bilal went directly to his apartment. He reviewed the discussion of the afternoon and decided the next move belonged to him.

I will cautiously open the door to show Emir I am a dissident. I have to know where he stands. If he's a terrorist, he could assist me against HuM. If not, it might be the end of my mission and me.

Saturday they met at noon in front of the ticket office, entered the stadium, found their seats, and bought chicken tikka to munch on before the game. Most of the crowd emptied the stands to seek food or toilettes between innings. Bilal found himself sitting alone with Emir.

Now is the time, he decided.

He leaned into Emir and said in hushed tones, with a slight edge to his voice,

"You know what angers me? The West, especially the United States. They treat us as if we are dirt beneath their shoes They send arms and money to our enemies, and then claim they are fair to both sides. They claim they accept our culture, but they lie. Ever since 9/11, we are their enemy, no matter what they claim. They hate all Muslims without knowing anything about our culture. I wish I could do something to fight them, but I'm only one man."

Bilal recalled the valuable lesson ExecProtect drummed into the heads of the recruits.

"If you want to be successful as a security guard or a mercenary, you must learn to listen carefully with your ears and watch even more carefully with your eyes. The eyes will reveal all you want to know about the person. The eyes will reveal if a person is lying, if they are afraid, or they are your enemy."

Bilal hid the fact that he was intently watching Emir's eyes.

"I know what you mean. I feel the same," was Emir's immediate response.

What Bilal saw, or thought he saw, were eyes empty of suspicion or anger. Instead, they quietly shouted,

I accept what you are saying and I agree with you.

"I was thinking of joining one of the homeland fighters, but I'm not sure if that's the right path for me. What do I know about fighting? I'm a carpenter. I work with wood. How would that help me?" uttered Bilal.

"Perhaps I can help," said Emir "I know someone who has contacts. Would you like to meet him? I believe I could arrange a meeting in the next several days."

"Contacts? What kind of contacts?" questioned Bilal.

"People who know how to make things happen. People who feel the same as you and me," replied Emir

"Why haven't you contacted them before this?"

"I wasn't sure if I should do it alone. Now that there are two of us, it will be easier."

"What do they do?" asked Bilal.

"I'll let them explain everything to you themselves, since I don't know." Emir replied.

"I guess it can't hurt to talk, can it? Set up a meeting," Bilal instructed. "The sooner the better."

"Done. Give me your cell number. I'll call you when the arrangements are made."

And so it begins, Bilal thought. *He is the one. My heart tells me yes. But I must remain alert until all is revealed.*

The next evening, Emir called to tell him to come to the teashop directly across from the Pearl Continental Hotel at 2:30 PM on Wednesday. His contact would be there.

"Will you be joining us?

"No, some things are better done privately. A man named Farook will be sitting at the far corner of the coffee shop. He will be wearing a white straw hat with a wide black band. He is 5'10. His skin is light tan with a thick black and gray mustache resting above his lip. He will be smoking a long cigar. A second cigar will protrude from his right breast pocket. Look for a black onyx ring with a center diamond on his left hand, fourth finger. He'll be in tan pants and a light blue shirt. You are to sit on his right, and say to him these exact words:

"Typical hot day in Karachi."

He will reply "Not as hot as in Iraq. Then you will know he is your man," stated Emir.

"I thought you wanted to join together. Why will I be alone with him?" Bilal questioned.

"I already met him briefly I know he prefers to meet face to face, one on one. After you have met him, then we can talk with him together."

"I understand. Thank you for helping me and thanks to Allah."

They departed at the end of the cricket match and headed in opposite directions. Emir reminded him about the meeting with Farook.

I do not know who this Farook is, but I sense he's the key to my path to HuM. I cannot wait to meet him. I feel in my gut that he will help me to fulfill my vow to Nasrin.

13

BARROWS AND THE PEACE ENVOYS:

Barrows first met with each of his Peace Envoys members individually before holding the group meeting. It took nearly two months of continual International travel for him to finish the task. Nine transcontinental flights, twenty-three local flights, twenty-three capitals, and twenty-eight meetings later, he completed the first phase of his PE effort. Each member of his team had similar financial arrangements with their own governments: Personal Swiss bank accounts, a yearly salary, and diplomatic immunity. Each person was committed to helping the world become a healthier and more productive place.

Many joined the Envoys out of dedication to their government and their ideals. Others because of personal loyalty to their leader. Each had been hand selected with similar profile requirements: they enjoyed the excitement of being in the forefront of a history-making event. A deep-rooted passion, coupled with their belief they were protecting their families from future terrorists added to their reasons to work under the PE auspices.

Except for Barrows. His base motivations were quite different. He held no ideology, no slavish obedience to the President or his country. He wanted to be independently rich, enormously famous, and to become President of the United States. The most compelling force was to be free of his father's suffocating control. If being a hero happened, it would be icing on the cake. To become President would be both the cake and the icing. He realized the International recognition he would receive from the Peace Envoys work would help his image at home. All he had to do was to develop plausible programs to assist the poor nations in their quest for economic and political independence.

Barrows understood many of the programs that his group might recommend would take years to implement and more years to be successful. He innately recognized that he stood to be the beneficiary of any good press and good will generated through the Peace Envoys. He called it his political collateral.

He held his initial Peace Envoy group meeting at the five star Washingtonian Hotel in Washington DC on Tuesday and Wednesday, March 30 and 31, 2010. Frequent spring rains had cast a pall over the city. It had rained seventeen days in March, one of the wettest in recent Washington history. Everyone waited anxiously for April to bring sunshine and lift the funk the people felt.

The FBI, the secret service and the Washington DC police teams cooperated to sweep all meeting rooms for bugs or explosives the evening before each meeting and once again in the morning and afternoon. Armed Marines provided 24/7 security. Guards staffed the front and rear entrances to the hotel. Anti-terrorist and armor- piercing weaponry waited, their chambers filled with live ammunition.

President Schuster, concerned attempts might be made to sabotage the meetings, ordered the most sophisticated US communications and detection systems be deployed to present a wartime armada of impenetrable security. The Peace Envoys was his baby, and he was doing everything he could to prevent any disturbances or attacks. He didn't expect terrorists to be so blatant to attack the hotel. He feared the lunatic element might.

By 8:30 AM, Barrows was in the ballroom checking the seating layout and the audio visual. He arrived first in the room to greet his team members as they entered. He instructed the hotel staff to set the table and chairs in "U" shape theatre style, with a dais for himself at the head, Microphones sat poised at each table and the dais. Padded red leather reclining swivel armchairs, rented for the meeting, were neatly tucked under each table. Pads of paper and carefully placed pens lined up like rows of yellow soldiers waiting for their marching orders. Water glasses and a cut glass water pitcher brimming with ice water complimented the yellow soldier-pads, as though they were reviewing the assembled troops before a battle. To all appearances, the room represented a typical corporate meeting room to exchange ideas, review projects, or to set new goals and attitudes. In many ways it was.

Pre-printed embossed cardboard nameplates were arranged alphabetically on a separate table inside the main doorway. Members retrieved their nameplates and took an empty seat, their name prominently placed in front of them.

Barrows closed the dual wooden doors and opened the meeting.

"Good morning. Thank you for coming. I'm Timothy Barrows, in case you have forgotten."

There was no acknowledgement from the audience.

"I previously sent each of you a CD that identifies every Peace Envoys member, their country of origin, phone numbers, and mailing address. Everyone receive their package?"

All nodded in the affirmative.

"Good. Because this is our first meeting, I would like everyone to introduce themselves and the country you represent."

Twenty-eight introductions followed.

Barrows again addressed the audience.

"Everyone here understands the risks and the rewards of our operation, so let's not waste time doting on those issues. Please be sure to state your name before you speak until we get to know each other better. We understand the stakes and the difficulties we face. Our roles as Peace Envoys will be demanding, confusing, possibly dangerous, and sometimes lonely. Our mission demands results in the form of recommendations and actions to create a more homogeneous and globally connected world. We will have to travel to these countries, and talk with the leaders and the people to get a sense of what they need. Every country will be different; each will have a different set of issues and problems to overcome. If we do not fully understand the essence of the culture and the real needs of the people, we will surely fail. We must work on those issues in a credible and professional manner. The world has opened their minds and hearts to us. We must earn their continued respect.

Therefore, we obviously need well-conceived plans to accomplish our mission. I firmly believe we have an opportunity to accomplish our mission. I envision a day when we will submit a global plan to meet the lofty goals outlined by President Schuster and the heads of your respective governments. I envision a day when our recommendations will help the third world countries to compete with the rest of the world. I envision a time when peace, prosperity, and happiness will be the norm rather than the exception. We can make a difference, ladies and gentlemen, we can and we will make a real difference.

Our governments are ready, the people of the world are ready, and we too must be ready. This morning I hope to establish an initial plan that will guide us towards these goals. I certainly do not wish to minimize the obstacles we face. Although our governments have given us an enormous amount of seed money with which to begin, the money is the least of our problems. When you think about changing people's way of life, their thinking, their forms of government, and the military and political foes that will vigorously oppose our efforts, it can be daunting. Nevertheless, I am of the opinion that these obstacles can be overcome, providing our governments use their collective power to back our efforts. This is the first time in modern history that there is such a high-level of commitment to work together towards a common good. I believe our leaders will not let us down.

We however must do our part. It will take hard work, significant time away from your families and long and difficult negotiations with the people we wish to help. We will meet stiff resistance to change. Many of the leaders of these third world nations are used to having unchallenged power within their countries. They often use the state treasury as their personal sandbox. We know we will be fighting tradition, massive corruption, inefficiencies, and many open and secret hostilities. It will not be easy. We may be risking our lives and our health because of the places and people we will encounter in our travels. The road will long and challenging. Yet, I expect that we will change the face of history by teaching and working with those less fortunate.

That was a great speech, if I do say so myself. Everyone needs a motivational jolt, and I gave them a good one. Now, I have to keep them pumped up, be sure they work, and keep them on their toes. They do their job, and I'll be on my way to the Presidency! Barrows smiled to himself, proud of his latest manipulation.

His slide presentation specified his agenda and his expectations of the group for the two-day meeting. The Peace Envoys broke into various sub committees according to their regional interests and capabilities. Each group was asked to generate a list of the countries that warranted placement on their potential support list. From these lists, Barrows instructed them to select two or three countries that they felt would be most receptive to overtures from the Peace Envoys. He wanted their efforts to have a good chance to succeed. Each success would then build on the other. It seemed a reasonable and logical approach. They diligently worked the two days to develop their "to do list."

14

BRUSSELS, APRIL 2010:

A heavy workload that week tempered Ed Walker's hyperactive feelings about the future. Tons of paperwork and intelligence field reports needed attention, plus he had to finish his personal project. He was one of two invited papers to be presented at the annual Conference on Terrorism in Brussels It was a distinct honor to be an invited speaker, and Ed felt this was an excellent opportunity to boost his International image, which would not go unnoticed by the Agency. His topic was how to maximize the technology developed jointly by the US and England. He intended to discuss how to track the money trail of terrorists, and methods to use that knowledge to shut down terrorist organizations. His title: "The Money Trail- How to Track Terrorist Funds."

Without revealing national security issues, his proven methods would assist second and third world countries to become adept at locating and freezing funds of any organization within their borders. Unfortunately, the larger terrorist organization such as al Qaeda and the Taliban were smart with their money. They avoided most commercial banks, and instead relied on less efficient but more secure ways to move their money. They primarily relied on informal hand-carried transfer networks called *hawalas*. The bulk of their funding came from drug dealing or wealthy sympathizers.

Smaller splinter terrorists organizations still relied on the banks mostly located in Saudi Arabia to launder their money. These smaller accounts remained open mainly because their size didn't attract much International attention. It was those smaller terrorist groups that drew the attention of Ed and his CIA team.

His group wasn't as glamorous as other CIA branches of Homeland Security. Although his work had minimal impact on the war against terrorism, it was steady and the government pay scales were comparable with other high government employees. Regardless of your efficiency or impact on the country's security, as long as you did your work, you received your semi-weekly paycheck and had excellent opportunities for advancement and pay increases. Ed was happy not to be in the spotlight.

Without their own resources, second and third world countries relied on outside intelligence techniques from the US, England, France, and Japan to assist them in their fight against terrorism. Even with Ed's techniques, many Middle East and Asian countries lacked the facilities, the capabilities, or the desire to stop the terrorist's cash flow. He hoped more countries would be able to employ his money tracking techniques. He hoped, but knew most countries would ignore his efforts.

Of course, when Schuster implements my plan, this won't mean shit. Once terrorists are destroyed, it won't matter where they hide their funds. They will be dead.

The conference began in three weeks.

Though he had finished the paper a month ago, he still needed clearance and approval from the State Department to sanitize it for outside presentation. He expected approval shortly. He booked his airline tickets and hotel reservations in anticipation of final approval, which based on experience, would come about four days before the conference start date. Ed worked diligently to complete the paper and 35 mm slides, under the assumption he'd be in Brussels. Everyone understood the business of terrorism. Secrets were secret, even among friends.

Over 350 worldwide attendees had registered for the four-day conference. The agenda called for multiple meetings and presentations, one of which was Ed's paper. He planned to attend several morning sessions of particular interest. His presentation was scheduled for 8:30 AM on day three.

The fourth day was intended to be semi-casual. Attendees could meet privately with colleagues for more intimate discussions where they could freely exchange new ideas or techniques. The Thursday evening end-of-conference group banquet usually drew a majority of the attendees. It was their last chance to meet for another year.

Ed planned to arrive in Belgium Saturday evening before the plenum session of the conference Sunday evening. The organizers decided to start the conference Sunday to maximize the number of sessions for the four days. The Belgium Secret Service suggested that multiple small or ad hoc committees meet in the evenings. This kept the attendees close to the hotel and maximized coordination for their security.

Ed liked the arrangements. He preferred to spend minimal time in Brussels. He wanted to be the Washington area in case President Schuster summoned him. When Ed agreed to attend, he had asked Janice if she wanted to go with him. When she realized how little time Ed would to spend with her, she declined.

"If I'm going to fly eight or nine hours each way," she said. "I'd like to know that we would be able to spend some time together. From the looks of your schedule, you'll be too involved with the conference. Not much fun for me," she reminded him.

He was glad she refused. He only asked her because she would have been pissed if he hadn't.

"Sometimes things do work out, if you're lucky," Ed chortled to himself.

As much as he loved and relied on her, when it came to terrorism, she took a head- in-the-sand approach. He concluded she wasn't able to handle the prospect of terrorists striking her family, her home, or her country.

Ed believed that if she truly understood the real danger she might change her mind. For now, he decided to shield her from the fear and anger that he felt because of *Red Sunset*. Should things dramatically change, he'd have to tell her. Today was not that day, nor did it look probable in the near future.

It would destroy her, and I'm not about to do that. I'm committed to protecting her, and if I have to lie, I will. This is my battle. Mine alone. There is no other way.

Thus resolved, Ed began his second life, alone with his fears, his determination, and his newfound backbone.

Early Saturday morning, Ed took a taxi to Dulles International airport. The United flight, scheduled to leave at 5:57 that morning, would arrive a little after 7 PM, Brussels time. His CIA credentials and security clearance mandated that Ed proceed directly to the tarmac and board the plane from the ground stairway, bypassing the extensive airport security systems the average citizen endured.

The flight was tedious and long. He found it difficult sleeping.

Perhaps the President was already formulating his plan to put my plan into action, he thought. *And when he does…*

His reluctance to travel to Brussels was exacerbated because he suspected he'd return home more frustrated than when he left. "These conferences usually solved nothing and were a waste of time and the taxpayers' money," he said to Janice before he left. The disillusionment and disgust gnawed in his gut the entire flight.

It was a rainy spring evening in Brussels when the plane landed, which fit Ed's gloomy mood. He had hoped that his arrival in Brussels would allow him to stay focused on the conference and leave his troubling emotions behind.

The Belgian Secret Service took over from the moment he arrived at the Brussels International Airport. Government orders were to "prevent an embarrassing incident on Belgium soil" before, during, or after the conference. They hustled Ed from the tarmac into a private security check area and into a waiting limo. Two unmarked vehicles rode shotgun at the front and rear of his limo as it sped to the hotel.

Concrete barriers and double police roadblocks erected at the two ends of the street leading to the entrance of the five star Royal Brussels hotel on Rue Duquesny protected the hotel area. Lights illuminated the entire street and roof top areas. Brussels Secret service units examined paperwork and verified his identity using hand held digital cameras that fed his image into a central data bank. His identity confirmed, Ed entered the entrance to the hotel.

The 24/7 security force had been deployed since early Friday morning. They swept the area twice daily for hidden bombs, snipers, or potential hazards. Observation stations on the roof of the hotel and other buildings in the immediate area were visible reminders of the potential danger. Lesser security measures might have given him a good excuse to avoid the conference.

Ed smiled because he realized he had dramatically changed in a short period. Until *Red Sunset,* he was content to track terrorist funds and make recommendations to stop the cash flow. That paled to his current intensity and passion.

I wanted to cut off their funds. Now I want to cut off their heads. The only thing that matters is the absolute destruction of terrorists. Jail? Trials? Public commendation? Pathetic! Each of them. I have the answer, if President Schuster will only recognize it.

The more he thought about it, the greater his distain grew.

Don't they see the terrorists are winning? All the government intelligence, all the money, all the talk, and for what? Their approach stinks; they haven't made a dent. No government has the balls to do the right thing. They fart around with investigations, jail, and the rest of that crap. Still terrorists are running free, killing at will, and no one can stop them. That has to end!

He felt edgy, coiled like a spring, waiting for the holding clamp to be released. He worried how he would function during and after the conference. The uncertainty unnerved him. He hated disorder, and he was experiencing the epitome of chaos.

Why is everything so damn difficult? he lamented to himself.

The first two days of the conference were worse than imagined. He found himself continually dwelling on the President's possible reaction to his proposal.

The wake up call the third morning startled him. At first he was disoriented, and wasn't sure where he was. After a few seconds, he remembered his presentation was this morning. He showered quickly, dressed, ate a continental breakfast, and went to the speakers prep room to review his notes and to check with the AV (audio visual) people. His proposal remained foremost in his mind, though he knew he needed to focus on his presentation.

He toiled through his presentation in a monotone and disinterested voice. Three ten foot screens displayed his computer-based slides. He showed no emotion, no excitement, and no interest. He reviewed the multiplicity of problems each country faced. He examined the International programs that failed and those that achieved partial success. He conceded much more remained to be done to claim success against the terrorists. He managed to finish his presentation without a major blunder. The words left his lips, but his concentration was minimal. His own presentation bored him. He resented even more having to attend the conference because he had to talk, hear, and see the frustration of the attendees.

He made a cautious reference that obliquely implied other methods than the traditional ones "should be considered to win the battle." He wasn't bold enough to venture into his proposal. He knew it would trigger a major tsunami in Brussels with the attendees.

He desperately wanted to shout that the world needed to execute terrorists if they wanted to win. Fortunately, prudence prevailed. He bit his lip to insure the unacceptable words didn't escape. He knew he was right. His plan was the only possible solution. It would quickly resolve the terrorist problem. All that remained was for the President to take action.

Fortunately, questions at the conclusion of his presentation were limited to five minutes, which he answered by rote. No one challenged him enough to make him think hard or asked for an in-depth explanation of his efforts. He received the standard level of polite applause, and sat seated on the dais for the reminder of the session. He found it difficult to be attentive to the other speakers who *obviously didn't get it. Their words and schemes were pure bullshit. The tragic part was they couldn't recognize the crap they were foisting on each other. Conference after conference. Strategic meetings by high-level government and intelligence officials. Ad hoc committees. They all mean nothing. They accomplish nothing, they solve nothing, they knew nothing, and they did nothing.*

He pretended to listen to the other speakers but his eyes and body language sent a different message. He drooped, he fidgeted, and he fought to keep his eyes open. He asked no questions, barely participated, and desperately wanted to escape from the room and distance himself from everyone and everything. He heard meaningless questions, idle suggestions, and tried to act as his colleagues did, concerned with terrorism, willing to exchange ideas to combat them, willing to learn how and what others were thinking, and searching for that one drop of magic dust that would solve everyone's problems. However, there was neither magic dust nor any discussion of radical or new ideas.

He heard more of the same: A few technological improvements that made slight changes in methodologies and communications. The usual meaningless International agreements to share intelligence data. Etc., etc.

In spite of the pledges, he knew that nations never shared all their intelligence, a reality fact that probably prevented the formation of a unified front against terrorism. Limited intelligence sharing was *de rigor*. Terrorism was certainly on the rise. That was a no brainer. In spite of this growing threat, governments' restrictions couched under the blanket of national security, always prevented real cooperation.

Nothing this group can do will change the situation.

He doubted al Qaeda or any other organization wanted to risk unifying the world against them again as they did during 9/11. They were already achieving their goals without the necessity of a cataclysmic event.

He couldn't envision any tragedy that would band countries together again. He noted sarcastically that the world had already endured 9/11, tolerated massive attacks on US troops and property, train bombings, and hundreds of suicide attacks on civilians, and they still hadn't found the courage to work together.

Ed reluctantly conceded that mental avoidance was his only solution, his safe harbor for his rudderless ship, a place where he didn't have to think or worry. By the end of day three he decided being isolated from the other attendees was good for him. The remainder of the day he moved about as though in a fog.

People may believe I'm sick, on drugs, or suffering from a hangover. It doesn't much matter what they think. I'm on a new and exciting course, on a space odyssey he reflected, *that no one here or home could have imagined, including me.*

Deep in his psyche, his fear of failing to stop terrorism, and the consequences, was quietly multiplying and giving birth to a new sachet of internal terror.

15

THAT EVENING:

That evening at the upstairs bar, Ed saw Farook el Habid enter the room and waved to get his attention. Farook, an Egyptian fellow conventioneer, founder of the conference, and noted authority on terrorism, acknowledged him and slid onto the adjacent chair. Ed and he had met several times before at different conferences, and seemed to share similar views. Ed marveled at how Farook always looked well groomed, even after a long day at the conference. Short, no more than 5'6", trim, full head of thick graying hair, black and gray mustache, and brown-tinged teeth. Something about antibiotics when he was a child. Ed never pressed Farook for details.

Ed liked Farook because he was a realist, with a hint of mystery. Farook was a private person who rarely spoke about himself. What little Ed had learned was shrouded in inferences and innuendoes. Farook grew up in Cairo. His father was a successful heart surgeon. Farook walked with a slight limp from a broken leg that was not set properly when he fell off a ladder. His marriage was pre-arranged. Four years ago while on a scenic boat excursion a boiler exploded and capsized the vessel. The impact killed his wife, their two year old daughter and his sister. Sixteen men, women and children died, fourteen others were injured. Farook's wounds proved to be superficial. Since their deaths, Farook lived with a constant yet suppressed anger and depression.

Authorities claimed the boiler explosion was accidental, but controversy shrouded the incident. Pundits claimed that terrorists were behind the explosion, supported by eyewitness accounts of strange behavior by several passengers. The Egyptian ship owners played down the accounts as mass hysteria.

Beyond that, Ed knew little about his life. Ed always counted on having a stimulating discussion with him, regardless of the topic. In the past, they spoke freely to each other, and as long as the topic steered clear of personal issues, they enjoyed each other's company. Ed, however, didn't hold back. He revealed his innermost thoughts and concerns about terrorism, his job, his family and his career at the CIA without violating security guidelines.

He and I make a great couple, Ed smirked to himself. *We're living proof that people can function successfully even when trapped by the heavy burden of depression. Mine is new; his was years in the making.*

"Hello, my friend, it's good to see a familiar face. How are you and the family?" asked Farook

"Well, thank you. And you?"

Farook paused before responding, his eyes focused on Ed's face.

"Personally I'm doing better than several years ago. But, I have to admit, I'm frustrated that we haven't found a way to stop these terrorist dogs from killing."

Ed replied, "Me too."

Ed wanted to confide in him about *Red Sunset*, about his proposal, and about his fears for the future. He had to make a conscious and difficult effort to avoid the topic.

Farook received his Medical Surgeon degree from Egypt University under an accelerated program for the gifted. At twenty-seven years old, he was the youngest Egyptian to receive an Ear, Nose and Throat surgical certification. He graduated high school at fifteen, completed his college undergraduate curriculum in three years, and breezed through medical school and his surgical residency in six years. Farook closed his successful practice after the death of his family to dedicate himself to fight terrorism.

He felt he could better serve humanity as a terrorist fighter than a surgeon could, and he joined the government task force focused on the Gama'a al-Islamiyya terrorists within Egypt. Gama'a al-Islamiyya is the largest militant group operating in Egypt. They recently split into two factions, one that advocates continued violence, the other a cease-fire. The group's main claim to fame was the 1992 bombing of the World Trade Center in New York. Now they focus on attacks against tourists.

Farook rose to the position of Head of the Directorate of State Security Investigation section, a part of the General Directorate for State Security Investigations (GDSSI), in less than twenty-two months. It was because of his efforts and persistence that this conference became a reality. In three years, it had grown to become the preeminent conference on terrorism. Regular attendees included representatives from every free world country, and some of the borderline Arab and Muslim states, which had as much to fear from terrorism as did the rest of the world.

They had met briefly on Sunday during the conference registration, but Farook begged off with,

"I have a meeting to attend. I will catch up with you Wednesday around 5-5:30 at the bar on second floor. Is that convenient?"

"Yes. See you then," Ed replied.

Farook seems more self-absorbed than last year, Ed thought. *Stress lines everywhere on his face. His demeanor. His dark brown eyes hiding behind round silver-rimed glasses shouted tension.*

Ed guessed the pressure was getting to him, the same as it was to him. Terrorism had everyone jumpy. The conference attendees were under constant and extreme pressure to develop workable plans to fight terrorism. They collectively received no leeway from their critics, despite the fact that a global solution was elusive, challenging, and highly unlikely. The world wanted answers. The attendees were looking for one.

"Farook my friend, I'm concerned about you. I haven't seen you smile once, and you seem highly distracted. Are you feeling well? Is there anything I can do to help?" a concerned Ed asked.

"Nothing more than usual. Except I feel very frustrated by the lack of progress in our fight against terrorists. We attend meetings like this and still we are no closer to stopping the killing than we were four years ago. Terrorists are successful and the more they succeed, the bolder they become. The world cowers before them. Yes, my friend, I am angry at the lack of resolve and leadership I see everywhere."

"I agree. I'm afraid things are going to get worse. Who knows if it will ever get better. Something dramatic needs to happen if we are going to win this war."

Farook slid his chair close to Ed and whispered in his ear,

"Perhaps there is a way, my friend. Can you come to my room to talk…. in private, away from these attentive ears? I have something of urgent importance to discuss with you."

Puzzled, Ed nodded his agreement. They agreed to leave the bar separately.

"Please follow my instructions. I will explain later," Farook whispered. "Do not leave the bar for 45 minutes. Go to your room. Stay there 15 minutes. Take the elevator to the ninth floor. After you are confident you were not followed, take the fire exit stairway at the end of the hall to the eighth floor, and come to my room, 805. The door will be unlocked."

Ed felt baffled. Farook had never acted this way, had never sought his private presence and never been so secretive. He imagined the worst. Perhaps Farook was leaving his position, was terminally ill and might be suicidal. But why this spy stuff? If it were personal, what difference did it make who saw him going into Farook's room?

I guess I'll have an answer in an hour.

Ed followed Farook's instructions. One hour later he entered room 805 and closed the door. Seated at the desk, looking quite grim, yet strangely anxious and jumpy, Farook motioned for him to sit in the adjacent chair.

"Thank you for coming. I take it you were not followed. I have taken the liberty to order snacks and drinks."

"Thanks. No one saw me leaving my room, or taking the stairs, if that's what you mean."

"Excellent. Before I answer your questions, I need you to answer some questions of my own. Trust me, all will be clear shortly," began Farook. "But, let's eat first and catch up with each other's lives."

They ate and Ed mostly chatted about family, health, work, and other mundane issues.

Farook finally got around to what was on his mind.

"We have known each other for three years, and we have become friends who respect each other. We share the same frustrations, the same passion to destroy terrorists, and the same desire to make changes where we can. We agree that something must be done, and quickly. If not, the world will become a sea of blood. Terrorists have made the first move, and there's no end in sight. I have an important question to ask, and I need your absolute honest answer. Agreed?"

Puzzled, Ed cautiously answered "OK."

"What are you willing to do to fight terrorism? I mean, beyond what you are doing now. We're accomplishing nothing, on that I know we agree. But if there was another way, something out of the ordinary, would you take personal action to get involved, beyond empty words?"

"I agree something has to be done. In fact…. eh… I have…eh…" Ed stammered.

Farook interrupted him, sensing Ed was not quite comfortable with the conversation.

"Suppose your family was in danger. Would you kill a terrorist to save them? Would you go further? Would you risk your life to save your family?"

Something in Farook had changed. He no longer seemed troubled or jumpy. He took off his glasses, placed them on the table, with fire in his deep brown eyes. He leaned forward in his chair, staring intently into Ed's eyes.

A startled Ed Walker wasn't sure what had just happened. His hand disappeared behind his head as he alternately rubbed and gripped the back of his neck. That familiar uneasy feeling returned. Light sweat formed on his upper lip. Something momentous was happening. He wasn't sure what, but he had a sense it was coming quickly.

"Why are you asking me these questions?"

His tone was slightly elevated and noticeably shaky.

"First your answer, please. You will understand shortly, I promise. Well?"

Ed sat quietly, nervously shaking his leg. He could feel his former sense of empowerment receding, just as the ocean waves retreat from the shoreline.

"I'm confused. Do you mean… eh…in reality? Or hypothetically?"

Farook replied, "For real."

Ed suddenly became highly guarded.

Is he saying he wants me to fight terrorists? I've never even fired a pistol or a rifle.

He was reeling mentally, searching to unscramble Farook's meaning.

"I'm not sure how to answer. I'm not even sure I understand your question. Are you suggesting I fight them myself?"

"No, you are jumping ahead. Let me finish. I will answer all your questions, after you answer mine. If no one is able or willing to stop them, then my question remains. What are you willing to do? Would you take an active role against terrorists? For the time being, I cannot say more. A simple *Yes* or *No* is all I ask," Farook insisted.

Ed stood up. His tension increased to an agonizing point where he needed to move his body for relief. He walked around the room, to the bed, to the window, to the door and back, all the while rubbing the back of his neck. Farook sat silently waiting for Ed's response.

Ed took several deep breaths before he returned to the chair. He leaned towards Farook, and cautiously responded.

"Farook… my friend, I understand your questions, but… excuse me for being so blunt. We….I… must be totally honest. You've experienced the horror of losing your family to terrorists. I know you have dedicated yourself to their destruction. For that I truly am sorry. I can't imagine how dreadful it's been for you. I understand why you want to fight terrorism. But, my wife and children are alive. I can't jeopardize everything without a solid reason. Does that make sense to you? Of course I agree terrorism must be defeated, and we need immediate action. I believe that with all my heart. I've thought of nothing else for the past three months. So trust me, I'm convinced. But…I'm not a fighter. I don't know the first thing about fighting. Our passions may be similar, or even identical, but our positions are entirely different. I need to understand where you are going with this. I don't have a clue."

Farook sat silently, seemingly lost in thought. Still, he never lost eye contact with Ed. The tension and anxiety filled the room. They realized they were sparing, neither willing to open the doorway to their feelings. Neither ready to share their true thoughts. In the past, they had never experienced this verbal scuffling, and the newness made Ed uneasy.

"Perhaps we should stop. We're not communicating very well. It may be me, but I feel totally lost. I don't get it," Ed said softly.

Farook paused, and said,

"You are right, but it is I who is not being clear. What I have to say is very delicate and explosive. You are in a unique position and at a special time of your life to do something concrete to act against global terrorism, but… there could be enormous risk, even your life, and possibly that of your family. What I am about to tell you will change your life. It could also change the course of history. So, I ask you again, perhaps more clearly, are you willing to take such a risk to help us to be free of terrorism?"

It was Ed's turn to be quiet. He was trying to digest what Farook had said, but the magnitude of it left him mentally gasping. This was certainly the last thing he expected.

Am I passionately against terrorism? Hadn't I proposed my own plan to stop terrorism. Didn't I submit it to the President?

Doubt trumped precedence. *Was I fooling myself? Am I truly that committed to stopping terrorism, or was it an exercise in mental masturbation? Was it OK to propose to kill terrorists as long as I didn't have to get directly involved or take risks?*

Reality concepts were exploding in his head. He felt his heart beating faster, perspiration collected on his upper lip. His armpits were drenched. His head felt like a stretched balloon ready to explode.

Ed nervously ran his hands through his thick brown hair, brushing it back, before returning his hand to his neck. He fidgeted in his chair, not certain if he wanted to bolt from the room or stay to hear more. During these few minutes, Farook never released his steady glare from Ed. He demanded an answer and he was prepared to wait until he got one.

Slowly, the shock dissipated, and Ed regained his ability to talk. Hesitantly he began,

"My first response is *Yes,* I think I'm willing to take that risk, but I need to know more. I still don't know what you have in mind."

"My friend, let me complete the picture. Then you will fully understand. Someone who represents an anonymous group of wealthy people approached me a year ago. Their goal is to actively pursue terrorists and destroy them, by whatever means possible. They operate outside the restrictions and laws of their governments. They are highly private, very rich, and very determined. They have a plan that will make a difference. Their vision and goal is to create a well funded and covert armed anti-terrorist organization to inflict maximum pain on terrorists. They believe that small incremental steps are ineffective. Force demands greater force, terror demands terror, and death of innocents demands swift reprisal killings.

"We call ourselves *Stop Terrorism Now*, or STN. We have nineteen worldwide regions, each controlled by their own regional team leader. These leaders recruit their own field cell members and field operatives. Our belief is basic. We are fighting the wrong terrorists! We are spending billions to kill those with the guns and explosives, while the true terrorists go free. Who are the real terrorists? People who finance them. People who train them. People who teach and preach to them. People who hide and protect them. People who provide them the materiel to damage us. They are the real terrorists! If we do not destroy all terrorists, the ones who carry the weapons as well as the ones who support them, we can never win this war!

Our plan is simple: Exterminate ALL the terrorists. Those who do the fighting AND their supporters. STN is a deadly response to terrorism, something like an eye for an eye, except we believe death before a death. We intend to hunt down every single terrorist and annihilate them. Our goal is to stop terrorists before they attack us or our friends.

For the past nine months, I have been assembling a cadre of key people throughout the world who have the passion, as do you and I, to fight terrorism through the STN plan.

Terrorists are terrorists, period. Regardless of their reasons to be terrorists, regardless of which part they play, the fact remains that they kill innocent people. They are promised by their religious leaders that they will find Paradise when they die as martyrs, fighting the enemies of Islam. They have no fear of losing their lives. Simple traditional tactics we talk about at conferences like this are useless. I think we both agree on that. When terrorists lose one funding source, they quickly find another to replace it. When they lose their operating base, they move to another. One door closes, another one opens. We intend to shut down these alternatives. They will have no funding, no place to hide, no hidden terrorists, and no more open doors.

We considered many ways to achieve these goals, and decided the best way was to make them fear us. Many believe terrorists only want to cause chaos. We understand their real goal is to impose Islamic Fundamentalism rule throughout the world. They want to impose their beliefs globally. STN is committed to create fear in the terrorists and to offer hope to the frightened masses.

However, STN recognizes killing one terrorist at a time is not the answer. We have decided to take more extreme measures. This particular part of the plan, which we call their Circle of Contamination, can only be revealed to you later, after you accept our offer and after you understand our rules."

"What offer?" asked Ed. "You're asking me to commit to a plan which you will not explain until I commit to it. Right?"

"Yes, it is somewhat unusual, but it must be that way for now. You will understand later, when all is revealed," softly responded Farook.

"I'm asking you to trust me. I too was in the same position when STN approached me to join in the fight. I understand it is not easy to make this leap of faith. It is a difficult decision, but one you must make on your own. Here. Today. Now. If you believe terrorism must stop, and you are committed to this with your heart and your energy, then the actual tactics should not matter. If you want a free world to exist, then you must move ahead with me, with STN, solely on your absolute determination to stop terrorism. Not tomorrow, not in the future, but now, before they take over the world and we lose our precious freedom. Are you up to it? Now Ed, your answer! If *No*, our conversation is over," sternly demanded Farook.

What Farook failed to tell Ed was that a *No* meant Ed's death, before he left Brussels. His death would appear to be from natural causes or an unavoidable accident. One phone call starts the wheels in motion. There would be no investigation, no telltale autopsy, nothing to indicate foul play. STN's irrefutable recruitment rule was simple. Anyone who knew they existed or knew of their plans and refused to join had to die. The success of the STN mission depends on absolute secrecy and control. Farook hated the thought of ordering Ed's death, but there was no other way. He prayed that Ed would say *Yes*.

"You will head the entire US and Canadian sector. What do you think?"

"Are you serious?"

"Deadly serious."

Ed paused, then asked,

"It sounds interesting, but what if we find that killing terrorists with your special plan, whatever that is, doesn't work? Wouldn't that make them more desperate and force them to seek revenge? That would make them more difficult to stop. Who knows whom they would target for their revenge, including me or my family!"

Farook scrutinized Ed's face slowly and deliberately for what seemed forever, then, in carefully selected words he responded,

"That is a risk, yes. Yet, you cannot lose sight of the ultimate goal. Think what it will mean to the world, to democracy, and to the lives of the people who no longer have to live in fear of terrorists. Think about that Ed, think about it," he strongly said.

"Go on."

"The evil face of terrorism is here. Will we fight or run away? Will we let them win? We didn't start this war, but it is one we must finish. We cannot allow fear and chaos to defeat us. STN will turn fear back onto them. Let them worry who will die. Let them worry they will never enter their precious Paradise. They cannot be free to destroy people's lives, as they have in the past. Not only must we insure that freedom survives, but that it wins. The future of the world is at stake, do you not understand that?"

Farook had taken control. He spoke with passion, with emphasis and steely determination. It was adamantly clear just how committed Farook was to STN and the defeat of terrorists.

He took his packet of Egyptian Standard Golden King cigarettes from his pocket.

"It's my one remaining vice. Do you mind?" he asked Ed without a smile.

"No, It's fine."

Farook took a long slow drag and blew the smoke towards the ceiling. It was thick, white, strong, and hung in the air like a puffy cloud in springtime.

"For me this fight is special. My fight is not about anger because of the destruction they inflict. No, I joined this fight for the people of Egypt and the people of the world. But I fight mostly for the children. They deserve an opportunity to enjoy freedom, to live in peace, without fear. They are the ones who need me, and you, if they are to have a chance in life."

"Although we haven't found a real solution, perhaps we will, one day. Isn't that a possibility too? Even without STN?" Ed questioned.

"Can you guarantee that terrorists will not attack in malls, on trains, or planes like 9/11? Isn't this the very problem we face now, every day?" countered Farook. "And what about the innocent people who are blown apart by a suicide bomber. The sad part is the bomber may not be sure why he had to die, or what he achieved through his death. The worst part is that the person who convinced him to die lives to find a replacement. The replacement strikes elsewhere. Kill one terrorist and another springs up to take his place. Is that the world you want to live in? You can't have it both ways. Do you want safety for you and your family? Do you want freedom?

If you want to live in fear, then do nothing. Go home. Sit in front of the TV. But, can you sit back and do nothing? Are you willing to wait until the terrorists go away on their own? I'm not willing to do that. What I'm talking about is making a major impact on the future of world history. Islamic Fundamentalist will rule the world if they are not stopped by committed people willing to risk everything to preserve our existence."

"What you say makes sense, but...," Ed interrupted.

Farook ignored him and continued,

"Sometimes a group of people, at a unique time in a unique place, can change the course of history. This is our time and place. We are that group, Ed. You, STN, and me. Think about this. One day, after terrorism has been defeated, the people of the world will welcome us as heroes. Those of us who joined STN will the ones who gave them back their freedom and safety, and the ability to live without fear. The Fundamentalists will not overthrow global governments, because STN will be there to stop them. Unfortunately, the time for more words has passed. It's time for action. It's time for your decision. It's time for your commitment. Is it *YES?*"

Farook was on fire. His eyes blazed like hot coals in the steel maker's furnace with an intensity Ed had ever seen before. Veins bulged in his neck; his face glowed from the increased blood in his head. He seemed to grow in height, in power, and in aura. The ferocity of his statements was like an attack of hungry lions ready to pounce on their Christian prey.

So intense, so inspiring was Farook, that Ed was stunned into silence. His eyes darted from one side to the other as he tried to digest Farook's words, to assimilate his passion. Transfixed by Farook's intensity, his words remained trapped in his throat, unable to form, and unable to escape.

This is not for me. What do I know about fighting? I'm not a fighter. This STN thing must to be done, but not by me. It's almost exactly what I proposed to the President, but I never thought I would be the one doing the killing! I need to think about Janice and the kids. They are my priority.

Doubt overtook his desires. He mustered the courage to address Farook.

Ed stood up, signaling that he had made his decision, and prepared to leave.

"Farook, I believe in everything you said. It sounds like it can work. But, it's not for me. I've thought about it, but I don't fit in. I'm flattered you think I do, but I know I don't. If there's anything I can do for you, behind the scenes, you know, you can count on me. I'll do what I can. I'm sorry, I just can't do what you ask. It's getting late, and I need to get some sleep. It's been a long day."

He extended his hand to shake goodbye. Farook refused.

"We are not asking you to do the fighting. Your team will have that responsibility. You will be their leader, the one who plans and designates, not the one in the field."

"Still, I know nothing about that type of work. It's not for me."

"I see," Farook said. He hesitated then softly said,

"There's one thing you should know."

He paused for a full minute before continuing. He wanted to be sure that he had Ed's attention.

"I completely agree with *Red Sunset*, but STN believes that things will happen two to three years sooner."

It had the desired effect.

Shocked, Ed stammered, "How...how... how do you know about *Red Sunset*? That's a top secret report. Only seven copies were distributed to key US officials."

"Eight copies."

"Eight?"

"Eight." Farook opened his briefcase that had been set beside his chair, and withdrew a black bound report. He handed it to Ed.

Ed scanned the report.

"Oh ... my ....God!"

He suddenly felt lightheaded, his legs weakened, heart thumping. He staggered back to reclaim his chair. His hand returned to the back of his neck.

"Oh my God! How did you get a copy?"

"It doesn't matter. STN has friends in powerful places, not only in the US, but also in the world. We also know you submitted a proposal to President Schuster, advocating killing terrorists, just like us. He hasn't read it yet."

He let Ed absorb the brunt of his words. Farook leaned back in his chair, his eyes narrowed to mere slits, a slight smirk on his face. Ed panicked. His shirt, saturated with sweat, stuck to his body from his neck to his waist. His hands shook in his lap. He barely blinked. His body limp, his head tilted back as he stared at the ceiling in disbelief. The only sounds in the room were the irregular panting of Ed's breath as he struggled to force air into his lungs, and the steady drip-drip of the bathroom faucet. Slowly, after regaining his ability to breathe, Ed, confused and badly shaken, looked at Farook. He sat down, weak from the sudden shock of Farook's words.

They stared at each other without talking. Ed too stunned to talk; Farook waiting. The rhythmic water drops added to Ed's sense that he was in a strange, unnatural, eerie, and frightening place, trapped, with no way to escape.

Four minutes passed before Ed managed to speak.

"I don't understand. How did you know about *Red Sunset* and my proposal? Who the hell are you?"

"How I know does not matter. Who am I? I'm the leader of STN and your friend."

"The leader of STN? What does that mean?" Ed shot back.

"It means death to terrorists. It means freedom for us. That's what it means."

"But how did you get the report? How did you know about my proposal?" Ed persisted.

"We have resources everywhere. You need to understand that we are not a group of idealists running off our mouths. We are deadly serious about destroying terrorists. We have the money. We have the intelligence. We have the determination, we have the people, and we have a plan that will work. With or without you, STN will succeed. It's a matter whether you want to join us or not. No more talk. *Yes* or *No!*"

I can't believe it. Farook wants the same thing I do. He wants to implement my plan. Do I feel as strong about killing terrorists? Especially now that I'd have to directly involved. I'm not a killer... or am I? I know Red Sunset is real and I believe in my proposal to the President. So what's my problem? Do I want terrorism to stop or not?

He remained silent as he tried to reconcile the chaos swirling in his head.

I do! I do! Farook's way is my way. I WILL join STN!

Caught up in the breathtaking moment, Ed's suppressed passion and determination inexplicably erupted from his lips.

"Yes, Yes, Yes!" he shouted unexpectedly. He had not logically made this decision. The decision resulted without his conscious approval. How could he reject his own plan to eliminate terrorists?

"Count me in! You know *Red Sunset* has been consuming me. I haven't been able to stop thinking how to stop terrorism. I believe in their immediate execution. It's the only way to stop them. I'm ready to join STN," Ed enthusiastically continued.

"I've got millions of questions, but please go on."

"First, are you absolutely positive? Are you sure this is what you want to do?" questioned Farook.

"YES, there's no doubt in my mind. I want to be a part of STN and history."

"Excellent. We will succeed together. This is a momentous day and an important decision. I applaud your courage, Ed Walker. There are many parts of the plan, too detailed to discuss this evening. I'll give you a summary of the key points. We'll cover the details later."

"Fine."

"First, the Bankers recognize that it could cost you your life. They are willing to place ten million dollars in a private Swiss bank account for you, or your family. If you and we succeed, your reward will be financial stability. Should you die, the money will insure your family is well cared for."

"Ten million dollars?"

"Yes."

"That's a lot of money."

"The task and you are worth it."

"You've got my attention," Ed said in awe.

"Next, we have placed another fifteen million dollars in a separate Swiss bank account for you to use as the Regional team leader. This is your operational money to implement and support your STN efforts and to pay your team members. You are responsible for deciding the pay rate of each member on your team. There will be no interference from the Bankers or me. Future contact between us must be at a minimum once you have your organization in place.

I am your only STN contact. The Bankers will remain anonymous. Each Regional Leader will operate independent of me and the other regions. This increases our security and our protection. You will not know the other team leaders, their plans, or their locations. They will not know yours.

This becomes your personal war. You will recruit your own cell leaders and team members. It's imperative to conceal your identity from them, and theirs from each other. No one is to use their real name or reveal any aspect of his life. Only team members who are needed to complete a specific assignment will meet together with their identities hidden, and they will only use their code names when they talk. No one, and I repeat no one, is to know your identity or mine, where you live, or anything about your personal life. We will discuss how to achieve this later."

"I understand," interjected Ed.

"As you know, Interpol has assembled over 15,000 names of terrorists, International thieves, gun smugglers, counterfeiters in their database. We have compiled our own list of comprehensive dossiers on them too, plus the names of religious leaders and heads of the madresses who promote terrorism. Our global list is approaching 38,000. Our list includes the names of terrorists, organizations, their sources of funding, suppliers, and their supporters. In addition, we have added many others who have been determined a menace to society. You will appreciate our thoroughness later. I promise. In case you cannot select a target in your region, we can help.

It doesn't matter where terrorists live or work. We draw no distinction between one terrorist or another. Naturally, it is best to plan your strikes against targets within your region for many practical reasons. Our plan is for every regional leader to have at least two or three designated targets before full STN operations officially begin. Once all nineteen teams are ready, I will designate one team to be the first to strike a blow against terrorism. From that point, you and your team will formulate your own plans, tactics and operational strategies. Then, when you are prepared, we'll give you the go ahead to proceed with your strike. Understood?"

"Yes."

"After the initial strike, an announcement will be sent to the media, including every major TV, radio station, and newspapers of every country in the world. I expect them to read my statement in it's entirety. My identity, of course, will remain secret. The announcement will declare the official existence of STN. We will take full responsibility for the strike. Our first strike will declare war on all terrorists and their Circle of Contamination. That includes anyone remotely involved with them. As I said before, we will decide which team will have the honor of the initial strike, and which one will be our initial target. We want to select a well-known terrorist whose death will immediately get the attention of terrorists throughout the world.

We will make it clear we intend to eliminate anyone who supports them. People will understand that involvement or associating with terrorists in any manner means they will be automatically marked for execution. They will receive no trial and no leniency. All terrorists will die.

Our statement will end with a warning that they will die if they refuse to renounce terroristic activities."

Farook excitement continued unabated.

"That will get their attention. But we both know them well enough to know they will not stop because we ask them."

"We expect to be tested soon after the announcement is made. We will be prepared to strike again. They will learn we are serious, deadly serious. Multiple strikes within one or two weeks of each other should convince them. We will unleash a wave of terror on the terrorists such as they have never envisioned and never imagined possible.

After our second wave of attacks, I will probably issue another media announcement repeating our message. From that point, I do not intend to make any more announcements. We'll merely unleash our power. STN teams will repeatedly strike global targets. Even I will not know when or where these attacks will happen. Over time, after enough terrorists die, the remaining terrorists and will understand. Death awaits them. They will fear for their lives. When that happens, terrorism will grind to a halt."

"But how will we deal with all the global governments, especially the US? Do you think they will sit by and just let us operate without trying to stop us? We'll be violating their laws," Ed questioned.

Farook continued,

"Remember, we operate outside government controls or knowledge. No government will be willing, or able, to take action against us because they know nothing about us, nor will they. They will not learn we exist until we make our announcement. What can they do? They have no information. Therefore they will not know where to start their investigation. We strongly suspect they will publicly vilify us, but behind closed doors, we believe they will praise us. Perhaps they will tolerate us instead of praising us, but the effect will be the same. Remember, we'll be doing their job for them that they haven't been able or willing to do themselves. They will certainly voice their indignation. They will call for investigations and the media will vomit analysis after analysis proclaiming we are barbarians, a bunch of dangerous lunatics, vigilantes, terrorists and everything else to distance themselves from us.

Some will claim we are another group of terrorists trying to eliminate our competition. In spite of the anticipated negative reactions from friends and enemies alike, the truth remains. They will be unable to do anything to prevent us from achieving our goals. They will only know what we choose to tell them in our announcements. As long as we retain our secrecy and independence, we will succeed. The Bankers have been planning STN for over three years. The time is coming to change history."

"I'm impressed!" Ed exclaimed. "You are prepared to win, aren't you?"

In his enthusiasm, Ed forgot about his proposal to President Schuster, an oversight that would one day turn against him, in the most deadly manner.

Ed asked, "What happens if someone is captured and talks about STN? Once the CIA or FBI is on the scent, it could be a major problem."

"We considered that. We understand the risk. Everyone in our organization understands the need for absolute secrecy. We have a strict rule, a code of honor, so to speak. First, no one can quit STN. Those who attempt to do so are to be eliminated no matter their position. In the unlikely event that the enemy captures one of our men, each has sworn to swallow a cyanide capsule that he carries. The same applies to you and me."

Farook dug into his pocket and withdrew a small capsule he showed to Ed.

"Just like this. We have a common goal, and we are handsomely paid to be successful. Not only must everyone be committed to perform with precision and determination, but to also protect STN with our lives."

"How can you make someone kill themselves to protect STN?" asked Ed.

"STN members are pre-screened to insure their beliefs about terrorism are genuine and deeply ingrained in their thinking. They understand what will happen to the world if we fail. By failing we place our family, friends, our country and our freedom in jeopardy. Therefore, we cannot fail. No one will jeopardize STN for the sake of his own life. We are insignificant as individuals. Our strength is in the continued efforts of our organization to succeed. If captured, or someone drops a careless remark that puts us in danger, and they refuse to use their capsule, they will be treated the same as a terrorist. We will execute them and those around them. We believe that will be sufficient motivation," was Farook's charged response.

Ed reacted immediately. He suddenly grasped the dark side of STN, the side that Farook conveniently failed to mention, the very ugly side of this secret organization. His heart raced when he realized the personal danger he faced.

I just joined STN to protect my family and my country. Now I've placed them in grave danger. I should have known, I should have known! All secret societies work the same way. That's how they can operate outside the law so effectively. No one from the inside would think of exposing the group. The penalty is too severe. Farook hid this from me!

It took every morsel of his strength not to show his fear to Farook.

If he becomes suspicious, Farook could decide I'm too risky to stay alive. Fuck, fuck, fuck! exploded in his head.

"As for the operational structure of each cell," Farook continued, unaware of the shock waves raging throughout Ed's body.

"We learned from the terrorists. Our team members will assemble only when a strike is imminent. Until that time, they will maintain a job in their community, live with their family and generally blend into society. We'll activate them when needed. Each man must develop a plausible reason to be away from his family during the planning, practice, and strike phases. Like the terrorists, we will be invisible before, during, and after our strike. At least the terrorists taught us how to fight them." Farook laughed. It was the first time Ed heard him laugh in three years.

"Now, for the practical aspects of our conversation. Later this evening you will receive an envelop containing two Swiss bankbooks, one for your personal account and the other for the mission. A courier will deliver additional information immediately before you board your plane for home. That way we reduce the possibility of someone stealing or somehow destroying the contents while you are at the conference. You will continue to attend the conference tomorrow, act normally, and begin your STN life after you are home in McLean. However, it's important we continue our normal dialog both here and after the conference as we have done in the past. To avoid suspicion, we should not change our pattern. Use my internet address as before."

Ed asked "What about cell phones?"

"Out of the question," replied Farook, "until we provide you with an encrypted phone. These phones and our incoming and outgoing calls cannot be traced to either of us. In any case, I prefer to limit our communications. No chatting, unless it's critically important."

"You can do that?" Ed asked incredulously.

"That's only the beginning. We cannot afford to have anyone, or any government, trace our calls and identify us, can we?" Farook answered with an amused look.

"I'm impressed. The CIA has a limited ability to hide our calls. How do you do it? Ed asked, trying to avoid any revealing voice tremors.

"Let's say we have special connections in the right places. The actual method is not important, only the results."

"Amazing! Absolutely amazing! Of course. I agree, Farook."

"Now leave. Walk down the exit stairs to the sixth floor and take the elevator to the lobby, go to the bar and have a drink or two. Wait about least an hour. Go to your room if you like. We will not meet privately again. Should we meet at the conference, act normally as two conference friends would do. Many of our fellow attendees know we are friendly, so let's insure they continue to believe that, and nothing more."

They shook hands and wished each other luck. Farook reiterated how happy he was that Ed had decided to join STN. He was happier he didn't have to order his death. Ed was happy to have stayed alive. He headed back to the bar as instructed.

He wasn't sure exactly what he felt, or how, or why. What he knew was that in the space of a hundred and thirty some minutes, he had placed his life and his family in jeopardy, avoided a serious blunder, and foolishly almost put them in danger again. He also had become a member of STN that would one day free the world of terrorists. He acted with a mix of scary trepidation and incredible fervor.

In his twenty-two year CIA career, he was involved with terrorism in one manner or another. He managed to endure three departmental changes, a move from Philadelphia to McLean, and four promotions. Now, as Deputy Director of the International Financial Investigative Department, Terrorist Section, he was one promotion away from the Director's job. He expected his boss, Len Winslow, to receive his cherished promotion within the next several years. As Director, he'd reach the GS 70 level, including a $120,000 yearly salary and a great pension. Not bad for a skinny Philly boy who delivered newspapers as a kid, he thought. Strange how quickly things can change. One blink of an eye, and your life is different.

Now I am STN. I'm not sure what the future holds, except if I get through this alive I'll be rich, ten million dollars richer. And my family will be safe.

16

LIZ HUNTER:

While walking towards the bar, he recalled how he had changed as he grew up. Ed recognized his views had changed from pacifist to hawk, culminating with *Red Sunset*.

Investigating terrorism will have that effect, he concluded. *I do desperately want to end terrorism and rid the world of these maniacs.*

Yet another piece of him, the uncertain piece, the frightened piece, wanted to run away, to hide, to not be involved, especially now, when he and his family were suddenly in danger.

What have the terrorists really gained? Nothing! One thing, I guess. Their families received money in 'honor' of their son or daughter's suicide death. Had their death enriched the lives of those around them, their families or friends? Have they run out of youthful replacements? Not that anyone could measure. They kill themselves along with their supposed enemies and still nothing changes, except they die. Can't they understand that? What about their parents? Why aren't they protesting against the sacrifice of their children? Youth will always react emotionally without clarity of thought because their elders prodded them. Their parents, friends, wives, or children, where are they in this? And their supporters? They remain untouched and continue to provide the money and arms to their expendable youth. Terrorists are not going to change. Therefore, we must stop both sides of terrorists by any means possible. Now, finally, I have the means, the direction, and the money.

This was the monster rationalization Ed used to assure himself that he made the right decision joining STN.

"I may not be any different than terrorists," he thought aloud. "Someone tells me how to fight the enemy, offers a plan and money, and then tells me to go do it. If I die, my family will have all the money they need to survive. Janice is young enough to remarry, and she will be able to afford a proper education for the kids. So, am I *really* that much different?" There was no answer for Ed Walker this evening.

He continued his rationalization.

Terrorists kill innocent people indiscriminately. Now, we'll be killing them in the name of preventing additional killings. I guess I'm fucked up. This is not the time to dwell on anything heavier than a drink. Hopefully tomorrow I'll be able to sort things out. First, a few drinks to dull the senses. Tomorrow will come soon enough.

He glanced at his watch. 9:22. Plenty of time to unwind.

The Blue and Gold hotel bar on the second floor served as a quiet retreat for visiting businessmen and women. No loud music, no TV's blaring idiotic images, and no garish lights bouncing from the ceiling or walls It's just a friendly quiet place to end the business day, a place to relax, and to meet with peers or clients to discuss the next day's business. Soft semi-classical music played in the background, low enough to enable people to talk across a table, but loud enough to mask private conversations.

Ed selected a table towards the rear of the bar, somewhat removed for the main bar. The pleasant looking cocktail waitress, after a friendly salutation, announced her name was Sophia and she would be his server. She proudly displayed the little gold nameplate with *Sophia* written in script, and attached to the vest of her jacket. The outfit was commensurate with the dignity of the hotel. Stylish, dark blue with gold piping around the collar and sleeves, and a matching loose fitting skirt hovering below her knees. Semi-high heels and dark blue stocking completed her outfit. Her brunette hair, neatly tied in a ponytail, swayed cutely when she walked.

"British?"

"American."

"Welcome to Brussels. May I take your order, sir?"

"Yes, I'd like an Absolute Vodka martini with two olives."

"Thank you, I'll be right back."

She placed a cardboard coaster and napkin on the table and left to place his order. He thought of ordering some bar snacks, but decided against it. He wanted nothing to dilute the expected effects of the alcohol.

His thoughts were still wildly bouncing in his brain, without consistency or direction. Time was his enemy. He didn't like it one bit.

Tomorrow I better be prepared to handle my new life. Now where is that waitress? I need that drink, he thought as he tried to silence the bombardment assaulting his head. *Too many conflicts and thoughts to resolve tonight*, he decided.

His drink arrived and he took several quick and deep gulps to settle his nerves, now tinged with a dark ominous deeply buried anxiety.

The buzz began with his second drink. Slowly he began to relax as the martini smoothed his rankled nerves and tense body. *Booze really helps,* he reminded himself.

He focused on no one or anything in particular. His eyes wandered around the room without seeing. The bar patrons seemed a sea of blurred lips responding to a hidden rhythm. Muted conversations elevated only when they rose to greet, embrace, or say goodbye to old friends. The bar people appeared fuzzy, without animation, and without a solid presence. Nothing was distinct, and nothing fit together, nothing seemed real. Their words and their actions became part of grand dream-like stage play. Ed was grateful he had selected a table in the rear of the bar, where the dimly lit lights complemented his emotions, hiding the softening explosions of his mind.

He drank in solitude, happy that no one from the conference approached him.

Two, maybe three drinks. Get the buzz and leave.

He decided on an exit strategy if anyone intruded his cozy haven. A quick apology *that he was leaving and perhaps another evening when he wasn't so fatigued.* Then beat a hasty exit. Fortunately, no one showed up. Ed decided to have a third drink to polish off the evening and complete his buzz.

A woman's voice startled him.

"Don't you live in McLean, near the Roosevelt school? I'm from around there too, and I thought I recognized you. Mind if I sit down? My name is Avery Hunter, but everyone calls me Liz. I'm here on business, beauty care products. We're trying to open the European market, and this is my first trip abroad. Wow, am I wound up. I'm sorry to intrude on your privacy." She turned to leave.

Ed almost offered his prepared apology, but hesitated as he did the man-thing and scanned the woman before him. Her sandy blond hair lay casually about her face and neck. She stood about 5'3" and was nicely built. Her silk lime green blouse offered a provocative but tasteful view of her pleasant cleavage. Sexy, but not beautiful, he decided. Her short above-the-knee tailored skirt accentuated shapely and athletic calves, wonderfully enhanced by single strap lime colored high heels. Flattered by her attention, he couldn't resist accepting her invitation.

After all, how often does a sexy woman enter your life, especially so far from home? It would be rude and stupid not to accept, he swiftly decided.

"Sure, have a seat. My name is Ed, Ed Walker. Nice to meet you." Ed took a closer look at her face. Nice skin, well groomed, attractive with great sex appeal.

"When did you arrive in Brussels, Avery...I mean Liz?"

"I've been here for six days, and I'm staying for another two. I'm leaving Saturday evening. What about you? How long have you been here?"

"I arrived Saturday evening. I'm with a conference."

"Oh, you're with the Terrorist Conference?"

"Well... yes," he responded. There was nothing classified about his attendance.

"Work for the government, I suppose?"

"Yes."

"Can I ask which branch?"

"Sorry."

"It doesn't matter. Is the conference any good? I've been to many of those things and if it wasn't for meeting old friends or the possibly of making new ones, they'd be a waste of time. In my business, it's usually the contacts you have that make a difference. I guess it's that way no matter what line of work you're in, don't you agree?"

"That's the way of business, I suppose," he answered.

"Been to Brussels before?"

"No, first time."

"And you didn't get a chance to see the Royal Palace Gardens or the antique market? They're within walking distance from here, you know."

"I haven't left the hotel. Security thing."

"Are you staying after the conference to sightsee?"

"No, really need to get back to work."

"Married?' Liz asked.

"Yes. You?"

"Divorced three years, no children, not going with anyone, happy in my job, and my life."

"That sums it up pretty quick. Do you do everything so fast?"

"Not the things that matter the most," she said with a wanton smile.

Her meaning was quite clear. He thought it was, though his head was beginning to spin from the whiskey. Here in Brussels facing an interesting woman, thousands of miles from home, he felt a familiar stirring in his loins. Not that he wanted to cheat, but the pressure, his meeting with Farook, his decision to join STN, and the martini, surely the martini, gave that thought increased credence. He thought more and more of the possibility as they continued to exchange light chatter over another round of drinks. Ed was reaching the point of no pain.

I could get drunk if I'm not careful. That wouldn't be smart.

Liz ordered a sipping sherry, which, after several drinks, she claimed, "they make me very mellow." He found himself wishing that she would become more than mellow, and fast.

She ended his fantasy by offering to pay for the drinks, said she was quite tired and needed sleep. But not before she took a business card from her purse, put it into the top pocket of his jacket, and sweetly said,

"If you ever want to have a drink back in McLean, give me a call. I'd like to pay the bar tab. My company would be happy to know that they are supporting one of our local boys who are fighting terrorists. Nice meting you Ed," she said as she gracefully glided to the bar to pay.

He watched her walk across the room. Men and women tossed lustful glances as she walked past. Surprised and disappointed at the sudden turn of events, Ed left the bar feeling down. His fantasy of an evening of infidelity with Liz shattered when she left so abruptly.

It's for the best. Now, I don't have to cheat, not that I wouldn't have if she wanted a Brussels adventure.

He removed her card from his pocket, reread her name, and placed it in his wallet, hidden between several credit cards. He wasn't sure what he would do about Avery "Liz" Hunter. He knew he did not intend to throw her card away.

He couldn't sleep, in spite of the buzz. His thoughts, if you could call them that, struggled between being convoluted and distorted. A snapshot of what was inside his head would look like a terrorist bomb had exploded and left a pile of twisted brain cells, skull fragments and miles of mangled veins and arteries.

His thoughts randomly drifted between his new mission, his family, his CIA job, the money, fear of death, his presentation tomorrow, and Liz. He finally drifted to sleep a little after 2 AM.

The last day of the conference was a blur. He sleepwalked through the few sessions, his emotions swinging from excitement to despair. STN vs. the danger he and the family faced. He talked with only a few attendees, saw Farook once, and generally prayed the day would end without a meltdown. Thursday night sleep came and went.

The wake up call Friday morning startled him. He awakened with sleeper's disorientation. He couldn't remember where or why he was there. After a few seconds his yesterday returned.

He smiled at how, until Farook, his only thoughts were on *Red Sunset* and his proposal to the President. Now neither mattered.

What I'll achieve with STN will surpass everything I've ever done! I'm on a new and exciting course, he reflected, *one so critical and important that no one here or home could have imagined, including me.*

Yet, in spite of his excitement about the future with STN, his mind was building a barrier to his happiness. Deep in his psyche, his lingering fear of failure, and the consequences, was lurking, waiting to giving birth to more anxious moments in his life.

While packing his suitcases, Farook's courier knocked at his door handed him a sealed large manila envelop.

"Farook sent me. Lock this in your briefcase immediately, and do not leave it for a minute, even if you go to the bathroom. Read the contents after you return to the United States. You will find everything you need to get started. May we all be successful in our mission and our lives. May Allah be with you."

The courier left as quickly as he appeared. Ed locked the envelop in his briefcase, called the bellman station, took the elevator to the lobby, paid his bill and immediately got into the waiting limo for his ride to the airport. He passed through customs and boarded the steps of the waiting United flight. He clutched his black leather briefcase in his hand, found his first class seat, buckled up, and settled in for the longest flight of his life.

17

THE RULES, APRIL 2010:

Tempted to peek at the contents of the envelope during the flight home, Ed found the resolve to resist until he returned to his office three days later. Farook stressed the envelope should be secure at all times and he had no wall safe at home. The office won by default.

Monday morning he quickly dispatched the usual assortment of office letters, information briefs and phone messages that accumulated during his absence.

"Hold my calls," he spoke via the intercom to Alice. "I need about ½ hour."

Impatiently he removed the manila envelope with its four single-spaced typed pages from his briefcase, and read:

Hello again,

This will be our last written correspondence. Future contacts will be through a secure phone line, and that is only for extreme emergencies. My number is 1-800-919-1919. Call me only when you have your own secure phone. From now on, refer to me only by my code name, el Berubi. Only use your cell phone, never a land phone.

When you have finished reading these instructions, shred everything, including the delivery envelope.

I have outlined the specifics of your assignment and your responsibilities. You have absolute freedom to conduct your operation as you see fit. As we discussed, you will operate independently from every other STN team. I will contact you if we need to talk. Be prepared to live in STN isolation. There will be no direct contact with any other STN members. Contact me for your financial needs, advice, or information about a target.

REMEMBER, SECURITY IS PARAMOUNT. ONE LEAK CAN DESTROY THE ENTIRE OPERATION.

Financial: You now have $15,000,000 US dollars in a Swiss bank account number 29L7-9877352 with Credit Suisse in Geneva. This will cover your operation for the first year. Also at Credit Suisse is your personal account for $10,000,000. That number is 33M0-4439059. Write these numbers down and place them in a secure place. Over time, you will probably memorize them. Other than insuring transfer of your personal funds to your wife and children in the event of your death, leave no traceable record of the operational account. Use what you need. No accounting of your expenses is required.

Code name: Select your code name. Call me three weeks from today, Monday at 10:45 PM sharp, your time. State your code name and hang up. Say nothing else.

General rules of operations: Your responsibilities are:

1. Select and train your cell leaders. Cyanide capsules will be provided for you, your cell leaders and your team members. It is important that you notify me immediately of anyone who wishes to resign from the cell or who undermines our mission. Call 1-800-202-2020 and say the person's code name. We will respond quickly. You do not need to be involved any further.

2. Decide the number of cells you need and where they will be located.

3. Cell leaders and members will operate only by a code name of their choice. No one, not even you, will know their real names. Cell leaders will only know the code names of their cell own members and, of course, yours. Do not give anyone my cell number. The Bankers will maintain a secure record of every team member. I have attached a list of potential cell leaders and member recommendations. Each has a number assigned to them. After they select their code names, you will prepare a list matching their code name with their number when they commit to STN. I do not know the people on your list of potential recruits. The Bankers generated the list.

4. Establish Swiss bank accounts for each cell leader for their operating expenses, according to your assessment of the funding needed. Each team member will have their private bank account established by the Bankers for their service. Select your cell leaders and let them decide on their team members from the attached list. They too must supply the matching list of code names and numbers for the Bankers. The rules of recruitment always apply. You will identify that person to me.

5. Funds for operating expenses for cell operations will come from

your operation account. You will set up the mechanics to facilitate these transfers.

6. Requests for additional funds come through me. We will discuss your requirements. Additional funds will be placed into your account.

7. Cell leaders are responsible for their own budgets and operations.

8. Instructions on how to obtain an encrypted phone for you and your team members is: Call 1-888-555-5515. State your code name to hear the instructions. Every team member must use an encrypted phone to conduct STN business.

9. Keep phone communications to a minimum.

10. The Bankers have access to a vast database. Should you need assistance in obtaining the names and locations of terrorists or their associates, contact me. The information will become available within a week.

11. Target selection: The time and the place for the execution of terrorists are the sole domain of the regional leaders. Each leader will plan and execute their strikes as they see fit, after the initial strike has succeeded.

12. No attacks from your organization will happen until I decide which team will make the initial encounter. The next series of attacks will occur after we have made our announcement to the media. Once the terrorists are on notice, you will be free to plan and implement your attacks whenever and wherever your team is ready. Meanwhile continue with your recruitment and training.

13. All STN members must have and maintain a job. Members must remain part of their community.

14. Recruit from the pre-approved list provided. They will make excellent recruits. The Bankers have provided a list of 159 potential STN recruits in your region. The list is enclosed for your review. They are prepared to join us. It's up to you to determine who you feel best fits your organization. Their credentials are impeccable. With them, you will be able to quickly build your organization and have them prepared to serve STN.

15. All preparations must be in place, ready to strike within one year. The experts on your list are field proven and will be able to assist you in all phases of your operation, especially planning the attacks. Trust them. They will help us both to succeed. Destroy the list after you have completed your recruitment. Until then, safeguard these rules and this document with your life.

Rule 16, *Mandatory Targets* hit him like a flash flood of mud and debris. So violent was his reaction that he nearly fainted. His blood felt sucked from his body. For the first time in his life, he experienced the meaning of pure horror, worse than *Red Sunset*. It was so sudden and devastating, that he became instantly nauseated. His heart ferociously thumped in his chest;

he felt he was having a heart attack. He threw up twice in the space of two minutes, just missing his desk as he blasted the area rug beneath his chair. Splatters of red and gray vomit soiled his white shirt and his pressed back suit pants. Somehow, his tie escaped the eruptions. Seven minutes later, after what seemed an hour, Ed regained some control of his body. Involuntarily, between the vomiting, he shouted in anguish "Nooooo, Nooooooo, Nooooo." so loudly that Alice rushed in to see what was happening.

"What's the matter? Do you need a doctor?"

She saw a pale shaking man, glazed over eyes, pools of nasty smelling vomit on the rug and his clothing. Ed looked as though death was moments away. With his mouth agape and his body shaking, he was holding onto the edge of his desk so he would not collapse onto the mess in his office.

"No, I'll be alright," he weakly replied. "Just get someone in here to clean up this mess. I… need some air. I'll be fine."

"But…"she started.

Ed cut her off.

"I swear I'll be fine. I must have swallowed saliva. It went down the wrong way. I'm feeling better now, really."

"Are you sure you don't want to go to the hospital? I think I'd better call 9-1-1. You look really sick."

"No, that won't be necessary."

"Do you want me to call Janice to pick you up?"

"No, just get someone in to clean up my office. I'll sit outside until it's done."

"Really Ed, you look sick, and I don't think you should take a chance. Better be safe than sorry. Let me call 9-1-1. I really think you need medical attention."

"No, I tell you that won't be necessary," he insisted. He stumbled shakily to his desk to scoop up the scattered STN papers. He quickly placed them into his briefcase, in no particular order. He willed his body away from his desk towards the open door of his office, desperately clutching his briefcase tightly to his trembling body.

"Are you sure?" she called to him as he staggered out the door.

"Yes, call me on my cell when it's cleaned up. And Alice, don't mention this to anyone, especially Janice. I don't feel like answering questions right now. I'll be fine, really."

He left as quickly as his shaky body allowed him. He found an isolated wooden bench not far from the main entrance and flopped onto it with his last bit of strength.

"I need Farook," he muttered. "He'll clear this up. I can't believe it. I can't believe this is what he wants. What have I gotten myself into?"

He gripped his briefcase and held it close, as though the mere thought of it not being in constant contact with his body would inflict a slow torturous death. He sat there for twenty minutes, trying to recover mentally and physically.

Mandatory Targets. Mandatory Targets.

He dialed Alice from his cell phone.

"I'm going home."

"Are you OK to drive? I'll be glad to drive you or call a cab. I'm worried about you," she pleaded.

"No, I can manage. Thanks anyway. How's the clean up coming?"

"You're better off going home. The crew has been working for the past ten minutes. They're making progress, but they need more time to do the job right. It's taking longer than expected. I'll cancel your last two appointments. Just take care of yourself. See you in the morning?"

"Thanks, yes. Bye."

He shuffled slowly towards the garage to his car. His knees felt shaky, his heart continued pounding, and his body was weak and uncoordinated. *Mandatory Targets* filled his thoughts.

It's still early. There shouldn't be much traffic. If I drive slowly, I won't get into an accident.

He realized that some vomit had hit his shirt and pants. The smell began to make him feel nauseated again. The four windows of his Cutlass came down simultaneously. The crisp rushing air somewhat lessened the heavy repugnant odor. Thirty-three minutes later, he pulled into his driveway.

Fortunately, Janice was out for the afternoon, so he didn't have to dream up a plausible explanation for her, at least for the moment. He quickly got out of his clothes, threw the disgusting shirt into the washing machine, washed his pants as best he could, sprayed some deodorizer on it to lessen the odor, and rinsed his mouth out three times with full strength mouthwash. He managed to walk to his office and flopped into his rolling desk chair. His hands trembled so much he had to redial the number three times before he got it right.

"It's me, Ed," he whispered into the phone.

"Why are you calling me? I told you not to call until you had your own phone," Farook demanded sternly.

"You've gone too far. How can you expect me to be part of this? I can't believe you are serious. I never imagined… I never thought that…killing terrorists is one thing. But I never bargained for anything like this!"

His voice, affected by his anger and his disbelief, quivered when he spoke.

"You need to listen without interruption to what I say. When I'm finished, then you can decide whether you are strong enough to continue our mission. Can you do that?" demanded Farook. His tone left little doubt that he expected Ed to listen.

"First, I want you to hang up. I will call you right back. My phone is secure, and yours is not. Hang up now!" he commanded. They both hung up. Eleven seconds later they were reconnected.

"Well, what is it?"

It's the *Mandatory Targets* thing...RULE 16. I can't do it!"

For the next eleven minutes, Ed absorbed Farook's anger and sarcasm. Ed meekly tried to interject several times with questions, but Farook cut him off with another tirade. It took the tone of a one way dialog by a strong-willed and determined parent holding court with his recalcitrant son.

"What did you expect? Hugs and kisses? You know what's at stake. What don't you understand?"

"But... I...."

Farook was in no mood to hear whining. Instead, he repeatedly bombarded Ed with references about terrorism and innocent people dying. He talked at length about the need to instill fear into the terrorists, by whatever means possible. Especially the Circle. He reminded Ed of the despair of the families of innocent victims of the suicide bombers. How the world has lost hope for enduring peace and security. How STN is the last and only hope. How STN will inspire the civilized world a renewed sense of hope for future peace and prosperity without fear.

"Men who do evil will die. Through their deaths, we will restore the hopes and dreams of civilized society, your society and mine."

Farook abruptly ended the lecture.

"There is nothing left to discuss. What remains is your decision. Will you accept the rules, *ALL* the rules?"

Ed suddenly remembered. No one leaves STN alive. That's the other rule, the one not written, the one no one learns about until it's too late. He was rapidly falling apart. He was drowning in his own fear.

I can't, but if I quit, I'm, dead, and maybe my family too. What have I done? I'm fucked, totally fucked. Answer him you idiot, answer him before he orders your death.

"I...err....err... agree with you. The world needs to have... to have hope and to believe they will survive," he meekly responded.

The tone of his voice indicated he had just submissively acquiesced to Farook's demands. Ed felt conflicted and confused. He had difficulty accepting Rule 16, and stubbornly refused to accept the logic and explanations that Farook threw at him. But, he understood the situation. Unless he could convince Farook he was completely committed to STN, he knew he would suffer the consequences. With death possibly close by, and in spite of his intense panic, perhaps because of it, he managed to answer in a convincing voice,

"You're right. I was temporarily confused, but I'm fine now. Yes, I'm ready to fulfill my destiny."

"OK," Farook flatly replied.

"Don't lose your way again!" The threat hung over him like the Sword of Damocles. The connection was broken.

In spite of his re-commitment, Ed could not grasp everything that Farook said over the past 55 minutes. Except for the insinuated threat! *That* he remembered. Deep down, he worried that he would never accept what his mind was screaming for him to reject. Rule 16 was his Mount Everest. He was compelled to climb to the top, but he lacked a security rope around his waist. To go up or down spelled danger. Still dazed, he found his way to his deep-seated reclining chair in the living room, extended the footrest, and dozed off from exhaustion. He was deeply troubled. Sleep helped to avoid the pain of thinking about his dilemma.

He awoke with a start. He had slept a little over two and a half hours. Janice would be home in another hour, the kids twenty minutes later, and another typical middle class American family evening would begin-noisy dinner, clean up, homework, teasing, cajoling, laughter, possible disagreements, baths, and thankful bedtime for the children. By then he'd have to come up with an explanation for Janice. He never came home early before. She would question him until he provided a satisfactory answer. He hoped "some sort of bug" excuse would suffice and he could get through the evening without additional questioning.

There is so much to do Ed thought. He felt disengaged from his body. His emotions seemed to hang in mid air, taunting, daring him to grab hold and forcibly propel them back into his body. His every thought, feeling and action seemed delayed. He felt foggy and disconnected. Vague images remotely formed outside his sense of awareness. Janice cooking. The babbling TV. The children complaining about something. None of it connected with his brain.

"Are you alright? You look terrible. Why did you come home early? Are you sick?" she asked when she saw him.

"Let's talk after dinner, after the kids go to sleep. I'm alright. Must be a bug or something."

Although concerned, she reluctantly agreed to wait for his explanation.

It took him over forty minutes to allay her concerns before she accepted the *bug* explanation.

"I'm tired. I think I'll turn in early," he said.

He retired to their bedroom, but could not sleep.

Rule 16 had just irrevocably altered his life again. Farook is full of surprises, unhappy surprises.

"I had to tell him. I had to!" he lamented.

Rule 16 deeply revolted him. He glumly said to himself, had *I only known! This is not worth ten million. My life and my beliefs are more important.*

The next several days Ed struggled with his new demons. He was grumpy towards Janice and the kids, grumpy at work, and grumpy to everyone and everything around him. He disapproved of the news and the newscasters, the Washington Nationals who had just began their 2010 baseball season, President Schuster, Congress, and Farook. Especially Farook. He still hated and feared terrorists, and he worried about *Red Sunset* and the *Rule*. Nightly he talked to himself before falling asleep, trying to convince himself that Rule 16 was only a small blip in the fight against terrorism. He recalled Farook's words, repeatedly, trying desperately to make Farook's passion his own.

Gradually, out of necessity for survival, Rule 16 became less revolting, almost acceptable. He reminded himself of the bigger picture. Slowly Ed convinced himself that the ends do justify the means. By the end of the week, it was almost over. He had successfully negated all STN rules as a byproduct of the war against terrorists. He regained his composure and re-committed himself to Farook and STN.

Though convinced he had forced a remarkable turn around in a short time, he guessed that sometime in the future, his psyche would not be able to continue suppressing his feelings. He relegated his debilitating concern to a deep place in his subconscious, a place that gave him permission to bury his personal terror, a place that allowed his confidence to gain the traction and confidence he sorely needed to be the North American Regional STN leader.

Ed Walker, CIA Deputy Director, father, husband and good guy, morphed into… "Thunder", head of the North American STN region. His initial inclination was to immediately call *el Berubi* and shout "Thunder" as soon as Farook answered. He wanted Farook to know he was now totally committed to the mission, that his former concerns had been resolved, and that he was prepared to fight terrorism any way required. He picked up his cell phone to dial, and hesitated. Though invigorated by his transformation, he was not ready to put it to the test. Not yet. He feared the sound of his own voice might rekindle his nascent horror, and his resolve would crumble. He put the phone down.

"I better wait until I have my encrypted phone before I start making that call. I don't want Farook to think I can't follow the rules," he gladly convinced himself.

Unable to sleep for more than a few hours, Ed decided the best way to strengthen his newfound resolve was to work on developing his STN master plan.

He lay in his bed, eyes open, diligently pinpointing critical issues to be resolved in his mind. He slipped into a deep exhausting sleep an hour later. The rhythmic sounds of the heavy spring rain hitting the window had its numbing effect.

18

BILAL, MAY 2010:

Bilal easily visualized the next phase of his life. Meet this stranger, Farook, join a terrorist group, find the HuM leaders who ordered the deaths of my family and kill them. Death to the dirty dogs!

He removed the picture of Nasrin from his pocket, just as he had done so many times, to see her, to talk with her, to weep over her, and once again to swear his vengeance. The vision of the fulfillment of his vow to his family excited him. Sleep was impossible. He barely managed three hours a night for the next three nights. As exhausted as he was, he would nod off only to find himself wide-awake. Daytime was no better. His thoughts focused on his meeting with Farook.

For the first time since he arrived in Karachi, he started to believe he was drawing closer to the revenge that motivated his existence.

This is why I live. My first contact is my opportunity. I will not fail.

He thought of Bruce MacCardle, and of calling him to share his good fortune, but decided to wait. A wave of caution forced him to reevaluate the situation.

"I have not spoken with this stranger. I have spoken only with Emir. Emir could be leading me to my death. Suppose Farook is misleading Emir? Then what? This stranger might be a dead end without terrorist connections. Even worse, he could be working for the government, looking to obtain information to arrest me as a terrorist or an infiltrator. No, I must be certain before I raise my hopes too high. In truth I am a combination of terrorist and infiltrator, but not the kind they might think," he openly mused.

Suddenly he grew angry with himself.

I am being foolish. I am allowing my hopes to become facts. I have no facts, no knowledge, and no proof. I cannot indulge in the pleasure of dreams. They will not help me to avenge Nasrin and my children. Truth matters. Nothing else.

He kissed his wife's picture as he always did, reverently returning it to its normal resting place in his shirt pocket, next to his heart. His feelings subdued, he returned to his revenge mentality.

As time inched slowly towards Wednesday, Bilal did little else but impatiently wait. He barely slept or ate. He felt highly wired at the prospect of the beginning of his revenge. His anger, his pain, his commitment, remained his constant companion.

"With luck," he muttered, "HuM will soon die."

An hour and a half before his meeting with the stranger, he took a taxi to the Pearl Continental Hotel on Club Road, in the heart of Karachi. He directed the driver to leave him a block from the hotel. Bilal took precautions to insure he wasn't headed into a trap. He walked to the entrance to a clothing shop diagonally across the street from the hotel, where he could be lost among the tourists, businessmen, and the local shoppers. From there he could observe the entrance to the hotel and observe anyone who approached from either side. He also had a clear view of the roof, a traditional place for snipers to hide.

He felt confident he would spot any possible assassin. He visited three shops along the block to be sure that anyone stalking him could not easily pick him out of the crowd. An hour and twenty minutes later, satisfied no threat existed, he entered the massive glass sliding doors of the Pearl Continental and found the small coffee shop.

The shop was nearly empty, except for two young men and a family of four sitting at tables near the floor to ceiling windows. He saw the man who fit Farook's description. Tan pants, blue shirt, mustache, smoking a big black cigar, a second one protruding from his pocket, an onyx ring with a diamond in the center, sitting alone in the far corner. The straw hat perched jauntily on his head cast a shadow over his eyes.

That is Farook. He matches Emir's description.

Bilal sat to the right of the stranger, and without looking in the man's face, said,

"Typical hot day in Karachi."

The reply came back, "Not as hot as in Iraq."

"I'm Bilal"

"I know. I'm Farook. We need to talk in private. Would you be willing to come to my room at the hotel across the street so we can talk privately?"

Bilal studied him, hard.

Is this a trap? Is Farook his real name? Is he a decoy leading me to my death?

Bilal studied the face and the body language of this stranger. He decided he had to take this chance. If Farook is a terrorist recruiter and he refused to meet, his opportunity to join them might be lost.

He is not a threat. His eyes tell me that.

"Yes," he unhesitatingly responded. *But I will be watching your every move.*

"Good, it takes a man of strength and conviction, or a fool, to go to a stranger's room in these times, don't you agree Bilal?" Farook challenged him.

"Which do you think I am?"

"Obviously you are not a fool, so you must be the other," Farook responded.

"Perhaps a bit of both," was Bilal's smart retort.

"Perhaps. I'm sure that will be unveiled shortly. But, let me assure you that you have nothing to fear from me, and much to gain. I am leaving now. Wait twenty minutes, then walk across the street to the hotel and go through the lobby to the rear entrance. There you will find steps leading to the upper floors. Walk to the second floor, pretend you are looking for a particular room. Be sure no one is following you. Take the service elevator adjacent to the stairs and come to the fifth floor, room 523. I'll be there, waiting for you. You are coming, aren't you?"

"I'll be there."

Farook left. Bilal waited the prescribed twenty minutes, walked through the small dingy hotel lobby, down the wide worn-carpeted hall until he found the service elevators. He found room 523 and knocked. Farook opened the door.

Old and cheap Pakistani furnishings crowded the tiny bedroom. A round 42" rosewood shaky table sat in the corner with two wooden chairs facing each other. A sagging bed covered with stained and faded bedspread filled the small room.

Bilal considered his dichotomy. He was convinced that the IB was not involved, since government agencies never stay in a run-down hotel like this. But, terrorists might. Still, if the IB wanted to hide their identity, this is the perfect place to complete their ruse. Concerned yet curious, Bilal resolved to stay alert and keep his defenses high.

He noticed the two packed suitcases resting on the bed, apparently ready for a quick departure. Both were of what looked like high quality leather that reeked of money. Quiet money.

This man is used to luxury and is not afraid to show it.

A black leather briefcase, partially opened, prominently sat in the middle of the rickety table.

"Please sit and make yourself comfortable. I took the liberty to order bottled water, flatbread, and tea, no milk, just as you prefer."

Farook looked directly into Bilal's steely eyes and began,

"My name is Farook el Habid, and I'm here to make you a special proposition. Please hear what I have to say before you ask questions, for you will have many. I have the answers. Let me start from the beginning.

You met Emir. Not his real name as you probably suspected. We know much about you, Bilal Maqsood Ahmed. We know of the tragic deaths of your family and your vow for vengeance. We know of your time in the ExecProtect, and the skills you demonstrated. We know about your work in construction, how, when and why you joined EPA. In fact, we know everything about you."

"But how and why?" questioned Bilal without emotion.

"In due time. Please hear what I have to say. I promise all will be clear shortly. We already were considering you for this position. We learned more about you quite accidentally from your friend Bruce MacCardle, which saved us a lot of time. An agent of mine overheard his conversation. We learned you planned to move to Karachi. From then it was easy to find you. We sent Emir to make the initial contact. We wanted him to assess your feelings, and to see if you are still committed to avenging your family. Emir, from his brief conversation with you at the soccer match, concluded you remain focused. You made that quite clear through your rather feeble attempt to determine if he was a terrorist contact. Your references to the United States and the Pakistani politicians were an obvious ruse to convince him you were angry and ready for a change.

We understand this was your way to try to penetrate a terrorist organization. We know you hoped it would lead you to Harakat-ul-Mujaludin. So far correct?"

"Yes," answered Bilal, stunned that this man, this stranger, knew so much about him. He had always been a private man, and for a stranger to know so much about him was quite disturbing. He felt betrayed by Bruce, who may have put his life in danger unnecessarily by blabbing about his mission.

Bruce probably was at a bar, drunk, and needed a friend, so he talked. But why is Farook interested in me? Bilal wondered.

"What I am about to tell you will possibly shock you. You understand this is highly confidential. If anyone learns about me, my organization, or that you and I were talking, both our lives would be in peril, as well as my organization. Do you understand?"

Bilal nodded *Yes.*

"I represent an organization called STN which stands for *Stop Terrorism Now.* Our mission is to destroy global terrorism. These so-called Lions of

Islam are a deviant minority section of Islam who is forcing us to fight a war we did not start. We are in a battle of ideals. They wish to rule the world. We are fighting to win the hearts and safety of the people. We are creating worldwide teams with trusted leaders to carry out this mission. We have access to information about every known terrorist. We know who they are, where they are, their families, friends, sources of money, and their contacts. We can track anyone we please. Our database is more extensive than that of the United States and Interpol combined. We are well funded and prepared to spend as much as it takes to defeat the terrorists.

Each global team operates autonomously from each other and me. We pay our members well to be successful. This gives them the incentive to perform efficiently with deadly force.

Farook reiterated the same speech about who the real terrorists are and that they all had to die, just as he did with Ed Walker in Brussels.

"Our mission is to wipe out terrorism completely. We foresee a time when terrorists, their supporters, and their sympathizers will be destroyed and no longer pose a threat to mankind. We believe they will realize the risks of being a terrorist are too high and they will stop. We will bring lasting peace to the world, free of the terror that these dogs impose on the innocents of every country. We know the next big terrorist threat will likely be in Europe. We intend to prevent this from happening."

Bilal remained flaccid and indifferent.

"That is a noble goal, but not one that interests me. My only interest is in HuM, to kill them for what they did. Thank you for considering me, but I must decline. However, it sounds as though you can help me. If what you say is true, you must have information on HuM members. I would be happy to pay you whatever you ask for the information. It is worth every Rupee I have. It will bring me closer to my goal."

They sat in silence, neither speaking. Bilal waiting for an answer; Farook offering none.

Bilal spoke first. "While you are considering my request, I am curious. How were you able to learn so much about me from fragments of a conversation in a bar?"

"As I said before, we are well funded, and have been collecting information for years on our enemies and our friends. You are our friend. Allow me to give you some more details about us so you can have a better understanding. Anonymous wealthy people, The Bankers, are funding our operation. The Bankers are committed, through STN, to the total destruction of global terrorism. They are highly disturbed that governments are unable or unwilling, to take more decisive actions. Governments take baby steps and refuse to use their strength to stop this terror. They talk, hold meetings, support corrupt régimes, repeatedly make stupid mistakes, waste money and lives, and what have they achieved? Very little. Many innocent people continue to die. Terrorists are out of control and gaining strength. Since governments are weak, our wealthy friends have secretly been funding and developing STN. We maintain our own network of data on terrorists and their supporters.

We already have teams strategically placed and operating throughout the world. We are forming the Pakistani team and want you to be the leader. Your background, your Army experience, and your EPA training, prove you will make an excellent Regional leader. Also, the tragedy of your family's deaths is reason enough to join our group."

"I am flattered, but still, this is not what I need to do. I only seek to destroy those who murdered my family. My energies must be devoted to their deaths. This I have sworn," responded Bilal.

"Consider this," Farook replied.

"Being part of STN will allow you to achieve your goals more quickly. We have the financial, technical, and manpower resources to help. What could take you years to accomplish on your own, you will achieve much more quickly. Alone you might never find the people responsible for murdering your family. We can provide you a direct path towards your enemies. In fact, they should be your first targets for execution. You can satisfy your revenge and still provide a valuable service to families just like yours throughout Pakistan. Together we will wipe out terrorism and protect people from experiencing the anguish they bring. Is that not worth considering?"

"Perhaps, but I have no interest in helping others. My life only has meaning to kill HuM. Nothing more. Nothing less. Will you help me find them?"

"No, we will not do that. We are not interested in selling our information, nor can we afford to have outside people know of our capabilities. I'm sorry, Bilal, but those are our rules."

"So, my choices are limited. Join STN and go after HuM, or not join and hope I can find them. If I join, you say I must also kill other terrorists, correct?"

"Yes."

"Suppose I join, find and kill HuM, then quit and go my own way. Wouldn't that be the same if you give me the information about them?"

"On the surface, it seems that way. However, that is not acceptable. I will quickly learn if you join us just to complete your revenge. However, I have a question for you. Suppose you join us, kill HuM, and then quit. What will you do then? Your reason for living would disappear, wouldn't it? Are you prepared to sit in a room the rest of your life? I know you are not a devout

Muslim, but you are still Muslim. Therefore, you will not kill yourself after you kill HuM, is that not true?"

Bilal clenched his fists to control himself. He hadn't thought that far ahead. In his mind, his only thought was the death of HuM. He stared at Farook searching for an answer within his mind. He had none.

"What you say is true. I have not thought that far ahead. I assumed I would kill them or die trying," Bilal pensively replied.

"Perhaps it is time to consider life after HuM."

A pensive Bilal sat in silence, reflecting on Farook's words. Neither man spoke, each giving the other his own space. Farook sat back in the chair and closed his eyes. This simple gesture told Bilal he would not interfere until Bilal had decided on his course of action.

For Farook it was a simple decision. Accept our offer or die. Bilal's dilemma was more complex. Confusion clouded his thinking.

How could I have not considered life after HuM? Could I kill myself if I had to?

He thought about Nasrin. About his children. About Syed.

Suicide is out of the question. I cannot dishonor my family. I have no option but to accept Farook's offer. The most important thing is to destroy HuM. After that, if I am alive, then I will kill all terrorists in Pakistan. By this decision, I bring honor to Nasrin.

Bilal broke his silence.

"Do you agree that I can target HuM first if I join STN?"

"Yes, without question."

"After that, I could destroy any terrorist organization I choose?"

"With restrictions. You have full authority anywhere in Pakistan, Afghanistan, and Turkey. Other leaders have jurisdiction in other countries. Pakistan and Afghanistan have enough terrorist organizations to keep you very busy." Farook smiled at his humor.

"Our goal is to rid the world of terrorism now, not later," Farook authoritatively continued.

Bilal narrowed his eyes evaluating Farook's words. He sat for several minutes, focusing at the Egyptian's eyes and face. He stared blankly, without emotion or excitement.

Bilal, the machine-man, in a steely cold monotone voice asked,

"When do I start?"

"Immediately."

They discussed setting up the operation in Pakistan, the Swiss bank accounts, recruitment and training, use of a secure cell phone money, his personal pay, the two Swiss bank accounts, and use of code names. Bilal chose to use what he felt. ICE.

Farook explained to Bilal, as he had done with Ed Walker days earlier, his media plan that would begin when all nineteen STN teams were ready. Farook indicated he would decide on which team would make the initial STN attack.

"It could be your team, Bilal, so you must be ready. It should take about a year for us to be fully staffed and prepared to start our war against terrorism."

"There is much to discuss. We should meet again. Emir will contact you with the arrangements, within a week or so. Until then, maintain a low profile. Continue to be new to Karachi. Explore your community, make friends with the local shop owners and go to teahouses. I want you to become part of the community. Let them see you and accept you, just as you planned before. Make only small talk, and do not discuss politics or terrorism with anyone. Is that clear?"

"Yes."

"I will make the Swiss deposits shortly. Meanwhile, if you have any questions, contact Emir and he will contact me. We will provide you with the answers."

Farook fished a card from his pocket and slid it across the table to Bilal.

"Emir will let you know where and when we will meet again to discuss the details of your assignment. Leave now. I'm happy you decided to join us. We'll do well together, I promise."

They stood and shook hands. Bilal left the room and the hotel. Emir joined Farook moments later.

"How did it go?' asked Emir.

"As I hoped. He has decided to cast his lot with us. Yet, he could change his mind after he has to reconsider. Eliminate him immediately if he does."

"Done."

It was April 2010, the beginning of Bilal's revenge.

Bilal walked the two miles to his apartment, feeling energized by his conversation with Farook. Once there he stripped and stretched out on his bed. For the first time since Nasrin died over nine months ago, he gave himself permission to sleep.

Now it begins. I know I am on the right path for my revenge. I will inflict immense damage to HuM and their leaders. The more who die, the closer I will be to repay them for the slaughter of my family.

Satisfied, he fell into a deep and satisfying sleep, the first since he received that fateful letter from his father.

The early morning dawn light awoke him. With a clear head, he examined his decision to join the STN, not with doubt, but with a steely determination.

"This is where I belong. To make them pay, to have them suffer," he said triumphantly.

He wrote a list of questions and items he needed. Selecting targets was the easy part.

I need to recruit the right people. There are others, many others in Pakistan, who are angry enough to take action against terrorists to join STN. If STN is as powerful as Farook says they are, he will help me recruit the men I need and trust. The quicker the better, he proclaimed to himself. *Revenge has no patience and no boundaries. All terrorists must die. As long as HuM dies first, I will be satisfied.*

He yanked the pull chain to turn on the 40-watt lamp and peeked in the small refrigerator for something to eat. Cheese, tomato, and lettuce on a roll suited him fine, especially when washed down with his favorite strong tea. That's all he had available.

Hunger is my companion to pain. Unlike others who do not eat when they are disturbed, my anguish connects to my stomach. I eat to sustain me for my work with STN. He almost smiled.

He munched on his sandwich, drank his sweet tea while making mental notes.

I must get a job. However, there are other troubling questions. Who and where do the other eighteen leaders live? Who are the Bankers and how powerful are they?

He withdrew the now tattered picture, stared into the photo- creased face of his wife, and spoke aloud,

"I have not forgotten my vow to you, Nasrin. I will fulfill it, whether by my hand or by another. I swear those who will die in your honor will avenge your death. This I also know. The violence that surrounds us must cease. Terrorists cannot rule the living. After the death of the HuM dogs, I am committed to destroying all terrorists where I find them. I hope you approve."

His thoughts turned to Bruce MacCardle. Surprisingly, his anger towards Bruce softened to forgiveness.

Had he not talked at a bar, Farook would not have talked to me as quickly. For that, I am thankful, he thought. *Bruce could be a valuable asset to STN and me. In South Africa he offered to share in my revenge. Now he can. He will come as promised. Bruce and I will be together again, fighting side by side.*

Twelve days later, his cell phone rang. Emir informed him the meeting was arranged for the following day, at Kahn's, a small tea/coffee house three blocks from the Quissa Khawani bazaar. Tourists and locals tended to meet and mingle in the bazaar. The bazaar was two blocks long and was home to many stores, restaurants and sidewalk vendors. The small street made the area crowded, even when the people traffic was light. The chance of someone observing a stranger with prying eyes and attentive ears was especially risky at the packed bazaar. Kahn's, on the other hand was far enough from the hordes of people and afforded more privacy for those who need to discus topics that could cause trouble if overheard.

"A meeting with Farook will take place in two days. Here are your instructions. Take the northbound 1-C bus tomorrow at 8:14 AM. Get off at the National Museum stop. Walk ten minutes ahead on Dr. Ziauddin Ahmed Road to house #114. You will easily recognize the house. It is sand stucco with a double door painted in dark brown, and is distinguished with a large camel's head knocker. Knock twice, and come in. There you will receive the information you need. As usual, take great caution to be sure you are not being followed."

Two days later, Bilal did as instructed. He took the bus, and walked to #114 Dr. Ziauddin Ahmed Road. The building, like all the buildings in the area, needed repair from years of neglect. The sand colored stucco, bleached by the sun, had large chunks missing from the walls, both from age and old scars from rifle fire. The wooden frame, exposed to the elements and poorly maintained, had significant decay around the window areas. A straw mat heavily clogged with the red area dust made it appear as an extension of the broken brick pavement.

He knocked twice and opened the door. He found Farook seated at a large table in the middle of the sparsely furnished but surprisingly well-lit room. Heavy dark cloth shades blocked the two windows. They covered the entire window to prevent prying eyes from peering into the room. Three empty yet comfortable looking faded brown armchairs hugged the table. Farook was in the fourth. A pile of papers awaited Bilal's arrival.

"Welcome again to STN, Bilal. We have many things we to discuss. I have arranged for lunch, since we should be here 4-5 hours. Any questions before we start?"

"Only one. What would you have done had I not accepted your offer?"

"Emir would have killed you."

"I'm not surprised. It's a good thing I made the right decision, then, isn't it?" he said without a smile. He decided to inform Farook of his decision to bring Bruce to Karachi.

"I have forgiven Bruce MacCardle for betraying me, though he should not have spoken so loosely in the bar," Bilal stated. " I want to bring him here to help me. How do you feel about that?"

"First, allow me to set the record straight. Bruce did not give you up. We already knew of you and we had planned to learn more before your family was tragically murdered. We needed to wait while you settled your affairs. Bruce's conversation merely accelerated our interest in you. Bruce confirmed that you were unnerved and badly shaken, but in control. That is why I sent Emir to contact you to determine if you were able to function properly. We do not want an unstable person running the Pakistani operation. That is why we are here today. You passed Emir's test. He recommended we recruit you. The last piece of business was to see if you would join us. Let me think about Bruce."

"Thank you for that. I didn't want to believe that Bruce could not to be trusted."

"Now we can focus on the details of your duties as the Pakistani Regional leader. Here is a list of our mission and rules that we give to every leader."

He pulled an envelope from his open briefcase, and handed Bilal the same rules of STN he had three weeks previously presented to Ed Walker in Brussels.

"Read this and let me know if you have any questions," Farook demanded.

Bilal read each paragraph. His stoic demeanor did not change. Only after he finished reading Rule 16, *Mandatory Targets*, did he speak.

"I understand your rules. I will destroy the terrorists and their Circle of Contamination."

"Do you have any problems with Rule 16? Some people say we are being cruel."

"Frankly, I find no part of your rules that are cruel," Bilal curtly spoke in a hateful and sarcastic tone that surprised even Farook.

"Cruel is their willingness to murder innocent women and children like my family. An eye for an eye is not cruel. It is the ultimate and the only true punishment for their crimes. There is nothing more to consider. You get what you want. I get what I want," strongly proclaimed Bilal.

"Excellent. Yet, let me suggest you take a few moments to rethink your decision. You need to be sure that this is how you want to spend the next portion of your life. Are you certain you are willing to execute dozens of terrorists, not only Hum?"

"Yes," Bilal quickly assured him.

"Our operation and our rules must remain secret especially in this part of the world. Obviously, if word got out what we are planning, it could affect our entire operation and cost many lives."

"I am Pakistani. You don't have to remind me what can happen if the wrong ears hear too much."

It took four hours to review STN's operation, goals, and what Farook expected of him. Bilal learned about code names, how the funding was to be distributed, and the vast resources of the Bankers, the Bankers commitment, and the Swiss bank in which his personal fortune was deposited, along with his personal access code. Bilal remotely cared about personal money. His only concern was when he could start.

He grew impatient with the flood of details Farook was discussing. He wanted to shout at Farook to "give me the names of possible recruits so I can continue towards my destiny."

But, he restrained himself and begrudgingly gave Farook the attention he demanded.

"Any questions?" Farook asked when he finished.

"None. I understand and agree, but should any questions arise, I will contact you," Bilal replied.

"It is best to minimize our contacts in person and by phone. Any questions you have ask Emir, he will be your contact for operational issues. Reserve your questions about targets and other STN business for me, once you have your secure cell phone. Your first task is to assemble your cell members, and train them to fulfill our mission. The people whom we can recommend will not question their pay or their task. We have pre- screened them for their loyalty and mutual desire to exterminate the terrorists. Many carry a great deal of anger against terrorists, but they do not know specifically about STN's goals. Your job is to explain what is necessary and to insure they are properly trained and prepared."

"Have you considered my request to have Bruce part of my team? I can use him as my advisor."

"Bruce could be an interesting addition. Talk with him as soon as possible. He might prove to be a valuable addition for us in Pakistan. Obviously, I would have to establish a cover identity for him. Because he is not Pakistani, he'd have to operate more in the public's eye than you. Give me a moment to think," responded Farook.

Both men sat silently until Farook spoke again.

"I envision a role in which he could work within the International community in Karachi that is closed to you. The contacts he makes could prove to be highly valuable to our mission, assuming he joins. However, our recruitment rule remains. Are you prepared to give the order for Bruce's execution should he not join? If not, do not try to recruit him," Farook empathically stated.

"Bruce will not refuse my request. That I can assure you," Bilal offered convincingly.

"Then do it."

"Thank you."

After the briefing, Farook handed the list of possible recruits identified only by a number and their telephone numbers to Bilal, who promptly placed the four typed sheets into his shirt tucked between his shirt and the belt of his pants. As a precaution, he folded one end in half to prevent the papers from accidently slipping from his body.

They parted soon after.

Bilal did some desperately needed food shopping at the local open-air market, slipping between stalls to avoid the sudden early evening rainfall before he headed to his apartment. It was 5:20 PM in Karachi, and 2:20 PM in Africa. The outgoing message on Bruce's phone "promised he would return the call as soon as he was available, but not to be concerned if it takes weeks." Bruce thought of everything. Bilal left his message to call him on his pre-paid cell phone. Six hours later Bruce returned his call.

"Hello my friend, it's great to hear your voice again."

"Hello to you too. How are you? What's happening? How's your quest coming? Did anyone contact you?" asked Bruce.

"Yes, we spoke, and that is one of the reasons I am calling. I'm doing well. I want to ask you to join me in Karachi. I think the job I have in mind for you will suit you just fine. Are you willing to leave EPA and come to Pakistan?"

"You need to ask? What kind of job is it?"

"That will come later. For now I need to know if you are willing to come to Karachi."

"Karachi?"

"Yes."

"Does it involve killing HuM?"

"Yes."

"Count me in."

"Good. When can you come? There's much to discuss. I will explain everything when we are together."

"It will take me about three weeks to settle my affairs at EPA."

"Let me know when your travel plans are firm. I'll make the arrangements from here. How are things with you?"

"Better, now that we'll be working together again, my friend."

"I've missed you."

"As have I."

"I'll call you when I'm ready."

"I'll be waiting."

"Till then, take care of yourself, Bilal. Save some of the action for me," he laughed.

"There'll be plenty, trust me," Bilal responded in a deadpan tone.

"I'll start in the morning to process my paperwork. Till then, goodbye."

After speaking with Bruce, Bilal called Farook.

"ICE. Bruce has agreed to join us. He arrives in three weeks. Is there enough time to create Bruce's cover?"

"Yes, I have been working on it since we talked, anticipating that he would join. One note, are you still prepared for the consequences if he should change his mind and not come to Karachi?"

"There is no need to be concerned. Bruce will not change his mind."

"Excellent. I'll be ready. I'll make the final preparations and let you know what needs to be done."

All preparations are made, for the good or the bad, thought Farook.

*

Bilal spent countless hours recruiting his Pakistani team. He decided to have twenty-seven three-man teams in his Pakistani Region. He interviewed the potential recruits recommended by Farook. He found them all to be as Farook depicted-loyal, tough, and prepared to kill terrorists. Bilal became addicted to the planning aspects of his new career. He spent most of his waking hours developing his plan. One issue troubled him. He needed to find a job to blend into the Karachi society. Jobs were not plentiful, especially one that would allow him to pursue his STN activities when required. He naturally sought construction work.

It took him less than two weeks to find a job as a carpenter with ASIM, a small company with only seven employees. Their specialty was wooden framing for houses. The owner, Hanif Hafeez was a tough, thin, bearded Pakistani native Muslim who was content to earn small wages, enough to feed his family, run his car, and have a little left over to visit the teahouses. Neither political nor educated, Hafeez managed to avoid trouble in a city where trouble can find you. He knew construction work. He spent thirty-five years in the business and had simple desires. He asked for little. To be left alone, to tend to his business and his wife of forty-three years, and to pray as demanded by his faith. They had six children, four boys and two girls, who were married, dead, or living outside Pakistan. Infrequently they gathered as a family, mainly for religious occasions or birthdays. Other than that, he and his wife lead solitary and sparse lives, wanting little and getting little.

The job was perfect. Hafeez asked no background questions, requested no references, and offered small wages. As compensation for the peasant salary, Bilal was permitted to take as many days off as he wanted, without pay, providing the customers didn't complain because their work was delayed. Pakistanis accepted delays as part of their culture. Traditionally, all work was completed days or months after the projected date. Only people of high societal status had their work completed on time. That flexibility precisely fit Bilal's needs to tend to his STN business. Because Hafeez's business was unburdened with deadlines, Bilal could take time off as needed. Hafeez expected little from him. Bilal was happy to comply.

19

MAY 2010:

So many details, so many questions, and so many security issues. These concerns weighed heavily on Ed Walker. He decided to allocate an entire week working in the late evening at home to fine-tune his plan to insure their success. He attacked it with a zeal he never knew he possessed.

Ed enjoyed early May in McLean the best. The lush green manicured lawn of the CIA complex gave him a sense of energy and tranquility. It always reminded him of Fairmount Park in May in Philadelphia. Something about the abundance of deep greens, full bloom flowers, and lush trees made his life's burdens seem smaller and lighter. Because he disliked the April rains, and the pending heat and dryness of June, the contrast from April to May was most satisfying. The view from his office window was postcard perfect. He felt renewed and energized. Plus his STN plans were taking shape. It made him forget Rule 16.

At 9:23 AM Ed dialed the number Farook gave him.

After two rings a woman's voice answered and asked

"What do you need?"

"A cell phone."

"Who wants it?

"Thunder."

"In four days, this coming Tuesday morning, drop your personal cell phone in a toilette or a tub of water. Be sure it is inoperative after its bath. Since you already are a customer, go to the World Link store at 1603 Chain Bridge Road in McLean, bring your broken cell phone, and ask for Sheila. Tell her your friend recommended her. Act as a normal customer, explain what happened and that you decided to upgrade your phone. She will suggest a phone for you. Buy it, and have it activated to your old cell number. Purchase the largest call plan available, with full national coverage. The phone she suggests is secure and diverts all incoming or outgoing calls to a special database that will eliminate any trace of your calls. The World Link software will track your normal cell phone calls and bill you accordingly. Should you lose this phone, call Sheila immediately. She will activate a fail-safe mechanism that will deactivate the secure aspect of the phone. If you need to repair your phone, bring it back only to Sheila."

"Very impressive," offered Ed. "Thanks."

The woman hung up without another word.

"First task completed," he mumbled, pleased and impressed with the efficiency and ease initiating his secure cell phone. His appreciation of the Bankers was geminating and growing like a flower seed, slowly, but forcefully, as though propelled by a magic solution.

Today, it starts.

The following morning Janice awoke before the alarm sounded. She liked starting her day two hours before the kids left for school. The early morning stillness allowed her to do a load of wash, bag lunches for the children, and plan her day without the impending morning chaos. Sometimes she gazed at Ed as he slept before getting out of bed. At times he looked like a beautiful little boy whose only care in the world was if he would catch a fish or get a hit in a sandlot ballgame. Sometimes she felt sexy and wanted a morning quickie. This was the morning.

She wanted sex, immediately. She removed her nightshirt and reached for Ed. Even when in a deep sleep he usually instinctively responded to her touch. This morning was different. He wasn't there.

"Ed?" she called out softly to not wake the children. He came out of the bathroom as if on cue.

"What are you doing up?"

"Couldn't sleep."

"Well, now that you're awake, get back in bed. I want your hot body."

The towel instantly dropped as he leaped into the bed.

"Hello tiger," she coyly said.

"Grrrrrr."

They made love silently, passionately and quickly.

"What a great way to start my day, making love to you," he said to her as she went into the shower.

"Glad you think so," she laughed back.

Spontaneous sex was a huge turn on for him. It made him appreciate and love her even more. He jumped into the shower, got dressed hurriedly, gulped his coffee, and left for work, energetic, confident, and prepared to fulfill his multiplexed life.

Behind closed doors in Langley, he scanned the list of potential cell leader recruits. The list contained no names, just numbers, a phone number, and a lengthy profile of each person. He wasn't sure if they were men or women.

Farook's instructions did not surprise him.

Listed are only a number and a telephone number through which they can reached. Each person has a throw away non-traceable phone. If you do not reach your party after three attempts, no further contact is to be attempted. This candidate is no longer available to you. The person on the other end will answer with their assigned number. Make your decision on which ones you wish to recruit after you talk with them. Every person on the list has the capabilities and the desire to be a part of STN, so you should be able quickly decide on whom you wish to recruit.

Instruct each one to select their code name. Once you have completed your selection, call me with their numbers, code names, and the amount you want placed in their personal account. We will do the rest. We will open a Swiss account under their name with their designated amount. They will receive their passbook in the mail. The rest is up to you. Good luck!

Ed never before had served as an undercover field operative. Farook's instructions thrust him into a new life. The reality suddenly hit him. He was alone. Farook did not want to hear from him except for major issues. The only time he agreed to talk with his cell leaders is when they were actively preparing for a strike.

Janice could no longer be his mentor. There was no one to advise or deter him from making a fool of himself. Moreover, he'd have to be on his guard to insure he didn't accidently spill the beans about STN to Janice, friends, or his co-workers.

He winced from the thought of being alone. Throughout his CIA career, he had the luxury of airing his concerns, problems, and successes with Janice or his fellow workers. That comforting scenario no longer existed. The realization cast an ominous and cloistered feeling of isolation and abandonment. It ripped away his earlier good feelings.

I'll have to live with this, at least until we win, he reluctantly concluded. *I have to get used to making decisions on my own.*

Uncertainty and anxiety renewed their acquaintances.

Tuesday morning Ed "accidentally" dropped his cell phone in the toilette. After several minutes of loud cursing, Janice ran upstairs alarmed at the noise from upstairs.

"What's going on? Are you all right? she questioned, out of breath from climbing the stairs so quickly.

"No, I dropped my phone in the fucking toilette, and it's not alright."

"Is that all? I thought you slit your throat or who knows what the way you were shouting and carrying on. And, the children are still here, so watch your language," she admonished.

"Well, this really pisses me off. Now I have to get a new one and reprogram the damn thing again. What a pain in the ass!"

"What were you doing making a call in the bathroom anyway?"

"I wanted to leave a message for myself at the office to remind me of something I needed to do, that's all."

"Since when don't you remember? You're always on top of those things. I don't get it."

"Yeah you're right; I have so many things on my mind from this new project. I guess I'm a little tired."

"And grumpy too. Don't forget that."

"OK, OK, I get the message. I'll buy a new phone this evening, after work. I might get an upgrade depending on the price. Plan on a late dinner, will you?"

"And this is new?" she jokingly responded.

Satisfied, Ed left for work, feeling that being secretive wasn't that hard. In fact, he rather enjoyed his performance, even if it was at the expense of his trusting wife.

Three projects at work needed his immediate attention. The top priority issues focused on newest money sources used by terrorists. That morning he had to make a verbal presentation to his boss, the Deputy Commissioner, two assistants from the DOD office, and the Attorney General, Julie Melantere. President Schuster recently appointed her and confirmed by a speedy Senate confirmation hearing. She was a well-known and established entity in Washington, and had garnished the trust of both Congressional Democrats and Republicans. Her confirmation hearing and subsequent vote took three rather placid non-confrontational days.

Ed's report addressed the increasing proclivity of terrorists to launder money through drug deals and credit card fraud. The number of incidents was increasing. The FBI and the local police were investigating, with a keen interest from the CIA. The terrorists were concentrating on hiding their money better. Sometimes one of the investigative teams got lucky and uncovered a connection through another investigation. Usually the terrorists remained undetected. Nonetheless, Ed's report was eagerly sought by everyone, if for no other reason that to pick it apart.

After work, he headed to the Tyson's Corner Mall to the World Link store. He easily spotted Shirley. She was the only woman behind the counter. To his chagrin, the store had seven customers in varying stages waiting or engaged with the three clerks behind the counter. Two young males and Sheila busily tried to handle the customers as expeditiously as possible. He took a number to get into the queue, and moseyed around the store looking at the vast selection of wireless cell phones on the market. He marveled at the array of phones displayed and wondered how anyone his age could make a selection. Teenagers knew exactly what they wanted. Somehow, this knowledge escaped people over forty. Talk about a generation gap.

Eleven minutes later Sheila became free, and called his number He wondered how many customers were legitimate, how many were spies and if any were STN.

"Hi, can I help you?" Sheila asked, "My name is Sheila."

"Ed Walker, please to meet you."

She looked to be in her forties, with strands of gray intermingled with her fine straight brown hair. Her stylish eyeglass frames and the company vest made her look slimmer than she was, he speculated. Her brown eyes, slightly pug nose, and thin lips were rather indistinguishable. *One could readily look at her for an hour and still not be able to describe her face, but then who would want to,* Ed amusingly thought.

"A friend of mine said you were knowledgeable and that you would be able to help me make a phone selection, so here I am."

"That's nice to hear. How about telling my boss?" she jokingly responded as she flicked her head towards a short swarthy man sitting by a desk in the corner.

"OK, let's see how you do. I accidentally dropped my phone in the toilette this morning and it's not working. Any way to fix it?"

"Toilette? You must be a confirmed workaholic to have your phone in the bathroom," she smiled.

He shrugged his shoulders as if to say *I really fucked up*. He thought that was a nice touch for anyone who might be listening to their conversation.

"Unfortunately, once these phones get wet, nothing can be done to save them."

"And the numbers I've stored?"

"Gone."

"Damn."

"You need a new phone. Anything in particular you have in mind?"

"I was thinking of upgrading my phone. I'd like to see the top of the line. One that's easy to use. I want national coverage, too."

"Actually, we just introduced a new World Link phone that has full US and Canada coverage, and you can have extended International coverage too. With this phone, you can call Europe and the Middle East for a small monthly fee."

"That's interesting," Ed exclaimed.

"How much is it?"

"$295. Includes a two year national and international subscription. You get one month of free domestic use, a home and auto charger, and a belt carrying case. After the first month, there's a flat charge of $99 per month for unlimited national and 100 International minutes, with anytime usage. That means the rate is the same for peak or off peak hours. It that what you had in mind, sir?" she asked while looking directly in his eyes. The intensity in her eyes told him to say yes.

"Yes. Sounds perfect."

You can fill out the paperwork while I activate your phone. I'll put in a fully charged battery so you can use it within the hour. Do you want the same number as your other phone? We can give you a new one if you like."

"No, I want my same number, please."

"OK. Might I suggest that you purchase a spare battery? It will make your life much easier."

"How much does that cost?"

"$58."

"OK, throw it in."

"Since you're already a subscriber, let me check your records and we'll activate your phone with your old number."

"Great."

His information popped up immediately on the screen.

"It's all here. Give me about five minutes," Sheila said.

He sat at the counter stool to fill out the paperwork Sheila handed to him. Six minutes later, she appeared from the back with a box containing all his goodies.

"How would you like to pay, Mr. Walker?" she asked, checking his paperwork.

"American Express."

"The total is $380.92 including Uncle Sam's share."

She gave him a three-minute primer of the use of the phone basics to "cover you until you have had a chance to read the manual. I recommend you rotate the batteries to keep both batteries fresh."

Ed recognized Sheila was telling him to check the battery compartment for any hidden notes. She processed his credit card, he signed the receipt, thanked Sheila for her efforts, and left.

That night he became familiar with the intricacies of his new phone. Beneath the battery, there was a note from Sheila.

"The software is highly sophisticated and doesn't require a prompt or code to be secure. Just dial. Your outgoing and inbound calls from STN phones will disappear. Destroy this message after you read it. The toilette works for you. Ha-Ha."

He shredded the note and tossed it into the toilette.

After his favorite dinner of pork loin, sweet potato and broccoli, he explained to Janice he needed an hour in his den-office to finish some work. Then he'd be hers for the night.

"Tell me another tall tale, will you Sinbad?" She tossed a cynical look his way.

"I'm guessing you're trying to get out of helping the kids with their homework."

He knew she would be upstairs with the kids for an hour, which would give him the opportunity to use his new phone from his home office without fear of being overheard, or questioned.

"God, you're so smart. Can't get anything over on you, can I?" he shot back.

Later that evening he visited the bathroom, cell phone in hand. At precisely 10:45 PM, he dialed Farook.

He said "THUNDER" and hung up. It was his signal that his cell phone was secure and his code name was Thunder.

He appreciated the sophistication of the Bankers. It inspired and gave him added confidence. He was thrilled to see how detail oriented they were. In some way, his admiration for the Bankers and Farook lessened his own skittishness. The next two evenings, with Janice's tacit approval to do some "CIA work," Ed worked an hour on his STN plan.

Another evening, well after Janice went upstairs to sleep, he toiled for an additional two hours before he grew tired and joined Janice in their bedroom. He wanted to continue, but knew he had to pace himself. He listened to the logical side of his brain. He knew significant STN work remained that would demand his attention, attention he was anxious to satisfy. His concern that he might fall behind made him feel insecure. Farook demanded his team to be ready, even though he intimated it would be a year away. Still, he felt he needed more planning hours. Finding them would be a challenge.

The scary side of his mind forced him to question the wisdom of working from home on STN. His was a secret and dangerous mission. He wondered what would happen if Janice inadvertently discovered he was working on non-related CIA work. Once she sensed something unusual was happening, he knew he could not withstand her intense questioning. He knew the more he denied her, the more determined and angry she would become, and the weaker his defenses. He never doubted her questioning skills. There were times that he thought she would be a great lawyer. She would get the information she wanted, even with the toughest of them. What chance did he have? He felt nervous and apprehensive. A rapid series of spurious questions rattled within his brain

If Janice ever learns what I'm doing, she would be hysterical and become vulnerable. Am I jeopardizing my family by working at home? If I allow every doubt to infect my mind, only bad things can happen. They usually do.

He uneasily dismissed these troubling thoughts. The hard part, the hidden part, the part he knew but would not accept, was that his fears would remain part of him for the rest of his life.

Each week his plans became more refined and began to take positive shape. He was pleased. Ed decided that he would establish eight to ten cells, strategically located in San Francisco, Denver, Miami, Boston, Dallas, Detroit, Philadelphia, Washington DC, and Montreal, Canada, with the possibility of two or three cells added later. Determining the finances needed to start operations was more complex. He had no intention of asking Farook for additional funds more than once. He projected his cash needs over two years, including a detailed list for each six-month period. He determined the fifteen million dollars in his Swiss bank account was enough to meet his operational needs for recruiting and training his team for at least a year and a half and possibly two.

He smiled, in spite of his nervousness. On one hand, the Bankers were powerful, highly organized, and able to make things happen. On the other hand, any group that powerful demands great respect and even greater caution.

The Bankers have their shit together. They must be highly experienced businesspeople. How else, he reasoned, *could they have estimated my costs so accurately.*

He estimated that the Bankers probably committed $150 to $200 million dollars to fund STN. He wondered if the Bankers were alone or had other silent partners, perhaps even the US or other global governments. He wouldn't put it past President Schuster to authorize clandestine support for STN. It was within his purview to do so. He decided to stay alert for clues that might provide the answers to his suspicions. Not that he really cared. His CIA training had prepared him for this job, perhaps too well. His fine-tuned diagnostic capabilities made him confident he would discover the truth, someday. Yet, he questioned whether it was something he really wanted to know.

Too much information can be deadly!

Once the basic structure of his organization was completed, the next task was to hire his team. He carefully examined each person's profile, and selected the ten men he wanted as team leaders. Armed with only their assigned number, a cell number, and their profile, he made his selection based on a combination of their qualifications, his gut instinct, and the phone conversation he had with each one. Once selected, the cell leaders would have to recruit their own team members. Farook said he would provide a list of possible recruits when Ed was ready.

By the end of the week, he finished his selections. All ten cell leaders eagerly accepted his offer and selected their code names. He sent the list of numbers and code names to Farook and distributed the STN rules to his cell leaders. The North American STN Regional organization was now set. According to the rules, each man had to have a job that allowed them to blend into their communities, just as Farook instructed. He felt a twinge of jealously. His leaders had their members to interact with as they set up each strike. He remained alone and isolated, except when he needed to discuss potential targets and dates of a strike with them.

His team in place, he and his ten leaders begin to develop their list of potential targets and supporters, done by encrypted phone, late at night or early in the morning. Only the eleven of them knew the names of the potential targets. Ed determined his team would need about two or three months to complete their surveillance of the selected target, devise an extermination plan, and implement the training for each strike. He was happy to rely on Farook to provide the backup information on each target.

Slowly he acknowledged his actions and his thinking processes were aligning with STN and the Bankers. They remained a phantom group of wealthy patrons who committed multi millions of dollars to insure that global freedom would endure. That was good enough for him.

He constantly uttered his newly invoked leadership mantra:

Pay attention to the smallest detail. Think security at all times. Get results.

He could hardly wait to start. Still, he subconsciously struggled with Rule 16.

20

MAY 2010:

President Shuster never created a committee he didn't like.

His legacy was fast becoming a standard joke within his administration due to his favorite political maneuver, the creation of committees. He used this technique so frequently that the press began to refer to him as "Meeting Man," a characterization he seemed to enjoy. To his thinking, this was the best way to bring together diverse or warring groups within the government to resolve issues or to advance one of his favorite programs. His reward was immediate: Heavy media praise, accolades from his party supporters, and little risk. Since the beginning of his term as President in January 2009 he had created four committees in his first eight months in office.

Throughout the history of the US, one irrefutable fact that every President learned quickly. Most committees did little harm to the country because the public expected little from them. Once the hoopla of their creation faded, so did the actions of the committee. They published few reports, they held few meetings, and waited for the media coverage to vanish. No one was accountable. No one cared.

Members of the defunct committee returned to their home base, happy to identify with a new cause with which they had no involvement, no commitment, and little interest. Yet Congressional members readily signed up whenever the opportunity arose, mostly for political reasons. During re-election time, members trotted out their membership lists of committee names like boy scout merit badges to prove their involvement with issues important to the country or their constituents. In this game the score was always the same: committee one, public zero. The committee got the glory. The public paid the bills.

"What better way than a committee?" the President spoke as he typed his idea on his laptop.

"What we need is one that will resonate with the public. I'll call it *The Public Development Committee.* Their mission will be to suggest ways to stabilize and tweak the US economy. The public will love my commitment to fund public projects. This committee's focus will be on the US economy and improving our infrastructure. I can pattern it after the Peace Envoys, but it will focus on domestic issues. Has a good ring to it. The unions will love it!"

The more he thought about it the better he liked it. It took less than three minutes to convince himself how wonderful his latest committee would play to the public.

"Judi," he buzzed her on the intercom.

"Yes, Mr. President."

"Ask Senator Crossings to come to my office tomorrow morning between 9:30 and noon, whenever suits her schedule. Clear my schedule to accommodate hers. I'll need about an hour. Also, I want to dictate a memo to her before tomorrow's meeting."

"Certainly, Mr. President. Be right in."

"Call her first."

The President printed his thoughts on his office printer.

Several minutes later Judi informed him that Senator Crossings would arrive at 10:45.

"You had a briefing on the events in Serbia scheduled. Apparently nothing of great importance is happening, I pushed that into next week," she informed him.

"Good. I'm ready now."

She took her seat next to the President's desk, notebook in hand.

"Internal Memo to Senator Karen Crossings:

Karen,

We need a committee to recommend ways for us to boost the economy, and I want you to head it. I want a mix of corporate leaders, equal members of Congress from both parties, a representative from the intelligence community and Timothy Barrows, Chairman of the Peace Envoys. Work with Hannah Goldfarb in Justice to make the committee selections. I'm calling it *The Public Development Committee*. Has a nice ring to it, don't you think?" he nodded to Judi.

"I like it a lot, Mr. President."

"Good. Let's continue."

"This committee will define ways to divert funds from outdated defense or domestic activities into projects to keep our economy strong and competitive. I know we're funding some useless projects and I want you to recommend which ones to drop. Of course we need a replacement activity for the saved money. We'll handle the political fallout later. I want maximum media coverage and lots of press on this one. I'll announce the committee's creation after I approve the member list and everyone has agreed to participate. Be sure you invite some of our major corporate supporters like Steve Kepplingar of Boeing, Wilson Hanford of IBM, Dr. Aidan Turnaski from Health and Human Services, and five Congressional representatives from both sides of the aisle. I suspect a committee of about twenty-five will suffice.

Tomorrow we'll discuss the details. I'd like a preliminary list of your recommendations in two weeks.

Alan."

They met the next morning as President Schuster detailed his expectations of the committee. Their meeting lasted sixteen minutes.

Senator Crossings scurried off to compile her list of potential members. Eager to please the President, she had her preliminary list ready for approval six days later. It took three weeks for him to review the list.

"Let's see whom you've selected," as he perused her two-page typed list.

"Hmm. I see our corporate friends agreed. Kind-a thought they would," he chuckled. "Good choices from Congress, especially Kayla Pittman. She's a real worker and smart. Has a good following in the House. They're all good choices, Senator. One addition. Ask the Secretary of Treasurer Osterweiss, to appoint someone from his office."

He continued to scan the list and stopped to ask a question.

"Ed Walker? Who the hell is he and why him?"

"Ed Walker is with the CIA, Foreign Services, and has done an excellent job tracking down the International terrorist's cash flow. He's helped us shut down the holdings of Asbat al-Amar from Lebanon, and the Egyptian Islamic

Takfir wal-Hijra. I feel his expertise in tracking money will be an asset to the committee, me, and to you. We can rely on him to watchdog the cash flow of the Committee. I suspect he'd be very interested in participating. Should help us to avoid the normal pitfalls of other committees who screw up their funding, and then cause a stir in Congress when the GAO investigates them. That's one problem we can put to bed right now, sir."

"I knew there's a reason I selected you for this task. I can always count on you to cover my ass. What about Barrows?"

"He agreed, of course," Senator Crossings chuckled. "Did you expect anything less?"

"No, I didn't." President Schuster smiled back.

"I like your selections. Thanks. This committee should be fun. The public clamors for us to stop congressional wasteful spending. We'll give them what they want."

"Yes, Mr. President, I agree. It should be fun. Maybe we can do some good too. Thank you."

"OK. Let's get this thing started. Somehow, I believe this committee might be a winner."

"Has the makings of one. The members are the best and brightest, and if they can learn to work together, you could come out a big winner."

"If this one goes, do you think the press will still call me Meeting Man?" Crossings shrugged her shoulders, smiled and placed her hands in a praying hands posture. Schuster's stomach shook from laughter.

"Don't want to touch that one, eh?"

She smiled.

"Keep me posted on your progress."

"Yes, Mr. President." She left the Oval Office.

Senator Karen Cynthia Crossings had become a favorite of both sides of Congress. A two-term Republican Senator from Oregon, friends and foe alike recognized her as a tough negotiator, but one who displayed a remarkable openness to ideas. Her powers of persuasion were legendary in an institution noted for its silver-tongued strong-armed members.

What she lacked in height and looks she more than compensated with intelligence and a fierce determination. Standing tiptoed, and by tilting her head to the maximum she laid claim to being 5 feet tall. In actuality, 4'11" was a stretch. She endeared herself to Congress as a junior Senator when, during a heated debate with Barry Shuttle, the 6'4" powerful majority whip for the Democratic Senate, she demanded a temporary pause in the debate for 7 minutes. Everyone assumed she needed a body function break, and were startled to see her dragging a wooden side chair behind her. She placed the chair beside Shuttle, stood on the chair, looked him in his eyes and announced,

"Now we can talk, Senator!"

The room resonated with laughter, so much so they almost adjourned without resolving the debate. Shuttle laughed so hard he almost came to tears.

"You win, Senator, you win!" he sputtered between laughs.

"Not until we finish." She remained on the chair, standing defiantly, for the next six minutes. It didn't matter to her that she won the argument. She wanted to express her views in front of her Congressional peers. For one of the few times in many years, Congress worked together without animosity or the debilitating and counterproductive atmosphere that bipartisanship compromise and humor offer.

From that moment her congressional colleagues affectionately called her "Eye to Eye" Crossings. She was the darling of the Senate. Her ability to understand both the Democratic and the Republican sides of issues, and to tirelessly and diligently work towards a bipartisan solution, made people forget her height limitations and her junior status in Congress. Over the years, as she progressed to a senior role after three landslide reelections, her power and charm gained admirers throughout the country.

She began the arduous task of soliciting the potential members to join her committee. She expected and received no resistance to participate. Some people might decline a Presidential request; no one dared to refuse "Eye to Eye." The first meeting was at the Presidential Plaza in Washington.

Senator Crossings, her slightly graying brown hair peeking from the tightly pulled ponytail hair, opened the meeting. She usually dressed in a tailored suit, a colorful shirt, matching medium high heels, and always made a favorable fashion impression. Divorced, no children, fiercely independent, she owned a modest townhouse in Alexandra, VA and drove the eight traffic filled miles to her office in her black 2007 Toyota Prius. She preferred to use a portable lavaliere microphone for public speaking. She never used a lecture podium. She felt it made her look small.

Growing up in a tough neighborhood of Chicago, being small meant you were destined to suffer from bullies, unless you stood up for your rights. She learned early to act big, think and talk big. Like a king cobra that expands its hood when angry, Karen Crossing waved her arms wildly to intimidate her antagonists. Sometimes it actually worked.

The *Public Development Committee* convened in the Truman room. Among those attending were Ed Walker, Jeanine Leatherman, VP of STR, an energy conservation group, Ellis Waxman, President of Waxman Enterprises, a software simulator company, Tim Barrows, Ethel Tarvechkian, CFO of

Ambreset, a manufacturer of high frequency communications jamming devises, and Killian F. Mankus, CEO International Metals Inc., ten Congressmen, and nine other educators, religious and charity leaders.

After the formal introductions of all twenty-five members were completed, Crossings addressed the attendees.

"Thanks for coming. You represent the most trusted, knowledgeable, and experienced leaders of our economy and our society. You have intimate knowledge of the good and bad issues of our country, and, equally as important, the deficiencies in governmental programs about which you've been complaining for a while."

Nods of agreement and smirks quickly spread through the room.

"You understand the impact these issues have on our economy and our global image. With that in mind, it's incumbent on us to analyze the current Washington projects that need trimming or cancelled. The earlier spread of terrorism, coupled with some disastrous domestic policies from the previous administration, has created a ton of unhappy people in Washington, in the business world, and with our citizens."

Laughter and nods of agreement again rippled through the room. Karen smiled, as she usually did when she achieved the effect she wanted. This time she wanted everyone to understand she both understood the issues and felt the same as they.

"President Schuster would like to streamline our budget, rebuild our infrastructure, and bring back some economic sanity by eliminating useless or bad press spending."

More laughter.

"We understand that we cannot operate without full cooperation of everyone involved. Without cooperation, we will surely fail. We have all seen that, haven't we? As part of our group, we also have Tim Barrows, Chairman of the Peace Envoys, who brings his foreign experience to help us avoid domestic policy pitfalls that could have International implications. Too often we have operated as though we live in a vacuum and what we do on our soil will not impact other countries or economies.

Each of you has a green book handout. It contains a list of the members of our committee, a brief profile, and their areas of expertise. This will help you become acquainted with your subcommittee members.

When you were "TOLD", I... eh...mean, "INVITED" (she emphasized the two words while smiling at her audience) to join this committee (more laughter), our mission is to identify the obstacles we face in the US over the next decade, and recommend programs or methods to minimize their impact. Our intent is to recommend long-term solutions that will reshape the United States economy into an economic powerhouse, one that will solve our current and future problems, provide maximum security, and reestablish our global leadership.

I understand this is a huge task, but that is precisely why you have been hand picked by the President. You have our future in your hands, and the President and I have the confidence that you will succeed. And, we WILL succeed, that I promise."

A round of applause followed. Eye to Eye had done what she normally does; create an atmosphere of cooperation and enthusiasm.

"I've assigned each of you to a subcommittee. Let's take a short break and convene in your respective breakout rooms noted in your handouts. Look for your sub committee assignments on page two of your handout. If you feel we have misplaced you, or you wish to work on a different committee, please let me know and we'll work it out. For the remainder of today and tomorrow morning, I'd like each committee to identify the problem areas in your area of expertise, and make a list of preliminary recommendations for their solutions. Those will be the starting points for future discussions. Let's use this time strictly for brainstorming. We'll sort them out later. Any questions?"

There was none.

"I've made arrangements for us to have lunch and breakfast tomorrow morning as a group, and I promise you'll enjoy the selections. No rubber chickens!"

Laughter.

"By the way, you're on your own for dinner. One final item before we break. I've listed several potential meeting dates for us to meet again as a group. I know everyone is busy, so I suggest we meet twice a year. Sub committees should set your own agendas and timeframes for your own meetings. The important thing is to apply some energy and thinking to what needs to be changed, along with your recommendations for new programs. There's no excuse about being too busy. We all are. But, this is so important to out future well being, I believe we can find some time to move our country forward. Most of you already have voiced your...eh... OPINIONS, as she emphasized the word, about what are wrong and what needs to be changed. Here's your opportunity to address them and dictate a new direction for our country.

Please respond by email within the next several weeks on your availability for the suggested meeting dates. If not, I'd appreciate three or four substitute dates. I'll let everyone know which dates work after I receive your input. Again, each sub committee should set your own agenda as you see fit. Thanks again for your support, and let's have a great meeting. Lunch is served in the adjacent room."

At lunch, Ed Walker turned to Barrows.

"Join me for a drink after the meeting? It seems we're on the same subcommittee."

"Well... alright. Right after we break for dinner will work." Barrows didn't seem interested, but still agreed.

"OK. What about dinner?" Ed asked.

"No, I'd rather not,"

"Some other time then?" responded Walker.

Barrows indifferently nodded his head.

Snooty bastard. Screw him. I'm sorry I asked.

The subcommittees continued their brainstorming ideas, finished for the day at 4:15, and promised to start early the following day to finish before they made their presentation to the full committee.

"See you in the lobby bar," Ed reminded Barrows. Barrows nodded his agreement. He looked bored as he announced,

"I'll be there shortly. Have to make an important call."

Ed headed for the bar, found an empty table and ordered a Vodka martini with two olives.

I hope the son-of-a bitch doesn't keep me waiting. He's an arrogant shit. I wonder how the President could've selected him for this committee. He's libel to start a war before he gets anything done.

Barrows entered the bar twelve minutes later, spotted Ed and sat in a chair opposite him. Rather than face him directly, he sat at an angle slightly away from Ed's face. It spoke volumes to Ed. To him, Barrows was saying,

I'm more important than you. You should feel honored that I agreed to meet. I know you don't have anything important to say. Let's get this over with.

Ed's anger made him nervous. His muscles tensed and he placed his left hand beneath the table to hide his clenched fist. As always, his right hand worked its way to the back of his neck.

Stay cool he reminded himself. *He's not worth creating a scene, not now, not here. The shit can't even face me!*

Barrows ordered an expensive glass of Chateau Margaux wine from the waitress.

"How long were you with Homeland Security before you became Chairman of the Envoys?" asked Ed as cordially as his anger would allow.

The right side of Barrows mouth said "Three years. And you?"

"Over twenty. Congratulations on your appointment to the committee."

"Thanks."

"Have any ideas that'll make a difference?" Ed asked, trying to act friendly.

"Of course. I have some excellent ideas that can make a big difference to the country."

Arrogant prick. He deserves to be on my hit list. I'd love to put his name at the top of my list. Farook wouldn't approve. Not that I need his approval, but he would consider the Chairman of the Peace Envoys off limits.

"How do things look on the terrorist front, you know, from Homeland Security's viewpoint?" Ed asked.

Barrows moved his chair to face Walker once his interest was aroused.

"I don't like all their policies, but you've got to respect them for trying. The fact that people think they're doing a crappy job tells me a lot. Of course, its none of my business any longer, is it? What do you do at the Agency?"

"Tracking terrorist bank funds."

"Really? I thought they were avoiding banks and using cash."

"Well... that's true for the biggies, but not for the minor groups."

Barrows locked eyes with Ed and began to say something before he changed his mind. A noticeable sneer crossed his face.

"So, what good are...eh... I guess it's important to track them all, isn't it? If I was in your position, I would have made the 'biggies' my top priority. I guess everyone sees things differently."

I hate you, you arrogant bastard. You should be the first STN target. Too fucking bad you're not a terrorist! I don't need a piece of shit like you passing judgment on me or my work. Typical HSD attitude. They think no one is as important as them.

Ed allowed himself a brief moment of immense satisfaction as he mused on the possibility of Barrows' gunfire death.

If he knew, he'd shit in his pants. He talks big. With a gun at his head he'd change his fucking tune. Perhaps I'll ask Farook to look into this arrogant asshole. I might have a real reason to wipe his ass off the planet.

Controlling himself, Ed calmly replied,

"Terrorists are terrorists. They all deserve an equal opportunity to be investigated and stopped, not just the big ones. Even small groups kill people and blow up our soldiers and our buildings. What would you prefer? That the government stick their head in the sand and pretend they don't exist or they're not worthy of our attention?" shot back an angry Ed Walker.

"To each his own. I feel the government needs to look in earnest at al Qaeda and the Taliban, not the little terrorists who don't amount to crap!" Barrows was noticeably annoyed.

"Are you saying that the CIA hasn't been trying to learn about them too?"

"Not to my satisfaction," Barrows sneered again.

You're even more arrogant and egotistical than I thought! I've seen people like you before. Rich, powerful, self-serving. I'll enjoy nothing more than to see your colorless face when you learn that I will soon insure that our democracy survives. That would make me happy! I hope you're still alive to see my success, asshole.

Barrows glanced at his watch and suddenly stood up.

"Got to run. Do you mind paying the bill?"

"Sure, why not?" Ed disgustingly looked at him.

"Thanks. See you around."

Barrows walked away in disgust, thinking,

I'm glad to get away from that idiot. He's like all the other government dredges, Happy to be paid for being a follower and willing to accept a paycheck for being slovenly and lazy. Not my job, he said. People like him screw the government. They don't care. All they want is to be paid and retire on a fat pension, neither of which they earned. Lazy fucking bastard. We wouldn't be in this position if he had the guts to take the initiative against real terrorists.

Walker continued his own thoughts on Barrows.

He'd check on the biggies, my ass! He acts as if his shit doesn't stink. If he knew with whom he was talking, he wouldn't be so fucking arrogant. I've seen government people like him. He does everything that benefits him. If something goes wrong, he blames someone else. I don't trust that prick. If he thinks he's going to pick my brain and take the credit, he has another thought coming. He's all talk, and damn sneaky too. He shouldn't be working on this committee, or even with the Envoys. He still deserves to die. He's one man I truly despise!

Government drone, thought Barrows.

Arrogant asshole, thought Walker.

The next morning they were silently cordial. It was obvious to the other committee members they disliked each other immensely. In spite of this distraction, the sub committee did their work. They made their action list and recommendations.

Chairwoman Senator Crossing presented them to the full committee in the afternoon. One member charted the collective ideas on 2-foot by 4-foot paper note pad mounted on an easel. The taped sheets on the wall represented the complete work of the committee for the two days. Senator Crossing promised the entire list from each subcommittee would be typed and sent by email to the Committee members within a week. She reminded the chairperson of the five sub committees to hold their own meetings to work on open items.

Ed and Barrows grudgingly nodded goodbye to each other. They left the meeting with a foul taste in their mouth. Each hoped they wouldn't have to see or work with the other again. They never did. Though their subcommittee met three more times, both men's travel plans prevented their attending the same meeting. Each felt relieved to learn of the other's absence, with good reason. They vehemently despised each other.

21

MAY 2010:

Thursday, on the way home, Janice called and asked him to pick up dinner at the market. Ed preferred to eat her home cooked meals, but reluctantly agreed. The market had a full salad bar and various cooked entrees for the overworked, over stressed, or the laziest who weren't cooking that evening. She wanted a Caesar salad, a rotisserie chicken, and a melon of his choice. He decided to get cantaloupe, but finding one ripe to eat tonight posed a challenge. As he ritualistically squeezed and shook each yellow-skinned melon in search of *the* one, he heard a seductive female voice.

"You're doing such a good job of squeezing those melons that it makes a girl tremble."

Ed wheeled around to confront the voice and found an attractive blonde-haired woman dressed in a tight fitting pink sweat suit, hair in a ponytail, and a wicked smile on her face. While Ed was fumbling for words, she continued,

"Ed, Ed Walker? I though I saw you enter the market. Remember me? Liz Hunter, from Brussels. In April?"

"How could anyone forget you? How've you been? Weren't you involved in a big sale in Brussels?' he innocently asked. His words were friendly, but his thoughts were on the image of her in Brussels. Stunning and sexy then. Stunning and sexy now.

"I was, got the order, and received a huge bonus too. Do the terrorists have something to fear these days?" she said mockingly, her words cloaked in a seductive shell. Or was it his imagination? He wasn't sure, but it was always great to fantasize about a sexy woman.

"You never called. Why not? Aren't I attractive enough?" she challenged him.

"Well… you know I'm married and …"

"I'm attracted to handsome married men. You fit the bill," she whispered. She gave him her best bedroom-eyes look. She stood there, her lips parted slightly, sensuously, moist, and begging for a kiss.

He was aroused. He suddenly wanted to be with her, to hold her, to smell her, to make love to her. He wanted her, now. He no longer thought of STN, work, or Janice. Lust was in his pants, more intensely than he expected.

"Who am I to deny you your pleasure? Give me your number again. I'll call you from work tomorrow. I promise."

He wanted to stay and talk with her, but feared someone might see them together.

She removed her business card from her Gucci purse, handed it to him and said "Call between 10 and 12" and walked away, without looking back. Ed had to restrain himself from chasing after her.

He managed to finish shopping and drive home without having an accident. In one instant of time, he felt renewed. It didn't matter that he would soon be ordering the death of many people. It didn't matter that he was married to the love of his life. Nothing was more important than possessing Liz Hunter. Nothing could be more exciting.

"Hi, honey, did you get everything? I'm starved and so are the kids," Janice asked when he came in the door.

"Yeah, it's all here. I could eat a horse," he managed to utter. He wasn't sure how they escaped from his lips.

Tomorrow. Tomorrow, Tomorrow.

He ate, lost in his fantasy of Liz. He barely talked.

"Are you alright?' Janice inquired. "You're out of it. Anything wrong?"

"No, just thinking about work, that's all. Sorry for being such a s..." he stopped before he said shit in front of the kids.

It was the longest night he had experienced in a while. Sound sleep was out of the question. He visualized Liz and him making furious and consuming love. Sleep or no, nothing could prevent him from being with her tomorrow.

A quick shower, no breakfast, and an automatic drive to work started his day. He fiddled with papers all morning, anxiously glancing at his watch so frequently that it pretended to ignore him.

I should wait until a little before 12, just to make her a little hungry. She's the one who made the first move. She's probably just as anxious as I am. A little uncertainty will make her want me even more, he reasoned. *On the other hand, she might leave thinking I'm not coming.*

At quarter to ten, he pulled her card from his wallet and stated at the number. He already had committed it to memory, but he wanted the card in front of him. The digital clock moved to 10:00. He picked up the phone and punched in her number. Three rings later, there was no answer. His heart began beating fast.

Perhaps I misread her. Maybe she was just toying with me, just flirting, or teasing me as some women like to do.

By the fifth ring, he felt foolish. He started to hang up the phone when he heard a voice, her voice.

"Don't hang up. Sorry I was on the phone with my boss. He wanted to talk about an account. I'm soooo glad I caught you," she seductively extended the word.

"Me too, I was beginning to feel you didn't want to get together."

"You didn't believe me?" she asked incredulously.

They agreed to meet at her house in Vienna at eleven-thirty. She gave him the directions and said seductively,

"I can't wait."

"Me neither." He disconnected the call and buzzed Alice.

"Alice, I'm leaving at eleven. I'll probably be back between two and three. I think my calendar is clear. In case I missed something, reschedule it for tomorrow. Thanks."

He tidied up his desk and locked his working files in the wall safe. Fifty minutes later, he was driving towards Vienna. To Liz. The 50 miles per hour speed limit annoyed him, but resisted the temptation to push the accelerator to the floor.

What the hell am I doing? I'm skipping work to have an affair with... who? Who is she? Why am I so attracted to her? Do I want to do this to Janice? I swore I would never sleep with another woman, and here I am. Am I stupid or what? he questioned. The lack of an answer didn't stop his foot from pressing the gas pedal.

Twenty-six minutes later, he pulled up into her driveway. It was a single, white aluminum siding two-story structure, colonial style, with blue shutters on both levels. A soft blue copula sat defiantly at the peak of the house, with a heavy brass rooster weather vane seemingly directing traffic. *Modest landscaping, but in good taste*, he observed. He recognized the wispy butterfly bushes, the miniature weeping cherry and arborvitae trees. A bordering flowerbed showed the remnants of the summer bloom. Most of the flowers had withered in the heat of early August and September. Brown spots of dying grass threatened the green of her lawn. That summer, rainfall was barely a tenth of an inch throughout the Virginia area. Virginia Governor Brad Poynter declared a state emergency in June because of the lack of rainfall. Watering lawns and washing cars were limited to once a week. To complicate matters, a persistent heat wave of 90 degrees or more had gripped the Eastern seaboard for thirteen straight days.

He parked, rushed out of his car and hastily leaped the two steps leading to a small open porch.

There's still time, he thought. *Just turn around and get the hell out of here!* Nobody was listening.

The natural cherry wood double doors, with their curved window glass inserts at the top gave the house an air of elegance. The focal point of the front of the house was the highly polished elaborate brass door handles.

A large purple post-it note caught his eye.

Door is open. Find me.

His lust, already threatening to explode, nearly took his breath away. He fumbled with the door latch, flung the door open, slid into the well-appointed hallway, and closed the door behind him.

The interior was well coordinated, tastefully done with an eye towards harmony and comfort in a warm and soothing manner. Her white furniture accented the light lavender painted living room. Several red accent lamps graced two small tables. Lithographic artworks and figurines completed the décor. A three-picture grouping of original oil and watercolor paintings depicting French urban scenes lavishly adorned the walls. Although beautiful to see, it was not what he had in mind.

He quickly panned the living room and the kitchen. No Liz. He moved throughout the rooms like a big cat stalking its prey. The sunken family room was empty, as was the den. Neither revealed the elusive Liz Hunter.

Upstairs. So, she likes to play games, does she? He smiled.

The dark wooden steps in the hallway led upstairs. He bounded the steps two at a time, the scent of his prey tantalizing his nostrils.

A door slightly ajar caught his eye. He gently pushed it open. There was his treasure, standing by a full-length mirror. He saw both the front and the back of her luscious body at the same time. Her sandy blond hair hung loosely about her face. She was wearing only three things. A seductive smile, high black strapped shoes with 5" heels, and a clear plastic wrap. His eyes riveted on her body and her image in the mirror. She had meticulously wrapped herself in clear plastic wrap. His eyes sensuously feasted on her feminine curves and well toned body. Large breasts, larger than what he expected from the clothes she wore, billowed out from her body. Her brown-reddish nipples, already erect, projected from two perfectly formed white breasts. Tan bikini lines accentuated her breasts and her groin. Big breasts and tan lines were a major turn on for him. Clean-shaven, she sported a tattoo of a silver-green fire-breathing dragon pointed towards her hairless crotch. She had it all. He wasn't so sure of the dragon.

He scanned her hourglass body. His eyes focused on the dragon, whose open claws seemed to cling to her tanned sexy legs. He examined the mirror view of her from the back. There he found a well-shaped ass, shapely shoulders, and exquisitely long legs. Her bikini lines barely covered her crack.

"Found me, didn't you?"

"I think I died and went to heaven."

"Well?" she teased, encouraging him to make his move.

Without a word, he took a few steps into her waiting arms. They kissed passionately. Long, wet, and fierce. He tried to rip the wrap from her body, but failed.

"Hold here," she said pointing to one end of the plastic wrap.

She began a slow spin as though she was a concept car perched on a rotating platform. Only she was the car, the platform, and the beautiful model, wrapped in one. Her movements were slow, sensuous, and exciting. Each movement allowed his eyes to devour her luscious body from every angle. Ed was near ecstasy as she tantalized him, slow turn by slow turn. Finally, after two and one half spins, the wrap released and he tossed it aside. They quickly came together locked in a scorching kiss. She helped him out of his clothes while they continued welding their lips together.

The next two hours they spent making love, giggling, holding each other, caring neither about the time nor about the problems of the world. What mattered was this moment. They locked their bodies together, their passion enflamed though their mutual and intense sexual attraction.

"You're incredible," Ed said to her. "I have never been with anyone so sensual and so accomplished at making love."

"You're no slouch either, stamina man," she giggled.

"You bring out the best in me," was Ed's smiling reply.

"It's my talent," she laughed.

"When can we get together again? I have to get back to work. It's getting late."

"So, is this a case of fuck and run? I never pegged you as that kind of guy."

That brought out a hardy belly laugh from them both.

"At least I haven't over eaten," he joked. "I'd like to see you again, Liz. Is that in the cards?"

"It's definitely in my plans. But here's the deal. I like married men mostly because there's no pressure for commitment. I don't want to be committed. I have important goals that I want to achieve. For me, this is a sexual relationship only. I don't want you to leave your wife. I don't want your money. I don't want romantic weekends away, and I don't want long phone conversations. I travel quite a bit, I eat at exclusive restaurants, and I like my space after a hard week of work. A relaxed dinner, some nice conversation and great fucking is my limit. I won't call you to chat. Don't call me except to set a time and place for us to meet. If you're comfortable with that, we can get together as much as our schedules allow. Honestly, you really turn me on, and I know you're turned on by me, aren't you?" She looked at him not expecting an answer.

"Slow down, that's a lot to digest. But...yes, sounds perfect," he chuckled.

"I can't think of a better arrangement. A beautiful, sexy, independent and exciting woman wants to use me as a sex toy. Who could pass that up? Unfortunately, I really have to get back to work."

"Thanks for an exciting lunch," she said. "I'm back to Europe to kick off another campaign. Might be away three to four weeks. Call me in a month."

"Can't wait," he responded exuberantly.

Ed dressed, kissed her a lingering goodbye, and left. On the drive back to McLean, he reflected on the events of his life for the past six months.

I attend a conference in Brussels, became part of an organization that will save the world, and I just fucked a magnificent love machine. Best of all, she wants no complications or emotional involvement. I love my life. This is great!

Not only did he not feel guilty about being with Liz, but he also acknowledged she added another layer to his already complex life. He had just cheated on his wife, and could not wait to do it again. Now he had two things he had to keep secret. STN and Liz.

22

EVIAN SANDERS, MAY 2010:

Bruce called Bilal to tell him of his travel arrangements. Bilal promised to meet him at the Karachi Jinnah International airport. The day of his arrival, Bilal rented a truck and drove to the airport to meet Bruce at the Eastern Satellite, the International facility. The plane was nearly three hours late.

Jinnah is the largest airport in Pakistan. Built in 1992 at an estimated 100 million dollars, it was beautiful, clean, modern, and secure.

The loading bridge was steered into place as soon as the plane arrived at the gate. When Bruce appeared in the doorway of the terminal, Bilal casually waved his arms so Bruce would more easily spot him among the crowd. It wasn't necessary. Only twenty some people were waiting for the plane's arrival.

They man-hugged, each filled with the mutual admiration and friendship that was missing from their lives. They retrieved the luggage from the baggage area and headed for Bilal's truck.

"I have missed you," Bilal said.

"Me too. We'll be working together again, that is all that matters. It's damn hot here. Is it this way all the time?"

"No," replied Bilal. "Usually it's hotter. Wait until July and August."

Bruce laughed. It wasn't often that Bilal tried his hand at humor. This was one of those rare times.

"So," asked Bruce, "what's this job all about? Only for you would I give up my job with EPA. Tell me everything."

"In due time, but not here. Wait until we are alone, for what I have to tell you is for only your ears. It would better in a more private setting. Are you hungry?" questioned Bilal.

"Yes, I could use a bite to eat," responded Bruce. "So let's eat quickly. I can't wait to hear what you have to say."

They went to a local restaurant and ordered dinner. Bilal ordered sag oshi, a curry lamb dish with spinach, and Bruce tried biryani, a mixture of mutton and chicken served with rice and a yogurt sauce, on the recommendation of Bilal. They chatted incessantly, with Bruce doing most of the talking, to catch up with the events of their lives. After the meal, they left for Bilal's apartment.

Nestled in the security of his bare bones apartment, Bilal related the events leading up to and including his meeting with el Berubi and his commitment to join STN. Twenty minutes later Bilal made the offer to Bruce to join STN.

"If you decide to join us, you will be my right hand man and strategic planner. Are you ready?"

"Are you kidding me? Do you think I would turn down his opportunity? This is a dream come true. We'll be doing something important, together, instead of playing nursemaid to wimpy executives who mostly need protection from themselves. I'm in. What's next?"

"Don't you want to know the rules or how much you will be paid?"

Bruce smiled and feigned surprise.

"You know that as long as I have enough money to eat, drink, and get laid once in a while, that's all I need. Besides, I know you will take care of me, so why should I worry about some silly rules? Killing terrorists by your side are all the rules I need."

He was startled to learn that his pay would make him rich beyond his wildest dreams.

"And a Swiss bank account too?" Bruce said mockingly. "Can you image, Bruce MacCardle having a Swiss bank account?" His laughter filled Bilal's apartment. Bilal remained unaffected.

"So who is the head of this STN?" asked Bruce.

"His name is El Berubi. That is all you will ever know about him."

"You chaps are serious, aren't you?" A sneer crossed his face.

"Deadly serious," Bilal replied.

Farook had created a plausible and exciting cover for Bruce for his stay in Karachi. Bruce was now Evian Sanders. He was the point man representing private business interests from the UK who was interested in developing and promoting International business in Pakistan. They wished to remain anonymous. Bruce was to explain his employer's concern about creating unwanted speculation about their business interests in Pakistan. They want to remain invisible to their competitors. Also they, he was to explain, were concerned that they might attract attention from special interest groups, or terrorists, within Pakistan before they were ready to make their intentions known. Either one could kill their project. Because of the potential for unrest in Pakistan, Bruce was there on an exploratory mission looking towards the future. He was to tell whomever he met that his company was willing to move quickly for the right opportunity.

Farook secured a bungalow for him at an upscale complex in the Gulsha-e-Lqbal district, reserved for two years, with an option for a third. As part of his cover, he was to state he planned to stay in Pakistan for 2-3 years to insure his employers were well represented in their "special" project.

Bilal instructed him to go to the office of the Defense Phase V complex tomorrow and pay his three months security deposit with cash. This complex was host to many International financers, wealthy local politicians, and powerful businessmen, the kind of people who were privy to all manner of information and intrigue. They formed an isolated clique of people with common interests and social status, and often enjoyed sharing their knowledge and power with their peers. Bruce agreed to become a member as soon as he was settled in his bungalow.

Bilal gave him a cash advance and an additional 1,000,000 Rupees as seed money. With the money, he was to furnish his bungalow with high-end furniture, carpets and paintings. A man of his importance from a top UK company would settle for nothing less.

Bruce MacCardle became Evian Sanders.

Bilal gave him a box of pre-printed high quality business cards:

Evian Sanders
UK Representative
343 Nailcourt Lane
Coverty, GB CV7 7DE
Telephone :44-0275477814
Fax: 44-440247602275

Farook thought of everything. Should anyone elect to verify Evian Sanders employment, Farook arranged to have all incoming calls routed to a

24/7 STN operative who would verify Evian Sanders credentials to the caller. He expected three to five calls within the first several weeks. Some resident Karachi would feel the need to confirm his employment, while others who suspected that Sanders' activities fell in the realm of "needing to be examined further" would call in the hopes of selling their information.

Bruce's purported task was to locate suitable areas and opportunities for his clients. He was to investigate and purchase the best site or sites, issue contracts, apply for the appropriate local and government licenses, supervise constructions and/or renovations, and to monitor and insure that the projects were progressing in a timely and financially responsible manner. Bilal instructed him to bribe the appropriate people to insure a minimum of political interference. This would solidify his cover as a business agent looking to do business in Karachi.

"Money talks," Bilal reminded him, "and you will be able to do a lot of talking."

Bilal provided Bruce, aka Sanders, ample cash for bribes to establish his presence within the business and government communities. Most importantly, his contacts with the higher echelons of Karachi society would afford him the opportunity to hobnob with influential people from all sides of the local and International political spectrums. STN expected that Bruce would provide information to enhance their database and to identify potential STN targets. As a frequent International traveler, he would be able to move around the country without raising unnecessary suspicion. No one would question his travels within Pakistan or to the UK to meet with his employers. This provided the cover Bruce needed to justify his frequent absence from Karachi when tending to his STN duties.

"So, I will be living better than you, my friend. Perhaps I'll have you over at my place once in a while, just so you can see how the better half lives," chortled Bruce.

"That is not going to happen. We must insure that no one connects us to each other. You will mostly be on your own until it is time to plan our attacks," Bilal solemnly replied.

"After today, we will communicate only by our encrypted cell phone. If we need to meet, it must be in a safe area, which I will specify later."

Bilal handed him his new iPhone cell phone recently introduced in Pakistan.

"Of course. Just thought I'd play with your head."

Bilal ignored the reference.

They spent the next 5 hours reviewing Bilal's organization structure. They worked assiduously through supper. A pumped up Bruce could not wait to begin his new and exciting dual life.

"Bruce, it will be best for you to concentrate on your adjustment into Karachi life as a foreigner and to take the time to establish your business cover. You need to open a bank account with enough funds to demonstrate you are well off, but not enough to arouse suspicion. Open several accounts in different banks. You should purchase furniture, eat at local expensive restaurants, and generally act as a businessman with a secondary interest in touring the city. Take pictures, talk with the locals, but do nothing that would arouse suspicion. Many people in Karachi look to sell information to the government, the police, or terrorists, all of whom could have an interest in a rich foreigner looking to invest in Pakistan. You can become a target of their interest if you are not careful. As a precaution, do not drink in public. Especially not at the hotel bar or public restaurants. Too much whiskey can lead to careless mistakes. Drink in your bungalow if you must, but not before you go into public areas. Take five to six weeks to get your things in order. Then we'll talk about STN and what we will do together."

"Sounds good. Thanks Bilal."

"I told the apartment manager you would be arriving tomorrow to sign the necessary documents. I made a reservation for you at the Karachi Palace for this evening. When we are finished, you will take a taxi to your hotel. The room is reserved under Evian Sanders. Tomorrow go to your bungalow. Call me only if you have questions. El Berubi insists we not use the phone for idle chatter."

"I understand. By the way, what's your code name?

"ICE."

"That fits," he mumbled. "Talk with you shortly. Can you call a taxi? By the way, I think I'll use Scottie as my code name."

"Yes, I will." Bilal ignored his reference to his code name.

Ten minutes later the taxi arrived and carted Bruce and his luggage to his new life in Karachi.

23

June 2010:

Since April, Ed spent his time planning, training his team, working his menial job at CIA, and being a family man. Now he intended to find time for Liz too.

In spite of his heavy time demands, his home life with Janice and the kids flourished. He no longer openly worried about Rule 16. Ed remained hopeful Farook would soon call to tell him it was time for action, and that he had selected a team to begin the STN war.

The early morning thunderstorm pounded the window of his CIA office. The forecast of heavy winds and rain proved accurate. The lousy weather added to Ed's gloomy feelings. He had spent nearly two hours the previous night talking with his cell leaders. They collectively expressed their frustration. They were frustrated due to the lack of action.

Adding to their dismay was that the number and severity of terrorist attacks were increasing daily. Emboldened by their continued success, and sensing a weakening of the West's resolve to take the battle to them, terrorists struck with relative impunity. People, ships, ports, trains, buildings, and sports arenas in Europe and the Middle East suffered attacks. His team demanded answers. They had questions. So did him. The North America Region of STN waited anxiously for Farook's signal to attack. The wait seemed endless.

Ed was bored with his job. He sat at his desk, the same desk at the same office doing the same analyses he had done for years. He was ready to make his impact on terrorism. It was Tuesday, June 8, 2010. He stared at the rain, watching the heavy drops slide down the pane to… nowhere.

That's me, going nowhere very slowly.

He found it harder and harder to maintain his and his teams' enthusiasm. His cell leaders frequently called, hoping *Thunder* would have news.

The ringing of his cell phone jarred him from his lethargy.

"Call tonight. 1:20 AM," the voice said. The phone disconnected.

It was Farook. Could this be it?

Janice noticed and complained how jumpy he acted when he arrived home that evening.

"Even the kids mentioned it. You OK?"

"As usual, problems at work. I'll be OK. Just need some time."

"Can I help? We used to discuss your work before. Feel like discussing it now?"

"There's nothing to discuss, really. Think I'll watch TV before I go to bed."

"Fine. I'm going to sleep. Don't stay up too long." She kissed him good night He returned her kiss.

"Good night Jan."

Worried, she tossed in her bed. She had grown accustomed to the change in Ed, to his emotional withdrawal, his lack of enthusiasm, and even his lovemaking. He seemed distant, lacked passion, and generally troubled. She had tried many times in the past to get him to talk to her about his feelings, but he always rebuffed her.

Perhaps we need a marriage councilor. Maybe he doesn't find me attractive. Could he be interested in someone else?

She fell into a troubling sleep just as she had so many times in the past several months.

He called Farook from the seclusion of his den at precisely 1:20.

"Complete your plans. I have decided that you will make STN's first strike against terrorism. Keep your plan simple. We must succeed with this attack. Have you selected a target?" Farook asked.

"Ibn Sulimari. Sheik Majduddin ibn Sulimari from Jersey City. Do you know him?" Ed asked.

"No, but I will in a few days. I'll send the information you need shortly. Until you receive your packet of data, do not inform your team of your selection or that you will be first. It will be better to have all the information before discussing it with them. I will contact you shortly." Farook hung up.

"I'm the first! I can't believe it. I'm the least experienced and he wants me to be first!"

The prospect of launching STN was frightening and exhilarating together. The gauntlet had dropped, and it was up to him to take the challenge. Ed wasn't sure what to do with this sudden turn of events. Receiving the honor for the first strike was one thing. Actually having to perform scared the crap out of him.

Can I do it? Is my team ready? What if we blow it? What then? What in God's name should I tell Farook? Beg off and claim I need more time? No, Farook would surely interpret that as a sign of weakness, and that wouldn't work. Can't tell him I'm nervous or afraid. Is this a test of my strength and loyalty? Maybe he'll stop me at the last minute. Maybe Farook wants to see if I can handle the pressure. Is he convinced I'm up to the job? Regardless, I can't show a lack of resolve. He would take immediate action against my family and me. Farook could easily direct another team to be the first. He wouldn't have to worry about their mental state of mind, as he probably does with me. Ed was reeling from the pressure.

His fears and doubts sped through his mind immediately after Farook dropped his bombshell. He broke out into a panic-driven sweat. His head began to throb while his heart threatened to explode. His right hand sought his neck for solace, but found none. He sat glued to his desk chair, too shaken to stand up.

Uncertainly threatened. No matter his fears, he knew he needed to be positive and unafraid. There was no return. There was no escape, at least not alive.

I believe Farook is sincere, he concluded. *He believes in me and so do I. Now, I have to be sure I don't screw up.*

174

The unbearable prospect of failure was too difficult to accept. He elected to categorically rejected failure as a remote improbability.

Three days later the package arrived at his office in a standard inter-office manila carrier. Multiple names on the front of the envelope had been crossed out to create the impression of an inter-office envelope that had been used many times before. Ed was surprised and pleased to note that Farook's reach extended within the CIA mailroom. He put the envelop and its contents in his briefcase for safekeeping, locked it, and continued his business of the day. Reinforced and encouraged by the speed of STN's response, he could hardly wait to read Farook's information in the privacy of his home.

That evening, when the family was asleep, he went into his den-office and quietly closed the door behind him. With trembling fingers, he ripped the manila envelop open and took out ninety-eight pages of highly organized data. Each dossier had an 8" by 10" color head shot attached to the back of the report.

The computer generated forms read like a biography, with complete detailed information about ibn Sulimari and each member of his Circle of Contamination. Included was a physical description, their current employer, their business and work addresses, their cell telephone numbers, a description and photo of the car they drove, its inside and outside color, license plate, make and model, the VIN number, and even any dents or special markings. Highlighted were detailed descriptions of each person's typical daily itinerary, their work schedule, and any special personal habits. Comprehensive facts about every member of the group destined for extermination was there, in glorious detail.

Ed marveled at the comprehensiveness of the information. He scanned all ninety-eight pages into ten USB memory sticks for each of his cell leaders. Ed had every cell leader rent a post office box in his area to facilitate document or package transfers.

Just another STN security measure to protect the innocent, he mused.

Sulimari's Circle of Contamination included his personal secretary, the Chief Executive of his small self-proclaimed charity organization *Relief Foundation for Sick Islamic Children*, one bank official, and of course his three bodyguards. Ibn Sulimari's people lived and worked in three areas within the US, including his headquarters in Jersey City New Jersey, Norfolk and Richmond Virginia. That allowed Ed the luxury of assigning six of his ten teams to cover the three geographical areas.

Satisfied the plan was complete, he counted the number of people scheduled to die.

He was shocked. The number for execution was thirty-two.

Thirty –two reverberated in his head

Sweat. Trembling. Pounding. His nervous reactions reappeared. He struggled to catch his breath. The process of actually counting the number of people scheduled for death shocked him. Those partially submerged fears of his STN life uncontrollably rushed to the forefront. Sulking self-doubts threatened his sanity.

What the hell am I doing? I'm planning to execute thirty-two people! I never imagined so many would have to die at the same time. But, should that really matter? What difference does it make if it's one or a hundred? Yet, I'm the one ordering their deaths.

His head felt stretched to its physical limit. He halfway expected his body to shatter into thousands of shredded bone and blood fragments any second. He tried to use Farook's words for reassurance.

Peace is sought by many and denied by few. We must eliminate the few for the sake of the many.

Though he accepted them, they weren't enough to sooth his jangled nerves.

Waves of cramps and nausea came first. A few minutes later, vomit, repeatedly, followed by explosive diarrhea. The awesome responsibility and the overwhelming guilt joined forces to render him dysfunctional. He couldn't think clearly, he involuntarily shook from the vomiting and diarrhea and the cold sweats made him feel like death was paying him a visit… *perhaps as punishment?* A plethora of scattered thoughts raged through his mind.

Call Farook? That's stupid. How could I? No doubt he would order my death. Farook warned me that this would be difficult. I never understood it before now, not before thirty-two people will die, on my order. I know they need to be stopped, it's just that… killing them seemed so remote before. What kind of monster am I? What kind of man am I? How can I possibly accept the weight of their deaths, knowing that I was responsible?

Rule 16, Mandatory Targets, resurfaced. The words never failed to ring in his head. His subconscious mind released the imprisoned thoughts that were now blasting his brain.

He prayed he was dreaming, hoping he was a character in a violent nightmare, a nightmare he was creating with his personal demons. But, it was no dream. The air reeked of the sweat that poured out of his body, forming large globs of moisture on his shirt, pants and socks. Splashes of tiny puddles formed on his forehead, and on his lips. *STOP, PLEASE STOP.* The words bounced around his head like a ping-pong ball trapped in a steel sphere, endlessly pinging, pinging, and pinging. Louder and louder with each second.

Somehow, Ed managed to pull himself together. He focused on the ultimate goal to destroy terrorism. Terrorism threatened his life, his family, everyone, and everything he held sacred. To achieve freedom was a struggle. To preserve it is a battle against those who would snatch it away in a heartbeat, if given the chance.

I would...could...never let that happen he reminded himself repeatedly. The words, thoughts, and feelings that Farook had repeatedly shared with him once again fortified his weakening resolve. He managed to corral his fears, tie them into a tenuous bundle, and forcefully made them unwillingly agitated prisoners of his subconscious. For how long he didn't know, but for now they were contained, or so he hoped.

Awakened by the sounds of him throwing up, Janice met him at powder room door.

"What's happening? Are you OK? I heard you throwing up. It woke me up. You look sick. This time we're going to the hospital."

"No, it's not necessary. I'm feeling better."

"Yes we are. You look and smell horrible. Get out of your clothes, and take a shower if you can. What's going on?"

"I think I have a virus or something."

This is the second time you've thrown up in the last several months. I think we'd better go to the hospital. I'll call Denise next door to se if she can watch the kids."

"No, damn it!" he annoyingly responded. "I'm OK, and I'm not going to the hospital. Forget it. It's just a virus or some kind of bug."

"You're making a big mistake. The doctors can give you something. I'm really worried."

"I'm telling you, just forget about it. I'll be fine after I get some sleep," he sternly replied.

"What are you doing down here so late anyways?"

"Work."

"You haven't been to bed, have you? You're still dressed."

"I'm going up now."

"Is this the stuff you're working on? I'll put them in your briefcase. Go do what you have to." Janice said surveying the papers on his desk.

He needed to think of something quickly to stop her from reading his STN papers.

"I'm feeling a little weak. Leave the papers for the morning. I'll take care of them. Right now, I need your help to get up stairs."

She held him under his arms as they struggled to reach the second floor. Ed didn't have to pretend this time. He actually felt weak and was thankful Janice was there to help.

Even as he staggered to his bedroom, he recognized a new STN priority.

I need a safe place to work. I cannot risk another scare like this. If Janice discovered…

He chopped off that line of thinking immediately.

Tomorrow, I must find an apartment. I need a safe place to work.

Though still feeling like crap, he managed one of his personal jokes to himself.

I need a secret apartment, just like a real spy, that's me, Ed Walker, first class spy, second-class nerves. Tomorrow, I'll check out rentals in the Falls Church Times Community newspaper. Can't get an apartment in McLean. Too up scale for my needs. Falls Church is better and not that far away.

He took a quick shower with Janice's assistance, flopped into bed, and asked her to set the alarm for 5:30.

"Why so early? You're not planning to go to work, are you?"

"No, I don't think so. But I need to call Winslow at home before he leaves for work. He has an early meeting scheduled and won't be available until late in the afternoon. He needs the stuff I was working on before I became sick. I'll finish it up in the morning. I'll call him with the information if I don't feel well enough to go to work."

"Alright, suit yourself. Feeling any better?"

"Yeah, I think I am. I don't feel as nauseated anymore."

"Can I get you anything?"

"No, thanks."

"Good night. Hope you feel better."

"Thanks."

He prayed that Janice would be too busy in the morning to think about gathering his papers for him. Once he was up, he'd stuff them into his briefcase and make his call to Winslow to tell him he's not coming to work. Then, apartment hunting.

He awakened on his own without the alarm at 5:25, reset the alarm for Janice, quietly put on his robe and headed directly for his den-office downstairs. He breathed a sigh of relief to see his papers on his desk, where he left them. He noticed a slight odor from his vomit. He secured the papers in his briefcase before he went upstairs to tell Janice. She was awake, but lingering in bed until the alarm rang.

"How're you feeling?" she asked.

"Much better, thanks. The downstairs has a fowl smell from last night. I'll clean it later."

In addition to preventing exposure to Janice's inquiring mind, he realized there were added benefits to a hide-away apartment. Liz.

An apartment solves all my problems. I need to blend into a place where no one knows me and where I can come and go without anyone caring. Besides, if

I'm going to keep getting sick because of STN, it's better if I'm away from home, and Janice.

He congratulated himself for his strategic thinking. Logistically, he decided an apartment about a half hour from McLean, in a low rent neighborhood, would be perfect.

"I feel good enough to meet Winslow at his meeting in Alexandra," he announced.

"I don't need a suit because I'm not part of the meeting. Winslow might want me to hang around in case he needs to ask me questions. I'll relax there with a book or something," he lied.

He picked up a paper at the store and scanned it in his car. Three rental apartments in Falls Church caught his eye. Two apartments were on the second and third floor. He passed on them. The third had a first floor entrance. He arranged to see the apartment within the hour.

Early June springtime in the McLean area is beautiful, especially when the flowers first make their appearance. The plethora of budding plants reminded him that life existed outside the CIA and STN. He drove to Falls Church and set his GPS for Patrick Henry Drive. Highway 7.

He did a quick surveillance of the area and the locals before the GPS announced "At destination."

This is similar to Kensington in Philadelphia, he thought.

The Shellington sat back off of Patrick Henry Drive, on its own parcel of land. The nearest building was two hundred feet away, he estimated.

The neighborhood looked like the melting pot of America. He saw Asian shops, White, Black, and Latino people scurrying about, and scruffy teens hanging out at the corner McDonalds. Women with multiple children herded in and out of local grocery and drug stores, pushing carriages and carrying bags of produce and soft goods.

The Shellington Arms East apartment building and the manager were waiting for him. Both looked old and neglected.

The building was a converted large home that had seen better days. Its appearance mirrored the forsaken look that low-income buildings take when they begin to fall into disrepair. This one fit perfectly. It looked forlorn. He guessed that nothing had been repaired or painted for the past fifteen or twenty years.

The discolored concrete steps, cracked in many places including the joints, led him to a weather-scarred door that fed into a small interior entranceway. Two doors and a set of steps greeted him. On the left door was a hand lettered cardboard sign marked in faded black magic marker that sadly announced "Office." He knocked and waited until the door opened and an elderly overweight Latino man appeared. He had not shaved that day, and his gray stubble beard gave him a sinister appearance. Although unkempt, his threadbare clothes seemed clean. His salt and pepper receding hairline gave him a cartoon appearance.

With newspaper in hand, Ed asked

"Is the apartment still available?"

"Si, do you want to see it?"

"Sure."

"I'll get my keys. Be right back."

A few minutes later he returned with the key, led Ed down the dimly lit hallway and opened the door to apartment D. He gestured for Ed to enter. A small single room apartment with a sagging bed, a small wobbly white-painted table, and a tiny lamp that faintly provided the illumination greeted him; a sofa and small wooden chair completed the 1960's décor. At the far end of the room was an adjoining tiny bathroom, well equipped with a once white and now slightly stained tub, a green and white toilet and a small chipped and stained sink. The place was clean, but in need of repair, paint, new bedding, lamps, and brighter bulbs. Ed wasn't concerned about the looks.

As long as it serves my needs, I can tolerate the deteriorating surroundings. Hmmmm, he thought. *only one entrance into the building. Not sure that's good, but I guess it will be OK. This'll do. I'm not planning to spend my life here. Who cares how it looks. Janice would throw up if she saw it. I'll fix it up later.*

He planned to stay there only during an STN operational phase. He figured he would have to make frequent appearances even when STN activity was low to keep the landlord from thinking he abandoned the place. During the next three months, he suspected he would be there a lot to help plan the Sulimari attack.

"How much?" Ed asked.

"$775 a month, in advance, cash only," replied the landlord. "Includes sheets and towels, but you need to clean them yourself. Has an air conditioner in the bedroom that works. I charge $25 a month extra for electricity. I don't pay for phones or TV. That's up to you."

"I'll take it. But, I want you to know that I travel, so I may not be around often."

"Suit yourself. Your business is your business. The rent is due one month from today. If it's not on time, I change the locks and toss your stuff in the garbage. Understand?"

"OK. How do you want to do this?"

"Here's the key. It's yours." He held out a huge rough hand for the money. "Don't lose them. Costs 25 bucks to replace lost keys."

Ed gave him the $775 and asked for a receipt.

"You got the keys, don't you? This ain't the Ritz," was the terse response. "But I'll write one out for you if you want."

"Don't really need one."

He paid the rent and surveyed his surroundings. He checked out the view from the back window. The room overlooked a narrow space way that separated his building from a shabby wooden building on the other side. The window opened and closed, which made him feel better.

I would feel better if there was a back entrance to the place.

He decided to bring some basic toiletries, soap, and clothes on his next trip. A new mattress, several lamps, a 19" flat screen and a folding table would make the place easier to work and to sleep. Fortunately, his laptop computer was already equipped for wireless transmission.

No internet connection here, he correctly concluded.

I'll need to make up an ironclad alibi for Janice why I have to be away from home, especially as we get closer to the time of the strike.

Four days later, secure in his apartment, an excited Ed Walker held a phone conference call with his ten cell leaders. He announced,

"Gentlemen, I have fantastic news. El Berubi has selected us for the first attack. We will make the official introduction of STN to the terrorists and the world. The exact date has not been defined yet, but I do know it will be within the next three or four months."

A rousing cheer rippled through the airways. His team, filled with pride, anticipation and enthusiasm, were highly vocal in their support. They began peppering him with questions. Who, where, the number of targets, but Walker held them off.

"First things first. I have decided that *Sabertooth* will take command of the attack, since he is the closest to the target in North Jersey. *Sabertooth* will plan and coordinate the teams. I believe at least five other teams will be required. *Sabertooth*," he said addressing his cell leader, "select your support cell leaders from the list. You have the list of cell leaders, their profiles and their locations. Take a few minutes to review it and make your choices."

"Roger that," was the response.

Three minutes later *Sabertooth* returned on the line.

"Fang, Stealth, Iron Mike, Airborne, and Hangman are my selections."

"Excellent. I want to draw on the experience of this team to begin the planning process. Until el Berubi defines the actual date, we have quite a bit to accomplish. We don't have much time to prepare. *Sabertooth*, do you think we can put it all together in three months?" Ed questioned.

"Unqualified YES, *Thunder*. Anyone disagree?" inquired *Sabertooth*.

A chorus of "We'll be prepared and ready to go on your command," was the unified response.

"Excellent. The target is Sheik Majduddin ibn Sulimari from Jersey City and his Circle of Contamination," Ed announced. "I will send each of you by overnight mail a memory stick with the dossier and photos you will need. If you have any questions, call *Sabertooth*."

A murmur of approval and excitement came from the group. Each one already knew and deeply loathed ibn Sulimari. Ibn Sulimari, an Islamic preacher, had been was under the watchful eye of the FBI for years. The FBI suspected that he hatched the plot to destroy the shipping facilities at Norfolk, Virginia. In an early morning attack in February 2008, two heavily loaded cargo ships sank while docked awaiting shipping orders. Many suspected ibn Sulimari was funneling millions to al Qaeda in Iraq, as well as preaching violence against the Western countries. Rumors swirled within the Agency that he was also encouraging his followers to destroy the UN building in his weekly sermons. In spite of being a prime suspect, the FBI had no hard evidence to substantiate his arrest or trial.

Ed smiled to himself because of the unanimous approval of his team of his target selection. He smiled thinking,

We won't have to worry about a trial anymore!

The high-level experience of the team quickly became apparent. They chose the six 3-man primary attack teams who had the responsibility to perform the simultaneous executions. The remaining four 3-man teams served as backup in case of an emergency. *Sabertooth* specified the weapons needed. Collectively the cell leaders established tentative surveillance and attack plans, contingent on a comprehensive review of the Sulimari information.

They individually vowed that no one from ibn Sulimari's group would remain alive.

"No one!" they emphatically stated. They showed neither excitement nor fear. They were professionals preparing to do their job. They hung up without goodbyes.

I never should have doubted that Farook would give me the names of anyone not committed and extraordinarily capable.

Ed's self-confidence gushed skyward. His previous concerns about *Mandatory Targets* and the number of people scheduled to die became lost in the energy and focus of the phone meeting. Buoyed by the determination and professionalism he felt from his team, Ed Walker couldn't wait for the Sulimari operation to begin. He rationalized that his previous anguish over the morality of his actions has been stupid. Terrorists needed to be destroyed. Period! He embraced the fact that his team was composed of highly qualified and committed men. He could have closed his eyes, blindly pointed a finger, and not made a mistake. He quickly realized his North Region STN team was well coordinated and exceptionally well prepared.

"They leave nothing to chance," he sighed with vocal relief. The more he analyzed the situation, the better he felt. His newly acquired appreciation, reverence and inspiration for STN's capabilities instilled in him a new and unfamiliar level of exhalation.

They are doing everything to guarantee success. What an organization! Perhaps Farook was correct. Some day, after we destroy the terrorists, people will hail us as the champions of humanity. We are taking the risks and we are the ones dedicating our lives. One day, the time will be right to tell them. I need to keep my cool, be certain my team is ready and everything will work just as Farook promised.

For the first time in his adult life, and certainly since joining STN, he, Ed Walker, CIA Deputy Director, devoted husband and father, consummate American patriarch, and Regional Leader of the North American STN strike team, fighters for liberty and freedom, became imbued with a feeling of power and invincibility.

Many phone conversations later with their planning sessions complete, the North American team expressed total confidence that the Sulimari operation would proceed without a hitch. They worked and reworked the details, tested each other's preparations, personnel, and avidly reviewed their surveillance information. Ed directed them to continue their surveillance to confirm the movements, locations, and habits of their multiple targets. He and *Sabertooth* demanded verification and re-verification of all information about the targets. They had to be certain their targets had not changed their patterns. Their success demanded it.

He also instructed them to call him on his cell phone to confirm the kill as soon as they cleared the scene. They laid out the plan for the attack. It would begin in the early morning, somewhere between two and three AM, and take no more than seventy-eight minutes to complete the thirty-two executions.

Sabertooth requested weapons with silencers. He preferred the Steyr AVG Bullpup assault weapons with silencers because of their rapid-fire power, lightweight, short barrel and ease of use. Ed assured him that el Berubi would get him what he wanted. Once the details and plans were completed, Ed knew his army of dedicated yet itching-for-action STN mercenaries was fully prepared to take down Sulimari.

Thirty-two people listed as targets, and thirty-two people would die, as soon as I issue the order.

Ed reminded the leaders of el Berubi's insistence that no STN member is to know the identity of another. This precluded face to face meetings. Because the cell leaders and their team members had to be together to plan their attack, he instructed them to wear a ski mask when meeting. He reminded them to refer to each other by their code names, and only communicate with their encrypted cell phones. Even though he knew they understood the rules, he felt better reminding them. It was his way of contributing to the team. Beyond that, there was nothing else he could do to protect STN.

An unspoken yet generally understood benefit for the team members was the bounty available from their targets. Once the commander declared the mission a success, valuables such as money, jewelry and rolled up art works became spoils for the victors. Farook made it clear that equal sharing of the loot by all members of the team was his firm policy. To prevent traceability, all valuables had to be collected in a sack and given to the commander at the end of the mission. Farook would arrange to pick up the sack and dispose of the items on the black market. He would then deposit equal portions into the Swiss bank account of each member for future use.

For this first strike, Ed instructed his team not to loot the properties. They wanted to insure that no distractions would jeopardize the success of the strike. The initial attack HAD to be flawless. The team needed to execute their targets, minimize the time spent at each site, and disperse quickly. Looting will be permitted on future strikes, he assured them.

The date of the Sulimari operation was still unknown and listed as WITHIN MONTHS.

Ed called Farook with their weapons requirements. He had no clue how to obtain them without raising suspicions. He knew Farook would.

As time inched slowly towards the anticipated date, Ed Walker's resolve gained increased strength and confidence. He seemed impervious to the pressure of uncertainty and his lack of leadership experience. He no longer yielded to doubts and indecisiveness. He acted more focused at work and at home.

Janice loved his new energy and attentiveness to her and the kids, but faced a dichotomy. She loved his new strength and drive, but felt concerned because of the sudden change in his personality. She believed people reacted differently to stress. Some grew depressed while others pretended they hadn't a care in the world. One evening, after dinner she asked,

"What's going on with you? You're so full of energy."

"You want me to change back to the tired Ed? I can reduce the times we make love. Less sex. I'm convinced that's the answer," he said with a twinkle in his eye.

"Well that's the first time in months that you have shown some life, but you need to be serious." She was annoyed. "Why do you joke around when I'm serious? Sometimes you act like an idiot."

"You're right, sorry. I guess I just wanted to avoid discussing the topic. I do feel terrific. Everything is going great at work. We're making progress against the terrorists, and I'm one of the major contributors."

He really wanted to tell her that he was committed to killing other human beings; and that that his feeling of invincibility was reaching new heights, and that his sense of values was clear. He no longer felt intimidated because he had to make major decisions. That he did not have to differentiate right from wrong, from duty to one's family from duty to world salvation. One day she would be proud of his accomplishments. He wanted to share with her the wonderful things that were happening to him, to the family, and how strong he felt. He wanted to tell her to wait for several months. Then she would understand everything. Mostly he wanted to tell her he no longer felt confused or weak. He wanted to tell her how he had grown to appreciate Farook and the role STN was soon to play in securing democracy for the world. He wanted her to know they expected incredible success, in spite of the weak government leaders who refused to take the actions against the terrorists when they should have, and who now have their collective heads up their own and each other's asses. He wanted to tell her how difficult it has been for him living two lives, one so secret that she and the kids could be at risk if exposed. He wanted to tell her that he was prepared to meet his destiny and would never leave STN. He wanted to plead for her forgiveness for the lies and deception, and for taking time away from the family. He wanted and needed to do it all, but couldn't. Not now. Maybe never.

"I know you told me that these projects are important, but I never imagined they'd require so much of your time and energy. It does look like you've figured things out and that makes me so happy," she acknowledged.

He worried about Janice catching him in a lie. He furiously raced through several scenarios, debating which explanation to offer her to explain the increase time he anticipated being at the Shellington Arms.

After a few seconds of calculated silence, he responded.

"Yes, all this pressure began with these latest series of urgent reports President Schuster demanded. I think I am getting a handle on how to manage them now."

That one wasn't a lie, he assured himself.

"Jan, I have to tell you that things will be a little more difficult in the next three or four months. The CIA is coordinating activities throughout the country, and Winslow asked me to oversee these programs. That means I'll be traveling quite a bit. It stinks, but it's necessary. It's our best shot at making inroads against the terrorists."

"Well," she replied, "you will definitely need a vacation after that. We should plan on it."

"You're right. We'll plan one soon, OK?"

"I guess. It can't come soon enough."

Another bullet dodged, he thought. *One day, I might not be able to escape so easily. And what if it happens at work? Then what?*

They spent the remainder of the evening watching TV and making passionate love after the kids went to sleep.

*

The Sulimari attack time was growing closer. Ed felt assured and confident. His panic attacks had totally disappeared. He no longer experienced physical illnesses. His former visitors of guilt and indecisiveness lay shattered in a field of past memories and future glory. Never again would they be able to cripple his thinking and his actions. Never again would he be subject to their demonic directions. Never again would he wonder when his subconscious mind might explode to control his life. He felt in control, empowered, and consumed with bringing victory and glory to STN and him. These powerful feelings directly transferred to his personal life. He grew to resent that he had to work at the CIA to maintain his cover. He would have preferred to spend all his time on STN.

Janice was the unexpected recipient. She was thrilled seeing Ed walking around with a new and commanding bounce to his step. Even more exciting, Ed never refused her sexual invitations, regardless of the time of day or night. He functioned with decisiveness and authority.

One evening after making love, she turned to him and said,

"I love the new you. I just want to be sure nothing is wrong."

"Trust me, everything is wonderful. I'm feeling great. You and the kids are happy and healthy. My career is moving along. Though I'm working long hours and spending too much time away from home, I see the future, and I love it. Even Winslow has remarked how incisive and focused my analyses have become. Perhaps, I'm tired of being a worrywart. From now on, I'm letting that crap go. I'm focusing on major issues. I feel in control."

"Are you telling me the truth?"

He moved closer to her naked body, drew her close to him, and, looking directly into her eyes and gently responded,

"I swear to you that everything is wonderful. You are and have been my dearest friend and confidant, my strength, and my inspiration since the day we met. I would NEVER do anything to jeopardize our relationship or our marriage, NEVER! If anything bad was happening, I promise I will tell you immediately."

She looked into his eyes to find the truth. Today, she wanted to believe. She wanted to convince herself that Ed was telling the truth. She wanted to accept his explanation without hesitancy. Perhaps she was not ready to challenge him.

Perhaps she did not want an argument. Perhaps she felt enthralled with the strength and resolve she saw in her husband, for the first time in many years. Perhaps she was afraid to believe differently.

"I believe you, my love. I believe."

"I love you too. Thanks for being concerned. It's a new time of our lives, Janice, a new time to grow and to appreciate the wonderful things we have in our lives. We have each other, two terrific kids, a beautiful home, friends, and a bright and secure future. It's the American dream, and we're riding the crest of the wave!" he enthusiastically said.

"What more could we dream about or want? This is the prime time of our lives. Let's squeeze every joy we can out of every minute, OK?"

"OK," she excitedly acknowledged. "Every minute of every day," she echoed his words.

"If I had more time, I'd ravish you again, but we both need to sleep. I do love you, with all my being."

"Me too. I'm first in the shower," she said as she raced him to the bathroom.

Well done, well done, Ed smiled to himself. *Well done, indeed.*

24

THE DATE IS SET, JUNE 12, 2010:

Four days later Ed's cell phone rang with Farook's distinctive ring. He flipped open the phone, and heard,

"The date is September 11, 2010."

"9/11?"

"Yes, 9/11. The day al Qaeda began their war against democracy and changed the actions and thoughts of the world. We will use our 9/11 to announce the end of terrorism. They rejoiced at the date of their greatest success for the cause of terrorism. We will make it the date of the end of all terrorist fanatics throughout the world. We will reclaim 9/11 once again and restore it to those who choose to be free!"

"That's…that's…. fantastic!" was Ed's awe struck reply.

"Good. It's up to you to initiate our war against the evils of terrorism. Goodbye."

Farook wants to attack on Saturday, September 11, 2010.

Ed sat and just nodded his head repeatedly.

What an idea! Start our war the same day they started theirs. This will get their attention!

The news brought him to the height of excitement.

Nine-eleven! I wish I could see bin Laden's face when he hears the news. I wonder what he will say to his followers. Sorry I got you into this. I never thought...! Or, will he laugh and ask of anyone heard of STN? Who do they think they are? I am shaking in my boots. We will crush them as we do all the infidels.

Ed calmed down and thought about the final preparations his team needed before the attack. His brain rapidly scanned his team's previous plans and prioritized the outstanding items.

At least Janice will not be a problem. She understands I will be traveling a lot. Soon the Shellington will become my operational headquarters. I need to tell Sabertooth the attack date, review our strategy and finalize the details of the strike. Increased surveillance will be required between now and September 11. It wouldn't do to have the targets disappear before they face execution.

Exaltation blended with trepidation. Ed sleepwalked through the rest of the day. As time permitted, between CIA phone calls and meetings, he managed to call *Sabertooth*.

"*Thunder*. The date is September 11. Get the team ready, immediately. I'll speak with you tonight."

That night, Ed waited until Janice fell asleep before he called *Sabertooth*. They spent the next two hours reviewing the steps needed for Sulimari. They concluded little additional planning was necessary. The real issue would be fine-tuning their plans and practicing the assault execution. They agreed to conduct multiple practice sessions. They agreed it would take lots of hard work to insure they are fully prepared to attack Sulimari. As a precaution, they brainstormed to expose any flaws in their plans. They tried to assess what could defeat any action by their teams, including possible problems with the escape routes, inadvertent exposure, targets not where they were expected, illness within the team, weather conditions and anything else they could imagine. They established detailed contingency plans as a backup in the event that something went wrong at any target site. The backup teams would be in place, ready to take up the slack if required. *Sabertooth* did most of the planning while Ed made minor suggestions.

After their conversation, Ed wondered if *Sabertooth* felt as anxious as did he. *Sabertooth,* a seasoned paratrooper and special units operative, had been involved in complex covet operations before. *He probably shifted into battle mode as soon as he heard the news.* Ed thought. Ed imagined *Sabertooth's* brain sorting through the operation like a computer-cold, calculating, mechanical, and focused.

"*Sabertooth* is my best cell leader. I'm glad he's heading the attack. If anyone can insure success, he can. With him leading, I can smell success," he declared.

That evening, he told Janice that Winslow had firmed up his travel plans.

"It looks like I might be away three or four days a week for the next two or three months. I'm traveling to San Francisco, Chicago, Dallas, and Boston. I'm sorry, honey, but I thought it might come down to this a week ago, remember?"

Janice offered no resistance. It surprised him. He expected her to be annoyed or angry. They both understood his being away from home would put an added burden on her and the kids. He was prepared with a litany of explanations to relieve her anxiety, but none was necessary.

Thank God she accepted this so easily. It allows me to concentrate on STN.
Ed forged ahead with his lie.

"This is the big push for Schuster's reports, and I'll be working with several teams in each city to coordinate the data. Once the report is finished, things will be easier and I'll have more time to spend with you and the kids. Isn't that great?" he prodded her enthusiastically. The truth was more gruesome.

If this strike is successful, I suspect I will be working on the next attack very soon. I'll have to spend a lot of time at the Shellington. If we fail, I might be dead, but Janice will be rich. Either way, the pressure will be off, he morbidly laughed to himself.

*

Karachi, Pakistan:

Farook's call in June that the first strike would be on 9/11 heartened Bilal. He and Bruce conferred frequently by phone, or met secretly to mold their team into an efficient killing force. Farook purchased the items Bilal requested and secretly delivered them to his Pakistani cell leaders. Bilal narrowed his target selection to a manageable list, starting with four HuM leaders. He added five additional HuM terrorists, one that Bruce suggested, and three selected by Farook, for a total of thirteen targets on his list. It was still three months before 9/11.

Harkat-ul-Muyalidin, HuM, was Bilal's single passion. He scanned the documents Farook provided to learn what else he could about the HuM leaders. HuM, organized in 2002 after the bin Laden 9/11, made frequent attacks against Christians and Westerners in Karachi. Their main headquarters was located in Kashmir. They had forged strong ties mostly with al Qaeda. 1500 strong, they operated mainly out of the Kashmir region, with splinter groups operating in Karachi and Islamabad. Their biggest claim to fame was a failed attempt to kill President Pervez Musharraf in 2005. The Musharraf government immediately labeled them terrorists.

Bilal knew that Muhammad Yusuf Shah, also known as Syed Saluhuddin, was the HuM leader. Muhammad Jwron, the chief consultant for attacks. Saud Menon, of Sindth, and Dr Tofeeq Ikran Elahi, a prominent family doctor in Lahore, had funneled significant money into the organization through Jwron. The good doctor provided information to HuM that he learned from the hospital staff, patients, and informers. He lived in Lahore, in a substantial home with his wife, their three children, and his aging mother.

Bruce chose the well-known leader Imam Moshin Kamal as a main target. Imam Kamal advocated armed violence against the Pakistani government and the US in his weekly orations, and openly provided financial and leadership support for suicide bombings. He preferred massive and spectacular civilian deaths to punish "the infidels." His favorite targets included shopping markets on Friday, when the greatest number of people assembled. Although the government suspected he was responsible for three bombings over the past two years, they lacked the will to take positive action. Though totally convinced of his terrorist activities, the government failed to act out of fear of retaliation from his terrorist friends, or of causing further unrest within the Muslim faithful. Without substantial proof and public support, they sat on their hands, doing nothing, while Imam Kamal continued to advocate violence.

Bilal grew increasingly impatient with the inactivity. Things were not moving quickly enough. He understood that he could not push Farook to allow his team to have the first strike. He also knew he had to wait a week after the North American's strike. Still, he had to wait. Patience was not Bilal's strong suit.

"How could he make me wait?" Bilal questioned Bruce.

"You would think that I, above all, so willing to fight the terrorists, would be given the privilege to move first. It is only right. HuM demands my attention. An eye for an eye."

25

FALLS CHURCH, VIRGINIA:

Ed started his travel scheme the following week, two and a half months before September 11 and Sulimari. He informed Janice he was leaving Thursday morning for San Francisco, and would return late Sunday. Wednesday evening he packed his black pin stripe and gray suits, several shirts, underwear, toiletries for a four-day stay, kissed Janice goodnight, and crawled into bed. He set the alarm for 4:15 AM to allow time to drive to Dulles airport for a supposedly 7:45 AM flight. He told her he decided to drive his car instead of taking a taxi.

The first several days in his apartment, Ed concentrated on sprucing it up. He bought a new mattress, higher wattage bulbs, a floor lamp, and tons of cleaning supplies. He knew hiring a cleaning service was out of the question. No one who lived at the Shellington Arms could afford such a luxury. He spent four hours cleaning the apartment the best he knew how.

Ed began his systematic review of every detail with *Sabertooth*. He added some of his own.

They spoke a week later. *Sabertooth* declared,

"I'll include the changes in our plan and begin training the teams immediately. I will keep you informed weekly how we are progressing. That's it *Thunder*. I see no reason for us to talk again except to keep you informed of our progress. If I need your help, I'll call. Try not to worry. Everything is under control. We will be ready and we will succeed. *That* is a promise. Goodbye and good luck to us all." He disconnected.

Of course, he's right. All I'm doing is rehashing the same issues over and over again. I'm sure he wants me off his back.

Sabertooth continued the dog work to be sure everything of importance was noted and that the teams were prepared. Farook's announcement that 9/11 was the date placed Ed under enormous stress. He had to juggle his time at work, at home, and at his apartment. He used a combination of sick and vacation days to be away from his Langley job. Lies proliferated. He lied continuously to Janice, to Winslow, and to his friends so he could spend time at his apartment. He would have preferred not to lie. It concerned him that if he was caught lying his cover would be blown. If that happened, all hell would break loose. STN would be compromised and the entire operation jeopardized. Farook would probably give the order to have him executed. Yet, in spite of these harrowing problems, Ed concentrated on the impending attack. Lying and clandestine conversations had become his way of life. In many ways, Ed's lies had made him a conspirator who was about to violate the laws of the United States.

*

KARACHI, PAKISTAN:

Bilal virtually locked himself in his apartment during the next month, working exclusively by phone with Bruce. They worked tirelessly at a feverish pace, driven to complete the plans to organize the HuM attack. Their time was coming. His revenge would soon be satisfied.

"I am tired of waiting," he confessed to Bruce one day. "I know enough about HuM to attack. I need to fulfill my commitment to my family. The longer they remain alive, the more Nasrin is dishonored."

"I'm impatient too. We have the knowledge, we could be ready, but we are not the first to attack. I know how you feel, but our time is approaching. Have patience."

"My patience is finished. I cannot wait much longer."

"Bilal, remember that el Berubi ordered us to wait a week until after the initial strike in the United States. Are you planning to ignore him?"

Bilal offered no response.

"Please listen to me. The most important thing is to destroy HuM, is that not true?"

"Yes."

"Then, if we attack too early, without the proper authorization, we will win the first battle, but we will still fail. We will fail to kill as many of HuM as possible. El Berubi will cut us off, and we will have wasted our time and energy. The people we want are the leaders and the financial supporters. We cannot kill them all with one attack. There are too many of them. We must be patient and live to kill all the HuM leaders. Once the leaders are dead, HuM will have no strength. The people responsible for ordering the attack on your family are the ones we must destroy. This goes for all the terrorist groups in Pakistan, Afghanistan, and Turkey. Our best hope to destroy terrorism is to prove to them that being a terrorist is dangerous to them and those around them. The STN plan will work. I'm convinced of that."

"I understand. However, this is different. It is my reason to live, my only reason!" barked Bilal.

"No, your reason to live is to avenge your family. Anything less then that will make it meaningless. It is better to wait and finish off HuM then to fail by not killing the leaders who ordered the attack. Only then will Nasrin and your children be avenged with honor."

Bilal weighted Bruce's sage words. Bruce knew enough about Bilal to understand he needed time to think before he would respond to such an important issue. Bruce continued to remain silent.

"You are right. I will wait." It had taken Bilal nearly three minutes to agree.

Bilal and Bruce continued to train their team, plan the attacks, and wait. Bruce managed to temper Bilal's intolerance with the need for absolute secrecy and greater preparation.

"This is Pakistan," he reminded Bilal, "where people's movement or action can and will be easily misinterpreted. Any misstep could invite unwanted attention by the military or terrorists. It is imperative," he argued, "to protect you, STN, and our team members. Any crack in the organization will bring the wrath of the IB on our heads, and destroy us."

Bilal reluctantly agreed. They waited and waited and waited.

26

KARACHI, PAKISTAN:

A month before the HuM assault, Bilal informed Bruce he had decided to lead the attack himself.

"That is not a wise thing to do. You are our leader and if something happened to you, everything would collapse. It will be difficult to replace you. STN would no longer exist in Pakistan. As I recall, you made two promises to Nasrin. First, you vowed HuM would die. Next, you swore to her memory that you would continue to fight terrorism to prevent them from destroying other families. Don't you remember your vows? If you die attacking HuM, you will have broken your promise."

"My first and only promise was to destroy HuM, even if I died. I made no such other vows," Bilal curtly corrected him.

"The plans are ready and our teams are trained. Success will soon be ours. Your presence in the attack could jeopardize the future of this operation. Is that what you want?" Bruce questioned, his voice showing the mounting tension he was feeling.

"It will not change the attack plans. I want to be there. That is the way for me to complete the vows I made to my family," Bilal adamantly replied.

"Your presence *will* change it, no matter what you think! This I know," Bruce said with reverence and in a soft yet firm voice.

193

"I've been involved in field operations. I know what happens when military plans change. Changing the leadership is a major mistake. I beg you. Do not follow this path. Your revenge will still be satisfied when HuM no longer exists, whether it is from your hand or from your mouth. You know I speak the truth."

Dejectedly the voice on the other end whispered,

"You are right. I will not be part of the attack."

"Ra'id, the leader of the attack, knows to call you the minute HuM is executed and the attack is secure."

Bilal disconnected.

Bilal, the hardened machine, had two conflicting emotional issues that overwhelmed him: revengeful hate and remorseful sadness.

"I am trapped by my own making. I cannot destroy HuM myself. Others must do it for me. Because I cannot, I bring dishonor to Nasrin, my children, and me."

This burdensome mindset would haunt him the rest of his life.

Bilal selected the four principal HuM targets for execution. They were Shah, aka Saluhuddin, Jwron, Menar, and Elahi. Against Bruce's suggestion, Bilal decided these four must be the first to die. Their deaths would satisfy his urgency for revenge. Bruce wanted to strike a more visible person, one whom the public would instantly recognize and accept as a terrorist worthy of execution. He wanted the Imam to be first.

"No," stated Bilal. "These four. Their hands carry the blood of my wife and children. It will not matter whether the public accepts their deaths or not. Eventually, all terrorist will die. It will not matter in what order. The order matters only to me."

"You are right. Sorry I wasn't thinking clearly," replied Bruce.

They spent the next week carefully reviewing their HuM attack plans. The nature of the Pakistani society and the geographical areas involved imposed challenging difficulties and problems. The mental state of both the average Pakistani and the terrorists was to trust no one, to observe one's surroundings for suspicious people and packages, and to report unusual movements or activities. Some sold their information to the government, others to the terrorists. The surveillance of these four would require great stealth and patience. Ra'id selected the best men equipped to handle the assignment. They collected their data, slowly but precisely, in sufficient quantities to give Bilal confidence the HuM attack would succeed.

*

FALLS CHURCH, VIRGINIA:

The closer 9/11 grew, the more immersed he became. STN took precedence over his life. It became a labor of love, in spite of the increasing stresses. He used every available minute engrossed in STN conversations with *Sabertooth*. In spite of *Sabertooth's* assurances that the surveillance had turned up no new information, and everything was under control, he found it impossible to do nothing. So he called whenever he had questions or felt the need to be reassured. *Sabertooth* remained patient, answered his questions as briefly as possible, and pleaded with him to trust the professionals.

Three days before 9/11, Ed spent a restless afternoon at the apartment trying to stay focused on the positives. He told Janice he had to attend another meeting in Boston and would not be able to leave until Sunday, the day after the impending attack. He told her not to expect to hear from him too often, since he was attending marathon meetings in preparation for the final report for the President. With that out of the way, it freed him to concentrate on Sulimari.

He mentally reviewed every detail of the approaching attack. Though his conviction was strong, vestiges of doubt remained. He knew they would be quelled about seventy-eight minutes after the attack, assuming everything went according to plan.

The wait was intolerable. Alone in his apartment, with little to do, he anxiously paced from corner to corner. He turned the TV on, but he did not have the patience to sit still to watch. He flipped channels and stared at a book without turning a single page. He thought of calling Janice, but was concerned about what might happen.

"I've nearly screwed things up with her before, and I can't risk it again. Not when we're so close. She'll have to wait, for everyone's sake. But I'm going crazy," he mumbled. "Being a crusader isn't the easiest thing in the world, especially alone."

He tried to force an afternoon nap to no avail. He managed eighteen minutes.

"The next three days are going to be very, very long. I need to calm down. If I don't, who the hell knows what might happen," he said to no one in particular.

Visions of the terror that will soon descend on thirty-two people did not faze him. He pictured thirty -two people huddling in their beds facing unknown gunmen prepared to kill them. He ignored their terror, their panic, their desperation, their lack of comprehension about the events about to unfold. He visualized the blood spurting from multiple gunshot wounds silently administered, spattering walls, furniture and floors. Wave after wave of bright red blood exploding within the room, as his STN team emptied their weapons into their human targets. The carnage was his and his alone. He ordered it.

These images created an unwanted conflict. He felt sorry that innocent people would die along with the guilty. He also felt exhilarated that the war against terrorism was beginning. He tried to remain focused on the expected success.

He lay in bed sweating from anticipation. He wanted 9/11 to come more quickly, to know his team had fulfilled their mission, and to feel the exhilaration of success. Waiting was not something he learned to accept. In the past, he sought solace from those around him to relieve his anxiety. He wanted to scream out of frustration, but couldn't. He wanted to be close to Janice, to seek the refuge of her motherly bosom, to hear her calming voice, to feel her arms embracing his anxious body, to shield him from the drudgery of waiting, and to rescue him from himself. That was out of the question.

He focused on the benefits STN was bringing to civilization. He tried to visualize the future when terrorism no longer posed a threat to society. A time in history when civilization would laud him and STN for their courageous and valiant actions they took against those who would destroy democracy. He visualized the pride and joy Janice and the kids will feel because of the sacrifices he made for them, of his bravery, and dedication to their freedom and happiness. Yes, how proud they will be. One day.

But, I can't let my nerves get the best of me. Not now, not when I've come this far. I know I'm stronger than I have been in the past.

He awakened early Friday morning from a restless sleep.

"Tomorrow is 9/11. One more day of waiting. The next 24 hours are going to be the most difficult time of my life," he proclaimed to his image in the bathroom mirror.

Laughingly he conjectured that without a miracle, his impatience might kill him. He felt the burden of a 1000-pound weight perched on his shoulders.

"Success depends on my team's performance. Failure means the CIA will divert their energies to destroy STN. They'll share their information and coordinate their intelligence with other governments. All governments, whether they are free, dictatorships, Muslim, or Arab, would likely join in the hunt. Everyone will be out to destroy us. STN will disband. Lost will be our opportunity to secure the freedom of civilians who hate and fear the terrorists. And..."

He couldn't contemplate finishing these chilling thoughts. The images were too numbing.

September 11, 2010 was now less than 14 hours away. Ed remained wired.

He wanted to speak with *Sabertooth,* but decided against interrupting him. For the last five weeks, he had spent two to three days a week away from home. He often would go to work from his apartment just to prevent Janice from becoming suspicious. He missed her warmth, her companionship and the sex. They barely managed sex once a week because of his STN and CIA work schedules. He was used to more.

Debating with himself, he made a snap decision. He needed company, safe company. It would help him to survive the intractable time until Sulimari became a reality.

I'd feel better if I Liz was here. I need to stop thinking so much. It's driving me crazy. She makes me feel so special. No other woman, not even Janice, makes me feel that way. I have to call her.

To Ed Walker, Liz Hunter was his escape mechanism and his safe haven. She brought relief from the pressures and anxieties of his daily existence. Both willingly indulged the fantasy of their relationship. Neither passed judgment on the other. Each felt secure in the belief they were secure from the outside world. They formed the perfect compliment for each other. Their protective bubble rested on a single premise. They could enjoy each other's company, unconditionally, without complications, and without the baggage that accompany permanent relationships, like marriage. They were in it for the moment, for as long as each moment lasted, without vulnerability, without games, without restrictions, without expectations, without emotional ties, and without a future. They agreed to stay together as long as they both wanted to, or until one decided to move on. It would end one day, and that suited them both. Time together was all that mattered and all they wanted.

He dialed her number hoping she was home. She answered on the second ring.

"Hi, it's me."

"I was just thinking about you. I must be psychic or something. What do you think?" she said.

"Angels can be anything they choose, can't they?"

"I'm no angel, but I'm close."

"Trust me, you are an angel. You're my angel," he replied.

"So, I guess you're available… hope, hope, hope. I'm very horny. I'd love to see you."

"Great! I have some time, not much, but enough. I need to tell you something first. I'm working undercover on a special project. Unfortunately, I can't come to your house. You'll have to come here. My apartment isn't the nicest. Government restrictions, you know. Because of my undercover work, things are a little unusual. I order in most of my meals. I don't normally leave the apartment. Unfortunately, you can't stay overnight. I will be busy with long phone conferences. If you come, you'll have to be out of here by nine tonight. This isn't the best part of town, so you will have to take a cab here and back. I'll pay, of course. How's that sound?"

"Whoa, mystery man, that's quite an agenda. Are you sure you're working for the government and not some terrorist organization?" she chided him.

Ed felt his breath sucked out of him.

Does she know or has she guessed what I'm doing? Had I somehow let my guard down, made her suspect? If she knows, I'll have to have her killed. I can't allow anyone to jeopardize STN. I've got to figure out what she knows or suspects.

The pain of panic gripped his throat.

"You've got the goods on me. I'm the mastermind behind the plot to overthrow our government, then the world. I have people, weapons, and chemicals stashed and poised to wreak havoc throughout the country. Plans have been in place for years. I'm waiting for the right moment, then KABOOM! The best part is that I want you to rule the world by my side, just you and me. Are you up for it?"

"Sometimes you're silly, you know, but that's why I'm attracted to you."

Satisfied she knew nothing and that her reference to terrorism was coincidental, he quickly marshaled his composure, assured her that it was safe to come, and gave her the address and apartment number.

"Great! See you soon. Say around three."

"The door will be open, so come in. I'll be there, waiting for you," he offered.

"Can't wait."

"Me neither."

Ed tidied up the apartment, sprayed an air deodorant, and lightly dusted the furniture.

At least it was somewhat presentable, he thought. *Knowing her, she couldn't care less about the apartment décor.*

By 2:48 on a late sunny summer September afternoon, Ed impatiently waited by the door, in case she arrived early. Watching from his window, he spotted the taxi pulling up outside his building. He watched her get out, her long legs stretched in a seductive position. His heart skipped a beat, as it always did when he saw her. She wore a light blue pants outfit, a beige silk blouse, beige shoes, and was carrying a large picnic basket. Her hair, usually in a ponytail, hung loosely, caressing her shoulders with every step she took. The slight breeze moved her hair to create an illusion she was floating above the sidewalk. He yanked his apartment door open as soon as she entered the front door to the building. He was beaming. Her eyes and mouth seductively twinkled. He knew they would.

"Hi."

"Hi."

They locked lips before the door closed behind them. She pulled away and said.

"This is getting heavy. I've got to put it down before my arm gets separated from my body."

"What's in there?"

"Since we can't go out to eat, I thought I'd pack some snacks to carry us over. Merlot included."

"You're amazing."

"Of course I know that. That's my secret power over you, dummy. Now you've discovered it, what are you going to do about it?" she chuckled.

"Well I guess I'll have to torture you by fucking you the entire afternoon. I'll force you to divulge your secrets, and I promise not to stop until you squeal. Remember, I'm with the CIA, and we have our ways to make you talk. There'll be no relief until you tell me everything. Then I'll decide what to do with you."

"Have your way, but I'll never squeal, unless you force me to moan and groan. Then I'll consider doing anything you want. Is that the torture you're planning?"

"Exactly."

"I'll put this stuff in the frig so it doesn't spoil."

"Be quick, if you want your punishment."

"I do, I do." she wantonly responded.

Liz took a disapproving glance at her surroundings.

"From the looks of this place, either you're in deep undercover, or you're working for the cheapest department in the government."

"Probably a little of both," he meekly responded.

"Frankly, I'm not very happy being in this dump. I'm used to nicer surroundings. I really like being with you, but… if this is the best you have to offer, count me out! I'm sure someone else will be thrilled to treat me better," she said disdainfully.

"Look, Liz, I don't disagree with you. I felt the same when I rented this craphole. But it suits my purposes. I prefer to be in a classier place too, if I had my choice."

"That's not my problem. If you want to spend time with me, then you will have to make different arrangements," she pressed.

"OK. I promise the next time we'll get a hotel or meet at your place. I promise," he responded contritely.

"OK. You wouldn't want to make me unhappy, would you?"

"No, I want to keep you real happy. You're going to stay, aren't you?"

"I don't like it, but I'll stay this one time. Too bad, you deserve better. We both do. When this is over, if you want, I'll do what I have to convince your boss at the agency to get you better accommodations. That I promise! I have *my* ways."

Her threat had the desired impact. His face showed compliance and embarrassment. She squeezed his hand hard, her eyes dancing in amusement. It was her pacifying gesture.

They spent the next four hours alternating between making love, eating, drinking, and enjoying each other's company. Neither mentioned the apartment again. They giggled, they laughed, and they lost themselves in the ecstasy of the afternoon. Never once did Ed think of STN, his mission, or his future. His focus was on their mutual indulgence.

They finished their erotic lovemaking. Their energies depleted, they relaxed curled in each other's arms. Ed remarked with awe,

"I'm amazed at how you make me feel peaceful and serene. The whole world seems to stand still, and nothing else matters. Our time together may only be a fantasy, but it's a fantasy of unbelievable joy. I've never met anyone like you, let alone dreamed I would be part of such an incredible sexual journey. I love it, and I love you," he whispered in her ear.

"Yes, we *do* have something very special, don't we? But, let's not go overboard with that love stuff. Right now what we have is a great sexual thing. Let's not screw it up with anything else. Remember, I told you, I do not want complications and love is one complication that will ruin our arrangement. Understand?"

That was the second time she rebuked him. It didn't fit his new stronger persona.

"OK, I understand."

She immediately recognized the stress in her voice.

"Look Ed, what we have makes us both happy. Let's not make it difficult on either of us. I enjoy being with you, you enjoy being with me. Its better left there, don't you agree?" She looked caringly into his eyes.

"Yes it is. I guess I got carried away," he answered.

"Settled?"

"Settled."

"I'm famished. I have some food left in the frig. Hungry?"

"Sex with you brings out my appetite."

They moved from the bed to the kitchen, ate again, and made love one final time.

Eight-thirty he called for a taxi, walked her to the door of his apartment building, and watched as she slid into the back seat. The taxi sped away with his slightly tarnished cargo.

27

FALLS CHURCH, VIRGINIA:

Six hours remained before *Sulimari*, before the free world's 9/11, before his crusade against terrorism would begin. Waiting for *Sabertooth's* call was maddening. Waiting was all he had.

Everything's under control he reassured himself. *We've gone over every detail so many times I see them in my sleep. My teams are in place, our targets are where they should be, and the night sky is dark, with only a small amount of light from the quarter moon. Darkness works in our favor. Stop worrying. In less than six hours we'll hit Sulimari, and seventy-eight minutes later, I'll know the results.*

He reflected aloud on the contrast between him and his team. "Not one of my cell leaders expressed concerns about their ultimate success. They are confident, professional and prepared.

No one else seemed as nervous as I did. To a man, each one expressed overwhelming confidence without worrying about failure. The wait is almost over, thank God. The future is ours."

By midnight, he was a total wreck. His patience disserted him. His throat, drier than usual, felt scratchy and irritated. He kept a bottle of water by his side. Nervous sweat poured from him like water from a watering can. He changed his clothes three times in an effort to stay dry. He could not find a comfortable position. Standing, sitting, or lying down didn't help. He wanted to feed off the confidence of his team, but lacked the experience to take advantage of their energy and confidence.

He repeated, "We will succeed, we will succeed," in an attempt to buoy his weakening resolve. He acknowledged his role in Sulimari was a relatively minor one. His team, mostly *Sabertooth*, did the real planning.

Sure I helped to finalize the plans, but they are the ones in the field, and they are the ones who will pull the triggers. My teams are putting their lives on the line. I'm only the administrator. I manage the money and maintain contact with Farook. But, just like a corporate CEO, I rely on my people to get the job done. I mostly stayed out of their way and let them do their job. I did suggest the strike begin early in the morning when most of the targets are asleep. They liked that. And they loved the idea of 9/11. They responded enthusiastically when I told them. El Berubi couldn't have selected a better date to begin our war against terrorism.

His rambling thoughts did little to calm him down. The anticipation of the strike was overwhelming.

Farook made a ton of predictions on what will happen both in the morning after the news reports the death of Sulinari and his followers, and in the evening when he issues his statement about STN. It should be interesting to see how many come true, he mused.

Sabertooth called unexpectedly and said,

"We'll soon make history. It will set the standard for future STN strikes. Terrorists will finally get a taste of their own medicine. They'll understand what it feels like to be under siege from an unknown and invisible enemy, one they can't see and can't find. An enemy they will grow to fear. An enemy powerful and unyielding. We'll show them no mercy, for they are evil and deserve to die."

Filled with pride, energy, and confidence, *Sabertooth* helped to sooth Ed's nerves.

"I will call you the minute we complete our mission. Be ready! Good luck to us all, and don't worry!" He disconnected.

I know there will be no accolades, no parades, and no newscasters demanding interviews from STN or me. Not yet, but one day, it will come. Terrorism is finished, though they don't know it. They'll find out soon enough.

These lofty overwhelming thoughts were enough to sustain him as he waited for 2:32 AM, Saturday, September 11, 2010.

Filled with anticipation, his thoughts flittered from the mission, the aftermath, and the media responses, to how the terrorists will respond to Farook's announcement. His thoughts were varied and inconsistent. Everything felt jumbled. He was so nervous that he wasn't able to think clearly.

One thing I do know is that the world will be stunned when they learn of our commitment to eradicate terrorism. The public probably will not understand the real meaning and power of STN just from Sulimari. As our successful strikes mount, they will embrace us. They will understand we are fighting for them and for their future. They will welcome us into their hearts. One day, when they awake and realize the world no longer has to fear terrorists, and that we were the ones who fought for their freedom and peace. They will hail us as the true champions of democracy. We will have made history for them and for us.

Sulimari will force terrorists to look for a scapegoat. They'll blame their usual enemies they use to rile their people. Undoubtedly, the US will head up the list, followed by the Israelis and Arab collaborators. All will receive the threat of "great reprisals," words meant to assure their brother jihadists that they are unified against the infidels. They will promise an immediate response for any future actions by the STN Satan.

He remembered Farook predicting that a major attack would occur, perhaps a building, a ship, or a crowd of people at a sporting event.

That saddened both of us. We reluctantly acknowledged it might be an unfortunate and unavoidable consequence of our war against terrorism.

Remembering made him sad.

"But," Farook had said, "Terrorists and their supporters will accept that their reign of terror is over. They will learn STN is *the* threat to their cowardly actions. We will deny them access to their precious Paradise. They will fear us. I'm convinced!"

Farook's eloquence had mesmerized him when they spoke. They continued to give him strength.

"The hunter becomes the hunted. They are the targets, hunted by professionals who play by our rules. We will raise the stakes of their beliefs and existence. Their dreams of dying for the glory of Allah will be shattered into indistinguishable pieces. They will live in fear, and they will die. Over time, they will grasp the danger they bring to themselves and others. Terrorism will lose its power to draw on the youth to sacrifice themselves. They'll learn there are no safe havens for them to hide. They'll learn they cannot support or teach terrorism. We will find them, wherever they are. Terrorism will cease to be a global threat."

So spoke the Egyptian leader and so listened his American co-conspirator. That was their plan, their dream, their passion, and their vision for the future.

28

THE WAR BEGINS:

Ed usually spoke with Janice once or twice a day from the apartment. Today he broke the pattern. He feared Janice might sense his anxiety and pepper him with questions, questions he did not want asked nor wanted to answer.

A quick glance at his watch jolted him back to reality. It was 1:47 AM. The coordinated attack would begin at 2:32 AM. Within two hours, *Sabertooth* should call to confirm the success of Sulimari. Frozen in time. Ed Walker felt frozen too.

2:57 AM. No news. 3:10. No news.

Sweat dripped from his forehead.

"Where the fuck are you *Sabertooth*? What's happening?" he quietly swore.

His hands shook, even the right one on his neck.

"Has something gone wrong? Are they all dead? Come on call damn it, call."

Ring.

The sound startled him. He violently flipped his cell phone open and heard the most exhilarating words of his life: **MISSION ACCOMPLISHED!** All targets are dead! We met no resistance. We encountered no problems and the local police never showed up. All team members are safe at all locations. We're on our way home. Thank you, *Thunder,* for the opportunity to lead this historic mission. We make one hell-of -a good team, don't we? Let me know when you are ready for the next one. Goodbye."

"Yesssssss!" escaped his tortured lips wildly. He pumped his right fist on the air. He nearly swooned from exhilaration and relief. He erupted into a euphoric dance. He jumped, he pranced, and he twirled while quietly shouting, "YES! YES! YES! We did it! We did it! We did it!"

He laughed, he cried, in a near delirious state. It took him nearly seven minutes to regain his composure.

"We're on our way. Sulimari and his Circle are dead."

He called Farook to tell him the news.

"El Berubi, el Berubi, it's done! We did it! We did it! Sulimari, everyone is dead! They're all dead! Every last one, dead! Our people are safe and headed home," he screamed into the phone.

"That's fantastic news! Congratulations, you did a remarkable job. A great job! But first, I want you to calm down and stop shouting. Take a deep breath," he commanded. "Take a minute…."

"I don't…"

"No, we cannot talk until you are calmer. Understand?"

"It feels great. I feel great!"

"I understand, completely. I feel the same. You have accomplished the first step for world peace. Terrorists will soon learn of their fate. Early this evening I will unleash our announcement to the media. Soon STN will be a household word. Enjoy the moment, for you have started the avalanche of terror on the terrorists, one from which they will never recover. Relax, if you can, but remember, we must be prepared to keep up the pressure. Remain unrelenting. Prepare for your next attack as soon as you feel ready. From this moment on, you are on your own. Strike whomever and whenever you feel the time is right. I will be available to support you as needed.

I will alert the other STN regions to begin their attacks one week from today. We will wage war against them until total victory is ours. History will record your victory as one of the most significant events of the 21st Century. We are creating a new world order, one of hope and decency. Congratulations again for a job well done. I knew you could do it! It should be interesting to watch the evening new. Goodbye for now."

Flushed with the unexpected and effluent praise from Farook, Ed poured himself a double shot of bourbon and raised the glass.

"Here's to me, my team, and our incredible success. Look out, you scum, we're coming after you! This is payback for the thousands of people you've slaughtered, not only on 9/11, 2001, but for all the poor souls whom you killed or maimed throughout the years."

Ed bowed his head, and offered a silent prayer for those who died at the hands of terrorists. Tears welled in his eyes.

The second shot of bourbon had its quieting effect. He solemnly gave thanks to God for giving him the strength to outlast his anxieties. For allowing him to discover his persistence and intestinal fortitude; for protecting his family and his team; for surrounding him with wise and determined people like Farook and the Bankers; for protecting him from himself; and from Janice too, he added as an after thought. A Botox smile froze his face.

Ed wished he could see the startled faces of the terrorists, hear their hearts pounding, and see them sweat when Farook makes his announcement. What a magnificent day for STN.

"One day, I will be their hero. One day, STN will be hailed as the freedom saviors, as the protectors of the world, as men who recognized the problem and solved it in our own way, the right way."

He reminded himself again. Not that he needed prompting. He had voiced and thought about his place in history often enough. It was now 4:17 AM. Sleep was out of the question, nor was it needed. His adrenaline made sleep irrelevant.

"Nothing can stop me. I've proven that terrorists can be destroyed, they and their Circle of Contamination. Good riddance to them all!"

He couldn't wait to see the response from around the world. Nor could he wait to strike again. He wanted to begin immediately, though he begrudgingly acknowledged he and his team needed a break. A short one, very short, he decided. He discovered a new emotion surging through his body. He wanted to experience the adrenaline rush from another success. He craved once again to experience the thrill of a fresh kill. His newfound self-confidence felt exhilarating. Anything he wanted to do, anything he wanted to happen, anything he wanted to be, was possible. He believed it with every fiber of his body.

Early morning he called Janice to tell her the meetings ended earlier than expected and he was coming home. He told her he already booked a return flight and he would be home for dinner. *And, in time to see the six o'clock news.*

29

SEPTEMBER 11, 2010:

Ed set his alarm for 8:30 AM to catch the 9:00 KTX morning news. By 9:23, Levrone Williams gave his report.

"Good morning. This is Levrone Williams with a special report on a series of strange killings overnight. Although the details are sketchy, we hope more information will be available shortly. Sometime during the night, unknown assailants entered Sheik Majduddin ibn Sulimari's home in Jersey City, New Jersey, and murdered him. Mr. Sulimari is a long-term suspect of an FBI investigation. We also have reports from Norfolk, Virginia, and Jacksonville, Florida that people reportedly associated with Mr. Sulimari have also been assassinated in the same manner. Police have not released the details about these murders or if they are connected. What we do know is that an undisclosed number of people suffered multiple gunshot wounds and died in their homes overnight. The FBI and the Police in the three cities involved are cooperating in this investigation. The names or numbers of people brutality murdered have been withheld pending notification of the next of kin. Unconfirmed reports indicated that there are no clues or suspects at this time.

Sources not authorized to discuss this investigations informed us that the FBI listed Mr. Sulimari and his followers as prime suspects in the bombing of the Helms Federal Building in Richmond, Virginia in 2005. He was also reputed to be a source of substantial funding to terrorist organizations through his charity *Relief Funds for Sick Islamic Children*. The FBI believes this is a front for Sulimari to funnel money into Islamic Fundamentalist organizations in Pakistan and Iraq. Although suspect, the FBI apparently did not have sufficient evidence to bring Sulimari to trial.

Speculation, and it is only speculation, is that a rival or an organization angry with Mr. Sulimari and his associates wanted to punish them for their alleged terrorist activates. Until we hear from the police or the FBI, that is all we have to report. We will provide an upgrade on this story as the information becomes available.

This is Levrone Williams, KTX news, Washington."

Ed felt somewhat let down. He wanted to hear that officials feared a wave of killings might follow, or that the reporters would make a bigger issue than what he heard.

They really don't know enough to arrive at any conclusions. My team did a great job of escaping without leaving any clues. If the police have nothing to report, the newscasters also have nothing to report. The big news will be tonight, when they receive Farook's announcement. That's going to loads of fun!

He called Janice from the apartment.

"Hi, it's me. I'm boarding now. Should be home in a few hours."

"Great. I really missed you."

"Me too."

"How'd the report go?"

"Great. It's done, so the pressure is off, at least for a while."

"Does that mean you won't be so damn edgy?"

"Sure does. I'm relaxed and super happy."

"Really? That's remarkable, don't you think? Four days away and you're happy? What am I supposed to think?"

"Now, now, I'm happy to be coming home to you, and I'll throw in the kids for extra measure too."

"So what should I say?"

"A simple GREAT will do. What do you think about this? I'll take a quick shower when I get home and we can engage in a thorough ravishing of your body. I should be home before 2. The kids don't get home until after 3:30. How does that sound?"

"You know I don't like quickies, but we have had so little sex lately, even a quickie sounds good. I'll be waiting."

"That's my girl. Actually, I was kind of hoping you'd say that."

"I'll have to watch out for you, now that I know how devious you are."

"See you in a couple of hours. Love you."

"Me too."

"Bye."

"Bye."

He left his Falls Church apartment a little after 1:10 in the afternoon of the free world's nine eleven.

Funny, Ed thought. *I really miss being with her.*

Liz however infiltrated his thoughts.

Liz, Liz. You are such an interesting woman. I don't know why I'm so attracted to you. It feels like we've been together our whole lives. I think I love you, in spite of our agreement to have no complications. But, I love Janice too. Is it possible to love two women at the same time? You make me feel like a king. Maybe that's why I love being with you. But Janice is there for me too. We have history together, college, the kids, our home, and she makes me feel good too, but.... not like a king. I feel.... more like her partner.

This fundamental difference helped him sort his relationship between Janice his wife, and Liz his lover. He didn't care whether this comparison was right or wrong. It satisfied him. Ed Walker had grown to be quite hedonistic.

"Now," he reasoned aloud, "I know I can handle both the STN and CIA jobs. I've learned how to lead a dual life. Two jobs. Two women. One fantastic effort, if I say so myself. Yet, as much as Liz has become so important in my life, I really should consider the possible consequences of staying with Liz. Perhaps it might be time to break up. I do love making love with her, but I need to think about my future. Liz poses an added risk. I might say something when we are together about STN or my role in Sulimari. It almost happened with Janice, and it could happen with Liz too. That alone is a good reason to end it now. That way I'll be eliminating one possible danger.

Eventually, when the world learns of my role with STN, it would tarnish my image if my affair with Liz became public. The world may be ready to be saved from tyranny, but I doubt if they're ready to accept licentious behavior from their hero. The new Ed Walker, CIA operative and STN leader, is ready, willing, and fantastically able to move to the next step. Unfortunately, Liz may not fit into my new world.

I'll figure out the best way to tell her. I don't want to hurt her feelings. We agreed our relationship would last until one of us decided to end it, and I guess I'm the one. I'll find a way to be gentle," he vowed.

30

THE ANNOUNCEMENT:

"I'm home," he shouted moments after the front door swung open.

"Up stairs."

A quick kiss hello. Janice was wearing his favorite black lace teddy they bought together on a vacation in Cozumel two years ago, the one that cranked his passion and his fantasy. He almost didn't make it to the shower. They make deep, soft, and passionate love as only married people can.

By 5:30 PM, the family had eaten dinner and Ed quickly retreated to the den. He turned the TV on to the news channel. It was too early for the 6 o'clock news, but Ed wanted to be sure that he was watching in case Farook released his media blitz earlier. He knew that was not likely to happen. Farook never deviated from his plan.

Six o'clock. A special announcement headline flashed across the screen, accompanied by faceless voice to "stand by for breaking news."

He called Janice to the TV room.

"Something big is happening. Come and watch with me."

Minutes later, the senior KTX anchor, Dana Ross, appeared on the screen.

"Ladies and gentlemen, there is late breaking news of major significance. Forty-three minutes ago, we received, a communication that we have been requested to read to you.

I am highly shocked by what I am about to report. A group calling itself STN, short for Stop Terrorism Now, has notified us that they are claiming responsibility for the multiple massacres that happened early this morning. Earlier we reported that Sheik ibn Sulimari and his followers met a violent death. Until now, these deaths baffled the police. I am appalled that anyone or any group would resort to such violence here in the United States.

At 5:17 this evening, we received a typed letter from someone claiming to represent STN, asking us to read their statement on the six o'clock news. They claim responsibility for the thirty-two deaths of Sheik Sulimari and his supporters. Mr. Sulimari was an outspoken religious leader who has been under CIA surveillance for several years, and preached against the United States. Mr. Sulimari operated a major mosque and madras in Jersey City, New Jersey. He reportedly preached that the US was the enemy of Islam and advocated violence against the government. The government had information that linked him to the bombing of the Helms Federal Building in Richmond Virginia in 2005, but did not have sufficient evidence to convict him of the crime.

The reason for the killings offered by STN was that ibn Sulimari and his followers are terrorists and deserved to die. Unconfirmed reports from police authorities indicate that these highly coordinated attacks occurred early this morning, sometime between 2:30 and 3:00 AM. No information is available on how these murderers were able to enter the homes of their victims and execute them where they slept.

STN, however, claims that the attacks are part of the major strike plan against global terrorism, and Mr. Sulimari was the first of many terrorists scheduled to die. Police report that Sheik Sulimari and his family, including his wife and three children, ages eleven, nine, and six, their collie guard dog, three bodyguards, and two mosque workers died from multiple gunshot wounds at the residence in New Jersey. Police have not determined if the children were targets or caught in the crossfire. Mr. Sulimari also ran schools in Brooklyn, New York, and Chicago, Illinois. STN executed a total of thirty-two men, women, and children in these cowardly attacks.

STN has requested that we read to you, in its entirety, the statement we received from them concerning these tragic deaths. I warn you that what you are about to hear may shock you. It certainly did me. Immediately after this statement, our team of political analysts will offer their reaction to this slaughter and the STN statement. What it means now and for the future. We have reports that every major media outlet throughout the world received the identical message. STN requested everyone read their message at the same time. What you will hear is the same message the world is hearing.

Management at KTX TV, after receiving security clearance from Homeland Security, has decided to read this statement in its entirety.

Here is STN's statement:

Today we at STN, Stop Terrorism Now, have taken our first action against global terrorism. For too long, terrorists have threatened the lives of innocent men, women and children. You bring death wherever civilians congregate. You have bombed markets, restaurants, and buildings without regard to the people killed by your cowardly acts. This message is for all terrorists throughout the world.

From this day forward, we are your enemy. We will hunt you down; we will execute you wherever you live, work, or hide. From this day forward, there is no safe haven for you. Not only will you die, but your entire family, your friends, your business associates, your weapons supplier, and anyone who promotes or supports terrorism will die. We call this group your Circle of Contamination, because everyone around you is contaminated. Expect no mercy.

Early this morning, September 11, 2010, we executed the notorious terrorist Sheik Majduddin Ibn Sulimari and his Circle. They have participated or supported terrorist preaching and activities throughout the United States. Ibn Sulimari previously avoided justice because the government of the United States failed to prosecute him for bombing of the Helms Federal Building in Richmond, Virginia in 2005.

On September 11, 2001, al Qaeda terrorists flew three airplanes filled with aviation fuel into the Twin Towers in New York City and the Pentagon in Washington. You slaughtered over 2800 innocent people. You made nine-eleven your rallying cry against the West and the free world. You wildly applauded your success.

Our response to you is our own nine-eleven. September 11, 2010. From this date forward, we declare war against you, the terrorists of the world, the same date you declared war against democracy and freedom. Our nine-eleven will prevail over yours. THAT we promise.

We have teams throughout the world poised to strike again, this time with greater force and greater destruction. This is your only warning.

Stop your terrorist activities or die. You will bear the full responsibility for the many deaths that will happen because of you. We do not care if you are personally involved in violent acts. All terrorists are our targets. Any actions you take that supports terrorism, you are our target. If you plan or cause violence. If you preach terrorism, if you provide them financial support, or if you supply weapons, you are a terrorist to us. If you launder or counterfeit money, if you donate money, if you allow terrorist money to flow through your bank, you are a terrorist. If you teach hatred to your children, or if you train terrorists, you will die.

STN has the finances, the power, and the determination to defeat you. We will wage our war against you until you no longer exist, until you are dead, defeated, or you stop your terrorist ways. However long it takes, we will destroy you.

No amount of political pressure by any government, or by any group, can save you. We report to no government. We listen to no government, and we work with no government.

We will hunt you down like the dogs you are. No matter where you go, no matter where you hide, no matter what you do, you will not escape. There will be no safe haven for you or your family, in any country, in any part of the world. No longer will you be able to plot your evil against us. No longer will we turn a blind eye towards your barbarism. There will be no further warnings, no trial, no jail, and no mercy.

Stop or die. Beware! We promise you will hear from us one week from today, when other terrorists like ibn Sulimari, will be executed. Do not underestimate us.

We are STN: Stop Terrorism Now."

Dana Ross continued.

"At this moment, the person or persons who paid for this global ad in newspapers and TV is unknown. According to our sources, an unsuspecting teenager delivered the letter. He told authorities a man in jeans gave him $25 to deliver the envelope to the front desk, marked Urgent, with my name as the recipient. We have just confirmed that other global TV stations have read the same STN message to their audiences. Apparently, all other stations had their packages delivered in the same manner, by a local person paid to deliver an envelope to the news editor. Other media outlets such as global newspapers and radio stations were informed by email postings. The sender identified himself only as STN. We have with us our Mid East news analyst, Dr. Milton Framers, based in Boston. Dr. Framers, are you there?"

"Yes Dana."

"What do you make of this STN claim, and what can you tell us about them?"

"I'm as stunned as you. To my knowledge, no one has ever heard of STN before you read their statement. My guess is this is a real organization. It sounds as though they have the strength, money, and leadership to conduct simultaneous executions anywhere around the world. The three attacks this morning showed a high-level of sophistication and intelligence capabilities. They obviously knew a great deal about their targets. They coordinated their attacks with excellent precision. The amazing aspect of these assassinations is that no information or witnesses have been uncovered at this time.

These attacks surprised us all, Dana. It is astounding that no one seems to have known about them, or the fact that they exist. How that can happen is very puzzling. However, from the tone of their announcement, I would tend to believe they are prepared to carry out their threats.

They must have given considerable thought to the date of their declaration of war against terrorism. 9/11, 2010, exactly nine years after 9/11 and the twin towers disaster. That tells me they are quite serious about their intentions and their capabilities. I would like to …."

"One moment please Dr. Framers, sorry to interrupt. I have another incoming bulletin. Sources from within the White House tell us that President Schuster has called an emergency cabinet meeting to address the STN situation. Home Land Security Director Sidney Kleinerman has been designated to the lead the investigation to bring STN to justice."

"My apologies, Dr. Framers. Please continue."

"No problem, Dana. As I was saying, I find it extraordinary that STN has launched their attacks against terrorism on the same date Osama bin Laden attacked the twin towers on 9/11. This is certainly a direct challenge to bin Laden, one he will not ignore. I imagine he will be busy preparing for some retaliatory statement or attack. It is not hard to understand STN's motives, but my guess is they are trying to win three wars here. The first is the propaganda war. There is no better way than to declare that your own 9/11 supersede theirs. It diminishes the 2001 aura, doesn't it? Second, they seem poised to implement their own terrorist war. Third, the Circle of Contamination to which they refer obviously is disturbing. They're saying that everyone who is associated with a terrorist will die. To me that sounds quite harsh and I expect many, too many, innocent people will die without justification. In some aspects, they are correct that anyone involved with terrorism is a terrorist. But children and women? STN is taking the law into their own hands, acting like the judge and jury to decide who will die. They are merely a vigilante group who could cause more anguish and problems than they think they are solving. That's perhaps one of the more troubling aspects of STN's announcement, don't you think?"

"Yes, I agree," replied Dana.

Dr. Framers continued. "The next few weeks or months should prove to be very interesting and possibly very bloody. As I said before, I can only hope that no innocent people die in the crosshairs between the terrorists and STN.

Of course, it may be weeks before Washington knows anything, and it may take months before the information is made public. All we can do is to sit back and hope these unsettling threats from STN do not become a reality. The last thing we want is for a group of armed vigilantes to be running around the world killing anyone they want.

Frankly, I'm horrified that they blatantly and arrogantly promised to not only kill terrorists, but their wives and children, friends, supporters and anyone they designate. Friends, supporters, and their families? I cringe to think of the carnage that they might inflict on civilization.

In my opinion, we cannot tolerate a group of gun slinging vigilante terrorists in a civilized world, even if their purpose is valid. We cannot have people take the law into their own hands. The Rule of the Land must prevail if our society and our values are to have any meaning. I personally have faith in our government and our intelligence agencies. I believe they will identify and track down these new killers, this new bred of terrorists, and bring them to justice."

"Thank you, Dr. Milton Framers, our correspondent in Boston, for your usual valuable insight and opinion. Let's hope you are correct. We will stay on this story and bring you the latest developments as they happen.

For reaction around the world, we'll take you to our London based KTX news correspondent, Brien Witherton."

"Thank you, Dana. Brien Witherton here. We have limited feedback from Parliament. As you know, it's three AM here. We'll have to wait for most of the world to wake up for them to hear the news. We are, however, able to report, unofficially, that the Prime Minister, Mr. Jeremy Brownsfield, has been debriefed. Apparently, the ministry had advanced warning to alert Mr. Brownfield to listen to the tube. We understand STN delivered the same message throughout the world, in spite of the International time zone differences. Apparently, STN wanted the entire world to hear about them at the same time. Quite unusual.

I expect Parliament will shortly hold an emergency meeting to analyze this situation. I have no doubt they will express their outrage and concern about this STN group. It's too early for anyone to know what to make of it. Everything has happened so quickly. They will need time to sort out it out and to decide what should be done. I personally am stunned that such an organization exists, and that they feel they can threaten to murder anyone associated with terrorism. They have the audacity to boast they will succeed, and no one can stop them. One thing Dana, it will be interesting to hear the official reactions from the Muslim and Arab countries. Surely al Qaeda and other terrorist groups will have their own response to STN. It shouldn't be too hard to guess what that might be.

I find it intriguing and difficult to believe their claim to have no ties with any government. It is very hard to imagine they could exist without the knowledge and support from a wealthy country with vast resources. The most likely candidate would be the United States. I suspect accusations will fly that the US government is the power behind STN, true or not. It's possible other governments might be involved, but it's easy to point the guilty finger at the US for leading the charge. They have been known to act unilaterally in the past, so I'm would not be surprised to learn of their involvement. It seems to me the US government is in for a rough ride."

"Well Brien, that certainly is an interesting point of view. I suspect that President Schuster will issue a statement after his cabinet meeting. I'm guessing that the Arab countries will call for an emergency UN meeting," Ross interrupted.

"You're probably right, Dana."

Dana took control again. "All we know at this point what we just read. We'll have to wait for this to be sorted out. KTX's worldwide correspondents will stay on this for late breaking news. We are in for a strange ride. Brien, anything more to add?"

"KTX London will be going to the streets to get the reaction of the public later this morning, after London wakes up to the STN murders and their declaration of war on terrorism. The murders of ibn Sulimari and his followers, especially his wife and three children, will certainly appall Londoners, no question about that.

What intrigues me the most is STN's direct assault on nine eleven. They have made a very forceful point of demeaning the essence of the meaning of the original nine eleven of 2001, which has been a symbol of al Qaeda's success against the West. Nine-eleven affected the entire world, and ushered in a global atmosphere of fear and intimidation. Al Qaeda used their 2001 success as a major recruiting tool in Iraq, Pakistan and Afghanistan.

STN now claims they have initiated a new nine-eleven today, Saturday, September 11, 2010, which they assert is the start of the end of terrorism. This is a monumental slap in the face to Osama bin Laden and his organization. For nine years they basked in the glory of nine eleven, claiming it was their most significant achievement in their war against the so-called Infidels of

Islam. They used 9/11 as their major recruiting tool by claiming their success validated their fight for Islamic principals. I heard Dr. Framers' analysis and I agree with him. This challenge by STN will, I believe, solicit a direct response from all terrorist organizations, which I'm afraid could result in more useless bloodshed of innocent people. I suspect they will want to punish the US, and Israel, especially if they believe either or both governments are backing STN.

I believe it is only a matter of time before a major retaliatory strike happens. One has to wonder if STN will also retaliate, and if so, how? One also has to wonder if this is the start of global warfare. It's a frightening thought. We'll have to see what plays out over the next few days and weeks ahead. Just picture this. One terrorist group fighting and killing another. It makes for an interesting and scary time, doesn't it? Brien Witherton for KTX, London."

"Thank you Brien. We'll be back to you later today for an update.

This is Dana Ross, signing off from KTX in Washington DC. Stayed tuned for updates on the breaking news."

The 7 o'clock evening news continued discussing STN and the reactions from global government representatives. Tim Barrows, Chairman of the Peace Envoys and his former boss, Sid Kleinerman from Homeland Security, provided the official US response. Kleinerman read the prepared text stocked with statements of dismay, shock, and outrage. He delivered a wordy yet insistent disclaimer of any US government involvement or STN support. He voiced the expected vow to bring the perpetrators to justice. He finished his speech by informing the audience that the President, his cabinet and his security advisors, have held multiple security meetings throughout the day to assess the situation. His speech was properly brief, properly vague, with the proper overtones of official indignation.

Barrows spoke after Kleinerman. He voiced concerns that this sudden emergence of STN could disrupt the efforts of the Peace Envoys. He expressed concerns that some of his organization's efforts will be ignored by the third world countries they have pledged to help. These countries are in the middle of political unrest. They may fear a possible retaliatory attack against them. Any attack, big or small, will likely force them to ignore the programs we have already installed.

"It is my personal opinion, that although STN claims to be fighting for our freedom, we all would be better served if they joined our efforts to fight terrorism through aid, not through guns. If STN leaders are willing to join us, I believe we can accomplish more together than apart. In the meanwhile, my organization and I will continue to develop programs to help the poor nations achieve stability and economic independence. STN does not change that commitment." Barrows finished his short speech.

In spite of the International time differences, some foreign officials managed to issue hastily prepared replies to the STN proclamation.

Just as Farook had predicted, officials from the US, England, France, Russia, China, the UN, and the Arab countries of Kuwait, Saudi Arabia, and Yemen were the first to react. Each vigorously disclaimed any knowledge of this "outrageous act against humanity." Each vehemently vilified STN and vowed to prevent future STN executions within their borders. Each pledged full International cooperation to track down the perpetrators and to identify and bring STN to justice.

Muslim and Arab world leaders had similar reactions, though much more forceful. The "murderers," which had become the standard reference term, were strenuously denounced as being sponsored by the US and Israel. They vowed a bloody revenge through the escalation of hostilities.

"Blood will flow as the rivers of the earth," proclaimed Osama bin Laden in a video tape released through Al Jazeera, the Arab media voice. He went on to reaffirm his commitment to rid the world of the "power hungry infidels in the US and Israel, and vowed to fight until the last person is standing. I call for every Muslim to stand together against this escalation of war against Islam. I call for the start of a new International jihad, the likes of which have never before been seen."

Bin Laden promised to issue a more detailed message to his followers shortly.

The media jumped on the news. They continuously analyzed the two nine elevens parallels. They re-invoked the images and the terror of 2001, again as Farook predicted.

Ed, astonished at how well Farook "knows our enemies," masked his immense pleasure from Janice. Both watched intently as the news replayed the horrifying events of nine eleven 2001 while the reporters confessed confusion on what affect STN would have in the future.

"My God!" Janice lashed out in anguish. "Now there's another group of terrorists running around! What going to happen to us? Are they trying to start a world war? It's bad enough the terrorists are killing people over there. Now it's here in the United States. Who asked them to do this? Don't they realize they are inviting another attack against us, here on our soil?"

He wanted to reassure her that he and Farook had anticipated such a move, and however unfortunate it may be, in the end it is a small price to pay to insure global freedom for the future. He wanted to. He almost did.

The TV bottom line feeder, the one that plays at the bottom of the screen, repeatedly scrolled:

...A group calling itself STN declare war on terrorists....

Outwardly, he supported Janice in her shock and dismay of the events unfolding before them. They listened in relative silence as the talking heads continued their report and analyses on the deaths and the STN message.

"I don't want to hear any more about STN," Janice declared. "It's freaking me out. I'm going to do the wash."

"I want to watch more. I'll let you know if anything significant happens," Ed responded.

The TV commentators flipped their discussion to address the human side of the murders with comments of "I pity the family of Mr. Sulimari. They did nothing wrong. No one deserves to be murdered in their bed." The reporters did what reporters do: provoke the base emotions of their audience with the fear of the unknown.

"Who is STN? From where do they operate? Who is supporting them? Are they a threat to society? Are they a new bred of terrorists? Will they destroy our way of life? Will they bring terrorism to our shores?"

Expert after expert paraded on the screen to lend their views to the mass speculation. So many questions. No answers.

Meanwhile the Bankers, Farook, Bilal, Bruce, and rest of the STN International team watched the media circus with awe and anticipation. They watched with pride and adulation to hear of *Thunder's* success, and swore to themselves to be as successful with their own strikes. Soon they too would be participating in attacks against global terrorism.

Farook sat like a new father, proud, thrilled, and relieved with the arrival of his first-born. STN was his baby. Walker's first strike success validated his belief in the STN mission. He had purposely chosen the US for the initial attack because he knew the media cover would be comprehensive and unrelenting. Their perseverance and insistence in reporting the news would readily spread throughout the world. He relished knowing they would soon open the floodgates of STN to the world. Four other global teams were ready to attack. He had promised they would be free to strike one week after his announcement. He intended to keep his promise.

Bilal and Bruce separately watched from Pakistan as the events unfolded. Bilal stoic, Bruce highly animated.

They spoke by phone 20 minutes into the news program.

"Isn't this great? Will you look at the TV? They're all running around like chickens without their heads trying to figure out what hit them. They don't know what to make of us, do they? I just love it! I cannot wait to get started here. One more week, and we'll show HuM a thing or two!" gushed Bruce.

Bilal spoke in his monotone and detached voice.

"I'm not interested in the US success or what the TV people are saying.

It means nothing to me. The destruction of HuM matters. They need to die, for Nasrin, and for my five children. My revenge is what matters, nothing else. We will succeed, that I promise. I promised Nasrin, and my promise will be fulfilled."

Bruce wisely remained silent. He had nothing to say.

*

Washington, DC:

Dana Ross reappeared on the nine o'clock news. Ed remained glued to the TV. He had been there since 5:30. Janice decided to join him.

"Still watching that stuff? Anything new?"

"Not much. I find it interesting what people's reactions are to STN. It's fascinating!"

"What do you expect people to feel? Everyone's shocked and frightened."

"Not everyone. According to the reporters, the people are excited. They see STN as the only one doing anything against the terrorists, at least doing something important. I'm sure it will be on the news again."

"That's disgusting. Are you saying that people actually are happy with these killers?"

"Looks that way."

They sat quietly when the 9 o'clock news started.

"Good evening again ladies and gentlemen. This is Dana Ross reporting from KTX, Washington. Earlier we reported on the STN message broadcast around the world in which STN declared war against global terrorism. We now have reactions from governments and people around the globe. In general, the response has been unanimous. Governments offered their condolences on behalf of those who were murdered. Without exception, officials expressed their fear of an escalation of terrorist activities against their military, ports, rail systems, or their citizens. Some declared a national emergency and put their military on alert. Spain, England, France, and Germany have declared Martial Law. Leaders from around the world are vehemently disavowing any connection with STN, emphasizing repeatedly they would never sanction vigilante activities within or outside their borders."

Ed suspected those same officials were thrilled and thankful STN was taking actions they could not themselves.

Ross continued. "Reactions from people on the street can be summed up as shock, for various and unexpected reasons. Many feared retaliation and an escalation of hostilities. Many others seemed quite excited that someone was taking direct action against terrorists. Some publicly stated they felt, for the first time in nine years, a new sense of hope for the future. Over 93% of the people we interviewed expressed cautious support for STN. Some indicated a willingness to join in the fight. Some offered to send money to support STN."

"What do you think now?' Ed asked Janice.

"Think? I think the world has gone nuts. First it's al Qaeda, the Taliban, and their suicide bombers, and now STN. They're nothing but a bunch of hoodlums out to kill people because they want to. We live in a democracy, and no one, no matter how righteous they believe they are, can violate our laws. Who made them judge and jury? What's next? Another group who hates Blacks, Jews, Catholics, or whomever, will claim they have the right to kill them? Even the skinheads, with their absurd beliefs, obey the law to a certain degree. Sure, some get out of hand, but for the most part they don't go on killing rampages. What if they change? The whole country, the entire world, will be fighting and killing each other. Is that what STN is trying to do? What happens to us, and our kids? Suppose some gang decided that CIA members should die. There isn't enough CIA, FBI, or police to protect everyone in the country. This is worse that any nuclear attack could ever be. What do I think? I think this is a disaster, that's what I think!" she shrieked.

Taken aback, Ed had not anticipated such a furious reaction. He longed to tell her it wasn't STN's goal.

We're bringing freedom, freedom from the fear of terrorists. We're doing it for the future of civilization, he wanted to tell her. Instead, he said,

"Aren't you overreacting? I mean, we know nothing about STN. Many groups claim greater numbers than they really have. It may be a way to reach out so people will take notice of them. I'm willing to bet they'll disappear as soon as Schuster unleashes Homeland Security. They'll track them down and expose them for the frauds they are."

He tried to minimize STN to alleviate her concerns. Janice would have none of it.

"You think they're all talk? What about that Salumarti, or whatever his name is? They killed thirty-two people. They killed his wife and children for God's sake! It seems to me they're well organized. And if that's true, they frighten me, I mean, really scare the crap out of me. Did you ever hear of STN before, from work? Or this Suli…,whoever. Is he really a terrorist?"

"No, and I don't know. My group does not deal with that side of terrorists."

"Well who does? What are they going to do about them?"

"I'm in the dark as much as you. I just feel in my gut they will be caught quickly. It will be over before you know it. Do you think the President is going to allow them to run wild, to kill anyone they want? He can't and he won't. You'll see. Let's wait a while before we jump to conclusions, OK?"

"I don't care what you say. I'm still frightened, and I'll be frightened until they're caught. Don't argue with me. I know what I feel," she lashed out.

"OK, I won't. But I still trust our government and our intelligence agencies."

"You would."

"Want to watch the rest of the news?" Ed asked.

"No. I can't handle any more. Besides, I have to get the children ready for bed. School's tomorrow, remember? You watch. Let me know if learn anything about STN."

She left the den. Alone, Ed pondered what else he could have said to calm her down. Nothing came. He, however, was too flushed with victory, impressed with his own achievements, and anxious for more attacks and more success to be concerned about Janice at this moment. He no longer worried about *Mandatory Targets*. The world now knows that STN will not only exterminate terrorists and their families, along with their Circle of Contamination!

I agonized about killing the children, but no longer. Unfortunately, it is important they must die so they don't grow up seeking revenge against us. It has to be that way so terrorism can never threaten us again.

He remained glued to the TV until the 11:00 news ended.

31

SIX DAYS LATER:

Throughout the week, the media continued their focus on STN. They trotted out more and more experts to voice their opinions and baseless predictions. Global TV news networks solicited the reactions of Muslims, Arabs, and Islamic Fundamentalists. Reporters questioned whether the average person in the Mid East felt less safe because of the STN threat. They were angry that STN would dare to threaten illegal action on their soil, and vowed their determination to defend their homeland. Many promised quick retaliation. Shouts of "Death to STN. Death to the infidels. God is Great," rippled throughout the massive agitated crowds rallying throughout the Muslim world.

The opposite reactions came from citizens of democratic countries. By a wide margin, people lauded STN and hoped they would succeed, in spite of their difficulty with the STN callous willingness to kill anyone: men, women and children. Remarks such as "It's OK to go after terrorists, but not their families, their kids or their parents." And "It's not morally acceptable," exclaimed others. Many, perhaps most, felt killing the families of terrorists was "proper payback for their indiscriminate killings of innocent people."

Pacifists hoped the terrorists "would get the message and stop the killing and live in peace." They denounced STN as terrorists and murderers and demanded immediate government intervention to dismantle and prosecute STN leaders before they ignite a global war that no one can win. Agitated hawks vented their anger and frustration "They deserve it. They never worried about killing us, so why should we worry about killing them?"

Cooler heads supported the Rule of the Land.

"The world cannot tolerate vigilantes, no matter their supposed justification. They are no better than the Islamic Fundamentalists they want to eliminate. STN is irresponsible and equally as ruthless. The law must prevail if we are to succeed as a civilization."

Everywhere emotions ran high. Ed found it stimulating to hear of the overwhelming support at work for STN. Although most people with whom he spoke expressed a deep concern about their target selection, they nonetheless begrudgingly praised STN for taking direct action against terrorism.

Bin Laden issued a new video quickly displayed on global TV. In it, he angrily vowed retaliation killings to avenge the deaths of the "great martyr Sheik ibn Sulimari." US and Israeli security forces reacted immediately by beefing up security on all hard and soft targets. These actions only served to reinforce fears that the terrorists might try to make good on bin Laden's provocative statements and threats.

Three days after the STN announcement, al Qaeda delivered their own message in their own way. An aborted attempt on the life of Juan Hernandez Francisco, The Director of Security of Spain, and his two–man security team failed when he narrowly escaped serious harm. A grenade thrown from a speeding motorcycle exploded just as Mr. Francisco was walking from his home to his car. The swift thinking of his bodyguard saved his life by tossing him to the ground and out of the path of the blast. The car absorbed the brunt of the explosion. The unidentified motorcyclist sped off. The Deputy received only superficial wounds, thanks to his fast thinking bodyguard. Al Qaeda quickly took credit, through the assassination attempt failed. The West understood the message. Al Qaeda vowed more bloodshed if STN dared to attack Muslims.

Three successful terrorist bomber attacks in England, Canada, and Germany hogged the headline news during the week. Thirty-six people killed, fifty-nine wounded. Al Qaeda gleefully claimed responsibility. The people responded with their usual fear and anger. Spontaneous protest gatherings in England, France, Canada, and the United States blasted the headlines. In similar rallies in Muslim countries, crowds shouted their joy for the al Qaeda's rapid response, reminding the world that Muslims were strong and capable of protecting themselves.

Another terrorist bombing in Kuala Lumpur, Malaysia, occurred at the Shangri-La Plaza hotel. No one claimed responsibility, although al Qaeda was the prime suspect. The hotel was hosting a conference for the International Bankers Association, whose purpose was to address the economic conditions of third world countries and how they could help reduce poverty and corruption. The explosion occurred at 10:48 AM, killed eighteen people and injured another fifty-eight. The blast shredded the left wing of the hotel that housed the conference rooms.

Timothy Barrows had just arrived at the airport to attend the conference when the attack happened. He exited the plane, spoke with security, and was immediately placed under protective custody at the airport, pending next flight availability for his return to the States. He left within the hour.

Two days later, al Qaeda operatives struck again, killing twenty-three people in an open food market in Jakarta, Indonesia. Other terrorist organizations followed the al Qaeda lead. They increased both their propaganda and suicide bomber attacks. Following the mass carnage, al Qaeda unleashed a stream of statements threatening "to continue to wreak vengeance on civilians and governments." They vowed to defeat STN, and promised to fight until they achieved victory. STN conveniently provided the propaganda platform for bin Laden to denounce the governments of The United States and Israel. He called them the demon agitators acting through STN against Islam. Bin Laden's rhetoric fanned the fires of anger and demonstrated his renewed commitment to the warriors of a new jihad he promised to ignite.

People anticipated another STN attack. They were not sure if STN was able to fulfill their promise. The wave of terrorist attacks created chaos around the globe. People and their governments feared the world was entering into a new phase of conflicts, where killings on both sides would escalate until no one was safe. Unbridled fear described the emotion of citizens and governments, prompting rampant accusations of insufficient security, poor intelligence, and general incompetence of nearly every world government.

President Alan Schuster held a flurry of top-level morning meetings with his advisors. The topic: naturally STN. The President again vehemently and continuously denied any affiliation with STN.

One afternoon meeting focused on the current US strategy, security, and contingency plans. At 3:45 on Thursday, September 16, the President met with the heads of Homeland Security, NSA, the Joint Chiefs of Staff, and his Counter Insurgency Chief.

"Gentlemen, we have a threatening situation on our hands, one that must be handled with extreme care and security. Each of you has a briefing statement, which I will read to you personally. I want each of you to understand what I will soon make public.

I have instructed the heads of our intelligence agencies to apply maximum effort to investigate STN. I have ordered all departments to mobilize and officially placed on high security alert. Rest assured this government intends to do everything in its power to protect our citizens and our laws. STN has triggered multiple retaliatory attacks on our friends across the ocean.

As you know, we are on Red alert. I have ordered all agencies and the military to take defensive positions. SAC and the Coast Guard are operating around the clock to protect our waters and borders. The National Guard, recently mobilized under my orders, is cooperating with Homeland Security and the Army. We are on a temporary wartime alert. I am committed to insure our forces protect our soil and our people. For the moment, I feel we are under no immediate danger.

STN is a vigilante group who has violated our laws. We will deal with them accordingly. The crisis precipitated by STN has placed the entire world in danger. No one knows what they will do next, if anything. You are aware they promised more attacks within a week. Tomorrow is seven days. I have spoken with my counterparts and they assure me they have taken extreme measures to protect their citizens from either terrorist or STN attacks. Let's hope they are successful.

Hannah Stemsure, my spokesperson, will make an announcement late this afternoon reflecting our status and preparedness."

The President continued.

"Now let's get down to the non-public portion of what I have to say. We may be facing a national emergency because of STN. I am angry that our intelligence agencies were unprepared for the first STN attack on 9/11. Since we cannot undue the past, we can only move ahead to protect our interests. You and your departments will apply maximum effort to investigate and learn everything about STN. I want to know who they are, who funds them, and how they operate. I want your reports and recommendations within a week. I also want your inputs on how we are going to prevent retaliatory terrorist attacks against us domestically and abroad. This is a maximum priority. I want answers, and they had better be right!

I've been in touch with leaders of thirty-eight nations, including our Arab and Muslim friends and enemies, assuring them in the strongest terms possible that the Unites States had no knowledge or any association with

STN, and that I intend to maximize our efforts to track STN down and bring them to justice.

I have also agreed to share our intelligence with our friends, as they have with us, so we can work together to prevent an escalation of hostilities that no one wants and everyone fears. Every head of state has expressed the same concerns, even our enemies. We all are concerned about STN and its potential to create havoc in the world. No country can or will permit a rogue group to exist to kill whomever they chose. The same rules that apply to terrorists also apply to STN. Their actions are unacceptable and intolerable. World leaders agree that STN poses a potential threat to world stability.

This government will be in a pickle if we have to fight two different types of terrorists. Make no mistake STN is a terrorist organization, in spite of their goals. My counterparts and I have agreed to work together and put our differences aside to contain or destroy STN.

It is in our best interests for us to prevent this STN war from escalating into a battle that could potentially result in hundreds of thousands of casualties. That is our official position. A public announcement will follow this meeting after we sanitize the message for the public.

Yet this brings up an intriguing thought. Off the record, I suspect each of you have reached the same conclusion as I. Although STN violates our rules and our sense of morality, they could work to our benefit. Assume for the moment that they are able to back up their claims to eliminate terrorism. If we do our best to stop them from succeeding, then wouldn't we be foolish? Think about that before you hit the ceiling.

STN might offer the only real solution to terrorism available right now. We have failed miserably in our fight against them. I'm sure no one has to remind you of that. Not only cannot we stop terrorists, but what's worse is that we haven't been able to infiltrate their organization. Frankly, our intelligence sucks. We can't slow them down, nor have we been able to prevent them from wreaking havoc on our economy and our resources. This is not a knock on our intelligence people. I understand the problem, and I'm certain they are doing everything possible. However, the truth remains. We know little about them and their plans.

We have proof that Iran has been a base for recruiting and training terrorists. Terrorists used Iraq to gain combat experience and apply it to Gaza and Lebanon. The experience they gained has allowed them to expand their influence. We've done a piss poor job of containment, we're stuck in Iraq, and Pakistan is heating up. Wherever we look, another terrorist organization is creating chaos. We can't do shit to stop them.

When I received my briefing after their announcement, the hairs on my head stood up. I was outraged and pissed that our vaulted intelligence community did not know they existed, let alone knew they were planning World War III. I wanted to wring someone's neck, or kill them myself. I might have, if anyone of them was in the room with me. I said to myself,

"Here we go again. Another group of trigger-happy maniacs on the loose. Whatever gains we made to win the confidence and trust of the Muslims will disappear because of STN. We're the ones who will eventually suffer the most. Many believe we are supporting STN. Because we lost our credibility during the Bush years, our claims of innocence are ignored. Many people and I suspect many governments too, believe we *are* backing them. I don't know which is worse. Losing our credibility or being accused of supporting STN. Both stink.

If the Muslims and Arabs truly believe that, it will cause incalculable political damage to us. I can envision a world where death and destruction will be the norm. That was the biggest fear and gut reaction to the news about STN. We cannot allow that to happen, I said to myself."

The President paused long enough to allow his message to make its impact. Then he continued.

"However, after I calmed down, I realized there might be another side to the situation that calls for exploration. First, make no mistake; you sitting here have some heavy explaining to do about our lack of intelligence. Why in the hell didn't we know about STN? Why haven't we intercepted one message, one phone call, one letter that pointed us in their direction? Trust me, if I learn someone or some agency blew it, heads will roll. I'll discuss that aspect of this damn intelligence mess later in the week. For now, I want to focus on an intriguing thought about STN.

First, we must learn what we're up against. I am restricting the dissemination of any intelligence data to those of us in this meeting. I insist on no discussion of information, speculation, or policies outside this room. Is that perfectly clear? No news media. No unauthorized discussions. Nothing! If there is a leak, I personally guarantee that you will find yourself in court facing charges of being a traitor. Everyone clear on that?"

He looked around to examine the surprised looks on their faces. Satisfied he had their attention, President Schuster continued,

"Back to my thoughts. I have considered this STN situation from many angles. Suppose, for the moment, STN does not pose an immediate threat to us. If we can convince the world that we are not sponsoring them, that we're cooperating with our friends to stop this STN threat, then there is another aspect that might be our golden grail. Let's assume that things calm down and the rest of the world lets us off the hook with STN. There might be a positive side to STN. We know we suck when it comes to fighting terrorism. We'll kick their asses in any traditional military encounter, but that's the limit of our power. Now STN bursts on the scene, killers who are doing something we can't or haven't been able to do; hit the terrorists where they hurt. They can go after people we cannot without violating the laws of other countries.

Think about this. What if STN *can* stop the terrorists? One day terrorists are alive, the next day they're dead."

He paused again to allow his words to have the desired impact.

"Does that suggest any possibilities to you? Perhaps, a world without terrorists? Think what that could mean to us. STN has declared war against the terrorists. I'm personally impressed they chose 9/11 to begin their war. I feel that was a stroke of genius. It must be psychologically devastating to bin Laden and the global terrorist organizations. With one decisive blow, STN snatched away their claim to glory to which they have been clinging for nine years. I felt a sense of pride and gratitude to STN.

I am excited that someone has a new approach to ending terrorism, one in which I privately believe. Admittedly, the thought of them killing innocent women and children appalls me. Aside from that despicable fact, if STN succeeds, it has the potential to bring long-term benefits to us and the world. STN kills off terrorists and we're the ultimate beneficiaries. We will be free to act to preserve our economy, allow it to grow once again, and catapult us back as uncontested leaders of the world. Doesn't that sound sweet?

So what should we do? We are facing a huge dichotomy. To fight or not fight STN. Which path should we take? The moral one? The practical one? The answer is obvious, people. The practical solution wins. I say let them kill off the terrorists for us. As long as we stay out of their way, hopefully, they may have a chance to succeed. That doesn't mean I don't want to know everything about them for our own security and protection. No doubt we'll take some heat for not doing enough, which, do I need to remind you, we're already getting.

Expect criticism from our friends and our enemies and probably lots of pain. The risks are high, but so are the stakes. Yet, I believe the risks are worth taking. STN has the potential to wipe out terrorism without the baggage and legal restrictions we face. The real beauty of any non-action we take is that we are not breaking our laws. Who can blame us for poor judgment or incompetence? If we are able to reach our goal of destroying terrorism, then don't the results justify whatever course of action, or non-action, we pursue?"

The President paused, took a sip of water from his bottle and continued his monologue.

"Do I approve of their tactics? Certainly not! But, if we intend to give STN the opportunity to wipe out terrorism, we'll have step aside and let them do it their way. It may be difficult because it challenges our personal and national belief systems, but we must be strong. Remember our goal and our commitment is identical to STN's. Rid the world of terrorists.

Are you listening to the reactions from our citizens? Have you been paying attention to the 24/7 news casts? By a wide margin, the people of the United States support STN, not because they believe in their methods, but because they believe in their goals. People desperately want to see an end to terrorism. They want to see an end to our military personnel dying throughout the world fighting terrorists. They want to bring home our thousands of young men and women soldiers risking their lives in Iraq, Afghanistan, Pakistan and dozens of other places around the globe that no one can pronounce.

Our people crave and deserve peace, security, and the right to continue our way of life. That is clearly what they want. Don't we want the same thing?

This is my plan. We must go balls out to learn everything about STN, and I mean everything. I demand maximum effort here from each of you. However, as I said previously, what we learn will remain *Top Secret: For Your Eyes Only*, and on a need to know basis. This applies to everyone in this room, without exception. There will be no internal or public disclosures, not to your staff, not to Congress, and not to our allies. We cannot permit world opinion to believe that we are not supporting the global outrage against STN. We'll make the expected public statements expressing our horror and our uncompromised and vehement support. We'll promise to commit our full resources to end the STN atrocities. To the world, we'll be the leaders against STN with our unwavering commitment.

We'll show good faith by sharing some non-essential information with our friends, but not enough to allow them to dismantle STN. I want STN to have every opportunity to succeed. If we see they are faltering, or they lose public support, we can quickly step in and dismantle them. We'll deal with them appropriately when the time comes. For now, our mantra must be *Learn Without Action*. We will patiently wait and see. We will sit back and let them destroy global terrorism. We MUST secretly be resolved to embrace STN to give them the chance to succeed in their fight against terrorism.

That is my official position on STN. Does anyone have a problem with it?"

None was voiced. The President smiled and nodded his approval to his inner circle of practical thinking people.

"Thank you for your support. I believe history will one day accept this decision with respect and possible reverence. Imagine a world without fear of suicide bombers. A world free and at peace!"

They spent the next hour discussing the wording for the President's announcement. They openly endorsed the President's position to support

STN. Several silently questioned the judgment of the President and his followers, but refused to voice their concerns.

32

KARACHI, PAKISTAN:

Bilal, Bruce, and their field leader Ra'id talked on a conference call to review last minute details of their initial HuM strike. Ra'id's responsibility was to ensure the Pakistani teams were prepared and to lead the attack. He confirmed his teams were ready.

"I think we've put together an excellent plan," exclaimed an excited Bruce MacCardle after Ra'id dropped off the line.

"In seven hours we will unleash our part of this war. In seven hours, your revenge will be satisfied. Seven hours, Bilal, just seven more hours!"

In Pakistan, it was seven o'clock PM, Friday, September 17, 2010.

"It has taken too long already to avenge my family. It has been over a year since their deaths. A long time to wait to fulfill my promise," Bilal reminded Bruce.

Bruce could easily imagine his friend's face at that moment. Not like his, brimming with excitement and anticipation. He knew Bilal was stone-faced, serious, and seething with hatred. He also knew Bilal had descended into his inter-self from the time the letter reached him in South Africa, and there he stayed. His singular motivation was to see HuM destroyed.

Since his arrival in Karachi, his conversations with Bilal were brief and to the point. No friendly chatter, no laughter, no remorse, and no moral concerns about how many men, women or children were to die. To him, they all must die, without exception.

Bruce recalled how excited he had been when he first received Bilal's call to join him. He anticipated being with him, sharing their meals, their thoughts and their fears, as friends do. It turned out to be a fantasy. Yes, he was living the life of a wealthy businessman. He lived in relative luxury and enjoyed the perks that his cover offered. He mingled with the powerful, the wealthy, and many who sought his favor in anticipation of personal gains. Because of this, he had provided Bilal with extensive and valuable information on terrorists, their supporters, and government plans aimed against STN. His presence in Karachi was more than justified.

They worked together, but only by phone, and only with the briefest of conversations. They met only four times, away from Karachi, and away from attentive ears and eyes. Each time Bruce initiated the meeting. Each time Bruce felt the need to see his friend in person. Each time he led the conversation, about the weather, about his life in Karachi, and his feelings of continual isolation. They met at restaurants outside of Karachi. Bruce mainly wanted to mitigate his loneliness. Usually they parted within the hour and returned to their separate worlds. Bruce never received the companionship or the intimacy of friendship he desperately sought. Bilal always arrived with one foot out the door. He felt disappointed and frustrated. He deeply missed the old Bilal from the days at ExecProtect. He began to fear the new one.

Perhaps once HuM is destroyed he will rediscover himself. Then both our lives will be better, Bruce thought. *I need him to be my friend more than I imagined.*

Bruce was lonely in Karachi. He'd been there for a year, without real friends or family. When he wasn't in public selling his business persona, he spent hours in his bungalow, watching TV, reading books, listening to music, or planning an attack. Mostly he had time to think, to reflect, and to question. Many questions with no answers.

Who is el Berubi? The Bankers? How much did Bilal know about them or about STN? Is Bilal my friend, my boss, or my business associate? Why hasn't he confided in me? Does Bilal even care about me? Am I a means to his end? To fulfill his vow, and then to be discarded in this hot country? He's become a cold and calculating man, a death machine with a single purpose, one without guilt or remorse, someone I don't know nor understand. Perhaps I never will.

Bruce felt sad, unsure of his value or his future with Bilal or with STN.

Yet, he tried to look on the bright side of his dilemma.

I have a job to do, and I will do it to the best of my abilities, with or without Bilal's friendship. The future will be what it will be.

*

The American Region had struck first on September 11, 2011. The Pakistani media reporters dutifully read the message from Farook announcing the start of the war against terrorism. Government officials, including those from Pakistan, issued their statements repudiating STN, vowing to maintain their territorial sovereignty. The devastating successes of the American team rattled the area Muslims and angered the local terrorists.

Bilal's team was ready to impart the next blow against terrorism.

The teams reviewed their plans for the final time. Bilal remained on the phone to speak privately with Bruce.

"I want you to call me as soon as the attack is confirmed as successful. I've instructed Ra'id to call you as soon as his teams confirm the targets are dead. The entire operation should take less than ninety-seven minutes. I expect to hear from your lips that the head of HuM has been cut off, and the body is bleeding to death."

"I will call you," Bruce promised.

"Goodbye for now, Bilal. I am positive you will have the news you crave."

The line went dead.

*

PAKISTAN, SEPTEMBER 18, 2010:

Seven hours later Bilal's STN struck HuM. Two forty-one in the morning of September 18, 2010, seventy-two HuM leaders, their families, their supporters and their families in Pakistan and Turkey died from multiple gunshot wounds fired from weapons with silencers. Four other STN Regional killing teams attacked the same morning as did Bilal's team.

Two fifty-eight that morning, Bruce called Bilal.

Bruce answered on the first ring.

"Done! All targets successfully eliminated," Bruce excitedly informed Bilal.

"My revenge has begun. The first of the HuM leaders are dead." Bilal responded in a steady and monotone voice.

"My wait is over. My revenge will be complete. Were there any casualties?"

"No one from our teams," said Bruce enthusiastically. "I knew everything would work as planned. We make a good team, don't we?"

"Thank you on behalf of my wife Nasrin and my five children."

Bilal closed his flip cell phone without another word. He stared toward the sky and in a soft shaky voice said aloud,

"It has taken longer than I wanted, but your deaths will continue to be avenged with each new attack on the remaining HuM killers. Forgive me for taking so long to restore your honor." Bilal addressed Nasrin's picture he had removed from his pocket.

One single tear slid down his cheek. He suddenly felt tired, exhausted, in need of sleep. His vow partially completed, he gave himself permission to sleep, permission that he had consistently denied himself since the day of the letter.

His attack was the largest single death toll for STN, bigger than the

American's and the other four attacks. The HuM executions took slightly over an hour.

The spoils from the attacks, now permitted by Farook, were especially rewarding to Bilal's teams. The booty from the ransacked properties of Elahi and his supporters was highly profitable. Each team member had 29,000 Rupees added to their personal Swiss bank account. Bilal, man-machine Bilal, had his taste of revenge. Though it had been his driving force, it brought him little personal satisfaction or pride. He was hardened beyond emotion or feeling.

*

The morning of the seventh day arrived. People throughout the world had wondered if STN would or could fulfill their promise. The media hype continued unabated since the initial STN strike, debating STN's strength or their weakness. Meanwhile, Las Vegas got into the swing of things and set the odds at 1.5-1 that STN would attack as promised. Many had doubted they would be able to strike again because their enemies were on the alert and looking to protect themselves. People of the free nations were not sure how they should feel. Should they put their faith into STN's ability to attack or risk being a fool for believing in them? The pundits pointed out that if STN was able to attack, the one thing in their favor was that the terrorists did not know which of them was to die. The terrorists worried who would be STN's next target.

33

THE SECOND ANNOUNCEMENT, SEPTEMBER 18, 2010:

Few were disappointed. Within the space of two hours, global STN teams implemented their attacks at locations in Afghanistan, Gaza, Saudi Arabia, Indonesia, England, Germany, and Pakistan. Hundreds of terrorists and their Circle of Contamination died. That afternoon, at noon, Washington time, Farook issued his second announcement of the STN war on terrorists. It was simple and deadly:

"Believe us now? This is only the beginning. Terrorists beware. STN."

Dana Ross, KTX, Washington:

"Whatever doubts may have existed about STN were convincingly dispelled yesterday in daring executions in five European, Middle Eastern, and Asian countries. STN is for real, ladies and gentleman. Last week, they claimed they were capable of striking anyone anywhere in the world. Yesterday they proved it. By the latest count, they have executed 273 people in eight countries, including the thirty-two from last week. As before, there were no arrests or witnesses. STN was thorough. Not even family pets survived. These attacks have ushered in a new aspect of the battle against terrorism. Unofficial sources expressed their amazement that STN completed these attacks, in spite of the increased security deployed by both democratic and Muslim countries. STN managed to bypass them to execute the entire Al Jamiya organization, located in six of the seven countries. Another group, key members of Harakat-ul-Mujaludin, also referred to as HuM, in Pakistan, died at the hands of the STN assailants. Both are terrorist organizations that were responsible for multiple bombings and attacks on foreigners. Questions again arose as to how much the global intelligence community knows about STN. If any government did acquire any intelligence information, then, from here, it looks as though the promised data sharing did not happen as President Schuster originally indicated in his speech last week.

STN obviously knew where these people lived and worked, knew their habits, and knew how to overcome intense security. There is no longer any doubt in this reporter's mind that STN is highly deadly and very real.

We have reports from around the globe of a unique phenomenon, one we have never before seen. Crowds in the tens of thousands are holding spontaneous rallies in support of STN in almost every free country in the world. It's almost as though STN has developed an International cult-like following overnight. Excited and energized, crowds are singing songs and dancing in the streets, many carrying hand made signs proclaiming "STN, Our Heroes." "STN saves the World." And "Down with Terrorists."

Our information indicates that global police and military personnel are offering no resistance to these massive rallies. I am amazed that STN attained such a lofty status in just one week. My guess is that because people have been so frustrated and angry at the lack of progress against terrorists over the years, they are eager to latch onto anyone who promises them greater security and peace. So far, STN has delivered.

We are witnessing a political phenomenon of support for STN. Contrast that to the world leaders. Heads of States continue to respond with outrage and threats against STN. Their position is that STN is no better than the terrorists they are murdering. They continue to promise to bring them to justice for their crimes against humanity. It seems strange that governments are willing to pacify terrorist organizations and countries, the ones they have tried to contain for years, over an organization that promises to solve their most vexing problem.

Think about it. We have governments vowing to hunt down STN, while the people look to them as their saviors. If STN continues to make good on their promises, that puts most governments at direct odds with their own citizens. The greater the STN success, the wider the gap will become. Where this leads is anyone's guess. I do not believe any democratic government ever had to face such strident popular opposition. The real unknown is what the reaction of the people will be if their governments continue to oppose their wishes. The marches in the 60's against the Vietnam War were small compared to what might soon take place if this dichotomy remains unresolved. Moreover, the Schuster administration admits they have learned nothing about STN's operation. Yet, they continue to oppose STN quite vigorously. Very strange set of circumstances, indeed!

I leave you to ponder these disturbing thoughts. This is Dana Ross, KTX, Washington."

*

KARACHI, PAKISTAN:

Bilal followed the first HuM attack with two more executions within two months.

After the 9/11 attack, STN globally struck seventeen times within four months. Bilal's two attacks registered the most deaths by any region since the North American's initial strike.

With renewed fervor, Bilal, driven by his team's stunning success and with the taste of blood and revenge fresh on his palate, pushed Bruce for plans for more strikes against those on his target list. He drove Bruce and the team relentlessly with added intensity and a sudden sense of urgency. In spite of the heavy pressure from Bilal, Bruce heard no complaints from their team members. Why would they? They were becoming wealthy men. They understood that not all attacks would yield the bounty they looted from the first strike, but the opportunities remained boundless. They were ready to seize it. From September 2010 through February 2011, Bilal's group made eight attacks. The toll: 194 terrorists' dead, no STN loses.

*

Months passed with no new revelations, but with considerable bloodshed. STN continued their successful attacks on terrorists. Terrorists responded by attacking soft targets, mainly people in congested places. The high alert by global military forces prevented six infrastructure attacks.

STN remained the target of political pundits. They raised a series of questions that defied answers. Some aggressive media moguls cautiously hinted that information existed on STN, but governments were keeping it concealed, supposedly for security reasons. Well-known TV journalists including Howard Korantz, Kayla Walnut, and Aidan Killian, tried to intimidate President Schuster by alleging government officials already knew about STN, but refused to divulge their findings to the public. They made nightly editorials demanding a full accounting by the government. Despite continued disclaimers by the White House, the media suspicions continued.

People became highly polarized. Some brave souls picked up the nightly chatter, convinced that the US government was backing STN. Others raised the possibility the government has information about STN, but was actively blocking it. The vast majority of global citizens did not care whether their government was or was not involved. They were quite satisfied. They were enjoying the major inroads against terrorism by STN.

STN made no further announcements. They did not need to. Their actions said it all. Successful attacks on terrorists continued. The lack of information about STN gave vent to a plethora of rumors and conspiracy innuendoes. Conspiracy advocates had a field day. Theories sprung up like weeds, accusing one government, then another, of supporting or secretly controlling STN. They quickly escalated the rhetoric that the US government and/or the Israeli government, or both, were involved in a cover up. Fueled by the militant Islamic propaganda machine, jaded rumors persisted that STN was secretly directed and funded by the United States, Israel, Russia, England, China, France, Japan, and several unnamed Arab countries, all working under the direction of President Schuster.

Some creative talking heads went so far to claim that even the Muslim nations were cooperating with the US because they feared hostilities would spread to their countries.

In truth, these highly vocal government officials were indeed part of an inadvertent and unintended conspiracy, but not the one that their accusers claimed. Government leaders who purposely took no action against STN's reign of terror were the true conspiracy culprits. At some point, they all had made a conscious decision to violate their own rules by allowing STN to continue to exist. It suited their needs. STN was destroying terrorism, and that followed their plan.

The people of the world, however, were not playing politics. They had simple wants. They wanted to live in peace, free of terrorists. They didn't care who was involved with STN.

The public was hopeful, yet cautiously worried. They worried about the escalating bloodshed. They remained fearful that terrorists would be emboldened to take more catastrophic actions against defenseless people.

Yet, they reviled in the expectation that soon, the world would be safer now that terrorism was under attack. Many rejoiced because they felt terrorists were on the receiving end of fear, the same kind of fear they had created as they blindly attempted to destroy civilization. They adored STN and applauded their results. No one cared or thought what would happen when terrorism ended. No one wondered what would become of STN, and no one cared. No one except for the leaders of the free world.

While the world wondered, rejoiced, and worried, STN was busy planning their continuing series of executions. The seventeenth week into STN's war was the week from hell for terrorists. STN struck in eighteen countries, killing over 268 people. Six hundred and sixty-eight STN related executions were reported over a nine-month period. STN took to leaving a typed message at their site of each of their strikes. It read "Complements of STN."

By May of 2011, eight months after STN burst onto the scene, terrorism was beginning to collapse. Global terrorist attacks dropped from 250-300 per day to less than nine. Terrorism was on the run, or at least walking at a slow pace. Terrorists and non-terrorists alike, who previously enjoyed a semi-privileged existence before STN, pleaded with their Muslim governments to protect them. Families who before could boast of their children's bravery and martyrdoms, now cowered in fear least they too became targets. Neighbors and friends who used to gleefully speak with pride and praise for the exploits of suicide bombers, now completely shunned the families of possible terrorists. Afraid for their lives, they distanced themselves from dangerous affiliations.

Intelligence agencies clearly confirmed a marked reduction in total terrorist acts. Information collected from multiple sources corroborated that terrorist recruitment and funds were drying up. Young Muslims no longer were willing to risk their lives and those of their wives, children, parents and siblings. Persistent reports surfaced that dramatic reductions in funding, weapons deliveries, and the popular support previously enjoyed were also on the decline. Apparently, the news pundits suggested, the STN formula, however brutal, was having the precise effect they predicted.

High-ranking US officials congratulated themselves on their foresight to wait and allow STN to do their work against terrorists. Anticipating the inevitable demise of terrorism, government officials began to make long-term plans to address the domestic needs of their people, the issues of the world economics, and to provide additional support for the Peace Envoys.

As the best politicians do, they never lost sight of what it takes to retain their personal power. For the first time in years, businesses planned their future with confidence.

STN's stature and popularity continued to expand unabated. People from every country and from every occupation began placing ads in newspapers. They wanted to join STN. They expressed their desire to take an active role in the new wave of the future. They wanted to do their share to hasten the destruction of terrorism, now that the end seemed near. People pledged support funds, but had no address to send their checks. The entire STN organization remained secret, hidden and impenetrable. They continued to operate autonomously, while the STN team members accumulated vast amounts of money from the looting of their victims.

No global intelligence organization, including the CIA, Mossad, or M16, had produced a single clue or a shred of evidence about STN. Their personnel, their finances, how they operated and where they were based, remained a dark secret. There were no arrests. They expected none.

People began to track the number of STN related deaths on a weekly basis. Global citizens, delighted with the numbers, staunchly prayed the death count would continue to increase. They rightly equated an increased STN terrorist death toll with an increase in their own security. Global doubts about STN's viability completely disappeared. People put their unbridled trust and faith in this clandestine organization. World citizenry accepted that STN had devised the perfect formula to eliminate terrorism. They conveniently overlooked the fact that many innocent people also died. To them, the end justified the means, providing they were the happy recipients. As long as terrorism was on the decline, no one cared about the means used. That was the overwhelming rationalization used to accept the STN carnage. They wholly disregarded STN's vigilante and illegal actions.

Throughout the winter of 2010 and spring of 2011, STN remained the topic of conversation. They continued their successful rampage against terrorism. To the delight of the world, the number of global terrorist bombings rapidly declined even further. Still, the separation between government posturing and the people's beliefs remained polarized. Suspicion, adulation, fear, hope, anger, and conspiracy theories continued their emotional rollercoaster. Not a day went by without some mention of STN and their inspiring success against the extremists. By May 2011, over 1814 terrorists and their Circle of Contamination became STN victims. The people cheered while governments grew increasingly apprehensive. They knew they had lost control.

34

KARACHI, PAKISTAN:

The names of the terrorists or their organizations no longer mattered to Bilal. They were terrorists, and all terrorists must die. No terrorist group was more important than the last. None was more urgent than the next, and none more rewarding. Because of his determination, Bilal and his team experienced remarkable success with their strikes.

The Pakistani STN team continued to add the unlimited names of terrorists throughout the region as their targets. They managed one strike every six to nine weeks. Their strike frequency was nearly double that of any other STN region. Bilal wanted more, but planning and surveillance took time. That displeased him. He had become an insatiable killing machine, one with a boundless appetite, one that would or could not be satisfied, no matter the numbers or the frequencies of the attacks.

The accelerated pace sufficiently worried Bruce that he decided to talk to Bilal. He knew it would be tricky. Bilal was too driven, too blinded, and too isolated to accept change. Bruce worried if they did not slow down and allow their team adequate rest, their risk of failure would increase dramatically. The men were getting tired. He was tired. He feared the pace would result in insufficient or careless planning for the next operation.

Bruce worried how he should approach Bilal about his concerns. His hope of a more humane and friendlier Bilal after their initial success was quickly shattered. He had expected Bilal to feel relief, excitement and possibly less pressure after the successful execution of HuM leaders. Instead, everything reversed. Success fueled his desire for more killings. Bilal became obsessed and more bloodthirsty. Bruce suddenly felt very frightened. Of Bilal.

I thought I knew and befriended this man. But he's changed. He only lives for another conquest, and even that does not seem to satisfy him. More is not enough. He offers no thanks and asks for none. He never smiles, laughs or cries. He is out of touch with reality. He is a perpetual motion killing machine with a boundless appetite to destroy everything in his path. Perhaps, it is time for me to leave Karachi. Perhaps join another STN region. But how? I have no way of contacting el Berubi. I don't know who he is or where he lives. Yet, my heart goes out to Bilal. He was my friend, and the terrible tragedy of his family's death totally fucked him up. He deserves my loyalty, for now. But I need to watch him. I need to protect myself from this new man I neither like nor understand.

Bruce decided he had to talk to Bilal about the accelerated pace and the toll it was taking on the men.

"We need to talk."

"So talk."

"We need to slow down our attacks. We have been working continuously and we've been very successful. However there is a new enemy. It is us. We are pushing our team and ourselves too hard. The men are tired and need a rest. You and I can work long hours because we know we have experienced cell leaders who will compensate for any mistakes or deficiencies in our planning. But, we are not the ones who are in the field. We are not the ones..."

Bilal interrupted.

"Are the men complaining?"

"No, nor would they." replied Bruce

"So what is the problem? We've lost no one in the field. The authorities have no clue who we are or when we'll strike again. Things are working quite well."

Bruce took a moment to respond.

"We rely on our team to succeed. Without them, we no longer can exist. It's time to give them a break. As their leaders, it is up to us to protect them, even from us. We cannot send them on missions when they are at risk to fail. The terrorists are on alert. They are paying more attention to everyone around them. They are taking many more precautions, and our job becomes more difficult. Tired men make mistakes. We cannot afford one small mistake, not as STN, not now when we are beginning to have a serious impact on the enemy."

"What do you recommend?" Bilal asked. His tone was surprising. Bruce thought he heard some concern in Bilal's voice, something he had not expected to hear.

Bruce stammered. 'Let me... err.... think about that." He was shocked to hear Bilal responding.

"I think we should take two months off. We can still do our own planning while the men rest. They need time to tend to their lives."

Bruce was not sure why he selected two months. It was the first number that came to mind.

"I agree, but we too should take time off to refresh ourselves. Tell the cell leaders to take the time."

"Thank you, Bilal. I'm sure the men will appreciate your concern for them. I will let them know it came from you."

"Do what you want. I will contact you in six weeks to restart our war against terrorists. In the meantime, relax and avoid trouble. Goodbye."

Bruce scratched his head in amazement.

Who and what is this man? Friend? Something else? He's obsessed with killing. Yet he unexpectedly shows compassion for the men. I can't figure him out.

A perplexed Bruce MacCardle reached for his half-full bottle of his favorite single malt Balvenie scotch and poured a double shot. His thoughts returned to Bilal. Bilal the enigma. Bilal the killing machine. He took out a yellow lined scratch pad to make his Bilal list.

One: He is consumed with STN

Two: His appetite for killing is insatiable

Three: He's only happy when we talk about a new attack or he learns of the number people we killed

Four: He avoids contact with me and the team leaders,

except during our planning sessions

Five: He has no interest in anything. Not food,

not entertainment, not people

Six: He may be depressed. He's dramatically changed since the trauma of his family's death

Seven: We were friends. But now he shuns my friendship

Eight: He just showed concern for the welfare of the men, which I didn't expect

Nine: Perhaps he is ready to return to the old Bilal. Yet, I am not sure of our relationship. Are we friends? Associates? Am I merely a pawn in his personal war against HuM? I don't know where I stand with this man.

Seven bad things, only one possible good one, and one that is unsure. But seven bad don't balance the other two, Bruce enumerated.

Convinced his concerns about Bilal were well founded, he worried what he should or could do.

"I know who he was, but I'm not sure who he has become. There is only one thing of which I am certain. Bilal must be watched and feared!"

He continued to say out loud what was on his mind.

"He is different and dangerous. He makes me feel uneasy and uncertain. If I'm his friend, why do I only know one person within STN, and that's him? He told me of his Egyptian contact but only shared his code name with me. The STN trail ends with Bilal."

The real question remains. Will his obsession get both of us killed?

It was a thought that would soon define the rest of his life.

35

FALLS CHURCH, VIRGINIA. JUNE 2011:

His attitude flipped 180 degrees from the early days, before his 9/11. Ed Walker relished the thought of more attacks. He hated the dull and uninteresting time between each one. He marveled that STN remained an enigma to the world. By fighting for a noble cause, they had earned the respect of the masses. STN were phantoms, never seen, but always experienced. They achieved continual success without a single failure. Never had there been an arrest and each strike was clean. No clues ever left behind. Ed wallowed in his own self-importance. Success has a way of bringing that out in people.

I started the war for freedom. I proved STN was strong and ready. I burned the name STN into the minds of enemies and friends.

His ego peaked at full charge. Between the North American attacks, Ed was greatly relaxed with Janice and the kids. Inside he craved for more STN action. Outwardly, he knew he needed to act differently to continue to deceive Janice. He engaged in playful banter with her. He made a monumental effort to show more affection during their lovemaking. He proclaimed to her that it was more satisfying and more loving.

I love Janice, but I hate to admit it she has become less important than STN. I sometimes feel uneasy when we're together because I am afraid of letting my guard down.

One evening, just after they had made love, and they were resting naked next to each other, she turned to him and said,

"Do you realize we both have been soooo much happier? I love you more than ever. You're more attentive, your lovemaking has become more exciting, and you are more tolerant of the kids. Actually, and don't let this go to your head, you've become nearly a perfect husband and father, even though you are traveling all the time. These have been the happiest months of my life. I thank you for that. This is the way I saw our marriage from the beginning. Now that it's happened, I sometimes pinch myself to be sure I'm not dreaming."

"I love you too. I guess I had to go through that garbage for the President to realize how important you and the kids are. I feel much happier now. I promise it will never end!" he exuberantly lied.

He meant every word. Mostly they applied to Liz Hunter.

I love Janice, and I love Liz too. Perhaps more than Janice. How could I have even thought of dropping her? I'm glad I decided against it. She's as much a part of me as Jan.

Somehow, the thought of loving two women simultaneously made perfect sense to him. It validated his sense of self-importance.

Janice continued to accept his excuses for his time away from home. It became an expected and normal aspect of their lives. She believed that his CIA work was a major deterrent to terrorism. She preferred to ignore the part that STN contributed. She continued to resent STN because of their tactics. She concluded that her husband's work at the CIA was making the world safer. She was almost right. She merely had to reverse CIA with STN.

How easy it had become, Ed thought with considerable pleasure. *Janice accepts whatever I tell her about traveling. No hassles, no accusations of infidelity, no pleading for the "sake of the children." I'm amazed what can be done under the umbrella of love.*

All was well in the household of Mr. and Mrs. Ed Walker, their two children and their French poodle. Ed Walker was master of his universe. *Mandatory Targets,* killing the families of his targeted terrorists and their Circle of Contamination, no longer intimidated him or violated his sense of morality. He accepted the fact that they all had to die. He was thankful the Circle was out in the open. People seemed to accept their deaths as a necessary part of the war against terrorism. Ed believed that STN's *No survivors* policy was indeed only a minor inconvenience.

*

STN became a staple reporting aspect of the daily news. Continual hammering from the talking heads spouting their newest theories captured the public's avid attention. They could not get enough of STN. They loved hearing about their heroes.

Several newscasters were beginning to report a sordid yet obscure aspect about the STN attacks. They noticed that the police reported valuables had disappeared from homes and offices of the victims after each attack. Some questioned why such a well-financed organization needed to resort to petty thievery. Irwin Terpin, a reporter from the Washingtonion Today postulated a theory. He proposed that STN was removing the valuables so they would not fall into the hands of relatives or heirs of the deceased and used against them later. He likened it to the scorched earth policy employed in World War II: Leave nothing of value for the enemy.

No one suspected he was partially right. STN's intent *was* to prevent funding of retaliatory attacks. However, Farook had conceived another purpose for the valuables. Motivation. The fact that the STN teams were highly paid mercenaries, Farook also reasoned they suffered from the human trait of greed. He saw no harm in providing an extra incentive for the field personnel.   Valuables looted from each raid fueled that incentive. Farook understood that some percentage of those who fight in the field treasure tangible reminders of their success. Many soldiers loot or engage in souvenirs hunting as their reward. He made looting an acceptable STN behavior. He encouraged his global teams to steal the valuables under the premise it would prevent future retaliation. Whether they bought into his explanation or not, did not matter to him. It worked. The men were happy and he was satisfied.

His plan was simple. He wanted to provide the added incentive, but feared the influx of added money or jewelry would find its way to the black market, which then might be traced back to STN.

Farook deposited an equal share of the loot into the Swiss bank account of each member after an attack ended. No one objected to the arrangement. To the victor go the spoils. STN members eagerly embraced this concept as each man prospered.

Ed knew his team members were discouraged from lack of work. Their continued success resulted in fewer targets available in the US and Canada. The team grew antsy from both inactivity and lost cash. His cell leaders pleaded with him for more strikes.

Ed guessed they were on the verge of overwhelming success in the Western Hemisphere. He estimated that terrorists would be eradicated within another two to four months. Financial and emotional support for terrorists had dropped dramatically now that their supporters feared for their lives.

South America remained the sole area where STN had not attacked, and for good reason. Little known terrorism existed. Instead, massive and powerful drug cartels posed the biggest threat. Ed wondered if his days as STN Regional Leader might soon evaporate due to a lack of viable targets. He wasn't sure how he felt about that prospect. He knew his team would not be happy. He wondered if their real motive for more targets was to loot more valuables from their victims.

I can't worry about their motives, he thought. *My purpose was to eliminate terrorism and bring peace and security to the world. I'm almost finished. Nothing matters. Yet, this has been the best time of my life. I don't think I could return to my former life. I love what I'm doing.*

Liz remained part of his dilemma. Ed was emotionally torn. He vacillated between ending vs. continuing their affair. In some ways, it made sense to end it. She had helped him get through his tough times, before he became successful. Now that his confidence was elevated, his focus was on the future.

Why risk everything now? I've keep the affair secret, but, for how much longer? Eventually most affairs are exposed. I'm not ready to sacrifice my marriage.

But, I do love Liz. She's become a vital part of my life, and I cannot just abandon her. I like things as they are. I can keep the apartment with or without STN. I'll always find time to be with her. With both Liz and Janice, my life is complete. Liz stays! He liked his decision. It would prove fatal.

Liz's dilemma was not nearly as difficult. She didn't have one. She liked Ed because he was decent looking, a good lay, safe, and treated her with respect. Some of the men prior to Ed treated her like the slut she was. She felt Ed was worth some extra effort. She didn't care about a future with him.

She always made herself available whenever possible to accommodate Ed. She enjoyed being with him, even though he wasn't rich. She sometimes wondered why she didn't want to settle down like other women. The thought of staying at home, watching little kids run around, caring for them when they were sick, and being a homemaker repulsed her. She preferred the freedom of being a businesswoman, free to travel, free to sleep with whoever suited her, and do whatever pleased her. It used to bother her when Ed told her how much he loved her, and that she had to remind him that was not in her plans.

Men! Most are just plain dumb. Give them great sex and a little personal attention and they're out of control.

She worked hard not to allow the concept of love to complicate their relationship. No commitments, no future, no kids, and no marriage. That's what she wanted, most of the time.

Lovers, not a husband, are what I want. Marriage is too limiting. The present is what I have, for as long as it lasts. I can live with it, as long as I have my good looks. What happens then? Maybe I am just a dumb blond! she openly rebuked herself. *Maybe it's time to think of a future, for when I'm older.*

"Who really knows about the future?" she recently wrote to her college friend Ashley Morales in their weekly email correspondence. The two were roommates in Purdue before Liz dropped out in her second year. They remained good friends. Liz was a bridesmaid at Ashley's wedding. Their friendship continued even after Ashley moved to Barcelona with her Spanish husband seven years ago.

"Things can change, and I'm willing to live with that. As long as I have my looks, I'll take my chances on the future. I admit I like Ed Walker more than most of the men I've been with over the years. Frankly, I can't see myself married to anyone. The thought makes me nauseated. Ed is overwhelmed and intrigued with his undercover work. Even if I wanted to think about a long-term relationship, it would take him forever to decide what he wants to do with his wife. Frankly, Ashley, I don't know if I should hang around long enough to find out. What do you think?"

Ashley wrote back.

"Find an unmarried man; build a life filled with kids, a home, and love."

Liz replied, "Maybe I'll think about it later."

*

During June and July of 2011, Ed's team completed only one more strike. He was running out of targets in his region. One evening, he decided he needed to speak with Farook about his problem. At 1:32 the following morning, he called.

"Thunder."

"It is good to hear your voice. Thank you again for your commitment and the continual excellent performance of your team. Your success has inspired the entire STN organization. The Bankers feel equally grateful because of your achievements. They asked me to personally thank you. But, as always, we must be brief."

"I need your help. We're running out of targets. My people are growing restless. Any suggestions?"

"I've anticipated this for a while and I have a new category of targets. People other than terrorists threaten our way of life, especially the ones who take advantage of our society and who cause pain and hardship to others. I'm taking about criminals, drug dealers, murderers, hate mongers, rapists, child molesters, gangs, counterfeiters, and other scum of society. The list is endless. Now, that your terrorist target list is smaller, we can shift our focus on those who are just as threatening as are the terrorists. The group I just mentioned is a good place to start. What do you think of including them?"

Ed didn't blink as he answered, "Why not? Frankly I hadn't thought beyond terrorists. But, I see your point. Yes, I totally agree. They make excellent targets. What about their families?"

"As before. Nothing has changed. Do you have a problem with that?"

"I have no such issue."

"One day our mission will end, once we destroy all the evil people who wish to destroy civilization. It will end, but I cannot say when," Farook stated.

"I think another announcement to the media to define our new thrust against criminals will be in order. Your team will initiate our new plans. Much work remains in the Middle East and Asia against terrorists. As you know, since we began our campaign, we have seen a 72% reduction in global terrorism, and nearly 93% in your region. Quite a remarkable achievement in such a short time, don't you think? I'll make another announcement after your first new target strike. You may attack whenever you are ready. Call me when you select your target. I'll send you the necessary information. Goodbye, and thank you again."

"Goodbye," a joyful Ed Walker replied.

"There might have been a time when I would have rejected this, but no longer," Ed thought aloud. "Although I originally signed up to destroy terrorism, Farook is right. Our job isn't done. My teams will be happy to have more targets. This is an exciting development I had not considered!"

His self-designated importance prevented him from recognizing any other considerations. To him there was no difference between a cause with valor and the irrational behavior of vigilantes. He was unable to separate moral validity and moral bankruptcy. He saw no conflict between acting legally and violating the law. Consequently, he viewed his new target list as a natural sequence in the war for peace and democracy.

Anyone who takes freedom from us or threatens our security is the same as a terrorist. They don't deserve to live. My mission is saving the world. This is the final piece of the puzzle. First, the terrorists, now the dredges.

Ed delighted in the added glory that was soon to be his. The future was exploding, and was getting brighter and brighter.

Thank God I'm here to save mankind, he congratulated himself. *Thank God I'm here!*

Within the week, Javier Rialdo became Ed's first criminal target. Rialdo, a transplanted Brazilian, reputed to be the leader of the notorious El Porto (The Door) cartel in Miami, had established lucrative drug distribution centers along the Eastern seaboard of the United States. Like the Mafia in Chicago in the 30's, Rialdo had Judges and lawmakers on his payroll to protect him and his people. The FBI estimated he had over eighty-three operatives and bodyguards in the country, and controlled a 200 million dollar heroin empire. He used boats, seaplanes, and a submarine to smuggle his drugs into the porous coast of Florida. Some authorities believed he also smuggled into the United States over 170 Latinos, whom he recruited from South America, to assist moving the drugs around the United States.

The FBI had tried to penetrate El Porto and failed. Three undercover agents disappeared while on the job in Florida. No indictment had been ever served. Rialdo lived in a high tech security mansion on Jupiter Island in Florida, which served as his US headquarters. Ed contacted Farook to pass on Rialdo's name. He expected delivery of the computerized Rialdo portfolio within the week.

Five days later a three-inch binder profiling Rialdo arrived at his office detailing Rialdo and his operatives. Ed and his cell leaders worked diligently for six weeks on plans for the Rialdo strike. The team was ecstatic. This would be the largest and most complex attack of their team since it required all ten of the North American teams. It would be the first attack without the comfort of a backup team. Ed's confidence in his planning and the execution capabilities of his teams allowed him that luxury

He again selected *Sabertooth*, his best field leader, to head this attack, the one in whom he would entrust his life. They spoke by phone to separate the attack scheme into two segments, a necessity because they lacked the manpower to handle Rialto's large group on the same day. They planned the deaths of twenty-nine of Rialdo's direct staff in the first attack. Twenty-two people were scheduled for death in the second group. *Sabertooth* was happy the numbers were low, compared to the larger number of terrorists they killed on most of their attacks.

"It will make our planning and our attack much easier," he remarked to Ed.

Phase two of their plan, the remaining twenty-two, would be executed two days later. With a split attack, Ed worried that some of Rialdo's organization might escape if they determined they had become STN targets.

Ed asked Farook to withhold his media announcement until everyone on the Rialdo hit list was dead. Without an announcement it would make the remaining targets easier to execute, he explained. Farook agreed.

The teams received their assignments after Ed and *Sabertooth* completed their plans. Ed detected a renewed excitement among the men. The nature of this attack was different from the others. Before Rialdo, the principal motivation for his team was the destruction of terrorism and the preservation of democracy. The new emphasis shifted to something less esoteric. It was the first time the financial incentives of an attack outweighed ideology. It bothered him since he expected the bounty from Rialdo would make his team rich, very rich.

"Once they get their hands on Rialdo's money, they might decide to quit STN," he complained to *Sabertooth*.

"If they feel they've completed their original goal to destroy terrorism, and now have accumulated so much wealth, they might want to retire to lead the easy life. What then? Would they have to die? And by whom? El Berubi will blow a gasket if that happens."

"We might have to start over with a new team. That shouldn't be too difficult. The newspapers receive hundreds of personal ads a week from people who begged to join. We'll worry about that if it happens. In the meanwhile, we have a job to do." *Sabertooth* replied, while assuring Ed his thinking was accurate and clear.

Ed, *Sabertooth*, and the nine other cell leaders spent countless hours on conference calls planning and refining the Rialdo plan. Farook assisted him with one major obstacle to the mission. Rialdo had a highly sophisticated electronic surveillance system installed on his property that protected the grounds and the house. The entire perimeter and adjacent fences had the latest in motion detectors, closed loop video cameras, silent and audible alarms, and pressure sensitive alarms imbedded in the grounds around the mansion. Anything larger than a cat would instantly set off one of the alarms. Armed guards with assault weapons were looking for an excuse to justify their jobs.

Satisfied they had considered all contingencies and completed their surveillance and preparatory work, Ed selected Sunday, August 21 and Tuesday, August 23, for the two-phase attack. He selected these dates because they knew Rialdo, a Catholic, would stay close to home on Sunday and would be an easy target. His teams didn't mind a Sunday attack. Rialdo, his family, bodyguards, his financial and strategic advisors and their families were the main targets for phase one. Millions of dollars were rumored stashed on the grounds, waiting to be snatched by the assault teams. The teams knew it. They were like racehorses prancing at the gate, anticipating the explosion from the starter's gun.

*

RIALDO, FLORIDA. AUGUST 2011:

It was a steaming hot day the early morning of August 21, 2011. Florida was mired in an eleven-day heat wave. The average daytime temperatures hovered in the high 90's. Six straight days the temperature hit over 100 degrees. The normal Florida summer humidity lingered throughout the evening. Governor Max Conner declared a state of emergency, and called out the National Guard to go from house to house to check on the health of the poorer citizens who might be suffering from heat stroke or dehydration. Most Floridians avoided leaving their air conditioned homes, if they owned that luxury. The temperature had dropped to a sticky 93 degrees in Florida on the morning of the attack.

The strike teams were in place on Jupiter Island, West Palm Beach, Tampa, Pensacola, Miami, and Albany, New York. New York weather was a pleasant 74 degrees. Great weather for executions. The thought made Ed smile.

Rialdo's fortress on Jupiter Island breached easily. A jamming RF signal from the power company compromised the elaborate state-of-the-art electronic alarm and TV monitor security systems, without tripping the electronic backup system. Ed wasn't sure how he managed it, but he accepted Farook's assurances that the alarm systems would be disabled. They were.

Rialdo, his wife, their four children, and three bodyguards died first.

Within 47 minutes, the full force of Ed Walker's North American STN team attacked Rialdo's four outlet locations in Florida and one in New York. Twenty-nine dead, plus two unexpected overnight houseguests. The teams scrambled to position themselves for phase two.

The evening news heightened the mystery of the twenty-nine deaths. TV news anchors tried to link STN to the attacks, citing similarities in the execution style, the early morning attacks, men, women and children killed, valuables missing (preliminary estimates over $5 million dollars in cash), no witnesses and no clues. However, they reasoned, STN's fight is against terrorists, not criminals.

"Could it be a copycat organization? A rival drug gang? The Chinese? The Russians? The US government?" they questioned.

Two days later phase two ended in the death of twenty-two of Rialdo's people. It added fuel to the already rampant media speculation. FBI and state police in Florida and New York jointly agreed to cooperate in the investigation of these crimes. As a platitude to the anxious citizenry, they assigned their top personnel to investigate the murders.

Tuesday evening, August 23, 2011 the mystery was resolved. Farook, after receiving word from Ed that the Rialdo attack ended successfully, boldly flaunted STN's power with the following media announcement:

"Hello again from STN. In the eleven months since we announced our war against terrorists, we have reduced global terrorist actions by 72%. Terrorism is dying. We have eliminated virtually all terrorist activities in North America. In spite of our achievements, our work is not complete. There still exist elements of society whose goal is to destroy our life. They steal, murder people, sell drugs to our youth, and generally cause havoc. Today, STN is happy to announce we are expanding our operations. Drug dealers, murderers, pirates, counterfeiters, hate groups, prostitution rings, and gangs, we welcome you to our list. We consider you the same as terrorists. Death is your reward, for you and your Circle of Contamination. We know who you are. There is no escape. Abandon your criminal ways.

To our many international supporters, do not worry. We are continuing our successful operations against global terrorism. We will continue our war against terrorism as promised on September 11, 2010.

Today STN has eliminated the drug king Javier Rialdo and his entire organization. They and their 200 million dollar drug empire can no longer hurt you and those you love. Rialdo has the dubious honor of being the first criminal to learn about us. He did not deserve to enjoy the profits of his illegal drug business. Javier Rialdo's gang of drug and

slave dealers experienced our justice. Good riddance to them and the hardships they caused.

You and those around you are NEXT. You have seen what we have done to the terrorists. There will be no further warnings. Continue at your own risk!

BEWARE TO ALL WHO WOULD DESTROY OUR SOCIETY AND OUR SECURITY.

STN"

In the privacy of their offices, the top echelons of management of Homeland Security and CIA high-fived themselves, openly applauded, and endorsed STN for eliminating the dangerous and elusive Rialdo. It was, however, a bitter pill for the FBI to swallow. They had not lost sight of damage it did to their reputation. They had the original assignment to destroy one of the most powerful criminal groups in the East, and they failed. After four frustrating and fruitless years of FBI investigation, STN completed their job for them in eleven months. Their ineptitude was a source of embarrassment to themselves. It had the unhappy effect of casting a shadow of doubt about the capabilities of all US intelligence agencies.

STN's success was stunning. The announcement enhanced their image as the knight in shinning armor to the people of the world. To the officials in power, however, it had the opposite effect. STN was beginning to look tarnished and highly threatening. Their continual success against terrorists, combined with their new commitment to destroying the criminal element, added an immediate layer of doubt and fear in the minds of government officials. President Schuster was no exception. These concerns were beginning to approach personal fear.

Criticism in private quarters grew louder against STN tactics as their lawlessness and success became bolder and more assertive. Though always recognized as the ultimate vigilante anti-terrorism organization, courageous newscasters cautiously voiced their opposition to STN's expanded role. Media critics and doomsayers grew more vocal. They vigorously shouted their disapproval with the lack of government action against STN. They demanded more government intervention. They trotted out the traditional catch phrases they used to stir up the masses:

"STN was entering dangerous territory by usurping the fundamental tenants of democracy. No matter the crime, everyone is innocent until proven guilty. No vigilante actions should override our laws. Everyone is entitled to a trial, no matter the alleged crime. And, a man is innocent until proven guilty by a jury of his peers."

Newspaper headlines screamed in two-inch type,

"STN-The New Terrorists?"

Commentators quickly drew the parallels between STN and terrorists. They asserted that the only difference between STN and terrorists was that the original ones killed indiscriminately with bombs, while STN made conscious decisions as to who should die by assassination.

"That made them more fearful and more criminal than the Islamic Fundamentalists," they claimed.

Meanwhile, their supporters paid homage to STN for taking the fight to terrorists and now to the criminals. Energized youths continued to seek ways to join in the heroic STN fight. They referred to them as "brave warriors" who were defending the rights of people to "life, liberty and the pursuit of happiness." The United States had developed into a pot of boiling polarities. Those strongly in support of STN and those equally opposed

One enterprising newspaper, The Baltimore Sun Times Herald, did a feature piece by a junior writer, Debbie Tonner. She wrote that she had conducted an extensive investigation on the STN slayings and had uncovered one aspect of their attacks that received only moderate media attention. Valuables were always missing from the homes and offices of the STN victims. Little was mentioned about these activities, and, as far as she knew, no stolen merchandise appeared in the open or black market. She pointed out that the main items missing were cash, jewelry, and artwork cut from their frames. Other expensive and large items remained untouched.

She insisted that as much as four to five million dollars disappeared from Rialdo's estate. Untouched were high priced electronic gear including stereos, large screen TV's, weapons, and cars. Ms. Tonner questioned why no one had considered the STN thefts before.

Perhaps, she postulated, STN's motives were not what they seem. She postulated that they might be an elaborate gang of thieves and not engaged in the noble and commendable mission they so vehemently claimed. Instead, their attacks could be a giant ruse to cover up their real intentions. Instead, they might be, and she emphasized *might be*, the actions of a highly sophisticated criminal gang accumulating massive wealth, while hiding behind the guise of moral righteousness. She introduced robbery into the STN equation.

She titillated her readers with her speculation that STN might be the smartest criminal gang to perpetrate an immense hoax on a gullible world. If that was their motive, she wrote, it seems logical and natural to presume that STN turned their attention to the criminal element. Master criminals are flush with large sums of cash. For STN they are easy pickings.

"Modern day faux-pirates," she called STN. "Old time pirates made no bones about who they were or what they wanted. These modern day faux-pirates hide behind uplifting concepts, but their goal is the same. Wealth."

She concluded her article with,

"I offer this as food for thought, dear readers, just food for thought."

Within a week, the Herald's circulation dropped by 82% as angry subscribers hastily cancelled their papers in protest of Tonner's blasphemous accusations. The paper fired her for her "unwarranted attack on the people's illustrious and only savior."

STN remained an enigma, unpredictable, impenetrable, and deadly. Eleven months after STN burst on the scene, the US official STN intelligence dossier remained an empty folder. Politicians felt apprehensive and uneasy about their lack of knowledge of this vigilante organization operating so blatantly on their shores. Forced to rely on media announcements from STN to learn about their activities, government officials conceded their only source of intelligence was from news releases. Everyone had *that*.

These same concerns voiced by the media also appeared in secluded and secret caucuses of the top US officials. They questioned whether a free society could accept or survive the actions of a secret and ruthless organization. They questioned for how long their actions should be tolerated. It prayed on their minds that they had no means to stop this powerful enemy. Those who feared STN the most, the politicians, quietly added their voices to the growing media discontent. Reluctantly, they recognized that STN's existence could threaten the status quo. They feared that the influential image STN held over the people of the country was diluting their own power and control. The Rialdo strike reinforced their heightened anxieties. Reality suddenly struck home. They worried whose name might be on STN death list. They feared it might be theirs!

36

PRESIDENT SCHUSTER, WASHINGTON, DC:

STN caused massive fractures among friends and families. Everyone had an opinion, stridently in favor or stubbornly opposed. Another polarizing moment came with the announcement of the Rialdo attack and STN's new drive against non-terrorists. Families found themselves in the uncomfortable position of opposing each other. Eleven months before they were unified. People began to worry that this sudden change in direction would usher in a wave of lawlessness unseen since the days of the early West. Others maintained criminals were fair game for an organization that was dedicated to bring peace and prosperity to the world. The polarization extended beyond families. It was friend against friend, city against city, state against state, and government officials against one another. Passions ran deep and hard.

The camps split along the "Wait and see" and the "Take action now." The "Wait" people did not want to stop or restrict STN until they finished their mission. The "Action" people feared STN might turn on them and demanded immediate action. They questioned how STN could be trusted when they choose to ignore the rules that govern civilization, in spite of the benefits they brought. The citizens of the United States recognized that the decision was out of their hands. They hoped President Schuster and his team could sort matters out.

Within the government, confusion was equally as rampant. Officials acknowledged the absence of STN intelligence severely hampered their ability to take action. They agreed on one issue: they didn't know which position to publicly support because they didn't know what was right. They took the coward's way out. They straddled the middle. They weakly vowed to bring STN to justice, while begrudgingly acknowledged their success and the inroads they made against terrorism and now, the criminals. They felt trapped and they knew it. So did the entire country.

One week after STN's Rialdo announcement, President Shuster convened a top-level emergency security meeting in the White House. In attendance were his Chief of Staff, the Director of Homeland Security, The Military Chief of Army Services, heads of the CIA, FBI, NSA, and selected advisors to the President.

The President spoke:

"We all heard the latest STN announcement, and I'm sure everyone has their own opinion as to what this means to each of us and what it means to the country. In the past, we willing stayed on the sidelines and tried to gather intelligence when we could. We tacitly agreed to allow STN to do what we, as a government could not. Eliminate terrorism. Unlike the terrorists whose goal is to break our will through global chaos, STN has a direct purpose: to rid the world of terrorism. And I'd have to say, they've been doing one hell-of-a good job. My hat's off to them.

We've seen the number of known terrorists in the US drop dramatically, while the number of worldwide attacks and bombings has also been significantly reduced. According to the latest unofficial count, over 3000 terrorists, their families, and their associates, are dead. I feel pain for the innocent women and children, but I understand STN's concerns about potential revenge killings ten to twenty years from now. I wish it didn't have to be that way, but that is the reality of the situation.

I'm sorry to admit we have failed in the intelligence area. Its non-existent and we are not alone. My International counterparts also report the same. They also know nothing about STN, or so they tell me.

The few promising leads proved useless. As you know, we always use the national security umbrella to hide our lack of intelligence on STN. The public's blind acceptance helps.

During the week, I have revisited the entire STN situation. Initially I jumped for joy at STN's emergence. That is no longer the case. Their last announcement convinced me they have become a major threat to us, more than the terrorists, and I will tell you why. On the surface, it's easy to make the case that STN has not changed their mission, only their targets. Terrorists, criminals, what's the difference? Both destroy our society, costing us enormous amounts of manpower, money and effort. And our results are not nearly as successful as STN's. Best of all, STN's doing it for us, free. We don't have to lift a finger and we get what we want. Sounds perfect, doesn't it?

But therein is the hidden danger. When STN only focused on terrorists, we eagerly embraced it. Now they are concentrating on the criminal elements of our society. On the surface, that too makes sense. Who wouldn't want to see Rialdo's empire dismantled? God knows we've been trying for years, without success. But look at what is really happening. STN is defying us and our laws. They decide who is guilty of a crime and decide their punishment. Only their punishment is death... you know the rest. Our criminal justice system has been cut out of the process.

It would be easy to sit back and let them finish the job. Yet, as I said before, STN presents a real danger to us. In addition to trashing our most cherished principles of the Rule of the Land, STN poses a personal danger to everyone in this room. Suppose STN decides someone in this government should become one of their targets. It could be you or me, for no reason other than they disapprove of our policies or our actions. Perhaps not tomorrow nor the next day, but what about next week, next month, or next year? Are any of us safe? Can anyone sitting here claim that Homeland Security can protect our families and us? Unfortunately, you know the answer. You have seen STN's ability to defeat even the most complex securities systems. They could decide to turn on our religious leaders, our corporate men and women, or our military leaders. Unfortunately, it could happen! The truth is that we are unable to protect our citizens or ourselves. This has become our worst nightmare.

Each of us could one day be an STN target. We wouldn't know until one evening, some gunmen showed up at our homes to kill our families and us. You'd have no chance to defend yourself. You and your family would be dead. With our less than robust intelligence on STN, who would stop them or bring them to justice? And then what? Who takes command of our government? STN leaders? Their puppets? It's not a pleasant picture.

We can no longer hide our heads in the sand. This is not who we are. The principles of justice for all define this great nation of ours. Every man, woman, child, criminal, or politician, has a right to face their accusers in court. From the highest to the lowest levels of our society, everyone has the legal right to prove their innocence. The Rule of the Land prevails in these United States of America. They must continue to prevail if we are to live in a society that respects the rights of all people to live without fear of unwarranted incarceration, executions, or loss of personal properties. These are our own rules, and they define us as a democracy. We cannot causally trash them, nor can we allow others to trash them for us.

We cannot be hostage to others, even if they are doing our dirty work. That is unfathomable, irresponsible, and cowardly. To do so is a direct abrogation of our duties as elected representatives of the United States and as leaders committed to freedom and the principles of democracy."

President Schuster paused to take a drink of bottled water and to allow his audience to reflect on his words. Not one person spoke. They were hanging on his every word.

"It is therefore my decision," the President continued, "that the government of the United States will actively seek to disband and destroy STN from this day forward. By the end of this meeting, I will again charge the intelligence community to place maximum effort to gather all intelligence on STN, to actively work closely with and share all data with our closest allies, and to develop a realistic plan to stop them. I am open to discussions or suggestions on the best way to proceed, but I will not entertain dissent or proposals to ignore STN. The time for lip service has passed. It's time for action. What we decide to do may not be popular with many of our citizens. They revile in the hope for peace and security that STN has given them. Unfortunately, they don't understand the consequences. By the time they figure it out, it will too late. We must look beyond today and tomorrow for our people and our country. It is our duty and our responsibility. The people elected us to protect the present and insure the future. It is time to meet that trust with action.

History will someday acknowledge that we took the proper and prudent course to stop an emerging threat to our way of life. Let's hope there still is time. At this point, I admit I do not know the solution. However, make no mistake. If we fail, it could mean the end of our country and perhaps the world, as we know it. We need to figure it out, and soon. Before I continue, I want to know if anyone here disagrees with my position. You are free to leave. I will accept your immediate resignation."

He slowly scanned the room, waiting like a panther in the brush ready to spring at her prey. No one stirred. They were in survival mode.

"I ask now, and for the final time, if you disagree, you are excused from the meeting and my administration. Anyone?

No one stood.

"Good. We agree! This meeting has the highest level of security. There will be absolutely no disclosure of our intentions or our plans, even to our allies. For the time being, secrecy is of the utmost importance. I'm counting on you to find a solution before you leave this room. You are the brain trust of our country. We need your guidance and expertise right now. I'm returning to my office to give you time to come up with a plan to destroy STN. Everything is on the table. Leave no stone unturned. Explore every possibility. I expect a solution before you disband, even if it takes all night.

I'm appointing Sam Lancaster, CIA Chief of Operations, to lead this effort. Call me when you are ready with your proposals and recommendations. I'll be in my office. I want to hear the moment you are finished. This is war. Treat is as such. Think hard. Our lives depend upon it!"

He quickly walked out of the room to his private bathroom to throw up.

A little over four hours later Sam Lancaster made his call.

"Mr. President, we're ready. We have a plan."

"Excellent. I'll be there shortly."

President Shuster made his way to the conference room with a determined stride.

I have some of the brightest minds and most risk adverse people making suggestions to protect our future. I can only hope that their brilliance will outweigh their reluctance, he thought.

The Marine guard opened the double door to the room.

"OK Sam. Ready?"

"Yes Mr. President, we are."

"Proceed."

"There is one possibility. We recommend you call a special news conference as soon as possible. Publicly state your opposition to STN tactics, but show your agreement with their goals against terrorists. Acknowledge that STN has fulfilled their mission quite admirably and they deserve recognition for their accomplishments. Authorize full amnesty for all STN members if they disband and return to civilian life. Give them 90 days to comply. You could also hint that you would integrate them into our intelligence community. We could use their expertise to protect our liberties and our democracy. Possibly suggest a willingness to create a separate intelligence agency for them, reporting directly to you. We do not feel that you should mention their recent activities with the criminal element. We suspect they would be highly sensitive, especially so quickly after they announced their new initiative.

Frankly, Mr. President, we suspect they will ignore this offering. It is our collective belief that they feel empowered and immune from our authority. They have opened a new avenue to justify their existence. We are certain they will reject this offer. They have the capabilities, the intelligence, the motivation, the finances, and the independence to achieve their goals. They already have proven what they can achieve without us. Our own laws and limitations are often our worst enemy against terrorists and criminals. We believe it will be very difficult to convince them to disband. Yet, it's worth a try, though we should expect a resounding NO.

The other problem with this approach is our people. We all understand their admiration and allegiance towards STN. And, rightfully so. They delivered where we couldn't. They gave them hope and security and the American dream. We gave them nothing. We've spent over several trillion dollars fighting terrorism in Iraq and Afghanistan. Yet terrorism continued to cause havoc, until STN appeared. We cannot compete with them. We suspect the public will not understand why we are trying to disband them. We will appear power hungry and afraid of STN and their success. That's a tricky road for us, one that I'm afraid, Mr. President, we personally might lose. They could decide to throw us out of office in the next election.

We understand why our people look the other way even when our rules are broken. People only want peace and security. To make this approach work, we either educate our people to the dangers STN presents, or hope STN screws up and public opinion turns against them. Neither is likely, but it is a realistic option. We need time and a media blitz to influence our citizens. Even if we continually educate them that STN is a vigilante criminal gang who are in it for the money, we would have to tap into the element of fear to turn them against STN. We know..."

"Stop right there! I've heard enough!" interjected the President. His face turned a crimson red with anger.

"This is the best you can recommend, after four hours? I find it hard to believe. Your so-called plan stinks! You suggest we wait for STN to screw up, for us to spend years educating the people about the dangers of STN, and you call that a plan? It won't work because it's stupid! I'm not going to beg them to stop. I'll look like an ass when they don't. What else do you have to offer?"

"Actually, we don't have anything else. Perhaps if we can intensify the CIA and Homeland Security operations to expand our intelligence on them, we might be able to come up with another plan," Sam replied.

"Unless I'm badly mistaken," President Schuster said with sarcasm dripping with each word, "we've learned crap about them in eleven months. What makes you think things will change?"

"Well Mr. President, no matter what direction we take, we might be facing incredible obstacles."

President Schuster stood up and first glared at Sam and then directed his anger at the others.

"Over four hours and this is what you came up with? It's no wonder we can't do shit around here, with outstanding thinking like this!

I can't believe I selected you for my cabinet. That apparently was my first Presidential mistake. The second is not firing every one of you!"

He angrily stomped out of the conference room shaking his head in disgust. The brain trust of the government of the United States sat in silence, stunned at the President's indignation, uncertain of their jobs and the future.

Sam Lancaster broke the silence and spoke to the stunned audience.

"He's upset, but he'll calm dome once he realizes we don't have many options. I'll talk with him later and try to get him to understand. There's a possibility he'll say yes, after he has a chance to think about it. He's done it before, so, we'll see. It's a slim chance, but I'll try. Assuming he does change his mind, and we do implement our plan, I suggest we prepare an outline on a possible advertising campaign. Also, I want to estimate budget allocations, and the time it will take to maintain this blitz until we can sway public opinion. If this has a chance to work, we'll need to give him a sense of what it will take. The tighter the package, the easier it is for him to decide in its favor. Are you willing to stay and get it done?"

They unanimously agreed. They called for sandwiches and drinks. They worked two more hours.

"I think we've accomplished as much as possible for now. I'll see the President first thing in the morning. I'll email you with his decision after our morning debriefing." Sam announced. They adjourned, weary, bleary, and disenchanted.

At the conclusion of the daily security meeting the following morning, Sam Lancaster confronted the still angry President Schuster.

"Mr. President, can I have a few words in private with you? I need just a few minutes."

"Is it better than yesterday?"

"That's your decision, Mr. President."

The frown on the President's face told Sam his political clout was on life support system.

"Well?"

"Mr. President, we stayed after you left to see if we could think of another plan. Frankly, we are still convinced our proposal from yesterday is our best option. It's a long shot, but with a few breaks here or there we can succeed. Should another better plan pop up, we can switch. I suggest you might want to reconsider, Mr. President. For now, it's all we have."

He gave the President time to mull over his suggestion. They sat in silence for nearly forty seconds. Sam sat quietly at the winged side chair at the President's desk. The President took his favorite thinking position. Feet on his desk, hands clasped behind his head, eyes closed. Ritualistically, his eyes opened first, the hands moved to his lap, and then the feet cleared the desk, right leg first then the left leg. The President was superstitious, a little known personal idiosyncrasy.

"I'm still opposed to it. I don't believe that is all we can do. We're missing something. I don't know what, but my gut tells me we can do more. We *have* to figure it out. What's that you have?" he asked pointing to the envelope in Sam's hand.

Sam handed him their budget analysis.

"We've considered the funding levels required and estimated the time we need to make our point to the American public. I'll leave this with you for your consideration, should you decide to take this approach."

"I'll look at it and let you know. Don't expect miracles," the President disgustedly answered.

"Thank you, Mr. President. Let me know if you have any questions."

"I will." Sam left the President sitting in his chair, a worried expression plastered on his face.

I need some fresh air. This is big, and I don't want to make a wrong decision. I know their dumb plan will not work. My cabinet says it's the only way. But damn it, I know they're wrong. And stupid too.

President Schuster put on a light jacket and headed towards the Rose Garden, followed by his secret service entourage. The late summer air in Washington was a pleasant 73 degrees. The light blue cloudless sky seemed to be celebrating the last days of spring. President Schuster always sought the Garden when facing weighty decisions. He reviled in the calm of the outdoors. It reminded him of happy days when he visited the farmlands of Kansas with his parents to see his Granny Maureen, his mother's mother. She preferred to be called Granny Mo. He remembered the times she spent with him in her flower garden. To her it represented life's triumphs and joy. She lavished her garden with motherly love and devotion. Her greatest pleasure was sharing her achievement with family and friends. She focused her golden years on her garden. That was her life.

She used to hold his tiny hand in her strong work-like hands as she guided him through bed after bed of flowers and plants. His parents visited Granny three or four times a year from their home in Western New York from the time he was four until she died when he was twenty-seven. He loved those days with his Granny Mo, especially the times in the spring and summer when the plethora of bright yellows, reds, and violets and flowery smells transported him to a place of deep and glorious tranquility, uplifting his spirits to lofty heights. He felt as though she saved her private secrets to share only with him. He lost himself as she affectionately described the name of each flower, and pointed out the special beauty of her favorites. They were her babies, and she took pride in their growth to maturity. They were her most treasured possessions. He never forgot those special times with her, those precious times she shared with him. Throughout his life he sought to resolve his problems among the sights, sounds and smells nature willingly offered.

The White House Rose Garden was his spiritual Granny Mo. He sensed her presence, even with his secret service trailers hovering nearby. He allowed them to do their job of watching over his safety, but at a respectable and inconspicuous distance. Then he could enjoy the sense of well being the Rose Garden offered. His protectors learned to give him his space and time without interruption. He needed this time now more than ever.

Alan T. Schuster was not a pleasant man if his sense of order was interrupted, with, what he felt, were silly questions or intolerable idle chatter. The only exception, of course, were things of national importance that could not wait until his connection with nature was complete.

Today he desperately sought the sanctuary of the Rose Garden. The decision he had to make made weighted heavily on him. It wasn't the decision itself, but the fact that he believed the plan he heard had no chance of succeeding. It was especially troubling because he had no alternative solution. He feared for the survival of his beloved United States of America.

He returned to the Oval Office, highly troubled, with no resolution to STN.

"Judi, get Sam Lancaster on the phone. Thanks."

"Yes Mr. President."

As soon as Sam picked up the phone, the President barked,

"My decision is NO. Come up with something that will work."

He broke the connection.

A thought popped into his head an hour later.

"Judi, bring me the *Red Sunset* file."

She opened the "Archive Files" directory on her computer, typed in *Red Sunset* to find the location of the file box. She called Archives, who brought the partially filled box to her office thirty-one minutes later. It was on the President's desk at 2:14 PM.

He read Ed Walker's proposal for the first time. Over two years too late.

37

THE PRESIDENT'S DECISION:

"The President's on the phone, Mr. Barrows," buzzed his secretary Natalie.

It was three weeks after STN's announcement about Rialdo.

"Good morning Mr. President. It's a pleasure hearing from you."

"Likewise, Timothy. I need to speak with you on an urgent matter. Can you come to my office at 1:30 tomorrow? As far as my cabinet and the media will know, this is a routine discussion about the Peace Envoys. Tell no one anything. This is a private meeting between you and I. Is that clear?"

"Yes sir, Mr. President. May I know the subject matter?"

"No, tomorrow will be time enough."

"Thank you Mr. President. I will be there at 1:30."

"Good. See you tomorrow."

Stange, thought Barrows. *He's calling me to a secret meeting. Something big is happening.*

He arrived at 1:21 the following day. He and Judi exchanged greetings.

At precisely 1:30, the President buzzed Judi on the intercom.

"Is Timothy Barrows here yet?"

"Yes sir."

"Show him in."

The President seemed tense and agitated to Barrows. He walked Barrows to the two wing backed chairs that Barrows hated so much.

"Please sit, Timothy."

"Good to see you again Mr. President. How are you feeling?"

"Not as good as I would like. But, that is the reason I asked to see you. What do you think about the Rialdo situation?"

"If you are referring to the fact that STN is now going after criminals, then frankly, it scares the crap out of me. Pardon my language, sir."

"Frankly it scares the crap out of me too," the President shot back. "No apologies on *my* language."

"As you probably figured out, we're in a bind. The majority of our citizens love STN. The majority of my cabinet is just as afraid of them as am I, and for good reason."

One of he President's annoying traits was his flair for the dramatic. He couldn't wait. President Schuster withdrew a thin blue pocket sized book from his inside breast pocket. It looked like a typical bank savings account book. The cover displayed in embossed gold leaf the name "Union Bank of Switzerland."

"Open it, Timothy, to page three. It's the one with the red tab," said the President. Barrows nervously flipped to the pre-marked page. There, in bold print, was a bank statement with an amount of $35,000,000 in the Deposit Column. Barrows had to look twice to be sure that he read it correctly. Thirty-five million? Stunned, mouth agape, he slowly looked at the President, with a quizzical and dumbfounded look.

"That's some number, isn't it?" the President snickered. "Now, look at the name on the account, on the inside cover."

Barrows flipped to the inner cover and read,

Timothy Randolph Barrows Jr., neatly typed at the top of the page. Beneath his name was a seventeen alphanumeric number. He began to tremble. "What is …"

Before he could say another word, President Schuster interrupted him. "Yes, that is 35 million dollars in a Swiss bank account under your name. Confused? I would be too. Let me explain. As you know, before STN came on the scene a little over eleven months ago, terrorism was threatening to shatter the world political and economic foundations. When STN made their startling announcement to eliminate global terrorism, it created a conundrum for us. Initially, we were thrilled that they were on our side and wanted to do something that we haven't been able to accomplish. Our friends throughout the free world also recognized STN's potential value and agreed with our position. The best part, or so we all thought, was that STN is fighting terrorism and it doesn't cost us a dime. They proved repeatedly that they could succeed without our interference or our help.

Yes, we all wanted the terrorists dead, but we were equally appalled because STN indiscriminately killed innocent people along with the bad guys. However, STN was the perfect foil for us. They gave us the ability to take the moral high road to renounce their actions, pretend to be pursuing them with all our strength and intelligence, while secretly delighting in their success.

Although we wanted to collect as much information as we could, and in spite of sharing our intelligence with our allies, we never learned anything about them. To this day, we still do not have a damn clue who they are, from where they operate, their structure, or how they avoid detection. We've looked into computer records, cell phone conversations, phone records, bank transactions and anything else we normally analyze, and still nothing. We found absolutely nothing, anywhere. No one knows them, sees them, or talks with them. There is no paper or money trail. Frankly, we're in the dark.

Therefore, we, our allies and me, agreed to keep our incompetence secret and out of the public domain. It wouldn't look good to admit we know squat about STN, except for what we read in the paper, and who can believe what you read?"

The President chuckled at his own joke, especially since it was a well know fact that his administration often fed the media disinformation to mask their own mistakes, or to impress the public with one of his pet projects.

"Unfortunately, our well intentioned hands-off strategy worked to perfection. We gave them free reign to succeed, and they did it exceptionally well. Terrorist organizations are virtually non-existent in the US, and rapidly shrinking across the world. Terrorism is falling apart. They're unable to recruit new members, their funding essentially dried up, and they have no place to hide. Not even the crazy ranting of religious zealots can protect the terrorists from STN. Once their lives and their Circle of Contamination lives were at risk, terrorists began to listen, and the world took a collective sigh of relief.

Their success turned against us when STN announced expansion of their killings to include criminals. We had convinced ourselves that STN would be satisfied with destroying the terrorists. Once they accomplished their goal, we reasoned there was no need for them to continue their existence. Simple or perhaps foolish logic, except they didn't want to play in our sandbox.

Things changed. Their vigilante activates against our citizens, even though they are undesirables, makes our position untenable. How can we permit STN to violate our justice system? Now it's the criminals. Who's next? They could turn on people of race, color, or us, you and me. With their new actions, they fundamentally have challenged our way of life. We are a democracy. We abide by our Bill of Rights. Everyone is innocent unless judged differently by a group of his peers. They've trashed that."

The President was on a roll, and he had no intention of stopping.

"THEY decide who's guilty. THEY decide who will live. THEY decide who will die. THEY reject the basic rights of all our citizens to a trial by their peers. This is what makes us unique. This is our democracy, and STN is destroying it. Yet, we are stuck with a real fact. The average citizen worships STN. Who can blame them? STN made their lives secure. They restored the American dream of peace and fulfillment. Because the people were enamored with STN, they chose to look the other way. They didn't complain when STN destroyed innocent people while they were killing the terrorists.

You've heard all the arguments for and against. Yet, look at the results: Terrorism in the US is almost a thing of the past. People can live without fear of a bomb tearing them apart. They can shop, attend a sporting event, or go to a family celebration and feel safe. That's what you and I hear from the citizens of our country.

The old saying of beware what you wish for, you might get it has now come to bite us in the ass. We desperately wanted STN to succeed, mostly because we failed. We are now facing a situation far more treacherous.

As I said before, we have a conundrum on our hands. STN is totally out of control. We do not know when, where, or whom they will strike. In the future, it's possible they could decide a government official should die and attack him or her. They could also decide they don't like someone, anyone, and kill them. STN is a highly organized and financed group of outlaws who make their own laws and decisions. On top of it, they have the temerity to steal the valuables from their targets' homes. We downplayed that aspect of their operation because, at that time, we didn't want to ruin STN's image with our people. We didn't want them to perceive STN as a gang of thieves. It served our needs to suppress this dirty truth about them. In retrospect, that too was a mistake.

Before STN, we had our hands full fighting terrorists. We had a limited understanding why they participated as terrorists. We believe that they would stop fighting if we could discover the key reasons why they selected to be terrorists. This thinking empowered me to create the Peace Envoys. I still believe it is a sound approach for long-term peace and prosperity.

With STN, our knowledge is even less than what we know about the terrorists. The world's most extensive intelligence organization in the world, the CIA, toiled for months and… nothing. We've made some educated guesses about their structure, but as far as I'm concerned, any janitor could come up with the identical analysis. Stinks, doesn't it?"

The President grew noticeably agitated. His frustration had found a new height. His voice raised several octaves; his delivery rate became fast and crisp. His eyes burned with anger.

"So," he continued, "my cabinet and I agree we face a greater risk from STN than from terrorists. It would be irresponsible if I, as President of the United States, did not recognize the threat and refused to take immediate action. In the past week, I have been busy consulting with the leaders of the world, both friend and foe.

The 35 million represents contributions from twenty-six worldwide leaders who also agree that STN cannot continue. They decided to join us in a combined effort to eliminate this new bred of terrorism. To fight STN, we are initiating a top secret program called OPERATION DOVE."

Barrows sat quietly, wondering where the President was headed, or when his speech would end. He couldn't wait for the President to end his rambling and to get to the point.

"I imagine you're wondering where this is leading, aren't you?"

"Yes Mr. President, you have certainly raised my interest," Barrows replied as respectfully and as calmly as his nerves allowed.

"Without going into detail, which I will explain later, I want you to hear our plan. We want you to head this operation. The bankbook I showed you is your seed money to fund OPERATION DOVE. Now, I have to warn you about several things before you respond or ask questions. This is a very deep covert operation. And one that officially has no links to me or any official of any country. If your cover is blown, I will deny ever having talked with you. You will need to do the same. We already have a plausible cover, the Peace Envoys, but we need your commitment to maintain the highest security and absolute detachment from any official sources. Is that clear?"

"Yes, Mr. President. But… the Peace Envoys?"

"Yes, I'll explain that in a moment. To continue, there will be no official channels from us for guidance or instruction. You'll be on your own, with access to as much money as you need to bring down STN. You will have to make some personal sacrifices, beginning with the time you spend with your family. We expect you will be traveling extensively throughout the world to do both jobs assigned to the Peace Envoys.

You understand there will be people, even in my administration, who will do what they can to make this mission fail. As part of this operation, your life might be at risk. To compensate you for this risk, your family will be financially well off, if the unthinkable happens, you die.

There will be both financial and career compensations, assuming you succeed, which we discuss when the time is right. I don't want your answer right now, nor do I want any questions until later."

"Yes sir, I understand," Barrows responded. Though his lips promised to wait, Barrows mind was racing towards an answer.

He's offering me a chance to put my career on the fast track. But why the Peace Envoys? That's not our mission, to destroy terrorists or STN. Yet in truth, does it matter what the mission is? There's nothing to consider. I'll do it! If there's one thing my father taught me, it was, when opportunity knocks, you'd better be ready to fling the door full open, or it disappears. Damn right, I will accept Mr. President. Damn right! he committed to himself.

He knew he would say nothing less. Neither his ambition nor his ego afforded him the luxury of refusing.

"One moment," said President Schuster as he walked to his massive desk, unlocked a drawer, removed a folder and returned to his chair.

The President held a black folder marked TOP SECRET: FOR THE EYES OF THE PRESIDENT ONLY. It was the original study known as *Red Sunset*.

"Timothy, this is a study that prompted this new operation on which we are embarking. When we're finished, you can read it in private in another room. I will have Judi issue you your own copy later, if you want. Let me briefly summarize some key issues for you. I want you to hear them before you make your decision."

The President summarized the essence of *Red Sunset*, especially the projection that Islamic Fundamentalists will control the world within sixteen years. He reminded Barrows that two years had already past. He made no mention of Ed Walker's proposal.

"Now, things have changed, STN is the new terrorist organization on the block. They need to be destroyed. That's our job. You will operate from your Peace Envoy office. Naturally, you will continue to work with Tom Peaksman. I briefed him yesterday. Tom will assist you for all your needs such as surveillance, data analysis, computer analyses, manpower, and advice. Your title will remain *Chairman, Peace Envoys.* You will now have two roles.

You and your team members will continue with the public side of the Peace Envoys. You will continue to make recommendations to assist the poor nations, just as before. With terrorism dead in the USA and dying throughout the rest of the world, we want to remind the public of our plans to insure continued and long-term peace and prosperity for all people. Every major world power is supporting the humanistic aspect of the Peace Envoys.

The covert portion of your mission, and obviously the most important, is to destroy STN throughout the world. No one, not your family, not my cabinet members, not Congress, not any member of the intelligence teams are to know the existence of OPERATION DOVE. Peaksman will report to me directly on the covert side of your activities. It would not be appropriate for us to get together more than normal. You know how smart some of these investigative reporters are. One whiff and DOVE dies.

My friends across the ocean have selected one person within their government to work with you and the Envoys. Most of them you already know since they are already on your team. Those not acceptable for this mission will be reassigned a new task before you implement DOVE. They each have a counterpart to Tom Peaksman within their own governments. They will continue to report to you. They are prepared to follow your leadership and not interfere in your operation. Also, I have arranged for a selected group of highly trained intelligence and covert military operations personnel to support you when the time is right. They will come into play when you are ready to exterminate STN. Similar teams are in place within each supporting country.

Should I or any other leader die, or become incapacitated, this project must continue without interruption. You will be in charge of this world effort and will be responsible for coordinating all DOVE activities.

Timothy, you are the final piece of our plan. If you accept, we're ready to get started. Out of necessity, the level of secrecy and isolation within the government must be at the highest levels. First and foremost, we must insure STN does not learn about our... err... project. Second, as I said before, we will be virtually invisible from you. It wouldn't look good if we announced our collective intention to rid the world of STN, when the masses remain so grateful and enamored with them. No one, and I repeat, no one, is to know who you are and what you are doing except for the members of the Peace Envoys. Is that absolutely clear?"

"Yes Mr. President."

"Before I proceed, what do you think? Is it achievable and are you the right man for the job? Are you willing to take on this task? Will you put your life on the line? Are you willing to lead a secret life, one in which you can never discuss what you are doing with co-workers, family or friends, possibly for years? Do you understand, really understand, what I'm asking you to do?" challenged the President.

"I understand you need some time to consider this offer. Timothy, It's a big decision, one that will impact your life and your future."

"No sir, I'm ready to serve my country in any way I can. If you have selected me, I cannot refuse. I do not need any further time. I'm ready to serve the demands of my country. One question, Mr. President. Why me? I'm sure you have more senior and better trained people within the government, people whose experience might serve you and the country better."

"Two reasons. Your outstanding efforts with the Peace Envoys and you have the perfect cover already in existence. You have a combination of experience and leadership that makes you uniquely qualified. You have shown a quickness and agility of mind to digest vast amounts of data, logically assemble it, and deduce conclusions that are right on target. You're decisive, bright, aggressive, and strong-willed. That, plus I like you.

You're our man. By the way, the choice among the global leaders was unanimous. Every major International intelligence agency reviewed your credentials over the past week, and not one objection was voiced," the President said proudly.

"I'm flattered, sir, and frankly shocked. I didn't know that anyone was looking at me that deeply," Barrows offered.

While he remained calm on the outside, Barrows was jumping out of his skin.

I never planned on this, but here it is! My golden chance to head up a world task force on one of the most important missions of history. It boggles my mind. Once STN is destroyed, I'll be able to write my own ticket in life. This should almost guarantee the Presidency. I'll be famous and independent of my fucking father.

"Are you sure of your decision? Do you want to take more time?"

"No, sir, I've already thought about it. I'm ready."

"Good for you. I expected nothing less. I'm even more convinced I've selected the right man for this critical mission. If you're 100 percent sure about your commitment, then I'd like to continue to review our plan."

The intercom buzzer rang twice. An annoyed President Schuster held the talk button down and shouted,

"I TOLD YOU NOT TO INTERRUPT ME FOR ANY REASON. NOW GET OFF THAT DAMN BUZZER. I'LL TALK TO YOU WHEN I'M DONE!"

Barrows clearly heard Judi gasp. She meekly stammered her apology to the President.

"I hate when people can't follow instructions," he said in an exasperated voice. "I'll straighten her out later. Sorry for the interruption. Now where were we? Oh yes, secrecy, wasn't it."

"Yes Mr. President."

The President began to scan the document he was holding, obviously still angry with Judi.

Barrows took note of this previously unknown side of President Schuster.

I wonder how he acts when he's really angry. I don't think I want to find out.

"You already have full diplomatic privileges to travel freely throughout the world under the Peace Envoys protection. That will make things easier. Peaksman will help to settle any operational disputes from the covert side of this mission. Anything from the public side you will continue to handle as you are doing now. An International intelligence team specifically convened for this purpose has certified each member of your team, including the newest members, so additional background checks are not required.

It's important that your public Peace Envoys efforts appear quite normal to STN as well as to the rest of the world. Allocate and distribute the 35 million to your team. I suggest you use the Swiss banks to transfer the operating funds to your team. They are untraceable.

I reiterate this one imperative order to you and your team. Should anything go wrong, you will be on your own. No one from any government will admit complicity in this project. Especially me!" Is THAT clear?'

"I fully understand, Mr. President," Barrows replied.

"I don't need to elaborate on this any further, do I?" pressed the President.

"No, you don't, sir" Barrows emphasized.

"Good. Let's continue. You will continue to receive your $195,000 salary as the Envoys Chairman. That will satisfy the IRS that you are still serving a legitimate government function. Now for the best part, which I'm sure will interest you greatly! An additional five million dollars has been placed into a separate Swiss bank account, strictly for you or your family as, let's call it, pre-compensation. The other countries connected with this mission have similar financial arrangements determined for the people on your team. Additional funds will be available as needed. My partners and I have not set a time limit for this project. Just get it done!"

Five million dollars! That's enough to be independent of my fucking father. He'll never control me again, thought Barrows.

"There will be no communications with me after today, except in accordance in your official capacity as Chairman of the Peace Envoys. At no time do I want to discuss or hear about the covert portion of your job. If you need anything related to *OPERATION DOVE*, talk to Peaksman. Neither I nor the other global leaders want to know the details. We want results! We'll be happy to hear about it on TV, or by phone. You need to remember that our support for the PE's is unwavering, regardless of any public stance we take. You start immediately. Good luck and God speed to us all."

President Schuster leaned forward to the edge of his chair, looked at Barrows intently and asked "Any questions?"

"Several. Mr. President. Are there any written instructions or directives concerning STN?"

"Nothing is or will be written. Your instructions are coming from me, right now." President Schuster seemed surprised at his question.

"I understand. Am I to assume the 35 million dollars is for both sides of the Peace Envoys operation?"

"Yes, that is correct."

"To whom do I have to report my expenses?"

"No one. Spend whatever it takes to shut down STN.

"No questions asked and no paper trail is that correct, Mr. President?" asked Barrows.

"Yes, exactly. You manage the money for both missions. Keep everything simple and untraceable. Obviously, communications as Chairman of the public side of the Peace Envoys can and should be through normal diplomatic channels."

"You said there is no time limit. What about the money? Is there a spending limit before the money runs out?"

"No. More will be available if needed. Just get STN."

"Another question. If for some reason the mission is not as successful as expected, do I keep the 5 million dollars? And, how will the money be transferred to my wife and children if I'm not around to sign for it?" Barrows pressed the President.

"I thought you said you were shocked. You seemed to have recovered pretty fast, haven't you?" chided the President. "I always considered that to be one of your endearing traits."

Barrows' mind and his heart continued to race, though he somehow managed to stay focused and calm in front of the President. A plethora of thoughts collided in his brain.

So that bastard father of mine was right. His plan is working, again. After STN, I'll be rich and ready to make my move for the Presidency. And Schuster is going to help! The world leaders approved me for this assignment. That will put me in a great position when this is over. I, Timothy Randolph Barrows Jr., am about to save the world from the tyranny of STN, and to save the political assess of the elite. With my money and political capital, nothing can stop me. This must be my destiny, to make the world safe for democracy, from the office of the President. I'll whip this government into shape and restore our leadership role in the world.

"Not fully recovered yet, sir," he responded, "but for the moment I've asked questions that come to mind. I'm sure there will be more within a few days, after I've had time to review everything. For now, I can't think of anything else."

With a hint of a smile President Schuster responded,

"To cover your family, we have several surrogate signees prepared to sign for you and transfer the money to your wife, Lynette. If the need arises, the signees will withdraw the funds, close the account, and open a new one in her name. I have issued a Presidential Order to insure the money gets to your family, tax free, and non-traceable, of course. This Order transcends my Presidency or my life, and is non-revocable.

However, we naturally expect you to succeed and to survive. Therefore, the money can't be withdrawn until your mission is complete, and you are given permission to sign for it. That's reasonable, isn't it?" The President didn't wait for an answer.

"Thank you Timothy, and good luck to us all. Anything else before you leave?"

"Not now, Mr. President."

"Excellent. And, Timothy, when this project is successfully completed, come see me about your career. I expect to be around at least that long."

The President chuckled again at his joke. What he meant to say was if you take too long to destroy STN, I'll be out of office and who knows what can be done for your career, or even if the next President continues this operation.

"Thank you, Mr. President, for this opportunity and the confidence you have in me. I will not let you down. I'll take you up on that offer for the future. You can be sure I'll finish the job as quickly as possible."

"I'm sure you will. I'm sure you will. Good luck again, Timothy. Keep

Peaksman informed. He will tell me what I need to know, which as I said before, is damn little."

He stood up to shake Barrows hand. It was his message to leave the Oval Office. He took one more look at the President's office.

One day it will be mine!

Barrows' multiplicity of thoughts coalesced into concrete action plans even as he left the Oval Office. He quickly reviewed *Red Sunset* in a private office.

This is the first government study I have ever read that is accurate. The terrorists are trying to take over the world. Not any longer! STN took care of that, and I'm going to see that STN will never become the enemy we need to fight.

By the time he reached his car, he already had mapped out the initial steps needed to organize the STN portion of the Peace Envoys. He thoroughly appreciated his greatest challenge. As the President had said, the collective intelligence organizations hadn't learned a thing about their STN adversary. He would have to break that trend.

I'll need a different approach to uncover the STN structure. The most logical place to start is to determine how they've been able to avoid detection. I wonder if my PE team members have any ideas or information that will be useful. All governments desperately want to succeed. I don't need to so this by myself, at least for now.

The more he evaluated the spying aspect of the mission, the more he realized how difficult it would be. He had no espionage experience to prepare him for this job. He felt concerned, in spite of his overwhelming confidence in his ability to handle any challenge.

"It's no wonder they're giving me 5 million bucks to risk my life. This is not going to be easy, but I'm smart. I've been waiting for this opportunity since I was in my twenty's. I can handle it. Didn't the President and other world leaders think that too? They never would have agreed to have me lead DOVE if they didn't think I would succeed. I'll prove their confidence in me is right. The 35 million dollars to fund this operation ain't hay either," he chuckled aloud.

They're paying a bundle of cash to destroy STN. If STN continues to expand and succeed, who knows what will happen? Schuster and his friends may find their jobs or their lives are on the line. That's why they're so worried. We'll all be fucked if I don't succeed. Five million dollars is the price tag on my head whether I screw up or not. Succeed and I'll have a chance to become President. Fail and I'm dead, literally and politically.

That daunting thought put a slight damper on his emotions.

Next on his agenda was to break the news to Lynette about his increased travel plans.

She's not going to be happy, but she'll get used to it.

Lynette fit the typical Washington bureaucrat's wife model. She was politically unaware, focused by necessity on her own entertainment, caring for the children, staying out of her husband's way, and being involved with her favorite charity, Breast Cancer. A graduate of University of Connecticut with a BA in Business, she eagerly gave up the notion of furthering her education and career when she and Barrows married. She became highly dependent on her husband for the major decisions of their lives. Barrows dominated the household. He decided on major purchases, the household budget, where and when they went on vacation, where the children should attend school, and their social calendar. Her job was to care for the children, attend school functions, and keep the children out of his hair. He preferred it that way.

He knew that his added responsibilities as Chairman of the Peace Envoys would place an additional and heavy burden on her.

"She'll have to make more decisions on her own because I'll be consumed with fighting STN and satisfying my original PE commitment. I need her to be more self-sufficient and I'm not sure how she'll function. But there's nothing I can do about it. I'll deal with whatever happens," was his conclusive decision.

38

THE PEACE ENVOYS STN MISSION:

Barrows assembled his Peace Envoys team two days later. He addressed them behind closed and guarded doors. No reporters or observers attended. For public consumption, the meeting was labeled a working session of the Peace Envoys.

"Good morning. There are some new faces here today, so I would like to take a few moments for everyone to introduce themselves and the country you represent before we get started with our business," Barrows addressed the group.

Twenty-six introductions followed. In the process of their new assignment, the Peace Envoys lost two members. The number reduction did not bother Barrows.

Barrows continued.

"Everyone has already been briefed on our new assignment. I trust everyone here understands the significance of our assignment. The stakes and the difficulties we face are daunting. Our new role will be demanding, confusing, dangerous, and lonely. In spite of our added task, we cannot forget our public commitment. We agreed to submit recommendations and take actions to create a more homogeneous and globally connected world. We must continue to work on those issues in a credible and professional manner in addition to STN. The world has opened their minds and hearts to us. We must earn their continued respect.

STN presents a dire threat to civilization. They have stepped outside the boundaries by violating the laws and traditions of every country represented here. They are our number one priority. If we fail to stop STN, we cannot possibly succeed with our public goal. Therefore, we obviously need a separate plan to attack STN. This will not be easy. If it were, our governments would have taken the initiative and destroyed STN themselves. Instead, they placed the entire responsibility on our shoulders while directing us to keep them out of the loop. Just stop STN, is what my President told me. Sound familiar?"

A ripple of subdued laughter filled the room Barrows smiled at their response.

"I firmly believe we have an opportunity to successfully accomplish both missions. I envision a day when STN no longer exists. I also see a day when we will submit a global plan to meet our original goals outlined by President Schuster and endorsed by the heads of your respective governments. I envision a day when our recommendations will help the third world countries to compete with the rest of the world, when peace, prosperity and happiness will be the norm rather than the exception. I see a day when the children of the world will no longer suffer from malnutrition or disease. We can do this. We can do both. We can make a real difference. Our governments are ready, the people of the world are ready, and we too must be ready for both missions. This morning I hope to establish a plan that will bring STN to their knees.

The stakes are incredibly high. STN threatens our existence and our ability to govern ourselves. The collective intelligence communities have been unable to infiltrate them, or learn about their leaders or their members. We don't understand how they operate, how they are funded, and how they managed to avoid detection. That's our starting point.

After asking myself these questions hundreds of times, I believe I have identified a path that, hopefully, provide us the way to break into STN's veil of secrecy. Let's examine some of the facts." He turned on his laptop computer to display his power point presentation on the large screen at the front of the room:

1. We know absolutely nothing about STN except for what we learn from the news

2. STN is a global organization
3. We know they are communicating with each other, but we don't know how
4. The only plausible communication methods are through cell phones and/or the internet
5. It would be a simple matter for us to learn their secrets if we captured one of their computers. They certainly understand that we could mine their data and eventually track them down. Therefore, I feel strongly they are not using computers for their communications
6. That leaves cell phones. They could be using throw-a ways, in which case, the cell phone idea is also a dead end
7. However, we know STN is quite arrogant, quite intelligent and highly sophisticated. That leads me to believe they are using the highest technologies available. Our job will be to discover their technology base, learn how they are using it, and track them down
8. Another possibility is to track the weapons trail, although in the past we have also been unsuccessful. We know they are using advanced weaponry, based on the data we have on the wounds they inflict on their targets

Barrows paused and nodded his head in self-agreement and satisfaction. His brown eyes danced from side to side as he surveyed the room. His teeth glistened from his smiling mouth. He was a bolt of energy, gathering strength to explode, barely contained.

The audience nodded in total agreement. Barrows beamed.

"Comments?"

A chorus of "No" followed.

"Alright. Since we don't know where to start, I'm charging each of you when you return home to begin searching for the technology STN is using. I don't have to remind you to maintain the highest security. We must assume that everyone and anyone outside this group might be an STN agent, except the direct people to whom you report. Assume that STN has contacts everywhere and is watching and listening. I don't have to tell you what that means. Discretion and secrecy are the operative words. Is that understood?"

Again a wave of nods followed.

Barrows spoke again.

"We must assume that STN might somehow learn about us and our plans. Any assumption less than that would be fatal. I have given this issue serious thought. STN has taught me one thing, and that is how to defeat your enemy. It is my opinion and strong belief that, when we are ready to take action against STN, they must be destroyed simultaneously throughout the world. It will require us to act with speed and utmost secrecy. Only a simultaneous action on our part will guarantee our success. We must insure that no key person escapes as did bin Laden in the early days after 9/11. Is there a general agreement with my analysis? I'd like to see a show of hands, please."

All hands shot up instantly. Several voiced their enthusiastic support for Barrows' strategy.

Francine DeMoupassant, the French Envoy expressed it most succinctly.

"STN prides themselves on their ability to end other people's lives quietly, suddenly, and deadly. They deserve the same consideration from us."

The audience erupted into a rousing cheer.

"Thank you, Madame DeMoupassant. Well spoken," said Barrows. "I have another word of caution. We represent our governments in this mission. To refresh your memory, they told us, in no uncertain terms, they do not want any traceable connected to our operation. Of course, we understand their real reasons, don't we? If something goes wrong and we fail, they want to save their jobs and their reputations. If we succeed, they don't want the public to turn against them because we destroyed their precious STN."

A wave of snickering and laughter rippled across the room. They immediately formed a mutual admiration for having the truth of their predicament defined so succinctly.

"Should you uncover anything of significance, or have any ideas on what we're facing with STN, please contact me or Tom Peaksman immediately," Barrows instructed them.

"Whatever action we eventually take, it must be done in a systematic and purposeful manner. I believe that as long as we plan with purpose and coordinate our actions, we will defeat STN. We will fail if anyone takes matters into their own hands by acting too early or too late."

He gave them a few moments to digest his subtle challenge before continuing.

"Today is the beginning of both STN's demise and the start of a new world community. We will not and we must not fail either. Here are my suggestions that I feel represent a good starting point, both for the remainder of our time together and when you are back home:

-Review all STN reports to determine if your intelligence agencies missed anything. We will share all data and final analyses uncovered with each other

-Look for unusual patterns from phone records, especially for increased phone traffic patterns before and after each STN attack

-Announce through the media that we will create an amnesty program for all STN members who are willing to work with us to establish a better world. If we get any takers, we might learn a thing or two about STN that would help us

Frankly, I doubt if STN will respond, but at least it may establish we are not their enemies. Nothing like lulling the enemy to sleep. Hopefully they will not consider us a threat. We certainly want them to believe the Peace Envoys is continuing our work for the good of humanity. My opinion is that we should examine all three options, but I'm convinced that the second item, the phones, is the key to STN's demise. We know STN exists throughout the world. We honestly do not know how they interact or plan their attacks. Yet, they apparently communicate with each other quite well. Therefore, we need to look deeply into the phone records of the carriers in your respective countries. This could create a serious problem for us. We need to consider that a mole of STN might be working at one or more of the phone companies. If that is true, any investigation on our part will tip them off, and we can kiss this opportunity goodbye. We must find a way to look at their records without betraying our existence. That's a major challenge for which we need a solution."

Discussions about Barrows' suggestions consumed most of the morning, with a general agreement to devise a strategy to approach the phone carrier CEOs. They agreed to submit their ideas to Barrows before taking any action on their own.

The afternoon they focused on the STN money. Barrows opened the session with his thoughts.

"I am almost positive that STN has their money in Swiss bank accounts. They surely don't have it in a commercial bank. Of course, they might be using cash and human carriers, but it seems to me that STN is too sophisticated to rely on such a clumsy method of funding their operation. That leaves the Swiss banking system. They need a mechanism to transfer money from one place to the other, and the only known banking system capable of providing security is the Swiss.

We might be able to solicit help from the Swiss. When appropriate, I'm certain we will have to pressure them to open their records. Without a compelling reason, the Swiss will categorically reject our request to go on a fishing trip. If we can identify STN by name, then we might be in a position to force the Swiss to help. Until then, we must be patient. I wanted to share this with you to encourage your inputs and suggestions. Think outside the box."

They collectively acknowledged the Swiss would be highly resistive, but, with sufficient political pressure at the highest levels from the major powers of the world, the Swiss might cave. They also agreed that pressuring the Swiss was a distinct possibility. A suggestion from the floor was that if governments publicly banned their citizens from holding Swiss bank accounts, the Swiss would get the message and they would relent. They agreed the Swiss would not want global governments to interfere in their business. The Swiss banks represented the final key to the links that held STN together.

Before they could tap the Swiss, the Envoys members recognized their first order of business was to solve the communications issue. Without that, the Swiss option was dead.

Barrows smirked to himself.

We are advocating uncovering STN Swiss bank accounts, while we, and probably STN, are both are taking advantage of the Swiss secrecy laws for our own purposes. There's irony for you.

The STN discussions continued the rest of the day. Barrows ended the afternoon session with,

"I want to briefly remind every one here that we cannot ignore the public side of our mission, the part for which we are receiving a handsome salary."

He laughed. The attendees caught the joke and laughed with him. The wealth tucked safely away in their private Swiss accounts for their covert activities made their salaries as Peace Envoys look like pocket change. Such was the nature of their dual existence.

"As I said before, we still have a responsibility to develop plans for the third world countries. What we do here, as PE's, can make the difference. This is our moment in history, this is the best chance to steer civilization towards realizing its full potential, to eliminate poverty, hunger, and pain, as well as a method of fighting the evils of the future.

If we fail to make meaningful recommendations to our governments to improve people's lives, or if we do not eliminate the seeds of discontent, sometime in the future we'll again be fighting terrorists or other malcontents. We'll be no better off than before, and we will have achieved nothing. We cannot let that happen. We must succeed both goals. I know I can count on each of you for your complete support and effort, and for that I thank you."

Without the public piece, my chances of becoming the President become zero. The public needs to see I was the one, as Chairman of the Peace Envoys, who brought them peace and security. Once that happens, nothing will stand in my way. It has to work, he reflected.

The final hour of the meeting lapsed into a typical organizational meeting. Six working committees of three to five people met separately with the instructions to identify the most pressing issues that plague the world. From the list, Barrows asked them to recommend possible solutions. Barrows instructed each breakout group to continue to work together over the next several months to suggest refine their proposed solutions and to generate firm projects.

"We must be sure what we suggest can be implemented and can work. I also expect a full budgetary estimate and analysis of the money required to accomplish each portion of our recommendations," he challenged them.

"Sergey Vasilov, here, and I have a question. Timothy, do you think our recommendations will be accepted and followed, now that our governments seem only interested in destroying STN? Remember, when you talk about the poorer nations of the world, we intellectually understand there is a two-sided history that must be overcome. Poorer nations have a history of corruption, incompetence, and indifference. Wealthier nations have abused the poorer nations. They have their own set of incompetency's, inefficiencies, and corruption with which we must deal. The wealthier have demanded, dictated, broken promises of support, food, or money, and generally disregarded the real problems of the poorer nations. Whatever recommendations we make will require both sides to be flexible and tolerant. It worries me, though, that they will ignore our efforts because of our new directive.

I fully support the STN initiative. I believe that they represent the greatest threat to us all. Assuming we do destroy STN, then what? What if we cannot help the poor nations as we intended? What if our leaders decide not to honor their original commitment? Then, I predict another wave of terrorism will flourish and probably another STN will evolve to fight these new terrorists. What will we have accomplished?"

"That, Sergey, is the very same question I posed to President Schuster when he told me the leaders of the world decided to add STN to our mission. He gave me his assurances that every world leader, the ones who selected each of you as their representative on this committee, have also considered this possibility. He told me they have seen enough bloodshed, enough suffering, and enough unrest that they never want to experience it again. They each gave their solemn oath to support our recommendations and to finance the changes we propose. Do I believe him? Yes, I do. I looked into his eyes and saw that he is committed. That's all I can tell you. We don't know the future, but I'm willing to bet that we will make a real impact on history. If I didn't believe in him, and us, I would not be here."

I'm betting my career on it.

By 6:28 PM, the meeting ended and the PE's left to begin their discovery of STN and to pursue methods for a better world.

Barrows headed home quite contented with himself.

I just completed laying the foundation for my future. As long as we perform, I've got everything and everyone poised to support my push to become President. Destroying STN will endear me internationally to the free world global leaders.

And why not? I saved their jobs and their asses. I need to continue to be visible to the public. As Chairman of the Peace Envoys, everyone will know my face and name. As the public gets to know me better, their vote will be in my pocket. Even if the global leaders don't do everything they can to help the poor, I'm relatively insulated from blame. If they don't follow my suggestions, or if they manage to screw things up, they shoulder the blame. I can always claim the high road. My campaign will be easy. I will promise to take charge of these failed projects. I will promise to bring them the long-term prosperity they were promised and deserve. I'll be rich, independent, and the President. Good work Timothy, my boy, good work.

He called Lynette as an after thought from the car.

*

The following evening after his meeting and announcement, Barrows found himself home alone. Lynette and the children were attending a school play in which Steven, their son, was singing in the chorus. Barrows begged off. He hated all those school plays and recitals. He found them boring, meaningless and stupid. Only important events like a graduation warranted his presence.

After making a ham and cheese sandwich, he flopped in his green marbled leather recliner chair in the den, devoured his food, and sat back to let his mind free flow to its own destination. His thoughts played like a movie reel, displaying his life, one illuminating agonizing frame at a time. Each image was distinct, but not in chronological order. There were flashes of his near perfect childhood as one of three sons growing up in luxury that true wealth brings.

For some persistent and incongruous reason, he returned to the dreaded images of his father, Clark Barrows Senior. He recalled in detail their conversation, word for word. Try as he would, his free time always seemed to push him to the same place.

Must be that love-hate thing between father and son, I guess.

Barrows Senior was the founder and owner of a chain of specialty women's boutique shops, *Designers Heaven*, serving the very rich. His money came from his father who made millions in the stock market, and insured that his money passed onto his children through a series of legal and somewhat problematical trust funds that allowed the money to go mostly untaxed. Through a combination of smart, shady, and lucky investments, Senior parlayed his wealth into a 150 million dollar empire.

As much as Barrows hated his father, he begrudgingly acknowledged the impact he had on his career and life. He revisited fragments of their conversation he had when he was twenty-one years old.

"Have you thought about what career you would like to pursue?" asked his father one day during dinner.

"Actually, yes. I think I'd like to be an ambassador to Switzerland, France, or Spain. It sounds like fun and interesting."

"Ambassador? Are you crazy? Those are positions for political hacks, not someone like you. You need to aspire to better things, like the Presidency!" Senior bellowed.

"Of the United States?"

"Yes, That President."

"I don't think I could…"

"That's the trouble. You don't think. Do you think I'm going to let you be a sniveling ambassador when better things are available? Think again, and this time, look higher."

"Well… I…I… guess you're right. But the Presidency?"

"Why not? I'm quite rich and powerful, and that counts for something. I can hire the right people, when the time comes, to guide you and clear the way. Just imagine. A Barrows as the President of the United States!"

Barrows pushed his dark brown hair back from his face.

It's useless to fight this bastard. He'll cut me out of his will if I don't agree. He's threatened it before, and I believe him. He's mean, arrogant and overbearing, but he's got the money, my money, he recalled thinking. *I'll tell him Yes and hope he dies before anything happens.*

"You're right. Why not shoot for the top?" he quietly replied.

"If that's what you want. Are you absolutely sure? I don't want to force you into something you really don't want to do."

You don't want to force me? Are you shitting me? My whole life you've told me and everyone else what to do, what to think and when to take a crap. You arrogant son-of-a bitch!

"No, you're not forcing me. I wasn't thinking clearly. I guess I'll learn to go for the top and not settle," he had meekly responded

"Good. You have to write a plan, a detailed plan, on what you need to accomplish over the next 15 to 20 years to position yourself for the Presidency. Decide which college, what organizations you should join, and the kind of jobs you will need to gain work experience. I'll take care of the people you'll have to know and who should know you. That's my job. After you finish writing your plan, I want to review it. I want to be sure you've thought it out carefully and it makes sense, understand?"

Barrows recalled his father's face. It was illuminated. His normal frown erupted into a near smile. No, a sneer was more like it. The old man was excited. He wanted his son to become President. He was determined that nothing was going to stop it from happening, not like when he tried to get the Presidential nomination for himself. His message leaped from his face. His eyes blazed red in anticipation. His demeanor mirrored a warrior armed for the battle of his life, one he expected to emerge as the victor.

"I've had an outline ready for you for over two years, waiting for you to accept your destiny," said Senior.

"Y... You've had it for two years? How did you know I'd want to become President?" his stunned son asked.

"I just knew it, that's how."

Barrows thought for a moment and said,

"I'm not surprised, I guess. You've always known what's on my mind before I do. I'm impressed."

Two fucking years he's been planning this? I can't believe it. Oh well, what's one more lie.

"I'm happy for you. You've never shown that much of an interest in politics before," chimed in his mother, Brenda.

"It's been growing over the past couple of months. Ever since I was elected President of class council at school. I enjoy the discussions and making decisions that affect everyone. I really like that part. That's what started me thinking about politics."

"Good for you. It's good to see that you've been paying attention. These are the lessons you need to have a successful career. I'm leaving for Munich Saturday. I'll be gone a week or so. That will give you a chance to look over my outline. When I get back we'll review your plan. I'll do my part. You do yours. You've made me very happy, son."

"Thanks, father, that would be great," was his enthusiastic yet cautious response. Senior was smart, and a control freak, both of which Barrows deeply resented, but understood enough to cater to when necessary.

That evening they discussed politics, especially the mistakes that most Presidents had made over the past 20 years. Barrows' fertile mind became filled with bubbling ideas and new expectations. By the end of the evening, Barrows was convinced that he wanted, needed, and deserved to be involved in politics. He now accepted. it as his calling in life. He would be ready, he promised senior and himself.

Thirty-one years later, I'm poised to fulfill our plans. First STN needs to be eliminated.

He reflected on his meteoritic career development. The plan he and his father had developed was a good start.

I'm the one who made it happen, in spite of my father's incessant suggestions. I hated most how he made me feel incompetent, and how he cursed that I couldn't function properly. He scrutinized and criticized my every move. I really hate hm. Barrows reinforced his unending hatred of his father.

Barrows paused in his movie sequences to take a break. He felt unsettled, recalling how submissive he was and had been most of his life to his father.

"Things are different now. After STN, I'll be rich and won't need him or his money. I can't wait to stop him in his tracks when he tries to tell me what to do. Sweet revenge is coming." He chortled aloud at the thought.

Begrudgingly and reluctantly he returned to thoughts of his father. He recalled his father's dogmatic and intolerable advice, repeated so often he usually tuned out his bastard father.

Stay on target. Do not allow outside influences or distractions to make you lose sight of your goal. If you do, you will fail. Failure is not an option for a Barrows, especially not for YOU. I remember he stressed that the strategic plan should remain constant; only the tactics could change. That way, any political, social or financial opportunities that come along will be incorporated into the plan if applicable.

His simple two-page plan had grown to over twenty-two computer printed pages, single-spaced, thanks to Senior's constant revisions and updates.

Those were not the memories he chose to remember, yet *the old bastard was right. I stayed on target, and here I am, on the path to the Presidency.*

The following day Barrows informed Peaksman of the results of the Envoy STN meeting. Barrows told him he wanted a copy of the software codes of all US based phone carriers delivered to the CIA.

"Do you know what you're asking? You want me to violate almost every privacy law on the books?" Peaksman asked alarmingly.

"Do you have any better ideas?" was the terse response. "You know the stakes, and I don't care what you have to do, just get it done."

"I may have to go to the President for his permission for this, and you know his orders not to involve him unless it is absolutely necessary."

"You don't think this is necessary? It's your choice. Go to the President like a wimp, or do it yourself. Use the President's name if you have to. At this point, we have nothing and we know nothing about STN. The old methods have not worked. We need a new approach, and I believe this fits the bill. Yesterday, we agreed to reexamine the phone records and try to tie them to the STN global attacks. There's no time to screw around with what ifs. We need to examine the phone company software and their records before we ask the Swiss banks to get involved. We need a break. If you don't help, I'll find someone who will. I don't think President Schuster would want to hear that you refused to help, do you?" snorted Barrows.

"No, I... don't. I'll find a way, somehow. If anyone catches wind of what I'm trying to accomplish, we'll be fucked. It could blow the lid off of DOVE."

Peaksman uncharacteristically ran his hand over his baldhead five or six time, wiping away wisps of imaginary hair.

"It's a risk worth taking. We need action and we need it now! You know the problem. We cannot count on the support from the world leaders to hang in with us forever, without us showing some progress. We know that some personnel changes at the top levels will happen. They always do. When that happens, it could weaken our position, so why wait? We have their attention, their support, and their money. Let's take advantage of it," Barrows said.

"It's not that I don't agree with what you're saying. What you're demanding borders on the impossible. I can only promise to do my best. Are we still focusing on the public side of the PE's?" Peaksman asked.

"Yes. We cannot ignore that part of our mission. Both are important."

"You know what really bugs me about STN? It's the fact that they willingly kill children. That just pisses me off."

Barrows was taken aback. *So Peaksman is sensitive to the plight of the children, just like me!*

"Is that the only reason why you hate STN? I would think you are afraid of what they have become," Barrows challenged.

"No, of course there are many reasons, but that one makes me angry. You know Tim, I have been thinking about our plans to help the poor countries as PE's. I'd like to see us take on a more challenging role. Shouldn't we be trying to insure that the children of these countries become a priority? Shouldn't we put in place a mechanism to stop their hunger and to protect them from the evils of poverty? And, that applies not only to these poor kids, but children around the globe. What do you think about that?" Peaksman questioned.

The very images of suffering children that Barrows had managed to avoid his entire life flooded his mind. His body instinctively stiffened as he tried in vain to wipe out those damn images that Peaksman had just reawakened.

"I… errr, I..errr…, understand and agree, but we need to focus on STN for the moment." Barrows was anxious to change the subject.

"OK, but think about it, will you?"

"When the time comes, I will. The children are my concern too. Back to our real problem. The phones. I'm counting on you. Our success depends on how well you get the job done. You've got to succeed. You've just got to," demanded Barrows as Peaksman shuffled from his office, leaving Barrows confident yet apprehensive. It scared the crap out of him to know that he relied on a suddenly frightened and unsure wimp to do his bidding. He did not appreciate not having complete control, nor did he like to have his future depend on Peaksman. Nor did he appreciate his talking about the children. He still found it difficult to handle. It was also more difficult to forget.

Why did he have to talk about the children? I know they are suffering. But he needs to focus on STN. He could fuck up everything for me. I don't know if I can count on him to get the job done.

His lack of confidence in Peaksman frayed his confidence. How deeply was not clear. Barrows figured he would know more within the next several weeks. He worried it might not be soon enough.

Over the next week, an annoyed Tim Barrows found significant time alone with his thoughts. They usually begin and ended with STN and the damage the remaining terrorists had inflicted on innocent people. Pictures of the terrorist bombings flooded his desk. Many graphically depicted the plight of the children, the sick, hungry, and forlorn children of the world. Slowly, he found a new and unusual emotion beginning to gather within his body. He saw an increasing stream of pictures of staving children huddled with their mothers, blank hopeless stares in their large brown eyes. The images made him sad, reflective, and upset.

Look at these children. Hungry, bloated stomachs, and thin withering limbs clinging to a parent or another child. They are the ones that need saving. Between terrorists and corrupt officials, they are the ones who suffer the most. They live in despair and squalor. The Envoys must focus on the children. They must be fed! They must be saved! They deserve a chance to live, to be healthy, not victims of adults who don't give a shit about them. Save the children to save the future. Perhaps Peaksman is right. Perhaps I should make this my priority!

He pondered these thoughts further. After considerable time, he made another decision, one that would alter his life.

I WILL make the children the priority of the Peace Envoy. It is the only way to secure the future once STN is destroyed!

Barrows had to stop to take a break from his gut-wrenching thoughts. His breathing became more rapid. He felt slightly lightheaded. Light beads of perspiration formed on his forehead.

I can't believe how insensitive I have been. I have always had everything I wanted. It was easy to pattern my life after my father, to my detriment. I see now that my actions have been self-serving, even, no especially, with Lynette and my children. I can't live this way any longer. The children of the world demand it. From this moment on, I swear to try to learn to be more caring and understanding. It will be hard, but I'm smart. Now that I have a real purpose, I can use my strength to make the world a better place for everyone. What good will it do to destroy STN and ignore children? Schuster shoved an incredible opportunity onto my lap. I know that wasn't his purpose, but it doesn't matter. I can drive the PE's anywhere I want. I see the route. It's so very clear. This is more important than the Presidency. If I fail, I will have failed all of humanity and myself. First destroy STN. Next will be to insure the Envoys develop meaningful and workable plans for the children, all of them, everywhere, even here in the US. From this moment, I will try to dedicate myself to be their champion, fight for them with all my might. Being the President doesn't seem as important.

He went home energized by his new revelation and his promise of pursuing a new life direction.

39

THE DISCOVERY:

Timothy Barrows and Tom Peaksman were chatting in Barrows' office several weeks after the Envoys meeting.

"I'm frustrated, Tom. We don't have a damn thing on STN, and we have no idea where to start. I don't know, you don't know, twenty-six Peace Envoys don't know, and no global intelligence agency knows. In spite of your excellent work, we still don't have enough on STN. We're stuck in shit, up to our eyeballs."

'We'll get there. Just keep working. Something will happen, I'm sure," replied Peaksman.

Peaksman's cell phone rang.

"Excuse me. I need to take this call. Hmmm… no caller ID. That's strange."

Barrows stared at him. His brow wrinkled from thought. He unconsciously bounced his right leg up and down.

"No caller ID, no caller ID, no call…" It hit him like a flash.

"Tom, I've got it, I've got it!"

"Let me finish this call and we can talk. I'll be done in a minute." He ended his call, turned to Barrows. "You've got what?"

"It's so damn obvious! It's right in front of us! I can't believe we missed it! We know STN is globally organized and that they communicate with each other to plan their attacks. We suspected they were using cell phones, but we haven't been able to figure out how they avoid detection. But, you ask, how can they go undetected? There are phone records. Yet, we examined every record of every cellular global network and came up dry. Why? Think, Tom, think!"

He paused to allow Peaksman a few moments to gather his thoughts.

"Go on, I'm listening."

"OK. Just now, you received a phone call. Though the caller ID was blocked, there still exists a record of the call. If we wanted, we could search the phone company records and track the caller down. Here's where it gets exciting. Following me so far?" Barrows excitedly demanded.

"Not yet."

"So the million dollar question is this. If STN is using cell phones to talk to each other, why can't we track them? Answer that and STN is ours. Assume STN feels safe using their cell phones. Why? Obviously because they know we can't track them! Do you get it now?"

"No," an anxious Tom Peaksman answered.

"Ready? Suppose, just suppose, they found a way to block their internal calls. Wasn't your caller ID just blocked? IT'S IN THE SOFTWARE, Tom, IT'S IN THE FUCKING SOFTWARE," he excitedly shouted.

"That's how they're getting away with murder. That's how they remain invisible. Somehow, they've corrupted the phone carrier's software to erase traces of their calls. You can examine the records forever and never find a thing! We know because we tried that and failed."

"My God, you're right! All they need is a software guru who understands the code and how to change it. Since they know the phone numbers of their members, they somehow adjust the software to allow calls in and out, but conveniently drop the record of the call. It's brilliant. You're right Tim, you just broke the damn bank!"

Peaksman had never seen Barrows so animated and so enthusiastic. Not only was his smile electric, but his entire body crackled with energy. He was generating lightening bolts, ready to fling them out into the world. A real live Zeus.

"We're right, aren't we? There's no other explanation. But, we need to be careful how we approach this. STN definitely has a mole in the software group, so we have to get our hands on the controlling code in the software without raising suspicions. If the mole learns we are examining the software, we're done. Don't know how STN would react, but they are resourceful. I guarantee they'll figure out how to neutralize our information and use some other means to communicate. We can't give them that chance, not now! Tom, this is the whole ball of fucking wax. If we can make this happen, they won't know what hit them. The end is in sight, my friend, the end of STN is in fucking sight!"

Peaksman excitedly asked,

"So how do we do it, Tim?"

"We're facing some tough decisions and some tricky operations. We've suspected for a long time that some pretty powerful and wealthy people are financing STN. We don't know who they are, so we have to assume anyone and everyone might be a supporter. One of them could be a CEO of a phone carrier. We need to have an airtight cover story that will not make the mole suspicious. Unfortunately, there is no way to bypass the CEO of every global phone company. We need a copy of their software packages and the codes that cover cell phone records, but we'll need a plausible story why they should let us examine their precious software. You know how protective they are concerning their propriety software codes, even with the government. Let me think about it," Barrows said.

For the next several minutes, they sat silently trying to conjure up a believable story for the CEOs.

Barrows' face turned from pensive to satisfied.

"I think I have an idea that should work. Tell me if it makes sense. We may have to use the President's clout to pull this off, but it's worth getting him involved. The CIA has to make this call for us. I'm sure you can arrange that through the President. The message to each CEO is something like this:

The CIA has classified information that a terrorist cyber group is targeting them and are planning to infect their global cell phone communications links with a vicious worm. They are determined to demonstrate they have the power to threaten our society. Once the worm starts and corrupts their software, they are planning to trigger the infection in the software of all global carriers. Your company is the base for them to test the power of this worm.

Emphasize to the CEO that our sources tell us they may have already implanted the worm in his software, and we believe it will trigger within the next week or two. Tell them we believe that the worm has also been inserted in their competitors' software, and that because it is nested, some innocuous software operation in one carrier's software may trigger it's full destructive power in his. If that happens, it will effectively shut down his entire communications network. Tell them we have a copy of their competitor's software codes and we need to search the two codes simultaneously to detect and dismantle the worm. Tell them that, in the past, we only looked at the general coding of his software. This time we have specifics to follow. Remind them we don't need the entire base, only that portion that traces the incoming and outgoing calls. That should allay their fears about giving us the code."

He took a deep breath before he continued.

"Assure them that our software experts must be the ones to make the comparison for two reasons. We know what we're looking for, and second, they don't have to worry about a competitor stealing their internal codes. Tell them this worm is so sophisticated, that had we not been given the software pointers, we would not have known where to look. The company would never know what hit them. According to our sources, once initiated, it takes about three hours to infect the software before total shutdown occurs. Tell them our best guess is that he has less than two weeks before drop-dead time, and we'll need every minute to break the code. Tell him we'll be working twenty-four seven to save his company. Delays in delivering his software will be catastrophic. Insist he not inform his staff of the situation, just in case those people who created the worm still work for his company.

That should scare the crap out of any CEO. Should a CEO be an STN backer, the scenario is plausible and believable. He will not challenge the CIA or their authority. Don't forget to emphasize that President Schuster is deeply concerned about this situation. He is anxious to help them and the country avoid this cataclysm. Remind them that once we have their software, our intelligence people should be able to dismantle the worm before activation.

I believe we will get the phone numbers of the STN people operating under the non-detection umbrella. We may not learn every name that is associated with each number, but I'm guessing we should get most of them. After that, we'll trace every call that STN makes or receives without their knowledge. Find the guys on the ends of those conversations and we'll find STN." Barrows was near delirium with excitement.

"We need to alert the other members of the Peace Envoys to get their intelligence people involved in the same way and with the same story. Just in case anyone grows suspicious, we will have a common story. That should provide the credibility we need to pacify even the most curious. We can't be sure which carrier or carriers STN is using. We must check out every phone company until we find big mama. Is there anything I've missed? Does it all make sense?"

"Absolutely. You're a genius! But, I don't intend to tell the President what we're doing or why. It's better we handle this on our own, and surprise him with the news of our success. I can use my influence to contact a trusted person in the CIA to make the calls," Peaksman interjected.

"Good thinking. What about our friends across the seas?"

"I suspect they each have their own sources to get things done. Let's hope so," Peaksman replied.

Barrows immediately dashed off a secure email informing his team of his discovery and the action they need to take.

Peaksman left his office to start his search.

An excited Barrows called Lynette. He had committed to involving her more in his life.

This is one more thing I need to learn to do. Lynette is a good woman and I need to pay more attention to her and my children.

He surprised her with his call. He never called during working hours unless there was an emergency or a change in his plans. They chatted for several minutes about her day.

"Is everything OK? You don't normally call me," she nervously asked.

"Yes, I just wanted to ask if you would like to have dinner out this evening, just the two of us," he answered.

"Dinner? Tonight?" his startled wife responded. "Is anything happening?"

"No, everything is wonderful. Thanks to you, I realized you were right. I was acting just like my father, and I don't like it. I'm trying to make changes, and my first change is with you. You are a good woman, Lynette. I haven't shown or told that to you very often. I decided it's time to start. I'm sorry it has taken me so long to wake up. Are you up for dinner with a man who doesn't learn very quickly?"

"I can't wait," a jubilant voice answered.

*

Barrows received a call from an exuberant Peaksman a week later.

"Tim, its Tom. We need to speak as soon as possible. We broke through, damn it, we broke through! When can we meet?"

"How soon can you come to my office?

"I'll be there in 40 minutes."

Barrows struggled to contain his elation, though he was not sure why. He heard enough to understand that the news was big, no probably huge. He drummed his fingers on his desktop. He moved papers idly from side to side. He paced and did everything possible to occupy his unending torture as time stopped. He almost called Lynette to fill in the time, but decided against it. He scanned his watch with such regularity that it quickly became a mindless habit. He looked, but didn't see the hands moving. He was sure he had entered a time warp where time either stopped or no longer existed. The wait was pure torture.

Thirty-eight minutes later a bouncy and light footed Peaksman burst into Barrows office carrying a heavy cardboard box.

"We've hit the lottery, we've hit the STN lottery! Names and bank accounts. It's all here!" he excitedly shouted. "We had a major breakthrough with the phone company coding. I decided that STN could only pull this off with one or two International carriers. Too many companies would be impossible to control. So I started with the biggest global phone company, World Link. I was right and lucky! STN uses World Link exclusively for their global communications. The gurus at the CIA have been working on their software, and found altered coding that buried the STN calls, exactly as you thought! This code allowed STN to make and receive non-recorded calls. They had a free unlimited world-calling plan. It's no wonder no one could figure out what was happening! Instead of wiping out their in and out bound calls, the software routed the numbers to a separate and hidden memory file. Once we discovered the file and tapped its contents, we discovered a list of numbers that probably... no, I'm convinced, they belong to STN.

The next challenge was to match these numbers and their activity patterns with the Swiss bank accounts. A contact from the banking industry told me he suspected that the Swiss would probably demand a phone number to open an account. If we could match our numbers with the Swiss accounts, we might have the names of some, if not all, of the STN people. My guess is that the top STN echelon have protected themselves creating multiple layers within their accounts, so matching the numbers with names might be difficult. On the other hand, if we can positively identify some members, and analyze their phone call patterns, it might lead us to the right people. If nothing else, it's a place to start.

Things were moving quickly, I contacted the Swiss banks myself. I threatened them with global sanctions, and they caved. We matched names and account numbers. Then we went back and traced the STN phone call patterns with the dates of STN attacks, and BANG, we found some interesting matches. The CIA folks say they need time to do a complete analysis to get a better read on the match ups. It won't be easy, but they have the confidence they'll eventually crack it. They've assigned their top experts full time to see what they can learn.

So far, we have a list of eighty-two people from every country who have opened large accounts in the past two years. We should be able to match most of the names on these accounts to people with legitimate backgrounds. That will leave us with a short list of unidentified accounts. They should be STN. As I expected, the top account names are highly protected. We'll have to sort that out later.

The Swiss initially gave us a hard time. They refused to break their secrecy code. After I mentioned Schuster's name to apply pressure, they capitulated. The CIA is really being cooperative. Of course, I haven't told them the real reason we need the names, only that it's of the highest security. Dropping Schuster's name put the screws to them enough to decide to work with us, no questions asked. Some luck, some hard work, that's what they said. Our people and the phone company have broken their asses on this. I'm really proud of them."

"Tom, that's fantastic! I can't believe you accomplished so much so quickly. This is the break we needed. It sounds like we may have some of the STN contacts. From that we should be able to break the code names and learn the real identities of their leaders. I want maximum pressure on the CIA. We need to find out who is running STN. When that happens, we'll get everyone together, our team, the military and special operatives throughout the world, to prepare for STN's destruction.

What's scary is the level of sophistication and smarts STN have, don't you agree, Tom? Can you imagine having that kind of power to reach into the software of World Link without them knowing? It boggles the mind. All their outgoing and incoming calls disappeared from the records. That means someone has the power and the money to make this happen. Ingenious, don't you think?"

Barrows paused to catch his breath. He was euphoric.

"Thanks to you, we're on the right trail."

"Thanks Tim, it makes me feel great knowing I could contribute to our mission. I agree. We make a good team, don't we?" Peaksman beamed.

"How long before we can get started?" Barrows asked.

"We need to continue to monitor both the phones and the Swiss to see if anything pops from any recent high STN activity. That will help us to confirm STN's involvement. The hard part will be uncovering the identities of all the leaders. Perhaps we should arrest their underlings. They might lead us to the big guys," Peaksman continued.

"I don't think that's the way we should go. Our real concern is destroying STN. That means their leaders. Without them, we're only cutting off a finger. I want the head!" Barrows quickly interceded.

"You're right. It really makes sense to go after their leaders."

"What did you give the Swiss for their cooperation? I'm sure they wanted something."

"I offered 25% of the STN holdings," Peaksman replied. "That OK with you?"

"I would have done the some thing. I might have offered them even more, so it was a good thing you did the negotiating." Barrows chuckled. Peaksman nodded affirmatively.

"What did you tell them why we needed to open their records, I mean after they became wealthy?"

"I impressed them that we're only interested in selected accounts, not their entire depositor base. That, plus the threat that Schuster promised to pass legislation that would make it illegal for US citizens to hold Swiss bank accounts made them cave."

"Great work, Tom. I wasn't sure if we'd find enough this soon. It is truly stupendous," Barrows beamed.

"Time is on our side, Tim. STN doesn't know we have anything. They'll assume we're still a bunch of shits and they are safe. With a few lucky breaks we can move to destroy STN."

"Hard work makes lucky breaks. Stay on World Link and the Swiss. I want weekly reports on their progress."

"I'm on it. Trust me, I'll be all over their backs."

"Tom, thanks again. When this is over I hope you get an enormous raise."

Peaksman looked at Barrows with raised eyebrows, slightly amused.

"You think I'll need a raise after this is done?" I think the million bucks President Schuster so graciously deposited in the Swiss bank at the beginning of this adventure is jussssst fine."

"Right, just fine," Barrows echoed.

"What are we taking about, Tom, I mean, what's the total STN money in the Swiss banks?"

"We've identified many potential accounts. Twenty-six have a total over 76 million bucks. They're the ones we'll be monitoring. I'm willing to bet they are all STN, or at least the majority of them are. These guys make our money look like chump change. Maybe we should move to the other side. Then we would really be rich. You ready?" He laughed so hard his belly shook like ripples in a pond.

"I assume Schuster knows nothing?"

Peaksman looked incredulously at Barrows and answered,

"Why would he? He said he wanted to stay in the dark. I'm keeping him there," Peaksman sarcastically responded.

"Sorry Tom, no offense intended. I guess I just needed to ask."

"OK, I forgive you." The sarcasm disappeared.

"See you later. I have work to do. I can't sit around and chew the fat like some people I know."

Peaksman smiled, abruptly ended the conversation and walked briskly out of Barrows' office.

"Bye, Tom. Keep me posted. Thanks again.

For the first time I feel as though I can trust him. He's smart and loyal. I'm lucky he's working with me. I have a lot to learn about people. But, I'm making progress. I'm starting to understand and accept people for whom and what they are. Hopefully, it will become easier.

"Seventy-six million dollars!" Barrows muttered to himself after Peaksman was out of sight. "Incredible! I'd love to find out who is financing them. I'd hang their asses out to dry. I know we'll never find out. They are rich, smart, and powerful. Soon I'll be there too. But, I want to do good for the world, not to destroy it. Things are moving quickly for me. Soon, I'll make a real impact."

Barrows was euphoric with the prospect of his success.

He reviewed the data on his desk for over an hour. Coded names, phone numbers matching Swiss bank accounts, and nameless people identified as probable STN operatives. *We still don't know their names or have any links to the remaining STN people.* He deduced from the data that STN employed global regions, each apparently acting independently. The phone records provided the clue to their structure. He deduced that STN had nineteen to twenty-one regions, give or take a few. Barrows resigned himself that he still needed a little luck to get the people he wanted the most. The STN leaders.

*

STN success remained high and consistent. In Europe, the Middle East, and Asia, terrorist attacks continued, though greatly reduced. Terrorism appeared to be on it's death march, though some hard core al Qaeda and Taliban groups continued to avoid STN executions. In the meanwhile, STN ramped up to implement their global activities against their new criminal targets.

The US media extensively and continuously examined STN's attack against the drug lord Rialdo. They were unrelenting in their coverage, Barrows noted with great interest. So did Peaksman.

"Tom, Tim Barrows. Are we on Rialdo? This could be the break we're looking for."

"Could be. We've been monitoring both the phone calls and the Swiss 24/7. I'm guessing there was increased activity in the banks since the attack. That might be when they make their payoffs, after a hit. Once that happens I believe we should be able to match the phone calls to the money, and sort out which accounts belong to STN. We've been looking at this already, but I'll increase the pressure. You check with the other Peace Envoys members to see what they've learned. Till then, be patient. I'll let you know. Speak later."

Two days later Barrows called Peaksman to tell him exciting news from abroad.

"Tom, good news! We believe we've identified seven STN people in Russia, China, Indonesia, England, France, Nigeria and Uganda. We've linked their phones and their bank accounts. More than likely, they are the leaders. As we thought, it appears that the leaders don't communicate with each other. Each leader makes calls within the local area. There are no long distance calls, except to Egypt. All the same number. I'm certain that the leaders only talk by phone and only within a defined area. That pretty much confirms our original thoughts that STN is regional. We're tracking the STN soldiers along with the leaders. I understand that we have little to gain from the soldiers. But I'll be happy if they lead us to the leaders. I suspect they will scatter once their leaders are dead. STN will collapse from lack of leadership.

As I said, there is one number in common from these regional leaders though. Someone in Egypt. Don't know what this means yet. The info is too sketchy. I've instructed our people to pull a 24/7 surveillance on the seven we know. What pisses me off is we haven't isolated the rest of these bastards. There could be two more or fifty hiding somewhere. It's frustrating," Barrows lamented.

"We'll get them, eventually. You deserve a lot of credit Tim. You gave us the right places to look. We'll get the others, trust me. You're still new to this business. Have patience. This is a bitch of an assignment and it takes time to pull it together. By the way, I didn't mean to offend you the other day. That was my way of complimenting you. I think you're brilliant, and doing one hell-of-a job."

"OK. I guess I'm frustrated that we only have seven probable leaders. We know there are at least twelve more. We need to find the rest of them."

Within three days, the Peace Envoys team identified ten more STN leaders, for a total of seventeen. They knew their real identities, their Swiss bank accounts, and their regions defined. After a quick review, they shuttered because there were two noticeable omissions. Conspicuously missing were the leaders from the US and Pakistan.

"Damn! There are still two more out there. As soon as we identify the Pakistani and the US leaders, we'll be ready, " Peaksman replied. "But what if there are more we haven't indentified? What then? Do we wait forever? Can we afford to wait?"

Barrows thought quietly for a few moments and replied,

"We can't wait forever. We'll strike STN as soon as we identify these last two. When these nineteen are dead, I'm almost positive the entire STN organization will collapse.

Remember, when we launch our attack, the Swiss agreed to deny access to all STN funds. Anyone trying to withdraw money will get the shock of their sorry lives. I'm hoping it's that Egyptian guy. Maybe we can get him too. Wouldn't that be something!" Barrows happily declared.

"Nineteen is the magic number. I'll start planning our attack against the seventeen STN leaders we already know and have under surveillance. We'll include the other two as soon as possible. That way we'll be prepared to launch the attack quickly. It won't be too long, I hope." stated Peaksman.

"Do it, Tom. It makes sense."

"I'm on it. In the meantime, we need to light a fire on our people. I'll do the US, you do the Pakistanis."

40

Bruce MacCardle, Karachi, Pakistan:

"I'm tired of Pakistan. I hate this damn heat, I don't like the food, and Bilal worries me."

Bruce MacCardle sat in his bungalow lamenting his position. Bilal had agreed to take time off from their attacks, but it made Bruce feel worse. He was glad there was a break in the attacks, but he wanted more. Scotland was where he wanted to be, away from people who spoke, acted, sounded and lived differently. As much as he enjoyed the trappings of a wealthy investor, the constant demands of his continuously role-playing made him uneasy. He longed to sit at a bar with his friends, chatting and laughing, without fear that he might expose STN.

The outside temperature was a scalding 102 degrees, hot and humid. June and July in Pakistan were hot, usually the hottest times of the year. Though his bungalow had air conditioning, the heat kept him a prisoner. He was startled to hear a series of loud knocks at his door.

"Internal Bureau, Mr. Sanders, please open the door. We need to speak with you about your personal safety."

His first thought was to pretend not to be home, wait for them to leave, flee the bungalow, and call Bilal.

There are two possibilities. They are IB or they are assassins.

He grabbed his 45 mm Glock handgun, checked it was loaded, and pondered his next move.

Knock, knock, knock.

"Mr. Sanders, we know you are home. Let us show you our credentials. If you don't speak with us, we'll have your bungalow surrounded with reinforcements, and we will use force to break in. Things will go badly for you if we have to resort to force. Your cell phone is inoperative. We have temporarily shut down the transmitting tower. You have no signal. If you don't believe us, check your phone," said the voice.

Bruce checked. There were no bars.

So they are IB. At least they won't kill me here. But why are they here? Have I done something illegal? Do they know about STN?

He tried to recall anything that he might have done to warrant an IB visit. Nothing came to mind.

Knock, knock, knock, this time with greater authority.

"Mr. Sanders. We mean you no harm. If you have a weapon, please holster it. We need to talk. Please open the door, now."

"Show me your credentials. Put them up to the window of the door. The two men did as Bruce requested.

"OK. Let me see your hands."

Four hands wiggled at the window.

"OK, I'm opening the door, but I warn you, any false move and I will kill you both."

"We are not armed, so there is no need for violence. Is that understood?"

"What's this about?"

"We would rather talk to you in private. We don't think you want your neighbors to listen to our conversation, do you?"

With both apprehension and arrogance, Bruce opened the door, gun in hand, ready to shot if provoked.

If they accuse me of being part of STN, I will deny everything. If they try to arrest me, they'll have a hard time without weapons.

He steeled himself against…what? But he was certain about one thing. No one would force him to give up Bilal or STN.

"OK. I'm opening the door."

Two men dressed nearly identically, stood in the entranceway, looking serious but not aggressive. They both wore wrinkled tan cotton suits with open shirt collars. Were it not for the fact that one wore a pale blue shirt while the other had a white shirt, they could almost pass for twins. *Uniform of the day,* Bruce thought.

"What do you want?"

"May we come in for a moment? This involves your personal security,'" asked the tall one.

"Come in, but keep your hands in front of you. You won't mind if I check to see you're carrying weapons, will you?" he said sarcastically.

"You are welcome to check," replied blue shirt.

He frisked them quickly and verified they were clean.

"Satisfied, Mr. Sanders?" asked the short one. "May we sit?"

Bruce put his weapon into his waistband and led them to his luxurious living room.

"Nice place," said white shirt.

"You didn't come here to inspect my home. You mentioned my security. I'm listening."

"We have intercepted information, confirmed by a very reliable source, that there will be an assassination attempt against foreign nationals within Karachi, probably within the next 24-48 hours. We are taking immediate precautionary measures to protect all potential targets, you included. All resident foreign nationals are moving to a safe location until the danger is over. We need you to come with us immediately. It's for your protection. Please pack a small bag with your personal items and be ready to leave in the next five minutes. You, along with thirty-nine other foreign nationals in this area, will be under state protection. You will stay at the Resorts Karachi under maximum protective security. Sorry to inconvenience you, but your safety is our primary concern."

"But I'm quite safe here. I promise to not leave my bungalow until you notify me that the danger has passed," Bruce countered.

"Sorry, that is neither possible nor advisable. The government of Pakistan cannot allow ourselves to be open to International criticism from the UN or England for not protecting you while you are on our soil. We cannot ignore a valid threat. You must come with us, now," said white shirt sternly.

Realizing the futility of further discussion, and thankful that they did not search his bungalow, Bruce decided to comply.

Anything else might draw unwarranted concern and might force them to probe further. No reason to raise their antennas over something that should be over in a few days, he concluded.

"Alright, give me a few minutes to pack. I'll be right back." Bruce turned towards his bedroom.

"Take a seat, if you want," he shouted over his shoulder.

Once in his bedroom and out of sight of the two security police, Bruce placed his 9 mm Glock in the hidden headboard compartment. When he purchased the bed, he hired a carpenter to build a hidden compartment specifically designed to secure his Glock from prying eyes. He learned that from his EPA training.

Even if someone searches my room while I'm gone, it will be safe, he concluded.

He packed his essentials: cell phone, cash, toilettes, two shirts, fresh underwear and a second pair of slacks.

I'll let Bilal know what's happening as soon as possible.

Ten minutes later, he was riding in the back of a black Volvo S70 sedan with black tinted windows and the official seal of the Intelligence Bureau stenciled on the door. The car headed towards downtown Karachi. Surprisingly, there was a beehive of activity the closer they approached the hotel. He saw two armored jeeps stationed at either end of the street, a third in front of the hotel, and a squad of armed military guards positioned along the length of street, at the front entrance of the Hilton and spread out along either side of the adjacent buildings. His trained eye also detected military personnel, fully armed and ready for action, stationed on the roof of the Resorts and on three buildings on the opposite side of the street. Positioned to observe any movement in and around the building, they seemed prepared to protect the area from attack, by ground or air.

Bruce commented to an armed soldier seated in the front of the parked jeep as white and blue shirt escorted him into the hotel.

"They are serious about this, aren't they?"

"Yes sir, it is very serious," was the terse reply.

The elaborate preparations convinced Bruce that the Pakistani government knew nothing about STN.

As soon as this exercise is over, I'll call Bilal. Can't call him from here. They aren't stupid. They probably tapped the phones.

Three armed guards joined Bruce and his two escorts, who led them to the elevator and then to a large one room junior suite on the sixth floor, Room 615. The room had a rosewood desk and matching wooden chair, a king sized bed, a sofa, a matching side chair, and a 42" flat screen wall mounted TV, standard decor for a five star hotel. Not typical however were the two windows. They had been covered and sealed with a sheet of Kevlar, the materials used to make bulletproof vests.

Blue shirt spoke.

"Mr. Sanders, we hope you will be comfortable. It's not very large, but we are running out of suites. All your needs will be provided for you. Meals, towels, etc. There will be armed guards on this floor, at the stairways and the elevators for your protection. Our security personnel will serve you your meals after they inspect it and verify its safety. Unfortunately, the selections will be limited, but I assure you the hotel staff prepares excellent meals. Any needs, call the front desk."

"There are a few simple rules," said the white shirted agent.

"You cannot leave your room for any purpose, for security reasons. No phone calls allowed, incoming or outgoing. You will be able to receive calls on your hotel phone only. No cell phones. Please give me your cell phone. We'll return it to you when it is safe to leave the hotel. I will give you a receipt for it. Do not, under any circumstances, remove the Kevlar from the window or try to look outside. This will prevent anyone from outside the hotel to pinpoint your specific location in the hotel. Stay in your room regardless if you hear commotion in the hallway. It might not be safe. We will notify you when the disturbance is under control. To insure your safety, we ask you to make your own bed. We will provide fresh bedding and linens daily. We wish to keep the number of people in direct contact with you to a bare minimum. Finally, keep your door locked at all times. Only open it for your food or linens.

We have established a communication sequence to follow so you know it's safe to open the door and allow the person into your room.

They will ring your room bell two times. You ask, "Who's there?"

They will respond " Room service. We have the towels you ordered."

You respond," Why are you late?"

They will respond, "The towels were being dried. We also have your shampoo."

Then, and only then is it safe to open your door. This applies for anyone wishing to speak with you, to bring you your meals, or other things you need. The phone operator is our agent, so make whatever requests you have to her. Feel free to answer your phone. We will be on the other end. We will try to make your stay here as pleasant as possible. Any questions?"

"How long do you think before this is over?"

"We are not sure. As soon as we confirm the danger has passed," responded white shirt. "Possibly two or three days, I imagine."

"I have an urgent business matter to discuss and need to contact my office in London. When can I do that?"

"Sorry, not permitted. We can relay a message from you to them, if you would like. You will not be able to speak with them directly. Although we have taken extensive measures to insure your safety, we must be sure that no information on your precise location leaks out. It's just another security measure we initiated for every foreign national under our protection."

Bilal will not know I'm not home. We agreed not to talk for several more weeks. Yet, he should know what has happened to me, Bruce thought.

"What about computers?"

"No, and since you didn't bring your computer, it not a big deal, is it?" the white shirt said mockingly.

"What am I supposed to do to entertain myself?"

"Watch TV, we'll bring you books, magazines, and papers. Or catch up on your sleep," chortled blue shirt.

"Anything you need right now?"

"When is dinner?" sneered Bruce.

"Anytime you want. Just call the operator. We'll keep you informed about what's happening, and when it's safe to return to your home. Sorry again for the inconvenience, but there is nothing more we can do."

"Lock your door as soon as we leave." Bruce did several minutes later.

"What a mess. I can take better care of myself than they can, but I'll have to make the best of it," he mumbled to himself.

Through the Kevlar-faced window, he heard a constant cacophony of truck and car doors opening and closing, orders shouted from people with authority. This lasted for nearly 2 ½ hours.

"I guess they are still rounding up the foreigners. They put they put us together to make it easier for terrorists to kill us with a single attack. At least it will save them time instead of trying to pick us off one at a time," he sarcastically mumbled aloud.

"This is not too bad for a prison, at least for a while. Not like Scotland, for sure."

After a boring afternoon, dinner, breakfast the next morning, and a sandwich for lunch, Bruce began to experience cabin fever. He still was concerned about contacting Bilal, but wasn't exactly sure why.

They better end this quickly, Bruce told himself *or they'll have a loon on their hands, and I know where he is!*

Two-twenty that afternoon, the phone rang. The voice on the other end told Bruce that two security people would be coming to his room. Minutes later, he heard the doorbell ring twice. They performed the verbal security check, and Bruce unlocked the door. In walked two British men, dressed in suits and ties, flashing their World Force badges.

"Hello Mr. MacCardle, I'm Captain Harley Wiggins, and this is Lieutenant Harold Bellereger. We are with the Peace Envoys, World Force team section, and we would like to talk with you about a serious matter… STN."

"MacCardle? You have the wrong man. My name is Evian Sanders. I'm an executive here in Pakistan on business. I know nothing about STN except what I read in the papers."

"Let's not play games, shall we? We have clear proof that you are Bruce MacCardle and you are intimately involved with STN. Our information confirms that you have been instrumental in the deaths of over 300 people. We also know you have a secret bank account in Switzerland. In fact, we know the account number. The Swiss have cooperated with us and frozen your very considerable assets. You are between a rock and a hard place, Mr. MacCardle, so let me be brief and, don't try to swallow that cyanide pill. It will do you no good. We have the antidote here."

He produced a syringe and small bottle of milky liquid.

"All that will come of that will be a bad stomach ache and headache that will make you feel you want to rip your head off. Let's avoid these unnecessary pleasantries and get on with our business, shall we?" asked the Captain.

Without waiting for a reply, Captain Wiggins continued.

"We have broken the STN cell phone software that allowed you to communicate with your STN members. Our purpose is to destroy the STN operation, its global connections, and to end your killings. At first, when STN focused only on terrorists, our government, along with the rest of the world, stood by and were grateful that someone was doing something we could not legally do. But, when STN, and you, extended your killings beyond terrorists, the government decided that you no longer were operating in our best interests.

You made your decision to kill terrorists and their Circle of Contamination, a decision we initially applauded. However, you and your friends crossed the line. No civilized nation can function long-term when groups operate outside their laws. Now that we've caught up with you, your days and the days of STN are numbered."

A stunned Bruce defiantly uttered,

"Aren't you forgetting that in less than eleven months we have nearly wiped out the terrorist threat in a good portion of the world. If you remember, everyone claimed it was impossible to achieve. Aren't you forgetting that more people are living their lives in relative peace because they have little to fear from terrorists? The reign of fear by terrorists is on the verge of total destruction. Doesn't that count for something?" he defiantly countered.

"Had you stopped there, we probably would have welcomed you as heroes, but you didn't," retorted Capt Wiggins, showing his contempt. His speech had transformed from measured to staccato, from calm to anger, from quiet to tense.

"STN and you decided to rid society of anyone who was breaking the law or committing an act of which you did not approve. I'm not saying that it wouldn't be nice to rid ourselves of these elements, but you killed everyone around them. How do you feel about killing innocent children? Isn't that exactly what terrorists do? You are just as barbaric as they are. Don't you understand that?" Wiggins angrily shot back.

"But we do precision killings, not wholesale slaughtering. The people we eliminate are terrorists. They needed to die to achieve world peace. Don't you understand that? Isn't there always a balance between what is best or legal verses what is practical?" Bruce quizzically responded.

"There's never a balance for slaughter, for blatant unprovoked murder, or for barbarism," the Lieutenant shouted. "There never is, and thank God there never will be."

The three men glared at each other with equal contempt and animosity without another word spoken.

Regaining his traditional British composure, Wiggins spoke again, more measured and controlled.

"At this point it doesn't matter what you or I think. STN is through. Throughout the world, your fellow STN members are, or will soon be, arrested. STN is in the process of being dismantled. You and your friends are the real scourge of society. I trust you will get everything you deserve."

"What's next? The firing squad?" queried Bruce.

"No. we are more civilized than that. However, your reward will be prison for the rest of your life, in solitary, except for one hour a day, I assure you. Your Swiss bank account is frozen. The British government will thank you for your contribution after the transfer of your funds to the Treasury becomes official. The Court will decide on your final punishment."

"Don't I get a trial?"

"Yes, if you wish to call it that. A court lawyer will plead your case. He or she will do his level best to insure you get the lowest acceptable level of representation. Then, you will go to prison in England, probably Strangeways in Manchester.

They sat facing each other in complete silence, Wiggins and Bellereger with broad smiles on their faces. Bruce somehow didn't feel like smiling.

"Then I'll appeal."

"There is no appeal. Once and done, old chap," Captain Wiggins laughingly responded.

Silence was the only sound in the room.

"Actually," Wiggins broke the silence. "There may be *one* way to avoid this piece of nastiness. Are you interested?"

"I'm listening."

Wiggins continued.

"How would you like to walk away from Karachi, with no strings attached, no trial, no prison, no record, and still keep your Swiss bank account? You will be free to move anywhere you want, and to live the rest of your life in comfort, as long as you keep your nose clean."

"What's the catch?"

"We want just one thing. We have identified nearly everyone on your team. The one person we really want is your leader. We have his cell phone number, but can't track him down from that. Though we've penetrated the World Link software, we know nothing beyond that. He will walk away, free, while you rot in prison. Assuming of course you don't cooperate with us. We want his name and his address. The deal is simple: Your life and a life of financial security in exchange for him.

Regardless of your decision, STN will soon disappear and will never operate again. We currently have the goods on every STN leader and member in every country, except for your boss. Shortly all STN members will be imprisoned. The entire bank assets of STN have been frozen or turned over to the appropriate authorities. Except for one remaining account. Your leader.

We do not know who funded this unlawful scheme, and we may never know. They may have lost a lot of money, but they have their freedom and their wealth. They will continue to lead their normal lives, undetected, and never be accountable for their actions. They created a group of the most abominable terrorists the world has ever seen, even more heinous that al

Qaeda, the Taliban or the hundreds of Fundamentalist groups you tried to exterminate. They hired you to do their dirty work. Sadly, they probably will never be caught and never serve prison time. They will remain anonymous and continue to lead their extravagant existence that wealth brings, while you and others like you sacrifice your freedom, your money, and probably your life. Good deal, eh?

They have sufficiently isolated themselves as the rich and powerful can do. The rich *do* that, don't they?

Oh, bye the bye, you have ten minutes to make your decision. Once the ten minutes are gone, we will have no choice but to arrest you. You can kiss your ass goodbye. Plan to spend the rest of your life in a prison, and not to your liking, that I CAN promise you. Time is against you. You have ten minutes to make your decision. We have confidence your esteemed leader will eventually learn of your capture along with the other STN operatives. He will disappear, just like your rich friends. He too will be free to live as a rich man, while you die or grow old in prison. Isn't that a pleasant thought, Mr. MacCardle? We'll wait here with you while you decide."

"What about the threat to my life and the other foreigners?" Bruce quietly asked.

"Pretty good ploy wasn't it? Fooled you! This was a ruse to fool your leader and to prevent you from swallowing that little death pill we know you have. Frankly, old boy, we wanted you alive, for obvious reasons. Had we just picked you up at your bungalow, your leader would have figured out what was happening and he would disappear. We couldn't have that, could we?" asked the smiling Captain.

"No," was Bruce's sarcastic response. "We wouldn't want that, would we?"

"Nine minutes, Mr. MacCardle, nine minutes."

Silence.

Bruce pondered his predicament.

It's my life or Bilal's. Prison for me. Freedom for him. I'll go crazy in jail, while he will no longer have a mission for which to live. Bilal is a maniac and a killing machine. He's a dead man no matter what decision I make. With STN destroyed, what is left for him? I doubt if he can survive without a reason to live. He's half-dead now. If I give him up, he's not any worse off than if I don't. But is this what one friend does to another, even if it will not matter in the end? Hasn't he suffered enough? Would Bilal give me up? He'd probably opt for prison. Why does it have to come down to that? I could have killed myself and ended it for us both. I will die a slow tortuous death in prison. The first time it nearly killed me. Me or Bilal? My life or his?

"Six minutes."

Six minutes to make the best or the worst decision of my life. Can I live with myself if I give him up? But he's changed. Nothing is left of the man I once knew. Questions... questions, but no answers. What to do?

"Five minutes."

Perhaps I can rush them, get their weapon, and shoot myself. But he decided they were not carrying an exposed weapon. Nor was he. His Glock was safe in his bedroom.

"Three minutes, Mr. MacCardle, three minutes," counted Captain Wiggins

"Two minutes."

I need to decide. I'm running out of time.

"One minute to go and it's off to prison for you."

"Thirty seconds is all you have left, and not a second more."

"OK, OK, OK. I'll tell you what you want to know. His name is Bilal Maqsood Ahmed."

Bruce spent the next twenty minutes giving them the pertinent information about Bilal: his address, his habits, and the layout of his apartment. He pointed out that Bilal had rented a place without a rear exit, and should be easy to catch at home, since he hardly ever left. Only the need to buy food brought him out of his apartment. He informed them that Bilal lives alone, is armed, and very tough.

"He will not be easily taken alive, that I can promise you," Bruce said in a shaky and unsure voice.

"Excellent. Thank you. We intend to capture him alive. Once we have caught this Bilal and he's in custody, we will release you as we promised. You'll be a free man, you and your money. We'll take you to the airport and put you on a plane to any destination you chose. We expect to never see or hear from you again, understand? Once we verify your information, we'll take you back to your bungalow to gather your things, less your Glock, of course, your passport in hand. You'll be a wealthy man. Free to go or live as you choose."

"What happens to Bilal?"

"That will be up to the judge. Our job is to get the information, and pass it onto the World Court for judgment. Beyond that, it's out of our hands," replied Wiggins.

What am I supposed to do while you make your plans? I can't work with him again, knowing what I've done to him." Bruce informed the Captain.

"Good question. We'll figure something out. Perhaps you can become sick and have to stay in your bungalow."

"That won't work. We usually only talk by phone, so I can be sick and still able to work."

Captain Wiggins thought for a few moments and offered,

"Why not tell him you miss Scotland and decided to return home for a vacation. Will that work?"

"Actually, it's perfect. I am supposed to take a vacation, so why not Scotland? I don't even have to tell him, because we agreed not to call each other for six weeks. Is that enough time for you to make your arrest of Bilal?" Bruce asked.

"We can do it."

Lying to him won't hurt anyone. Bilal Maqsood Ahmed will be a dead man soon, Wiggins thought.

Wiggins felt quite satisfied that he had accomplished his mission. *This should mean a promotion.*

He immediately placed the call to his supervisor on his cell phone.

In spite of Wiggins lie, Bilal was not the last STN leader to be identified. The American leader remained unknown. The World Force placed Bilal under immediate surveillance. The search for the American continued. The Peace Envoys' master STN extermination plan grew by one name. The plan was a jigsaw puzzle, one unique piece at a time added to the puzzle as they identified each regional STN leader.

His expert global Para-military forces impatiently waited for their instructions from Barrows to begin the executions of the STN leaders. It was up to the American sector to find the missing leader to so they could do the job for which they were highly trained, and one for which they were anxious to fulfill.

*

Peaksman called Barrows with the news about Bilal.

"One more, Tim. Only one more."

"I know," he replied.

41

THE LAST TIME:

The news media constant chatter about Rialdo reinforced Ed Walker's gloating. He was thoroughly convinced that his place in history was now secure. He had scaled the largest mountain. He explored the universe. He felt close to God.

I'm impressed, if I do say so myself. I planned and executed the most complex of all the STN strikes. And, the most significant one too. This one is the final phase of making the US the safest place in the world. I've proven that scum can be eliminated as easily as can the terrorists. It took just three days for Rialdo, the worst vermin of the drug world, and his cartel to die. How long did it take the government to cripple the Mafia? Years, and it's still not done. It cost them hundreds of thousands of dollars for trials and jail time. I did it for free.

No longer did he agonize over the deaths of innocent women and children. No longer did he feel nauseated or frightened. No longer did Rule 16 obsess him. He had morphed from a caring law abiding citizen to a man whose thrills arrived in a different package. He loved the process of selecting his new targets. He rejoiced in the detailed planning sessions with his team. He soared to dizzying heights of near delirium when his team successfully executed their targets. Ed Walker had morphed into a thrill seeker. Ultimate satisfaction came from his successful execution campaigns.

His recent success against Rialdo really had him pumped even more than all the previous terrorist attacks. The continual media bombardment made it difficult to control his emotions. When he was home for the first four days after Rialdo's execution, he found it excruciatingly difficult to hide his rampart emotions from Janice. A few times, he had to catch himself from giving her a verbal dump. It made him quite nervous just thinking about his near blunders. He decided the safest place to hide was in his apartment.

It doesn't get any better than this. I can't wait for the next one that will be even more spectacular than Rialdo! He promised himself.

Exhilaration, invincibility, and all-powerful feelings dominated his emotions. Yet one issue continued to haunt him.

I don't trust myself to be alone with Janice right now. I'm afraid she'll want to know why I'm so damn excited. I need time to calm down. I have this overwhelming need to tell Janice about Rialdo, about STN, about everything. She would be so proud. I can't allow myself to think that way. Yet, I can't wait to see her face, someday when it is safe to tell her what I've done for her and the country. That'll be something! But I know myself, and she knows me too. I need a safe place to relax before I blab it all to Janice. I'm much safer with Liz when I feel like this. I think I'll call to see if she's available.

She answered on the third ring.

"Hi, are you available this evening?"

"Well, it all depends on who's calling," she teased him.

"This is Superman and Batman, in one dynamic package. Does that interest you?"

"Who wouldn't be with those credentials? Let me check my schedule. Don't want to miss anything important."

"Make it quick, before I have to fly off and save some highly exotic and beautiful woman from certain death."

"What if I told you that I'm in distress and need to be saved?"

"I'm here, beautiful lady in distress. Can you hang on until 6:00 tonight? I'd give my life to save you. Bring a bottle of your favorite Champaign."

"I hope I can hold onto this thin rope before I plunge into the waiting mouths of the hungry lions waiting to eat me."

"I'll be sure to eat you myself after you're rescued. That I promise."

"It better be more than that."

"I'll do my best."

"Where, our favorite hotel?"

"No unfortunately. I can't break away. It will have to be at the Shellington Arms, just for tonight. I promise you will never have to come here again. Alright?"

She did not answer.

"Listen, Liz. I know how you feel about this place. We've had a great time together. Since that first time, I haven't asked you to come here, have I? We've been at some really nice hotels and your place too. I'm begging you, please come here this last time. I'll make it up to you, I swear."

"Are you sure you can't get away? I really hate that place."

"Me too, but I really need to see you tonight. Please come!"

The new tone in his voice was strong and insistent. She liked when a man was forceful, and Ed fit the bill at that moment. She felt turned on.

Reluctantly she said, "OK, I'll come, as long as it's the last time."

"Great…see you soon."

She packed her new sexy lingerie, a bottle of Veuve Clicquot Demi-Sec NV Champaign, her travel makeup, toothbrush and fresh set of underwear and stockings into her Burberry red tote bag, called a taxi, and headed to Falls Church.

He sounds excited, more than I've heard him before. I hope it's because of me. I don't know what he does, other than he works undercover for the government, he's happily married, and he loves me. He is what he is, and I enjoy the entire package. Tonight will be incredible, I can sense it. She almost had an orgasm in anticipation.

Janice was next on Ed's call list.

"Hi, it's me."

"When are you coming home?" she asked.

"Sudden change in plans. I have to be in Boston this evening, so I'm going there directly from Miami this afternoon. Sorry, one of those things. You know how the government works, or doesn't. I'll be a day or two, depending on how things go."

"Do you have enough clean clothes?"

"No, but the hotel has overnight service, so it shouldn't be a problem. How are things there?"

"We're fine. We all miss you. Seems like forever."

"I know, but I expect things won't be as hectic for the next several weeks. I'm hoping the meeting will be only one day. I'm tired of traveling too. I miss you too. Have to run. Call you in the morning. Love you."

"Love you too."

There was no temptation to tell Liz so I can be with her without it being threatening.

Pleased that he had managed his latest lie to Janice, he hurriedly cleaned the apartment. Three hours before Liz would arrive.

Not bad for a skinny Philadelphia kid! he thought. He set the alarm and dropped into a much-needed sleep.

Strange, Janice thought after she talked with her husband. *I've never seen him so upbeat. He's been prancing around like a maniac. Something doesn't feel right. Probably just my nerves.*

She wasn't sure why, but something was different about Ed. It wasn't just his enthusiasm. Something in his voice. But what? Her uneasiness persisted throughout the evening until she fell into a disturbed sleep.

The alarm awakened him, an hour before Liz would glide through the door. He spent the time reviewing his thick dossiers of potential criminal targets. Disgruntled that he could not find the one that fell into the potential spectacular category, he showered to prepare for Liz. He knew his target was in the pile hiding, begging for discovery.

I'll look them over tomorrow, after Liz leaves. I'm sure I'll find what I want. For now, I want to enjoy my time with her.

He placed the papers into briefcase, locked it and slid it under the bed.

Her taxi arrived shortly before six. He heard the taxi stop, he leaped from his chair, rifled his hands through his hair, and ran to the door. She arrived simultaneously as he yanked the door open.

He reached for her hand, and practically dragged her into the apartment. Something seemed different to Liz, something about the look in his eyes. She wasn't sure, but it was unsettling. It wasn't his normal lust and passion, but something was very different. She tried to remember when she had seen that look before. The movies? TV?

His eyes seemed to glow with a brooding darkness, a hidden intent, and something even deeper, more sinister then she had ever seem in anyone's eyes before. And certainly never in his. He had the look you see in horror movies where the evil character is possessed by a demonic entity. She wasn't sure what it meant, but it disturbed her.

She had little time to reflect further as he pulled her into his arms. Within seconds, their lips locked together as they eagerly and passionately embraced. She temporarily forgot her concern, but quickly it returned.

His eyes, his eyes, what was it I saw in them?

"I've missed you, you beautiful creature," he said in a sexy voice as possible.

"Me too, passion man, me too. Can I put my bag down first?"

"I don't know if I'm willing to waste the time. After all, you're in distress, aren't you?"

"Save me, save me." She softly dropped the bag, forgetting the Champaign was inside. She heard the bottle thump on the floor.

"Oops, forgot the bubbly was in the bag."

"Forget it. Right now, it's time to ravish the damsel in distress."

"I thought you came to save me, not to take advantage of me in my time of need. OK, don't save me. I'd rather be ravished. Do it now!" she commanded. He readily complied. They made love: strong, furious, and intense.

They spent the next two hours lying in bed, drinking, touching and caressing each other.

Though he wanted to devote every moment enjoying Liz, he found his thoughts wandering to Rialdo. He reviled in his feelings of power and invincibility, smug in his role as the savior of humanity.

They drank and giggled and drank some more. Usually they talked in general about the things that had happened to them and their jobs, always avoiding topics like war, International conflicts, or any stressful topic. That kept their idyllic relationship pure and unfettered by the outside world. Yet, this time there was something different. After sex, Ed usually was thoroughly relaxed. Tonight, he wasn't. Tonight he also was getting drunk.

Despite their marathon hours of sex and drinking, Ed continued to be a bundle of high energy. Several times he started to talk, only to stop before he began. She did not challenge him. They polished off the Champaign. Ed drank more than his share. His words became slightly slurred, although the intensity of his lovemaking wasn't affected. Liz responded with her own passion as she again yielded to his touch and his willing body. She had expected this evening would be special. It was.

In spite of their passionate lovemaking, Liz could not dispel the strange feeling when she first entered his apartment. Something new intensified those feelings, something very powerful. Something highly unusual.

In the past, Ed usually built up his sexual excitement with foreplay. Tonight, he passed that phase. Tonight, his passion was immediate, long lasting, and almost selfish as he took her multiple times. He seemed driven to satisfy some deep-rooted sexual compulsion buried deeply within him.

She had never experienced his harsh love making before. The power behind his every thrust, the urgency of penetration, and his sudden and unexpected animalistic grunts during orgasm fulfilled her deeply hidden fantasy of rape. Together they created a volcano of continuous sexual eruptions. It excited and frightened her together, a unique conflict of feelings she never experienced before.

Without warning, Ed jumped out of bed, went to the refrigerator and returned with his own bottle of Champaign and two clanging glasses.

"Now, my love, we are going to celebrate," he slurred.

"I think we already celebrated. But just what are we celebrating?" she asked.

"Can't tell you. Instead, let's dedicate our celebration to our secret experiences and not tell each other. You celebrate yours, and I'll mine, but we will still be celebrating together, right?"

His look baffled her. The love and excitement normally so evident in the past had been replaced by an intense and disturbing flicker in his eyes. She considered saying something, but thought better of it. She instinctively masked her concerns with smiles and good conversation. Was it fear? Of what? Him? She wasn't sure and wasn't anxious to find out.

"Separate celebrations? I've never done that before, but why not? It will be fun. We'll have our own little secret celebration, separate and together. It's a little weird, but I love the idea."

They managed to drain most of the second bottle in less than 40 minutes. She reached an early state of drunkenness from their separate celebrations. Ed had passed that point at the end of the first bottle. Ed continued talking while Liz prudently sat back. And listened and wondered and watched.

Instead of conversation, it became a self-endorsing boastful drunken soliloquy.

"You know, what I'm doing is the most important thing I've ever done in my life. When it's finished, I expect the President of the United States will award me the Medal of Honor. Our freedom and our way of life depend on me. I'm almost done, and when I finish"... he never completed the sentence.

"Someday, history will note my brilliance and my remarkable success. I'll be listed along with the greatest heroes of our country: George Washington, Abraham Lincoln, Teddy Roosevelt and Harry Truman. My place in history is secure, only it will take a little more time before there will be no more terrorists or criminals in this country. They will all be dead, just like that scumbag Rialdo. You did hear about Rialdo, the drug dealer, didn't you? What do you think?"

"From what I've heard, he was an evil man and a drug dealer."

"He was more than evil. He deserved to die, him and all his friends. They ruined so many lives with his drugs. Can't do that any more, can he? The government tried to get him for years but couldn't. It took STN two days. Two days! That's something, isn't it?"

"Yes," she cautiously responded, not sure where he was going with this sudden talk of current events.

"But don't you think that everyone is better off without him?"

"Do you mean society or his family?"

"His family doesn't matter now, do they? No, I mean society. Wasn't he threatening our fucking society?"

"Why are you talking about him? It makes me uneasy and very anxious. Can't we get back to happy things? I don't want to think about it any more. Want to ravish me again?"

Ed ignored her attempt to change the conversation.

"STN executed him, and Rialdo's not the only one. More is coming. You'll see."

"I believe you. Let's stop, OK?"

"But what do you think of the guy who made Rialdo's death happen? What about him?" he insisted, ignoring her request.

"What difference does it make who he is and what he did? STN scares me because they kill anyone they want. Where will it end?"

Hearing her own words made her tremble. She suddenly had a clearer vision of STN and the future. The truth filled her with trepidation and anger, fear of STN, and angry with Ed for making her face the threat she was forced to acknowledge.

"You don't get it," he slashed back at her. His tone, though still slurred, changed. A sense of urgency peppered his speech. He was obviously drunk and highly agitated.

Annoyed, she shot back "Why are you talking to me like that? What's wrong with you?"

"Nothing's wrong. I asked you a simple question. What's so damn hard about that? I want to know what you think of the man who killed Rialdo. That's all."

"He must be very smart, or...", suddenly feeling very intimidated, she wanted to say "demented" but didn't.

Perhaps it's the Champaign talking. I don't know what's bothering him but it frightens me, she thought.

"Do you mean the way he was killed? In his home, with his family, bodyguards and everyone?"

"Partially, but not exactly."

"You mean STN?"

"Well, kind of... yes," he slurred, adding,

"What if I told you…No, I can't."

"Tell me what, Ed?"

"Never mind. Forget this whole damn conversation."

"If it makes you happy, we can talk about other things, or not talk. I'm happy lying next to you."

Her response seemed to agitate and frustrate him. He grew increasingly impatient with her and himself. Not with ugly impatience, but with the impatience of someone with a story to tell, yet is having trouble getting it out.

Still, his eyes drew her constant stares.

"They already made their official announcement. Just think, you're sleeping with one of the heroes of the 21st century. Isn't that something?" he continued.

Liz listened. And watched. But he wasn't talking to her, nor was he seeing her. He seemed to be addressing a non-existent audience, sitting in a hushed amphitheatre, a gaggle of microphones and cameras meshed together, fighting each other for the best position as hundreds of TV cameras transmitted his words to the world. He was the conquering hero, triumphantly leading his troops after a crucial battle in which he destroyed the enemy. His trance-like demeanor, made him look like a devout prophet communicating directly with his God.

Shoulders squared, his jaw jutting forward at a haughty angle, his ego bursting from his body, infinitely powerful and domineering, he was the essence of omnipotence; his eyes darting from side to side, scanning the audience for their smiles of adulation and awe. Never once did he look at her, or see the contrived smile on her face, or the terror in her eyes. He made her invisible the moment he started to speak. Her body might be invisible, but her mind captured his every word, gesture and expression. What he said and how he said it jolted her into sobriety.

He slumped onto the bed. Liz stared at the ceiling, too nervous to permit the sleep she desperately needed. She tried to remember his words and the way he looked. What did he mean by hero? Is he tied to Rialdo? To STN? She needed time to sort out the last few startling minutes. It would come, she hoped, when the effects of the Champaign were gone and she was safe in her own home. Her thoughts bounced like a rubber ball from one image to another. Slowly she recognized the one dominant emotion that had plagued her the entire evening. The one that made her uneasy. The one she now recognized she felt when she saw Ed's eyes. It was fear. Hers.

"There, was that so hard? Now, I want to tell you … I did it. I planned the entire operation against Rialdo," he uttered with total pride of his accomplishment. His next words elevated her fear to terror. She suddenly feared for her life, though she wasn't sure why. Her paradise was shattered; she had no place to hide, and no way to protect herself

"What are you saying? That you are a part of STN?"

Hearing her say STN was a jolt of lightening. Ed broke out into an instant sweat. He stopped talking, his shoulders slumped, the fire in his eyes extinguished. Samson the mighty had lost his power through drunken lips.

He looked like the boy who caught with his hand in the cookie jar, and now was going to be punished.

What the fuck have I done? I just told Liz about STN. Oh my God! I've fucked up, really fucked up! Now what do I do? Think! Think! he implored himself.

"Liz, I'm so sorry. I think I drank too much. I guess I was fantasying and it came out all wrong. I always wanted to be a hero, and the drunker I became, the easier it was to convince myself I was the hero of my fantasy. I wanted to impress you, and I lost control. I'm really stupid and sorry. I know how much it upset you. I'm embarrassed and very humiliated. Can you ever forgive me, please?"

Thankful Ed had calmed down, she felt the immediate danger had lessened, but was not completely gone. Her terror remained.

Be careful, very careful she reminded herself. *Say the wrong thing, or act frightened, and he might go crazy. Who knows what he's capable of doing? This isn't the man I admire. Something dreadful has happened to him. Is he really STN? It could explain a lot!*

Her experience with men high on liquor had awakened her sixth sense. It convinced her Ed was not fantasizing. Exaggerating some, but not without some level of truth. That only exacerbated her fear that her life might be in danger. She wasn't sure what kind of danger, but danger nonetheless. In spite of her fears, she knew she had to force herself to be calm and not arouse his suspicion.

I must convince him I accept his explanation. It may save my life!

Mustering her poise, she enthusiastically embraced and gently kissed his lips and whispered in his ear,

"You don't have to be a hero for me. I don't want you to be a hero. I love you just as you are. Intelligent, kind, considerate, and a great lover. What else could a woman want? Of course I forgive you. Booze has a way of making us all someone we're not. But…" she coyly said, "I will forgive and forget everything, except your love making. That was sensational, don't you agree?"

"Thank you. I knew there was a reason why I love being with you so much. You really understand me, and now, who I fantasized I wanted to be."

They giggled and held each other tightly. Ed felt caution. Liz felt repulsed.

"Maybe we both need to sleep it off. What do you think?" she innocently asked.

He nodded in agreement as they returned to the comfort of his bed. Their bodies intertwined, seemingly as one. Though exhausted from the booze and his boasting, he refused to allow himself to asleep. His eyelids drooped, but his mind was wide-awake. He knew he needed to watch her to be sure she wasn't trying to deceive him.

Liz also made the same choice to stay awake. She dreaded for her life. She pretended to be asleep so she could watch him and to protect herself, if necessary. She was not sure how, but being awake gave her an opportunity to survive. Terror dominated her emotions. She thought of trying to sneak out of the apartment as he slept, to run away as fast as she could. She thought of quietly dressing and leaving, but decided against it. The neighborhood was not the place to be alone in the middle of the night without her car. There could be trouble if he caught her trying to leave. She knew she could not match his strength. She would have to wait until morning.

There would be enough time, she hoped.

Ed pretended he was so sleepy he couldn't keep his eyes open. Although he was exhausted, his sense of danger demanded he remain alert. He caught himself dozing off several times, only to remind himself that Liz needed watching. He didn't know what she knew or thought, but he couldn't take the chance she would leave if he fell asleep.

What have I done? I let my guard down, and now… I don't know what she believes. Does she remember what I said? I'm fucking stupid. I've spent years creating an elaborate undercover life, and I blow it because I wanted to impress her. I let my ego and the booze control me. In the process, I may have destroyed everything. STN, she, and me. What if she really believes I'm STN? I can't trust her with that knowledge about me. She would have to die, and I would have to kill her. I wouldn't even know how to do it. I never killed anyone before.

But I love her. It's not her fault. I was out of control. Fucking booze! How could I live knowing that I destroyed her? Still, STN is the most important thing I have ever done in my lifetime. I'm a hero, even if I'm stupid. My team and I are the best. When Farook needs something done, he turns to me.

For the first time in months he experienced a deep, disturbing, and dark panic. His stomach turned into knots, sweat poured out of him, and he rested his neck on his hand. His mistake weighed heavily on him.

Should I tell Farook, wait, or say nothing? If I wait, and she believes I'm STN, she'll go to the authorities. If the government doesn't get me, Farook will.

I have no intention of dying, not yet. Not this way, not over a piece of ass. What to do?

Throughout the long, lonely, and sweaty evening, he waited for Liz to awaken. They both had pretended to sleep. For three hours, mighty Zeus was a trembling mass of inconsistencies and uncertainties.

I must find out what she knows. Then I can decide what to do. Hopefully, she was too drunk to remember. Dear God, don't let her remember what I said!

So he waited and watched. Liz never stirred. The longer he waited, the more he rebuked himself.

I will never forgive myself for being so careless and jeopardizing everything I love.

Finally a little after six, Liz began to stir. She grew tired of pretending she was asleep, fearful that her need for sleep might overtake her. The sun had not made it's appearance. It languished behind a gray sky. She opened her eyes. Ed was sitting in the chair facing her. Her head hurt slightly, she was hungry, and was still obsessing over what he said last evening. The fear never left her.

Play it cool she reminded herself, *play it cool, if you want to leave here alive.*

She coyly smiled at him.

"Have you been sitting there watching me all night? The Champaign was tasty but wicked. I haven't had a hangover like this for a long time. Be a dear and get me some aspirins, please. My head is throbbing like a drum."

He brought the aspirins and a glass of water, eyeing her as inconspicuously as possible.

She either a great actor or really got bombed last night. Don't know yet, but I will learn the truth before she leaves.

Liz remained haunted by last evening's events. She eyed him as he went for the aspirins, feigning to be woozy and disinterested.

Was he telling me the truth or was he just fantasizing being a hero? It's hard to believe that hero crap. Even an egomaniac wouldn't want to be known as a killer of women and children. He must be telling the truth. What if he is a killer... will he kill me? What am I going to do? I must convince him I don't remember what he said. If I'm going to leave alive, I'm going to have to learn how to be an actor, and fast. If Ed is working with STN, she reasoned, *he wouldn't hesitate to kill me if he thought I would expose him. My only hope is to pretend that I don't remember too much of what he said.*

"Take these, they might help."

Coincidently they each reached the same conclusion. The next hour would determine the course of the rest of their lives.

"God I'm hungry, hung over, and happy. The three H's." he muttered in an attempt to put her at ease.

She smiled, placed a gentle kiss on his forehead. "Me too. My head's killing me. Can't remember the last time I got this bombed. What did you put in that Champaign? Ecstasy? Everything's a big blur. I remember feeling good about something you said to me. What did you say? Do you remember or were you too shit faced too? " she innocently inquired.

"I vaguely remember something about you being my hero," she continued.

"It made me feel good because I know you're my hero, and I love you so much. Do you remember that? Oh crap. If these aspirins don't start to work, I'll never get to work. What about breakfast? Can you make it? Whatever you do, don't even think of scrapping the spatula in the pan. The noise will drive me crazy. Two eggs over light for me, and strong cup of coffee. Hmmm... That sounds delicious. Oh... I guess I'm not being a considerate lover. I was so into me that I didn't ask how you're feeling. How's your head? You look like shit, Nice shit, mind you, but shit nonetheless. Maybe it's that way because of the cotton in my eyes."

"You still look gorgeous to me, even if your eyes ARE blurry," he retorted.

"I know I was drunk as a skunk, and the Champaign made me nuts. I think I may have said some things that may have upset you, but frankly, I can't remember what it was. I vaguely remember talking, no, more like babbling, about drugs, or being a hero, wasn't it? Do you remember?"

He decided that coy probing was the best approach to determine what she knew or remembered.

"I told you before about the hero stuff, and I meant it. I'm not sure what else you said, but I do remember hearing the word hero. I don't remember being upset. Should I be?" Liz questioned, then continued,

"You know, I was feeling no pain last night, and kind of remember being worried about what you said, but for the life of me I can't remember it either. So why don't we just forget about it. I suspect we both were reacting to something, and made more of it than what we should have. I think it was something like that, don't you?" she lied.

"Yes, you're right. My head is pounding and I'm still a bit foggy. I truly love you. Let's promise not to get that drunk again. Deal?"

"Oh Ed, I'm so thrilled you feel the same as I. We almost made a mess of ourselves. I think I'm falling in love with you. I know I said no complications, but people can change, can't they? I don't want to lose you."

She fell into his arms as they passionately kissed and held each other tightly.

"Whew, I'm glad that's over," he whispered in her ear.

"Me too."

He waited for signs of nervousness.

If she's worried, it will show up. Her words, her face, her eyes. Somehow she will show me what she's feeling.

"What else did I say that made you happy, I mean besides the hero stuff?"

"I don't know, it's a big blur. I kind of remember something about rigatoni. Were we talking about eating? I guess it doesn't matter. But I do recall the best parts, when we made love so many times. I have to confess, as long as you promise you won't let it go to your head. That was the best sex I've ever had. It was delicious. I don't know what got into you, but I know what got into me." She laughed at her own joke. He smiled and nodded.

"It *was* special wasn't it, at least until I broke out the second bottle of Champaign. Two bottles is WAY too much booze. I'm feeling shitty too. Remind me never to do that again."

"The sex or the drinking?"

"I want to remember how great it feels screwing you, so I must mean the booze. Did you want me to say the sex?"

"You got it right the first time. Hey, what time is it?"

"6:18."

"Good, there's still time to make me breakfast. Are you up to it?"

"Coming up."

"I'm going to take a quick shower and get dressed. Give me twenty minutes before you start the eggs, will you?" She scurried into the bathroom.

I think she's OK. Everything seems normal. I know. Her smile says so.

He was only too happy to convince himself she posed no danger to him or STN. Mostly because he wanted and needed to believe that was the truth. He selected the only path that validated his sense of self-worth and his safety.

She's not a threat, thank God. I dodged a bullet, but I learned another valuable lesson. I'll never again let my guard down. I stupidly allowed my ego to impress a woman I love, and I nearly killed us both. Never again. Never! This time I was lucky. Silence is my friend; ego my enemy.

He repeated this new mantra repeatedly until he felt confident it was firmly entrenched in his memory.

He cooked breakfast and they ate in relative quiet, each respecting the purported thumping in the other's head. Liz finished first and said,

"It's too bad we don't have more time and less hangovers. I need another fix, but it'll have to wait until next time. I have an appointment at 10:30 that I can't break. Sorry my love."

"The way I feel it probably wouldn't have been my best effort, and you deserve the best."

"Your worst is still the best. Don't you forget it!"

"You say the truest things, you silver-tongued beauty. Let's plan on getting together in two or three weeks. If I don't spend more time at work and at home, it could become nasty."

"I understand, but I don't have to like it." It was her second protective lie.

"I have to leave too," Ed said with a trace of sadness in his voice.

"I promised Janice I'd be home in time to see the kids before they left for school. I don't want to get her pissed off or suspicious by not showing up."

"I know."

She called for a taxi, and gave him a long and sensuous kiss goodbye as soon as she saw the taxi pull up front of the apartment building. The sun was out, threatening to punish anyone caught in its grasp.

"Love you!"

That must have sounded good to him. He always wanted me to tell him I love him. I can't think of a better time to say it than right now!

"Me too. I'll call you," he responded.

"Think of me touching and caressing you when you're sitting in your office. That will be your punishment for making me wait so long before we get together," she taunted him as she exited the front door of the building.

He watched her slide into the taxi and closed the door behind her. The driver eased his way into the morning traffic without regard to the driver he cut off.

"Whew," he reflexively touched his head. "To think I might have been forced to end the life of such a wonderful woman."

He smiled at the dichotomy of this morning.

"I have no problem ordering my enemies to die. Yet to think that I might have had to order Liz's death scared the crap out of me. That would have been hard. Really hard. It's my own fault. I will NEVER let that happen again," he said loud enough to convince himself that his secret was still safe.

42

LIZ MEETS PEAKSMAN:

The second the taxi driver cleared the parking lot, Liz broke into tears of relief. Shallow breathing; racing pulse; head pounding.

The driver looked back at her through his rear view mirror, but wisely ignored her.

"Where to lady?"

"Towards Vienna. I'll give you the address later."

She was free from him, but not from the terror he instilled in her.

Thank God I'm alive and out of the apartment. He must have believed me. Otherwise, he would not have let me go. But, what if he didn't believe me? What if he called someone to have me killed? Or maybe they're waiting for me inside my house. I know in my heart he's guilty and somehow intimately involved with the execution of Rialdo.

She cringed thinking the worst about Ed Walker, who just might be the brains behind the monstrous STN killings. She grappled with the image of him as a cold-blooded killer who thinks nothing of slaying innocent people. *HOW COULD HE DO IT?* Her sense of what was right and wrong waged a fierce battle for her emotions and her conscious.

If he's involved with STN, I need to turn him into the authorities. But if he isn't, I might be ruining both our lives. Over what? Too much Champaign? It's not as if I'm in love with him, but he is a decent human being. Or is he?

Her conscious mind battled her subconscious mind as strongly as two enemies do on a tortured and bloody battlefield. She felt trapped and confused.

The truth is the truth, and I do know the truth about him. It seems so unreal, so hard to accept he's a killer!

Her fear of Ed clashed with her sense of duty to her country. She no longer cared about being his lover. She was ready to sacrifice those exciting moments of time with him. She wasn't sure if she was ready to sacrifice Ed Walker the man. She pondered her options as the taxi speed towards Vienna.

Survival and duty won. She made her decision. She had to report him, immediately.

She called 611 on her cell from the taxi, and asked for the McLean National Homeland Security office. She explained to the operator that she had information about STN. By executive order from President Schuster, all STN related calls automatically routed to Tom Peaksman's office.

After five frantic minutes explaining the purpose of her call to the woman on the other end of the line, the woman instructed her to tell the taxi driver to drive directly to the Homeland Security headquarters in McLean. Tom Peaksman would be waiting at the main gate to the underground parking garage. The woman warned her to neither make nor receive calls on her cell phone.

The taxi arrived thirty-four minutes later. Waiting at the gate was a somber looking short balding man in a rumpled suit.

"Avery Hunter?" he asked through the open taxi window. He flashed his badge to her.

"Yes."

"Tom Peaksman, special advisor to the President. Please get out of the taxi and come with me." He paid the fare and dismissed the driver.

He led her to a waiting electric cart. They proceeded through the garage to the back door of the building, Peaksman slid his electronic ID pass in the detector, and they entered the electronically controlled door. She saw suited men and women Marines strategically positioned throughout the beige hallway leading from the garage.

Security is really high here, she nervously thought.

Unnerved and visually shaken, she never imagined she would be walking the halls of the Homeland Security headquarters, and about to save her life and destroy the man with whom she had just spent the evening.

Peaksman ushered her into a waiting elevator without speaking, pushed the fourth floor button, and the elevator silently whisked her to her new role in life: informant.

They walked to his large office down the hallway. It looked like him. Papers and boxes haphazardly placed on the floor, his round conference table covered with some sort of chart with red, blue, and green markings, lines going every which way, and large black wooden desk equally cluttered. Beige drapes hung from the windows. They looked like they had not been changed in years. When presented the opportunity to redecorate his office, Peaksman declined, muttering something about he couldn't be bothered.

"Sorry for the mess. Let me make some room for you."

He pushed the piles of files to one side and invited her to sit by the cleared space.

"Before we start, you look as though you need to relax. May I offer you coffee and a doughnut?"

"Coffee, black, one sugar, please. No doughnut."

He waited five minutes while she sipped her coffee before he began the debriefing.

"Your name is Avery Hunter, correct? OK Avery, why don't you tell me everything you know about STN.

"Please call me Liz."

Fifty-seven minutes later Liz finished relating the events and conversation of the previous evening. He took over seven pages of notes. He offered in return a brief summary of the magnitude of atrocities Ed committed under the name of STN. Peaksman wanted to impress her just how significant was the information she provided on Ed Walker. She sobbed hard when he finished. Not because she felt anguish for Ed Walker, but from a sense of relief that he didn't kill her.

I guess I'm a lucky shit. His love for me probably saved my life. I glad I came here. They need to put an end to his killings! she thought.

Peaksman could hardly contain his exhilaration. He now knew the name of the man who ran STN in North America, the addresses of both his home and his apartment, his cell number, and that he worked in McLean for the CIA, in the same building as he!

He thought of two important actions that needed immediate attention. First, protect Liz from Ed Walker. Second, he had to convince her to stay in touch with Ed Walker, to deceive him, until the Peace Envoys were ready to take action.

"Liz, I need your help. I understand you're afraid of Ed Walker and what he might do to you. But we have a serious problem. We need you to maintain your relationship with him. If you don't see him or stay in touch, he'll know you gave him up, and that's not good for you or us. He'll know he's been made and will certainly go into hiding. Its imperative Walker doesn't feel threatened or compromised. We need him to believe you still trust and love him, otherwise we'll lose him and our chance to stop STN."

"Mr. Peaksman, I never loved him. We were together for other reasons, but love wasn't one of them," she said emphatically.

"Sorry, I just assumed. Regardless, we need him to stay put until we're ready to act. This is a national security issue and unfortunately, we desperately need your help. You're the only one who knows him. Will you help us?"

"You want me to see him again? I…I… can't do that. I'm too frightened. He'll kill me if he thinks I've turned on him. I can't and I won't do it! The minute I see him he'll know something is up. I know how important this is, but not me."

"I don't blame you," replied Peaksman. "I wouldn't feel safe either. Let me think for a moment."

He sat quietly, occasionally nodding his baldhead in agreement with himself.

"How's this. Can you talk on the phone without panicking? I mean, can you pretend you're in love, I mean you still … err… like him if you speak on the phone? I agree you should not ever be in his presence again.

Let me ask you another question. How do you feel about taking a vacation abroad, at the government's expense? You can tell Walker you have to go there on business, perhaps to open several offices for your company in Europe. That would take you out of the country for five to six weeks, or more if necessary. Then you can talk on your cell without being in danger. All you need to do is to pretend you miss him when you are talking. Can you at least do that?"

"I think I can, but I can't afford to miss six weeks of a work. I still have bills, lots of them. I'll be out of a job. I can't be away that long. My boss will fire me. I want to help, but I need to think about me too, don't I?"

He smiled before he spoke.

"Sorry, I forgot a minor detail. The government will be happy to deposit one million dollars into your bank account as your reward for your participation, after Walker is captured."

"A million dollars? Really?'

"That's right."

"When do I leave?" Liz managed to subdue her fears about Ed. She was instantly buoyant and ready to become rich.

"I do have one question… about Ed. What are you going to do with him?" she asked

"Once we have him in our custody, he'll be put on trial for his crimes. I'm sure he will be facing a long prison term."

"Oh… I… thought…I don't know what I thought. I guess that's what needs to be done, isn't it?"

"Yes, that's how a democracy works, Liz. Do the crime. Do the time."

She was satisfied with his explanation.

"I need to leave you alone while I set things up. Can I get you something to drink or eat?' Peaksman asked.

"Do you have any bourbon?"

"Sorry, I gave up drinking when I developed ulcers. More coffee?"

"Just a bottle of water, and a tranquilizer, if you have one," she seriously replied.

"I'll see if anyone has a Valium. Be right back."

Peaksman practically ran to another office and called Barrows.

"Tim, Tim!" he shouted. "We did it! The last piece! We have the American! I have Liz Hunter, who was his girlfriend, in my office. She became suspicious when he talked about STN while drunk. She panicked, figured out she was in danger, called Homeland Security, and came here. She gave him up, everything! You won't believe who he is!"

"Fantastic! Tell me who!" demanded Barrows.

"I'll come to your office as soon as I take good care of our Miss Hunter. I'd rather tell you face to face."

"Get the hell over here as soon as you're done!"

"I'll call when I'm leaving," Peaksman assured him.

"Make it quick," Barrows impatiently barked.

Peaksman jotted down an emergency plan of action for her while she waited in his office. He made a call and a team of FBI agents raced to her home to insure it was safe to return that night. He arranged a security detail for 24/7 home protection. He also arranged for her to leave in two days on an extended tour of Italy, France, and Germany. He wrote a cashier's check from his slush fund for spending money to cover her expenses. He and Barrows had created the fund for such an emergency.

He received the all clear call from his surveillance team, arranged for a "safe" taxi, and returned to his office. Liz was asleep in her chair.

"Liz…"

She awoke with a start.

"Everything's OK. You fell asleep. Sorry I had to wake you."

"I guess I was tired. Rough night."

Peaksman explained everything in detail to her. The trip, the $25,000 spending money, the round-the clock security, the surveillance of her home, and that a safe taxi would arrive shortly to take her home.

"It would be best if every thing looked normal. The driver is a highly trained agent used to protecting dignitaries, of which you have become an honorary member. I've also taken the liberty to provide security abroad for your protection. There will be no need for you to contact me unless you have a problem The one million dollars will be transferred to any bank account you select when we have Walker in custody. Any questions?"

"None, and thanks for helping me."

"On the contrary. It's I who thank you! You did the right thing by coming to us, and I can't tell you how much this means to the government. Thank you so much."

"How will I know when it's safe to come back home?" she asked.

"I'll contact you when it's over."

"Be sure you do. I would appreciate it."

"Of course. You can count on it. By the way, have you decided where you will stay in Europe?"

"The French Riviera sounds good. I'm sure there are a lot of available men there who want to meet a rich American woman," she smiled.

He escorted Avery Liz Hunter from the complex to the waiting FBI taxi.

He called Barrows the second Liz was in the taxi.

"I'm leaving now."

"Get your ass over here and get a police escort! I don't want anything to happen to you before we talk."

"And after?"

No answer. Barrows disconnected.

Peaksman charged into Barrow's office, closed the door and excitedly put his notes in front of Tim. "It's all here. It's Ed Walker from CIA! For God's sake, he practically works beside me!"

"Ed Walker? That son-of-a bitch! I didn't like him the first time we met.

To think that bastard was operating under our noses. I want him to die first. Understand? Do you think he's the brains behind STN?"

"Not sure. He certainly is in the right position. He might be, because the two important attacks, 9/11 and Rialdo, came from his group. If he's the brains we should be able to make this real simple. Take Walker out and STN will crumble."

Barrows thought about it and replied,

"Why take a chance. If he's not the leader, we'll have blown our only opportunity to destroy STN. We'll stick with the original plan. All nineteen die. Then we'll be sure. I think there's way too much money involved for Walker to be their leader. We're talking about 70 or 80 million dollars. No way in hell did he have access to that much money to finance an operation as huge as STN. Others are definitely involved." Barrows reasoned.

"What about them?" Peaksman questioned.

"I don't see any way to get to them. Even if we decided to capture Walker alive, I doubt he would talk. My guess is that once the STN leaders are dead, the money people will vanish. I suspect they will be damn glad they weren't exposed. Don't forget, they almost completely eliminated terrorism. They might be content with what they *did* accomplish. I'd be happy if I was they. Especially if I'm alive, not in prison, or dead."

"Good point. Let's finish the job correctly. All nineteen STN people die as planned."

They spent an hour reviewing Liz Hunter's information from Peaksman's notes. They quickly verified through the CIA that Walker's cell number matched the Word Link file.

They now had a name, a place, and a cell phone number.

Barrows' quest was nearly over. He was on the brink of eliminating STN. Barrows was coolly excited about his future. His career looked promising, very promising.

Once STN is destroyed, President Schuster promised to help me with my career. I used to want to become the next President of the United States. I'm not sure that's where I should be. I can continue as Chairman of the Peace Envoys. I might be in a better position as Chairman to help the children more than as President. I'll decide after STN.

The last piece of the STN puzzle was in place. They immediately decided on their course of action. Meet with their covert military operatives, the World Force teams, to structure a plan, conduct immediate and comprehensive surveillance on the nineteen leaders, select a date, refine the plan and get the job done. Soon STN would cease to exist.

The next five days, he and Peaksman toiled to organize the meeting with their operatives. The STN leaders had to die simultaneously, regardless of the country, obstacles, or time differences, as he had dictated at the start of the STN campaign.

"Ironic," Barrows said pensively to Peaksman. "We're following the same strategy to kill them as they used to kill their victims. Simultaneously kill your enemies. That's poetic justice, isn't it?"

Now that they knew the leaders, Barrows found himself facing conflicting emotions. He was euphoric with the latest information. Now he was ready to make the final preparations for the ultimate destruction of STN. Yet he worried that something dramatic might go wrong. If STN somehow discovered plans were in process for their deaths, the STN leaders would quickly disappear. That thought greatly disturbed him.

World leaders would surely blame him, and withdraw their support for the Peace Envoys poor-nation mission. Again, the children would bear the brunt of their actions. His plans for their salvation would evaporate quicker than water drops on a hot stove. Who would support him after his failure? Schuster? Not for a minute. The public because of his PE successes? Probably not enough, he conceded. Barrows shared his concerns with no one, not Peaksman, not Schuster, not Lynette.

Barrows forced himself to be optimistic, in spite of his lingering doubts.

The following day after Walker's identity was revealed, he called for a secret strategy meeting with his Peace Envoys team to strategize the details for the STN attack. Invited were the key special-force military leaders of every county that had the direct responsibly for the field operations. They had the skills to conduct covert or quick strike commando actions, and this would be their most important mission; to execute the nineteen STN leaders. Barrows intended to select a commander to coordinate and lead the global attacks.

He decided on Athens, Greece for the meeting. He knew Athens had multiple International flights into the airport from every country in the world. The meeting naturally had to be secret. Barrows wanted to be out of the public's eye, and he determined that Athens gave him the protection he wanted. The comings and going of world figures are less conspicuous than other major cities simply because of the large number of touchdowns and lift-offs that were part of the Athens airport daily activity. The meeting was scheduled one week later.

Peaksman invited seventy-eight people. He instructed each attendee to use their government connections to enter Athens quietly, secretly, and anonymously. Phony passports and names were essential and quickly created. Peaksman created a schedule of arrival for the attendees staggered over a five-day period. They made sleeping arrangements at non-descript hotels or inns to maximize their isolation. Their orders were simple. Make no calls to anyone, including family or friends. Remain in your room until the meeting.

Sightseeing, bars, women, and entertainment are prohibited. The meeting needed to be invisible.

Everyone was on a wartime footing. Each man could carry a throwaway International cell phone to be used only for communicating with Barrows or himself. Peaksman appointed himself as the emergency contact. He would resolve any problem that arose.

The meeting was scheduled for 9:00 AM on Tuesday, September 14. 2011.

"Be prepared to stay for three to five days," Peaksman warned them A fleet of taxis, manned by agents of the Greek Ministry of Public Order, the United States FBI equivalent, was hastily organized to transport the attendees to the meeting from their hotels or motels.

For two twelve-hour days Barrows and Peaksman worked to incorporate the US and Pakistani STN pieces into the extermination plan. They poured over the massive pile of paperwork, some typed, some handwritten, to isolate the pertinent facts. Included were surveillance reports, personal habits, bodyguards, travel patterns, eating patterns, work and home locations, etc. They laid out a giant matrix of the living and work habits, patterns, and locations for each STN regional leader.

When finished, they emerged with a ten foot by three-foot organization chart that offered a unified view of the entire STN organization, region-by-region and country by country. Their greatest attack asset was STN's decentralized organization. It gave them maximum attack flexibility. Still, they had no link to the central Egyptian figure. He remained a mystery.

"We'll be able to develop independent strike plans for each regional leader to accommodate the specific needs of the security forces. As long as we attack simultaneously, we'll be fine," declared a jubilant Barrows.

"STN kept their identities secret even from each other by using code names to communicate. It was the most logical way to maintain their secrecy. Frankly, it's a perfect setup for global vigilantes from which to operate. Fortunately for us it plays directly into our hands. We don't have to worry about inter-regional communications when our attacks begin, which allows us to develop nineteen individualized plans. They'll never know what hit them! How thoughtful of STN to accommodate us so nicely!" Barrows reminded Peaksman.

Barrows paused to reflect on their ingenuity.

"When evil people plan evil things, they always find creative ways to persevere."

Peaksman added,

"Let's not forget that when STN first exploded in our face, they had a noble mission that was eagerly condoned by our short-sighted world leaders.

Only after they decided to expand their targets to include criminals did STN become unacceptable and frightening. They violated laws and scared the crap out of everyone. Yet, where would we be if they had not broken the back of the terrorists? We'd still be sucking our thumbs, just as we've been doing for the past 20 years.

STN's mistake was they became worst than the terrorists. They threatened the essence of our society by hiding behind their lofty mission, only to stumble by declaring war on society's misfits. Yet their adoring public still regards them as heroes. Had they not violated our laws, do you think we'd be trying to destroy them? Between you and me, I'm thrilled they decided to attack criminals. The big question became where or when would they stop. They could have enjoyed their success if they would have just stopped after they destroyed the terrorists. They really fucked up, didn't they?

They forgot their main purpose. I suspect that killing may have become their eventual reason to exist. I suspect it became their joy and their thrill. Don't forget, they stole money and jewelry from their victims, probably to help with their finances. I know they had a lot of money floating around, but maybe it was not enough. I'm guessing that they probably couldn't stop even if they wanted to," offered Peaksman.

"Really? You sound like an STN sympathizer Tom."

"No, I'm not. Just being pragmatic. I appreciate the role they played in helping us to have a chance at peace, that's all," Peaksman warily responded.

This is not the battle I want fight with Tim Barrows.

"Any thoughts about their money source?" Peaksman shrewdly asked, changing the subject.

"Not a clue. Whoever they are, they were very clever. They funded STN with non-traceable cash deposits. How they amassed so much cash is intriguing isn't it? But the bastards are smart, you have to give them that. They left no trail. Nothing even remotely points to them. They've isolated themselves perfectly. I doubt if we'll ever learn who they are. I guarantee only a few people within STN know their names, including our Egyptian friend. Unfortunately, they will never come to justice," lamented Barrows.

"It's more important we break the back of the field operations. That's our focus, and that's what we're capable of doing. The rest is up to someone else," Peaksman reminded him.

"We're on the verge of accomplishing what many thought was impossible," Barrows philosophized.

"History might one day support STN as heroes and us as villains. Everything was acceptable until they forced government officials to fear them. They gave birth to their own demise. They scripted, no demanded, their own termination. They forced the politicians to come to us. They deserve what they'll be getting."

Barrows stopped talking and slumped in his chair. He looked like a partially deflated balloon, not limp nor puffed up. He looked fatigued and troubled, yet bore the demeanor of a victor of a bloody battle against a superior foe. STN was in their grasp. Shortly, success would be his.

But, where to from here? The Presidency? The Peace Envoys? What will happen if the funds for the Peace Envoys are turned off? What will happen to the children? Perhaps I'm better off working towards the Presidency. I would have 4-8 years where I could influence the funding for the Envoys.

Barrows insisted the execution date should be implemented as soon as possible, preferably in October. Intense surveillance on all nineteen STN leaders continued. Barrows insisted he personally wanted to know everything about them. Peaksman threw in,

"We'll soon know when and where they shit too." He laughed

"Tom, I've been thinking about the widows and children of these STN people. They will be the innocent victims. I don't want them to have to suffer for the stupidity of their husbands. I want to set up an anonymous trust fund for every wife and child. They need to survive. For them, survival means money. We will be endowed with over fifty to seventy million STN dollars very soon. I want each of them to receive one million dollars from the money we'll be getting. At least some good will come from their husband's evil. Can you make those arrangements? I don't want the suffering of nineteen families on my conscience. Is that clear?"

Surprised, Peaksman responded,

"Even Walker's family? You hate everything he stands for, I mean, he's among the worse. He worked for the government, for the CIA. He was the spy among us."

"True, he is scum. That's why he will die. But his family is not responsible. Are we going to act like STN? Are we going to kill the family along with the guilty? Not kill them with weapons, but by snuffing out any opportunity they have for a future. No. Walker's family must be included!"

"Tim, I'm proud to be part of this. It's a wonderful and caring gesture on your part. I'll make certain that NO ONE can trace the source of the trust funds, not even the CIA."

"Thanks Tom."

*

He flew first class to Athens, under the passport name of Simon F. Morgan. He reasoned that should anyone detect his travel, he can say that he was on a mission to discuss delicate issues with our friends and did not want the meeting to be public. Barrows poured over the data multiple times to be sure he had not missed anything important. Seven hours later Peaksman would arrive in Athens under his assumed name, Harvey T. Foster.

Barrows reviewed the STN organizational. His lingering concern was that the news media might somehow link the STN leaders' deaths together and deduce they were STN members.

If that happened, all hell will erupt! The public will go crazy if they learned we were responsible for the deaths of their heroes. It certainly is the last thing President Schuster wanted.

Upon closer examination, he realized he had little to fear from the attacks on STN. It wasn't an issue. STN had successfully isolated themselves from one another and the rest of the world. Because of that, their deaths will not draw any attention.

Who will know they are part of STN? It's unlikely their executions would make the headline news. No one is a public figure. That, plus the fact that they will die in nineteen different countries, gives us another layer of isolation. I doubt if anyone will remotely connect their deaths as part of an organized attack. Their deaths will probably be reported as unsolved murders and will be a footnote to the news. No one will notice. No one, that is, except the Egyptian, his financial people, and the Swiss bankers.

"The Swiss bankers will do their part, especially since they agreed to keep 25% of the STN money for their trouble," he mumbled aloud. "They estimated seventy-six million dollars was in the STN accounts. I'm sure nineteen million dollars of pure profit got their attention!"

Barrows anticipated the Egyptian and the other finance people would receive a double shock. *First, after they learn of the destruction of their carefully constructed covert STN organization. Second, when they discover they no longer had access to their money. Perhaps, with luck, they will have a heart attack and die. That would be a fitting end to STN. The beauty of my plan,* he chuckled, *was not one of the big financial supporters will complain. To complain meant exposure, and I know they don't want their money back that badly. The STN brain trust may not understand how their organization suddenly disappeared, but they will certainly receive the message, loud and clear. STN is finished!*

He smiled as he thought of the old saying "Here today, gone tomorrow, and a good morning to everyone." He laughed loudly.

How fortunate, he reflected, that the Hunter woman gave up Walker, and the Pakistanis had uncovered Bilal Ahmed's friend, MacCardle. They somehow convinced him to give up his boss. I wonder if they tortured him. From what I've learned, Ahmed was a good and caring family man who joined STN to revenge his family's deaths. It was his only motivation.

"I respect that in a man. Walker, on the other hand, I never liked him. He works for the CIA and double deals by being STN. He's a traitor and nothing but dirty scum. I suspect he was in it for the money and the glory. He's one STN leader I'm going to relish taking down," he said to no one.

*

ATHENS, GREECE:

The three days of secretive meetings in Athens resulted in comprehensive death plans by the special forces of the participating countries. The extensive covert experience of the military personnel in attendance allowed them to formulate detailed attack plans quite rapidly. Lieutenant Harrison Stillweather, Commander of the British Commandoes, was designated operational chief. He had the responsibility for coordination, synchronicity, and success of the attack plans.

Time zone differences were his major obstacle. Two AM in Washington DC was one PM in Pakistan. That meant some STN leaders would have to be executed in broad daylight. Covert simultaneous operations that involved individual executions in the daytime were more risky and extremely difficult to plan and to coordinate. Barrows insisted that the STN deaths happen within two hours of one another. He wanted to avoid any possibility of word spreading within the STN ranks that they were under siege. It would drive any remaining STN people underground and probably never seen again.

Convinced the attacks would succeed in spite of the time and geographical obstacles, Stillweather insisted on additional surveillance of all the targets. He selected three other prominent commanders as his direct reports. Barrows agreed with his selections. They agreed to communicate over secure phone lines as soon as the plans were firm and all potential obstacles identified. Stillweather promised to hand-carry the final plans to each member involved in the attack to insure coordination among the various global operations.

The attendees left Athens satisfied and confident they were prepared. They expected complete success, though each had their individual concerns. The military personnel accepted these doubts as normal for any covet undertaking. However, the civilians who lacked prior experience worried, as it turned out, needlessly.

43

TIMOTHY BARROWS, OCTOBER 20, 2011:

Timothy Randolph Barrows Jr. anxiously paced for an hour. He had been in his office on the morning of October 20, 2011, since a little after 12:30 AM. The "Beginning of my destiny," he blithely acknowledged. His Peace Envoy's office was the only one lighted in the dark and abandoned corridors of the West Wing of the White House. He was too nervous to be anywhere else. He had arrived three hours before his phone would ring. The Marine guard raised his eyebrows in surprise to see anyone return to the White House offices without a major crisis in the making.

Barrows impatiently waited for the phone calls from his World Force agents, the military arm of the Peace Envoys, calls that would determine the direction of the rest of his life. Each of the nineteen World Force leaders had a designated time to call in his report, between 2:45 and 4:25 AM, spaced five minutes apart. If all went well, within three hours he'd learn if one of the most daring execution plans in history, his plan, had succeeded.

His instructions to his team leaders were simple. "Call, state your location, and say *Yes* or *No*." A call not received meant that portion of the mission had been compromised, or failed. Failure to report initiated an emergency backup plan.

A single piece of paper sat prominently in the middle of his otherwise barren desk. It was his checklist. Two of the three columns had typed headings with nineteen entries labeled *Call Time* (five minutes apart) and *Locations*. The third column was blank. It's heading, "*YES/NO.*"

Barrows desperately tried to settle his nerves.

Calm down, he told himself *calm down.*

He unsuccessfully tried reading yesterday's Washington Post, tapped his pen on the desk, sat down, stood up, paced some more, repeatedly peered out of his window into the wet early morning darkness, checked to be sure the phone had a dial tone, and frequently glanced at his watch, waiting for 3:06, the first scheduled Call Time report.

"Damn, damn, damn! Too much time, too much time! Should've come in later. Damn it."

*

Falls Church, Virginia:

The five black-clad men had been sitting in the unmarked Cadillac Escalade SUV with tinted windows for over an hour. The van, parked in front of the Shellington Arms East apartment building at 5137 Patrick Henry Drive, idled in neutral. Three men in the back seat cradled the three-foot Kayo two-man battering ram on their laps. Each man verbally reviewed his role in the night's activity. No one spoke after that.

Ed Walker lay soundly asleep in his bed, unaware of the men huddled in the van. At precisely 2:46 AM, four of the five assassins exited the van, black ski masks pulled over their faces, and the 40-pound battering ram slung over the shoulder of the strongest. The driver remained in the vehicle with the engine running. They opened the unlocked front door of the apartment building and walked down the dimly lighted hall. Stale cigarette smells and dampness greeted them as they stopped at the green painted door of Apartment D. The two men assigned to the battering ram positioned themselves in front of the tattered and frail wooden door, waiting for the signal.

The leader focused on his watch. His team focused on his left hand. He began his finger count down at five seconds. At four fingers, the 40,000 pounds of force of the epoxy steel battering ram was poised at its highest arc, ready to inflict its devastating blow.

Three fingers.

Two.

One.

Zero.

The leader gave the "go sign" A loud THUD and the wooden door exploded from its hinges. The door and its splinters flew into the apartment. The leader and the fourth man burst through the doorway and headed directly for the bedroom. The battering ram men stayed behind to intimidate nosey neighbors.

The constant whine of the aging air conditioner slightly muffled the sound from the battering ram, but not enough. Ed Walker awakened with a start, struggling to unwrap himself from his blanket. Before he managed to get untangled, he saw the silhouette of two guns, one pointing at his head and the other at his chest.

"Compliments of Tim Barrows" were the last words Ed Walker heard before twelve bullets from the two F & N Herstal 5-7 pistols, equipped with special made silencers, riddled his body. One final twitch and Ed Walker lay dead.

The four World Force agents grabbed Walker's laptop computer and bolted from the blood soaked bedroom to the waiting SUV.

At 2:59, the Cadillac glided away from the curb and disappeared into the early morning darkness of Falls Church, Virginia.

It was the morning of October 20, 2011. The North American Regional STN leader was the first to die.

In Karachi Pakistan, a similar scene was unfolding at the same time. It was 11:46 AM in Pakistan. An elite security force of fifteen men, in two black unmarked Honda vans, sped to Bilal Maqsood Ahmed's apartment. They had been on alert for over three weeks. They waited, fully armed, for their signal to kill Bilal, the STN leader in Pakistan. When the World Force agents reached Bilal's apartment, the men spread out and immediately secured the entrance to the building. Several men took positions on the roof of an opposite building to prevent Bilal's possible escape. Five fully armed agents quietly ascended the stairs leading from the building entrance. They silently climbed the three flights to reach Bilal's apartment.

They positioned themselves for the assault, finger counted to three, and, with a single kick-thrust, shattered the door to Bilal's apartment. Seconds later, three agents entered the apartment, and caught Bilal just as he bolted from the chair by the computer table, trying desperately to reach his weapon in the bedroom. He never took another step. Seven bullets blasted open his chest and head. Several bullets pierced the two tattered pictures nesting in Bilal's breast pocket before entering his body. He fell to the floor, dead, blood gushing from his bullet-ridden body. STN Pakistan abruptly ended, in violence.

World Force agents simultaneously sprung into action in every major country in the world. It took less than two hours for the remaining seventeen STN leaders to die. Some died at work, some at home, and others while traveling. Many STN leaders found death in the privacy of their homes. Others were feasting at their favorite restaurant. No matter where they were, no matter with who they were, no matter what they were doing, their executioners completed their mission in a synchronized and flawless manner. Without police or military interference. Their lives ended from multiple gunshot wounds, just as they had ruthlessly executed their thousands of victims without warning or mercy.

*

BARROWS:

Dry from the pressure, he gulped three bottles of ice-cold Evian water without quenching his thirst. By 2:54, he forced himself to sit at his desk, hand poised on the phone, waiting for the first ring. He obsessively tapped his foot on the crystal chair mat. Precisely at 3:06, the phone rang.

He ripped the receiver off the cradle and heard,

"Falls Church, Yes."

His heart pounded as he heard each word.

"One down, eighteen left," he mumbled. The phone began its rhythmic ringing according to his pre-determined schedule.

"Cairo, Yes."

"Tehran, Yes."

"London, Yes."

"Karachi, Yes."

"Istanbul, Yes."

"Sanaa, Yes."

"Manila, Yes."

One by one, Barrows checked off the remaining eleven locations. It took precisely ninety-five minutes for the final call. The extermination of STN was complete. No STN survivors, no World Force deaths, and no contingency plans needed. He had achieved success beyond his wildest expectations.

Tim Barrows, Chairman of the Peace Envoys, had demanded that the executions of all STN leaders happen on the same day, within hours of one another, regardless of their global location. And they did! Their near simultaneous deaths were his only option. The political fallout and media heat would have been huge and unbearable with anything less.

Trials are messy. Lots of questions and unpleasant facts would surely come from that ordeal. Worse, the global powers did not want to make a public spectacle of STN, since public support for them remained high. The people believed STN were heroes. Under those conditions, it would be difficult to select a non-biased jury. In fact, the opposite would result. There would be so much sympathy for STN that the leaders might avoid conviction and walk away free men. The free world government officials concluded trials were not in their best interests. STN vanished that morning, without fanfare and without trials.

Ecstatic and elated, Barrows sat stunned in his chair. Though he hoped with every fiber of his body, he never imagined it would be so easy, so efficient, and so complete.

The sheet of paper containing nineteen hand written "YESES" was immediately fed into the eager mouth of the crosscut shredder.

Barrows slumped into his chair. For the first time in months, he felt total relief, exhilaration and pride. He spent months of intense planning and training, of secrecy, of lying, of continual anxiety, of hope, and of dreading failure. That was behind him now. All that mattered was that he had succeeded. He had accomplished what everyone in government openly wanted, but secretly thought improbable. His heart said it was possible. He believed he could do it…, yet those nagging doubts were always there, ready to tear his head off, to drain his energy, to ruin his dreams, or to destroy his career. Tom Peaksman, the President's liaison, said his anxieties would never leave him. He was right.

He thought back to June when he sat in President Schuster's office, recalling the President's words as though he heard them yesterday.

"You'd be a fool to think that a mission as complex and as secretive this isn't going to gnaw at your guts every minute of every day of your life until it's done. If you don't control your doubts and fears, we're all doomed." Barrows had nodded in agreement.

The task *was* daunting. The President wanted him to destroy STN, something not even the vaunted intelligence community of the US was able to accomplish. His reward came much sooner than anyone had a right to expect. He fully expected his immense success would catapult him into the career positioned he wanted, either the Presidency or Chairman of the Peace Envoys. Barrows allowed himself the indulgence of his achievements to energize his thoughts. Exhilaration replaced his trembling anxiety of only hours ago. Now was the time to gloat, to bask in his expected glory, his money, and his future.

STN is finished! I've done it, in spite of the doubters. I beat the odds. I knew I could do it. They thought I would never live to collect the five million they put in the bank. Soon I can devote myself to the children.

He smiled broadly. Life is good for a fifty-two-year old man at the zenith of his career.

*

Their leaders dead, STN instantly dissolved. As their executioners anticipated, the media virtually ignored the killings. There was no universal outrage or media frenzy. No protesters furiously demanding an explanation from their government as to why their cherished STN no longer existed. No one knew the nineteen global victims were STN leaders. No one had a clue the nineteen were linked together. They had no idea history had just been made. Nor would they.

Life went on, quietly, without a single raised eyebrow.

Word, however, spread quickly within the STN ranks. They learned that unknown assailants executed their leaders. Within 14 hours and 7 minutes, 151 of the 543 remaining STN members committed suicide. Some by cyanide capsule, some by their own weapons, and others by gas. A few leaped to their deaths from buildings or cliffs.

No one felt compelled to destroy evidence of their STN association before their death. What little they had could no longer hurt them. Only those who chose to live, those who could return to their pre-STN lives, only they destroyed what little incriminating evidence they had in their possession.

Fifteen days, ten hours and four minutes after Athens, Ed Walker and the entire STN leadership ceased to exist. The date was Thursday, October 20, 2011. The global vigilante group known as STN shattered into oblivion.

44

BARROWS:

One final task remained. President Schuster and the world leaders needed to know. But, he questioned,

Should I do it or let Schuster be the hero?

Moments of careful consideration dissolved into a political strategy he knew would play to his advantage.

I still need Schuster to help me. If he breaks the news, he'll feel indebted to me for giving him his moment of International glory. Besides, the world leaders know I'm the one responsible for saving their governments and probably their lives. I still will get all the credit!

He dialed President Schuster's private number the President had given to him with the instructions,

"Call me on this number any time of the day or night, but only for two reasons. First reason is to tell me STN is dead. Barring that, I'll need to know when I need to increase my personal security because you failed. And it better not be the second one!"

Two rings.

A groggy President Schuster demanded

"Whose calling and what's happening?"

"Tim Barrows, Mr. President. I have great news, the one you've been waiting for! STN is destroyed as of six minutes ago. All nineteen leaders are dead and the organization should begin to crumble within hours."

"Are you shitting me? That's fantastic, incredible amazing... I'm... lost for words," a suddenly alert voice responded.

"No sir, Mr. President, mission accomplished. Total success. No hitches.

My men executed the plan precisely. Well, Mr. President, congratulations to you. If it weren't for your insight, and leadership, none of this would have been possible. You recognized the threat, you got everyone on board, and you made the decision to go after STN."

"Can they be identified as STN?"

"I don't see how that is possible. Their own secrecy helps us. Since the public did not know their identities, there's little chance anyone could figure out the connection of their deaths. There are only three groups who can identify STN. Your people, my people, and STN people. I doubt if anyone from these groups will be interested in blabbing to the media."

"Excellent point."

"Now as far as who made it happen, most of the credit goes to you, Mr. President."

"No, the truth is you did all the real work, and it was you and your organization that developed the plan and executed their leaders."

"Thank you, sir, but without you, your dedication, and your vision, where would our government and our country be? No, no we both did great, didn't we? The world owes us both."

The President continued.

"Someday, history will record the credit we deserve. Of course, that is not possible now, nor, I suspect, anytime in the near future. Someday we might be able to tell the world what we've accomplished. Because people around the globe still believe in and idolize STN, the last thing we want is the media to roast us. You know, hearings, talking heads pointing their fingers at us. They could possibly precipitate a riot. For now, this will remain our secret. For now, we both have to live with the knowledge of our accomplishments. We need patience, Timothy, before the country or the world can hear about us. What we have... what you have accomplished, can only be described as truly remarkable. Thank you again and again!

Frankly, I'm flabbergasted! I never thought you'd do it. I hoped and I prayed for your success, but I never... I'm still stunned, Timothy, stunned, grateful and overwhelmed. This is the most incredible news I've heard since I became President! Congratulations, a million times over. Or should I say 5 million times over?"

President Schuster laughed heartedly.

"You've given the world freedom from tyranny, from lawlessness, and freedom from fear that a damn vigilante group might someday come after you, our families, or me. Well done, well done!"

"Thank you. There is one more pleasant task that needs to be finished, Mr. President. When you first called me to your office about STN, we agreed I would notify the leaders of the world as soon as STN was destroyed. I want to defer that honor to you. This is your moment in history. I would like to suggest that you personally make the calls. It started with you and it should finish with you. This is your moment, Mr. President. Take it, please."

"You're right. I will. I'll be in touch. Thank you once again. I'm forever indebted to you," the President quickly responded.

Schuster spent the next two hours and forty-seven minutes on the phone from the Oval Office, in his pajamas and robe, dialing the private phone numbers of the free world leaders to tell them the news. The collective global relief, appreciation, and respect Schuster heard, if bottled, would have been worth it's weight in uranium 235.

Behind closed doors, global leaders cheered at their success. They felt safe, now.

*

Barrows drove home in his 2007 Porsche. For the first time in months he knew he would finally get what had been missing in his life. Badly needed sleep. He was free from the most gut-wrenching assignment he had ever experienced. No longer would anxieties of a possible failure interrupt his sleep. No longer would he be on constant internal alert, and no longer would he hide his secret life from family and friends.

It was over, but he was just getting started. His emotional rollercoaster ended exactly as he knew it would. He doubted if he would forget the exhilaration that inundated his being, nor did he want to.

My experience as Chairman of the Peace Envoys will serve me well. I suspect that President Schuster will be re-elected for a second term. If I chose, I could be taking my Presidential oath the following four years in 2017. I will be sitting in his chair, living in his house, the undisputed leader of the free world. President Barrows. President Barrows. Has a nice ring. So does Chairman of the Peace Envoys.

Even President Schuster had acknowledged Barrows' ambition, though he had not made direct reference to a possible Barrows Presidency.

My singular troubling regret was the many lies I told my family and friends in pursuit of STN. Surely, he rationalized, *they would forgive me once they learn about my role in securing their freedom. Even if it takes a decade or more.*

I guess I am growing up. I do not want to be like my father. I understand more about people now. When I realized how important the children of the world had become to me, that's when I began to change. I like the new me. I'm better with Lynette and my own children, and I even can accept my father for what he is. He has his faults, but who am I to judge his actions? I can only be the master of me, and no one else. Yet, I can become the leader of the free world as President, if I choose. I no longer have to control everything and everyone, but I know I will make a difference whatever path I decide to follow.

45

BARROWS' FUTURE:

Barrows drove home, exhausted, optimistic and happy Lynette was still sleeping. He undressed without showering. He scrawled a note with instructions for his wife to let him sleep until he awakened. He quietly crawled nude into the bed, tenderly kissed Lynette on her forehead and passed out. Exhaustion overtook his pride and personal satisfaction. His last thought before falling asleep was,

Tomorrow will be time enough to determine what I want to do for the rest of my life.

It was nearly 7:21 in the evening when he awoke and walked downstairs, his blue velvet robe loosely draped on his weary body.

"I've never seen you sleep like that before. Are you OK?" Lynette asked when Barrows staggered into the den where she was doing homework duty with the kids.

"Everything is excellent. I'll tell you about it after the kids are asleep. I'm starved. What's for dinner?"

"Would you like me to heat up the leftover roast?"

"I'll do it. What setting on the microwave?"

"Try two minutes on 70% power. There's salad in the frig, and sesame dinner rolls in the breadbasket."

"Sounds fine." He allowed his starved body to catch up with his energized mind.

By 8:35, Lynette was finished with the boys. They were plastered in front of their own TV's. Lewis was playing Game Boy, and Steven engrossed in a sit-com.

"OK. I'm ready," Lynette said as she sat next to Barrows in the den.

One last lie. The money from OPERATION DOVE and the captured STN money will go to support the PE's mission for the world.

"My Envoy team has gotten the global governments to agree to fund multiple global programs. Our recommendations, when fully implemented, will make the world a better place for everyone. Men, women and children. It's been a long battle, mostly because of the power control and the money demands we've made. Some governments have balked at sharing intelligence data with other countries, and others are reluctant to allocate enough money to help the third world countries to establish a better educational and a better economic environment. We're on the verge of obtaining agreements from many who were reluctant to support us. Things could begin within the next two to three months. Many details have to be worked out. Everyone seems committed to supplying the labor, the effort, and the money.

These programs will eliminate the root causes of terrorism, especially in the Middle East and Africa. We'll be able to structure specific plans to make the changes needed. Most importantly, the money will go towards feeding and caring for the poor children. They will receive a better education, learn a trade, and hopefully climb out of poverty and depression. That truly makes me happy and excited.

That's what Tom Peaksman and I have been busting our humps on this the past months. This is a major breakthrough. Before I became Chairman of the Peace Envoys, governments, especially ours, paid lip service to the poor countries by pledging all kinds of support and financial aid. Once the politicians took their credit, they and the funds disappeared. The talked and did nothing, as usual.

This time it's different. Everyone has had enough of deaths and bombings. They pledged to make major changes so that the world can live in peace and harmony. I think they've learned their lesson. I'm proud of what I've accomplished with the Envoys. Damn proud!"

"I'm so proud of you too, Tim. You've worked so hard, and to see it pay off in this way is remarkable."

Barrows interrupted.

"Yes, it's been hard. But do you realize what this means for me, I mean, for us? Soon I'll have to make a major career decision. You know I have a real shot at the Presidency in four years. But, as I began to understand what is really important, I realized that without my family, nothing else matters. I can stay on as Chairman of the Peace Envoys, if I want. Think how much I can achieve from either position. My success with the Envoys has been a wonderful learning experience. I think I may have gained International recognition. Winning the nomination for the Presidency will be a cinch, if I decide to take that path. How does 'First Lady' sound?"

Lynette seemed puzzled.

"I thought after this that you might take a job less strenuous, something where we could spend more time together, you, me, and the boys."

"I would like that too. I've really missed you and would like to be sure I have your support before I make a move to either position. What do you say, Lynette? First Lady or … what would people call you as the wife of the Chairman?"

She was taken aback. He never consulted with her before nor had he included her in his decisions. Not since they were first married did he say he missed her.

"I'm so pleased. I guess I really have mixed emotions. I'd rather not see you in the White House. We'll see each other even less than now. On the other hand, I understand how much becoming President means to you. You've worked hard for this, and I want you to know that I will support you no matter what you decide. If you want to become President, I'll be there by your side. If you decide to continue as Chairman, I support you there too. And Tim, I really appreciate you asking for my opinion. It means a lot to me."

"It means a lot to me too. I know I haven't told you very often how I feel. I guess I never learned that part of life before. But these many months have taught me there is more to life than work, and my family needs to be considered in these decisions.

I've also decided on two more things. I would like you to help me, to work with me for the children. You can, if you feel you would like to be involved, be my point person with UNICEF. I want to involve them as much as possible. They already have the connections and organization to help stem the tide of continual hunger the children of the world face, including here in the States. Next, I intend to open a dialog with my father. He is what he is. It's time to let go of my anger and resentment. He may have been controlling, but in retrospect, his advice was sound and correct. He deserves to share in the part he played to prepare me for life."

Lynette broke out into tears.

"Why are you crying?" he asked tenderly. Have I said something to upset you?

"I've waited so long to hear you come to those conclusions. It just makes me so happy and so very pound of you. These are tears of joy and happiness. Yes, I would love to work with you and UNICEF. I always wanted to be a part of your political life. Working with you would be the most fulfilling thing you have even asked me to do. Thank you, Tim. I can't tell you how much it means to me. This proves you have changed. I love it!"

She burst into a new torrent of tears.

Tim pulled her close to him and gently and gratefully said,

"I'm glad you are happy. It makes me happy for us both. It's taken me a while to grow up but I think I'm finally getting the hang of it. You know, I've always envisioned me being in the White House. It's been my dream since I was twenty-one. I told you repeatedly the heavy hand my father had in helping me to look to the future. Our future is here now, for you and me.

I'm going to take my best shot; I just don't know which one. But, I appreciate your support. I love you Lynette. One day I hope you will forgive me for the bad way I have treated you in the past. I swear it will never happen again," he softly said.

"Are you sure? I don't want to influence you either way, you know, about what position to take."

"No, believe me. I appreciate and need your support and your opinion."

Her hands clasped together as though she was holding onto her last grasp of life. Perhaps she was. It was different, and so was he. She hoped it would last. She wasn't quite sure how to handle this new aspect of her husband of over twenty years.

Barrows accepted her joy.

I really have changed. I've learned about human frailty and human feelings. Something my parents couldn't teach me. I am different than my father. Everything I hated about him I was becoming. Thank goodness, I woke up in time. If I hadn't begun thinking of what I could do to help others, I might have become my father's duplicate. I would have been doomed to remain self-centered, arrogant and self-serving.

She wept, happily, with dignity. For the first time in his life, Barrow felt a sense of humility.

Barrows' remaining thoughts were on what he would to do for the rest of his life.

Decide which job I want, continue to learn how to be happy with my family, have a real relationship with my father, put all this STN stuff behind me, and work with all my energy and passion to help the children of the world.

The end